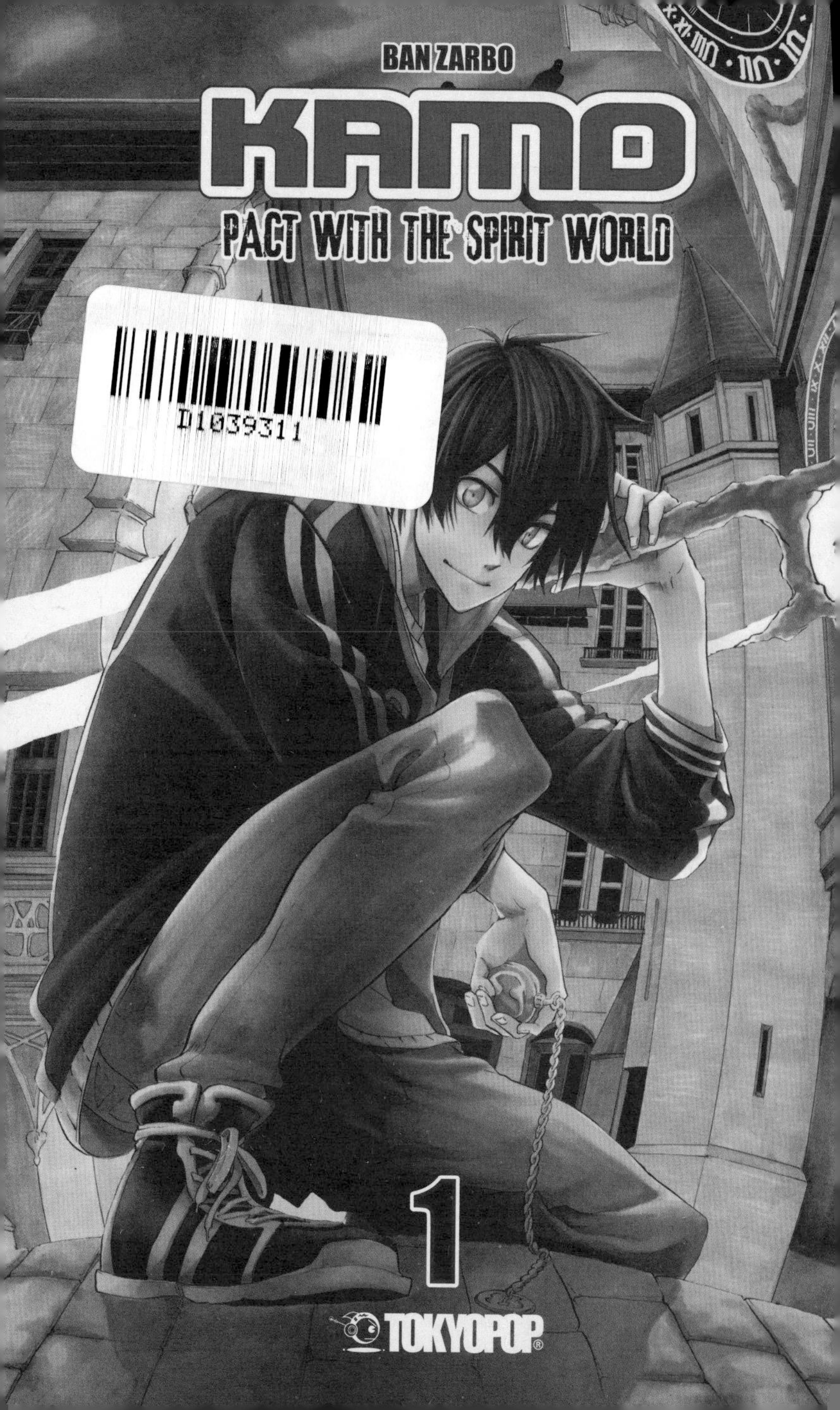
BAN ZARBO
KAMO
PACT WITH THE SPIRIT WORLD
1
TOKYOPOP

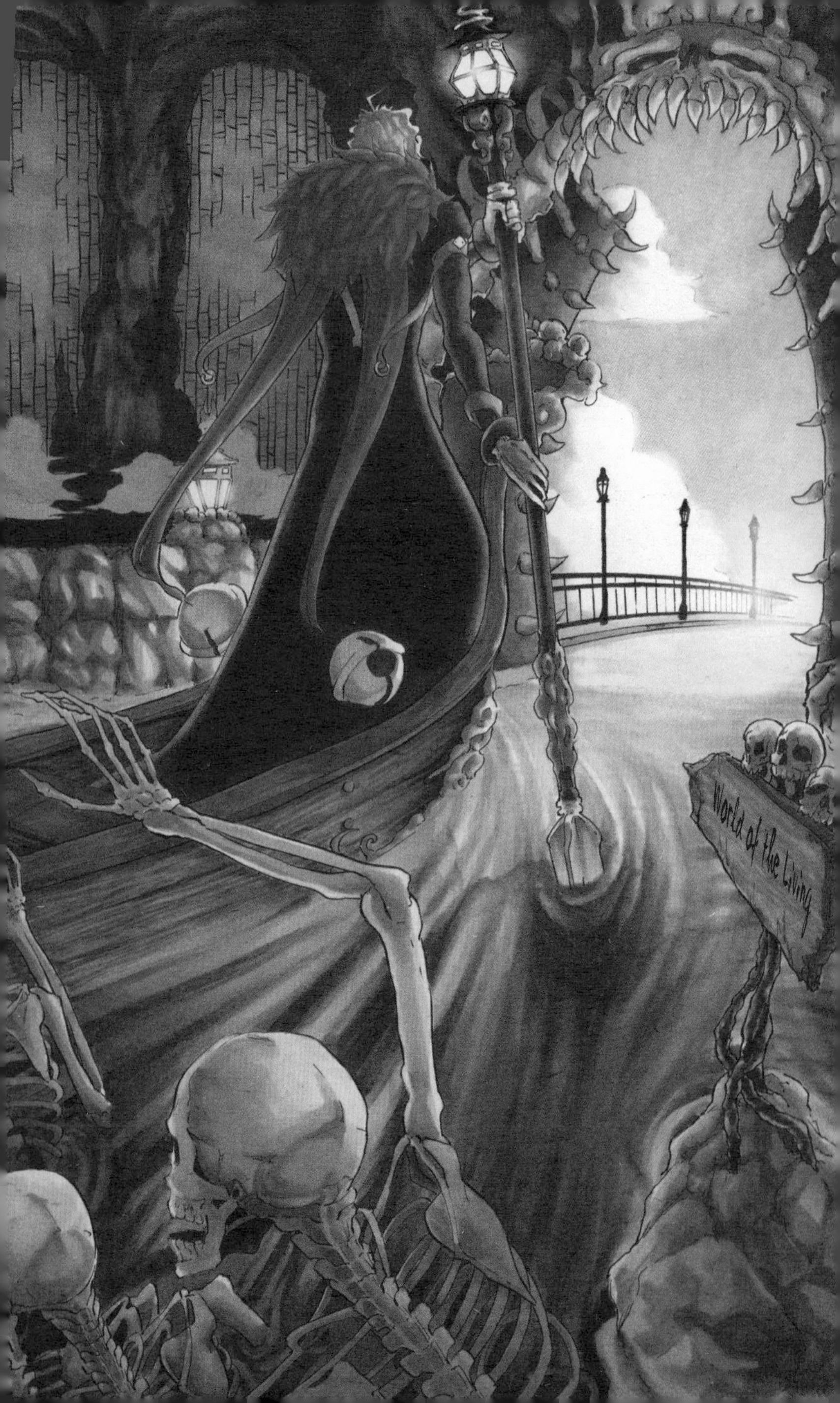
World of the Living

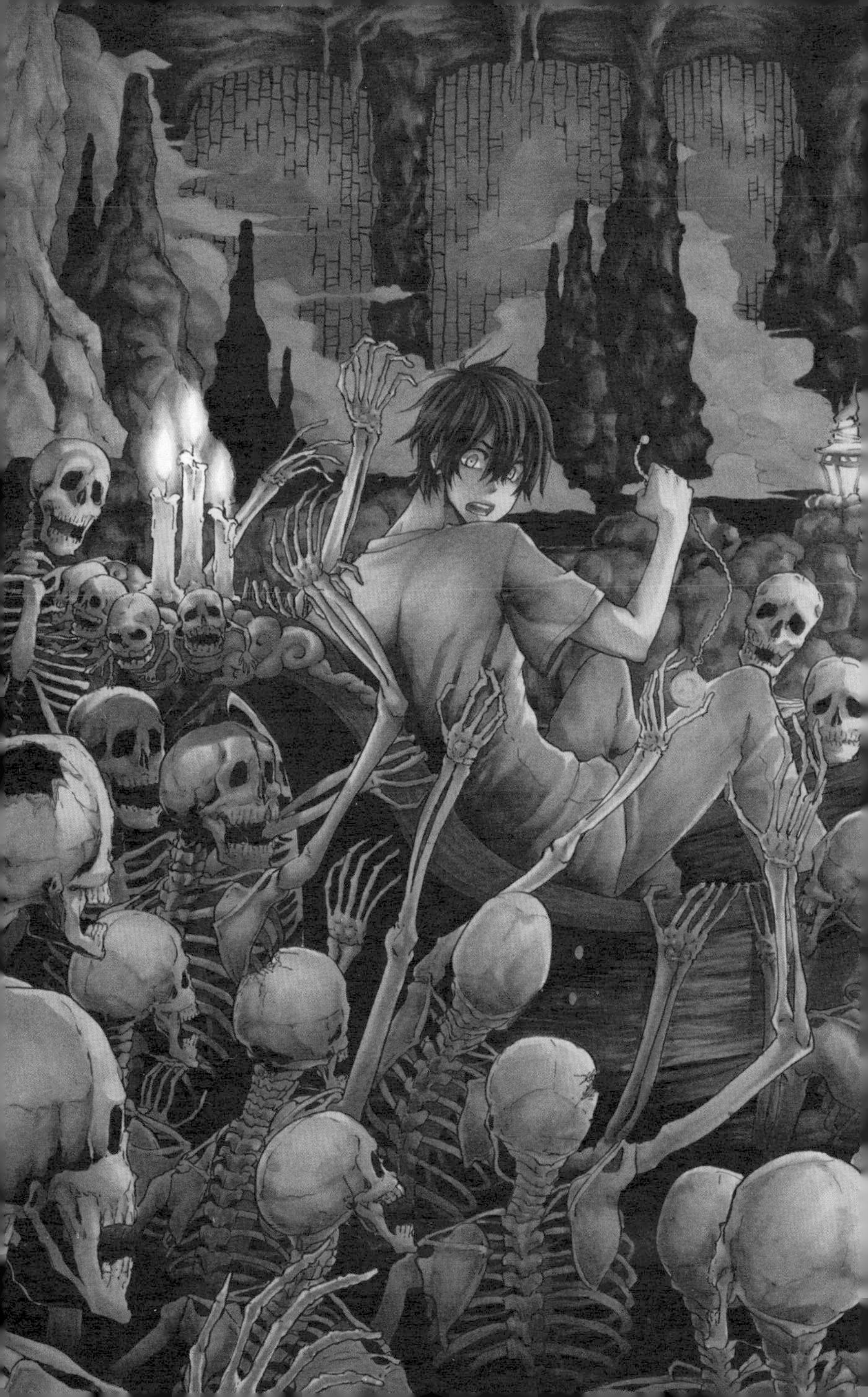

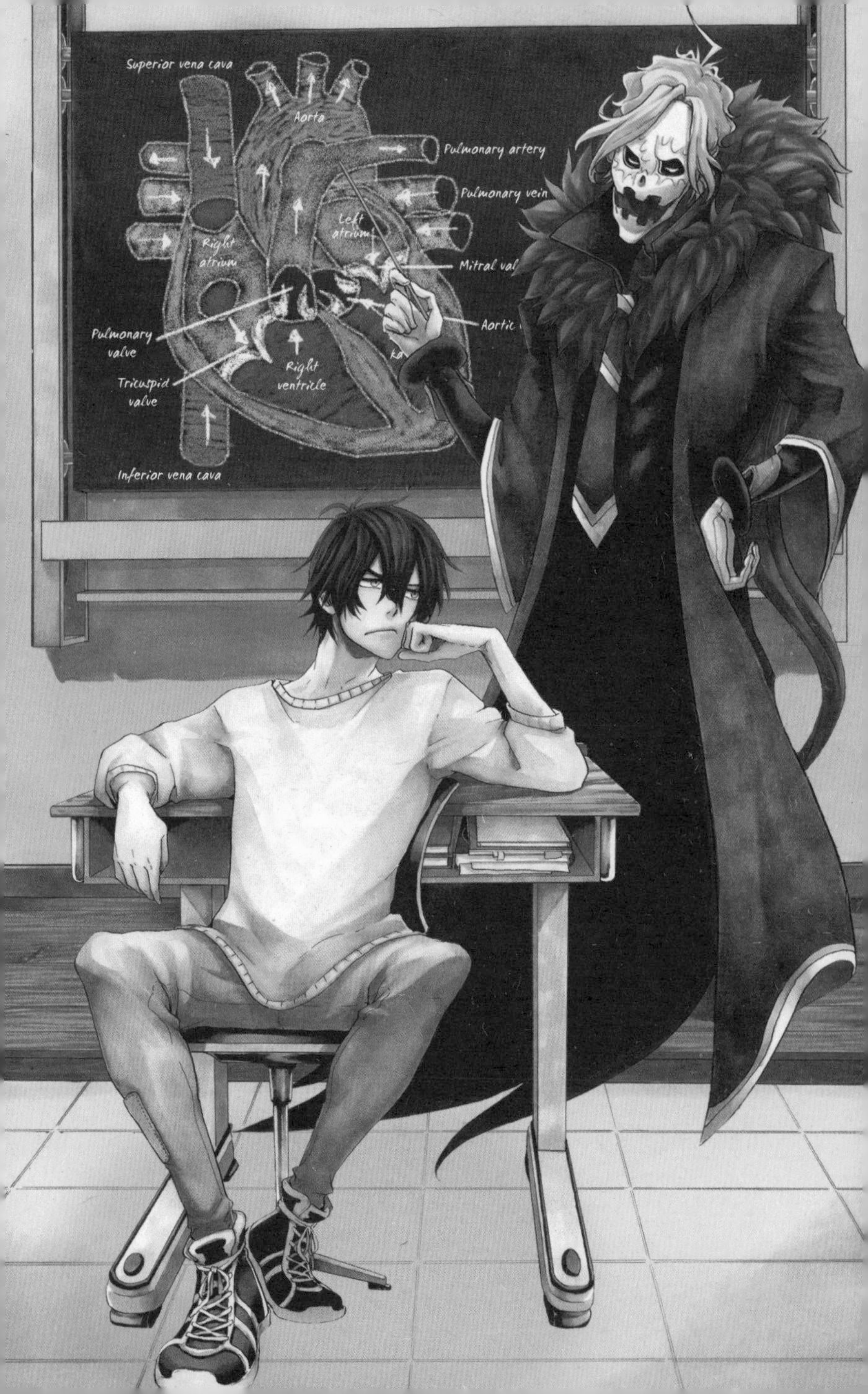
Superior vena cava
Aorta
Pulmonary artery
Pulmonary vein
Left atrium
Right atrium
Mitral val
Aortic
Pulmonary valve
Tricuspid valve
Right ventricle
Inferior vena cava

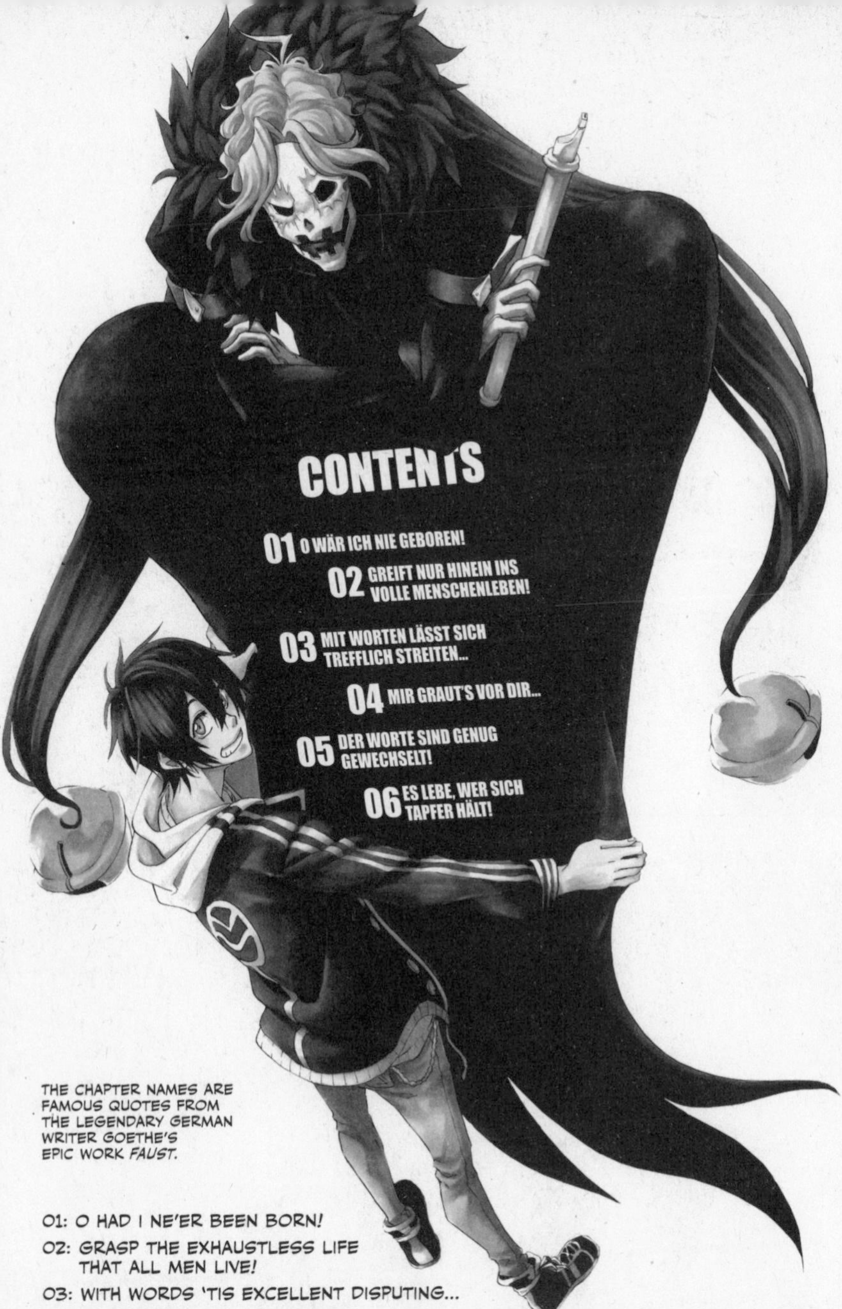

CONTENTS

THE CHAPTER NAMES ARE FAMOUS QUOTES FROM THE LEGENDARY GERMAN WRITER GOETHE'S EPIC WORK *FAUST*.

01: O HAD I NE'ER BEEN BORN!

02: GRASP THE EXHAUSTLESS LIFE THAT ALL MEN LIVE!

03: WITH WORDS 'TIS EXCELLENT DISPUTING...

04: I SHUDDER TO THINK OF THEE...

05: THE WORDS YOU'VE BANDIED ARE SUFFICIENT!

06: HAIL HIM, WHO KEEPS A STEADFAST MIND!

KAMO

PACT WITH THE SPIRIT WORLD

01
O WÄR ICH NIE GEBOREN!
O HAD I NE'ER BEEN BORN!

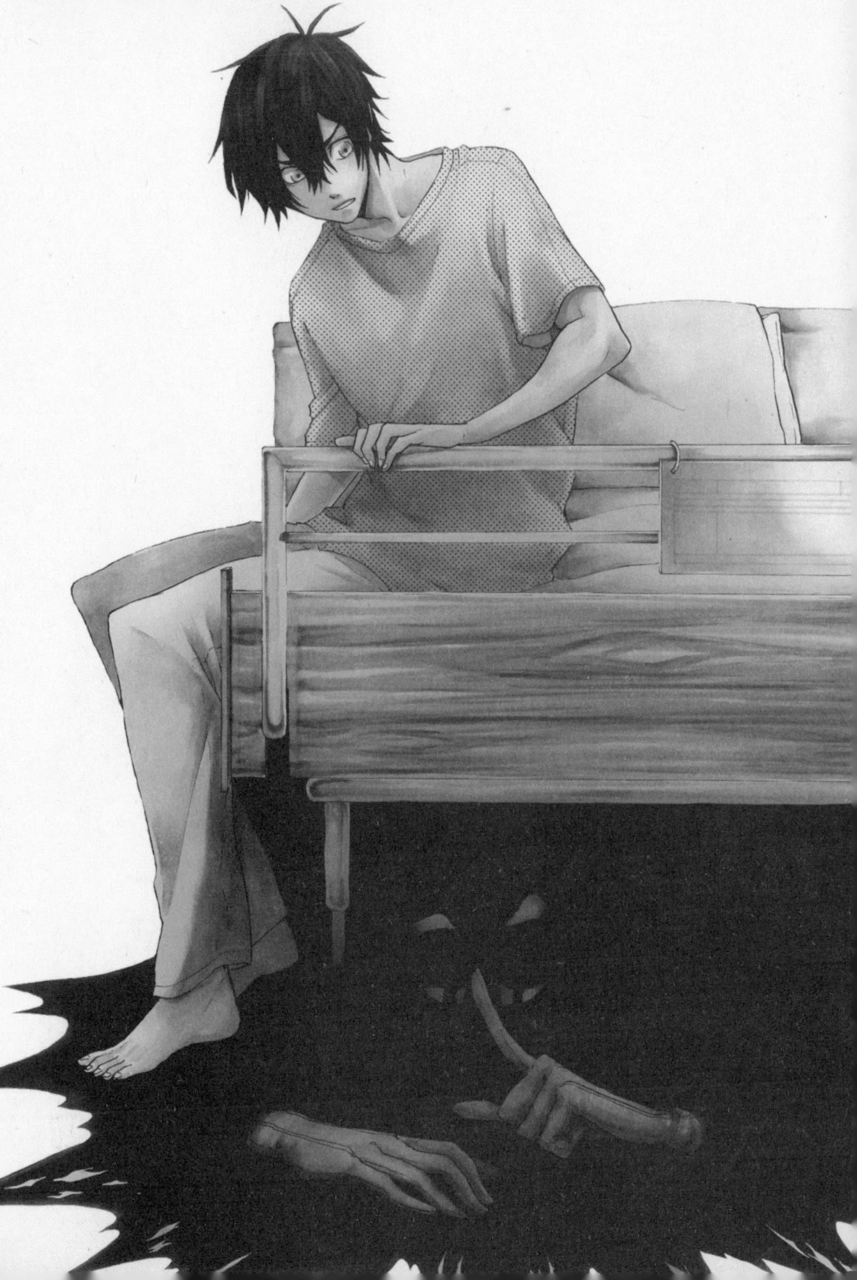

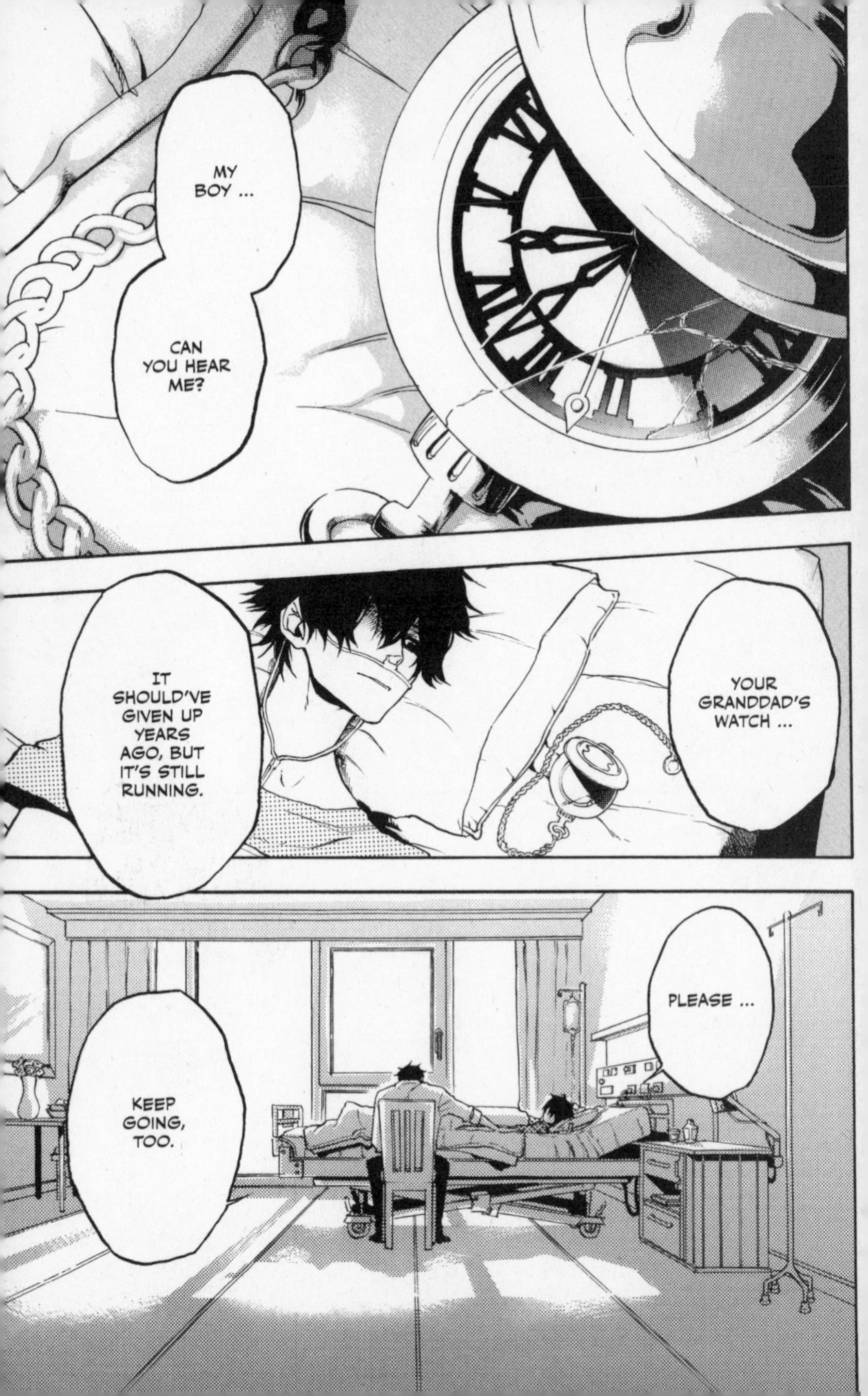
MY BOY ...
CAN YOU HEAR ME?
YOUR GRANDDAD'S WATCH ...
IT SHOULD'VE GIVEN UP YEARS AGO, BUT IT'S STILL RUNNING.
PLEASE ...
KEEP GOING, TOO.

YOU KNOW THERE'S NO POINT ANYMORE. YOUR TEARS BETRAY YOU.

DAD ...

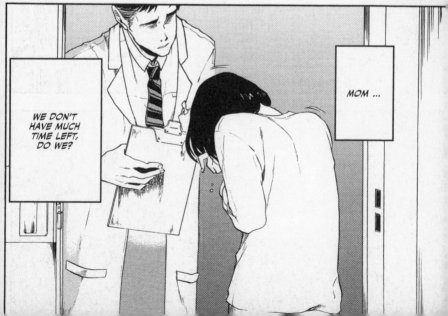

WE DON'T HAVE MUCH TIME LEFT, DO WE?

MOM ...

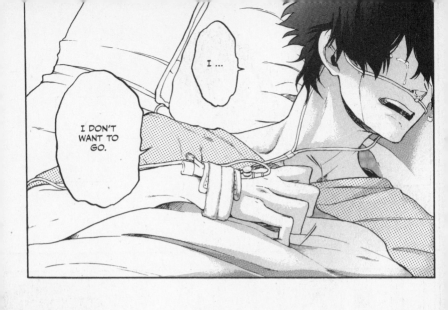

I ...

I DON'T WANT TO GO.

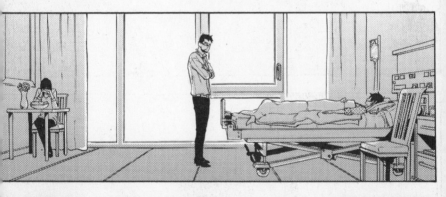

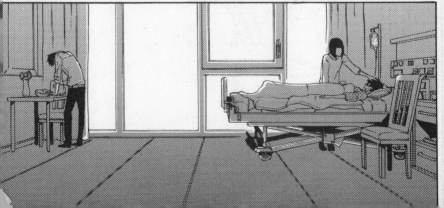

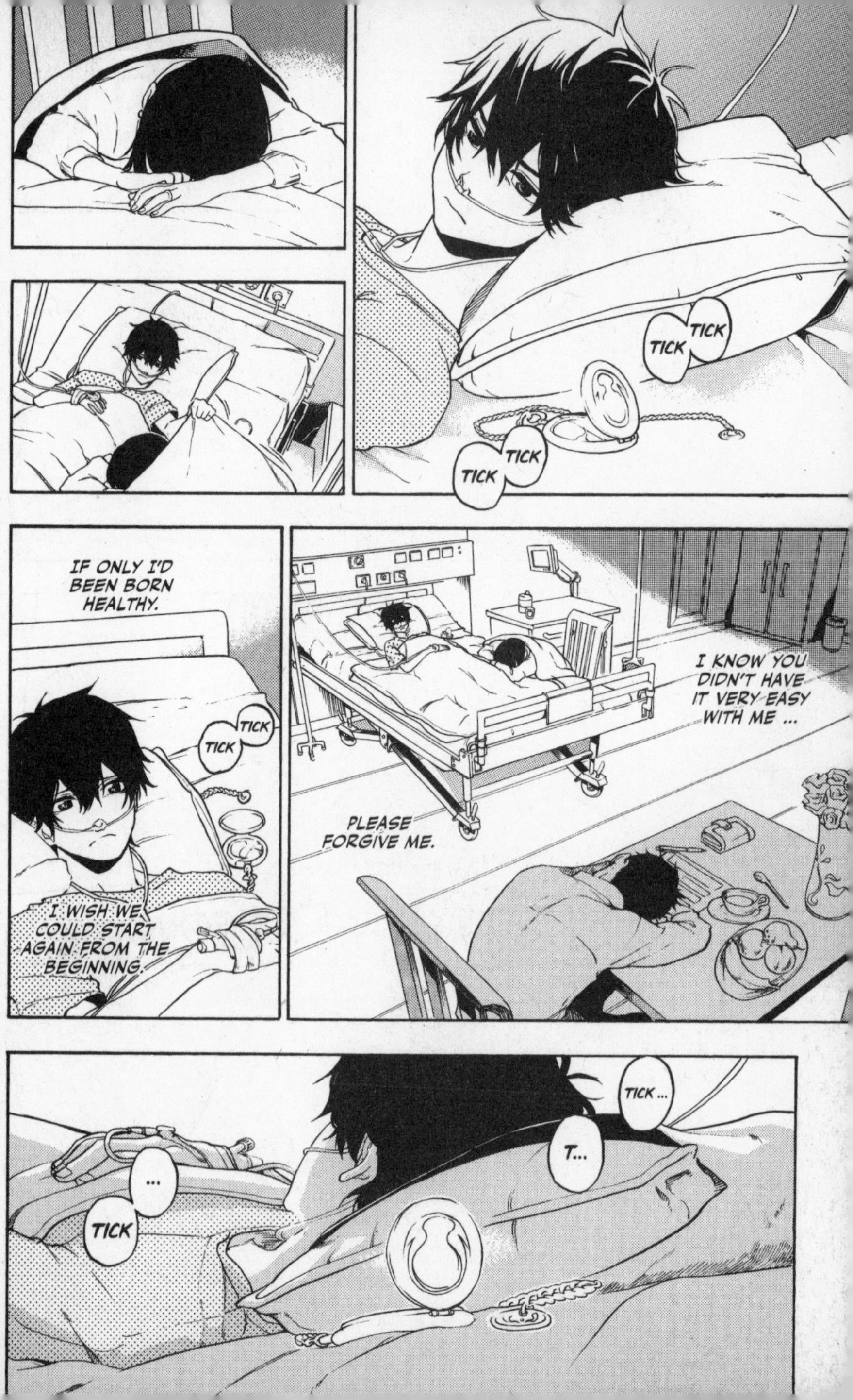
TICK
TICK
TICK
TICK
I KNOW YOU DIDN'T HAVE IT VERY EASY WITH ME ...
PLEASE FORGIVE ME.
IF ONLY I'D BEEN BORN HEALTHY.
TICK
TICK
I WISH WE COULD START AGAIN FROM THE BEGINNING.
TICK ...
T...
...
TICK

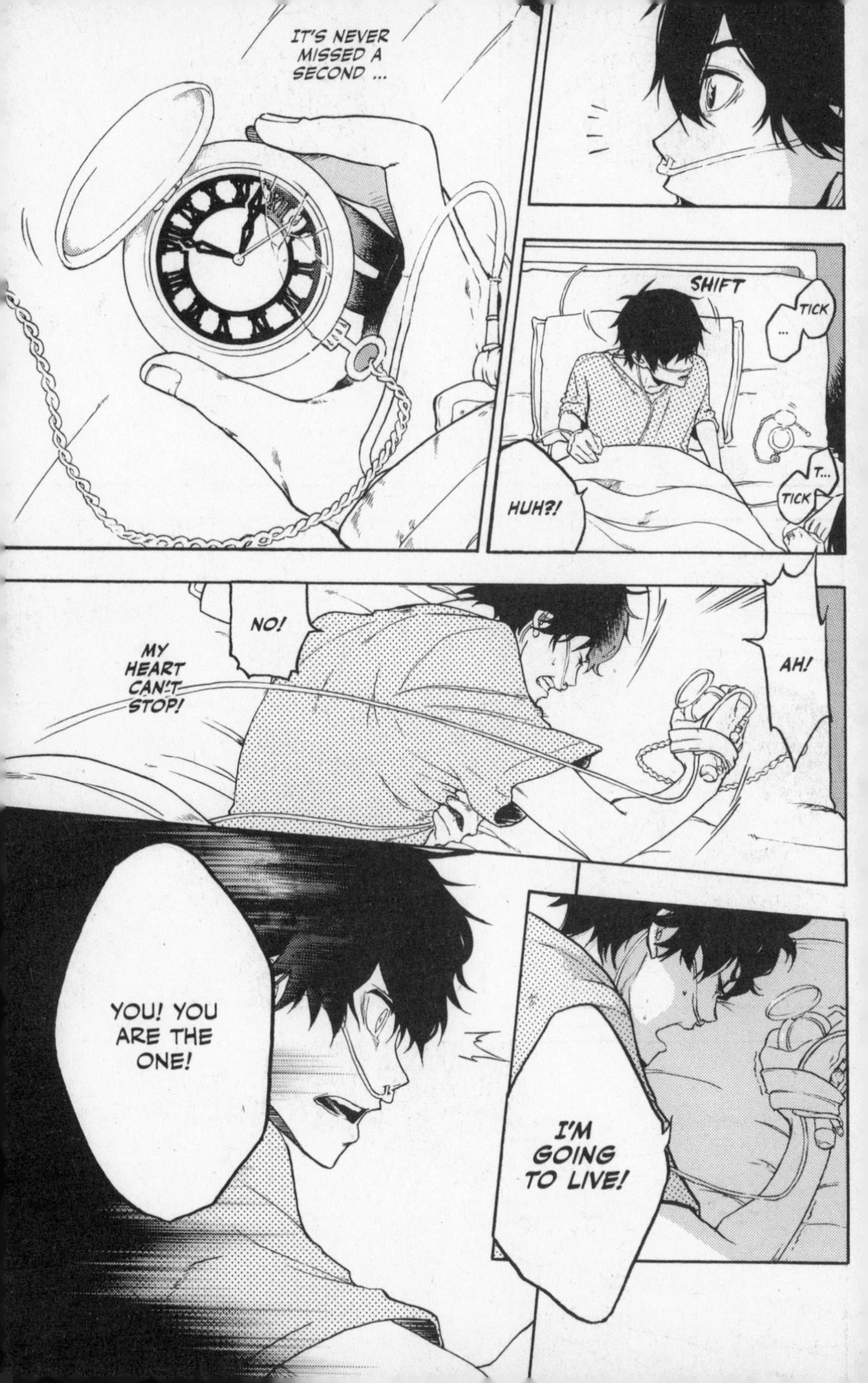
SHIFT
TICK ...
T... TICK
HUH?!
IT'S NEVER MISSED A SECOND ...
AH!
NO!
MY HEART CAN'T STOP!
I'M GOING TO LIVE!
YOU! YOU ARE THE ONE!

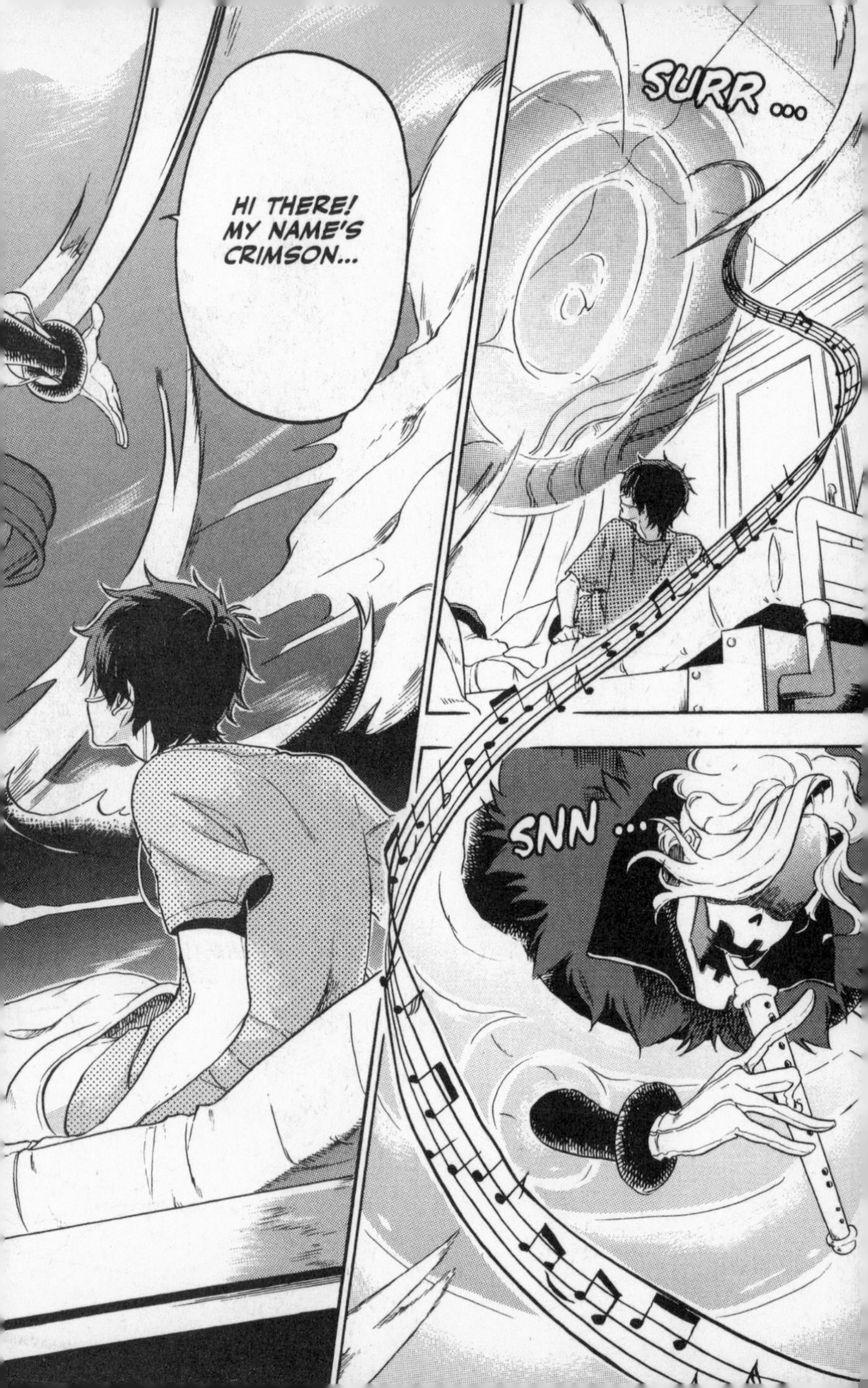
SURR ...
HI THERE! MY NAME'S CRIMSON...
SNN ...

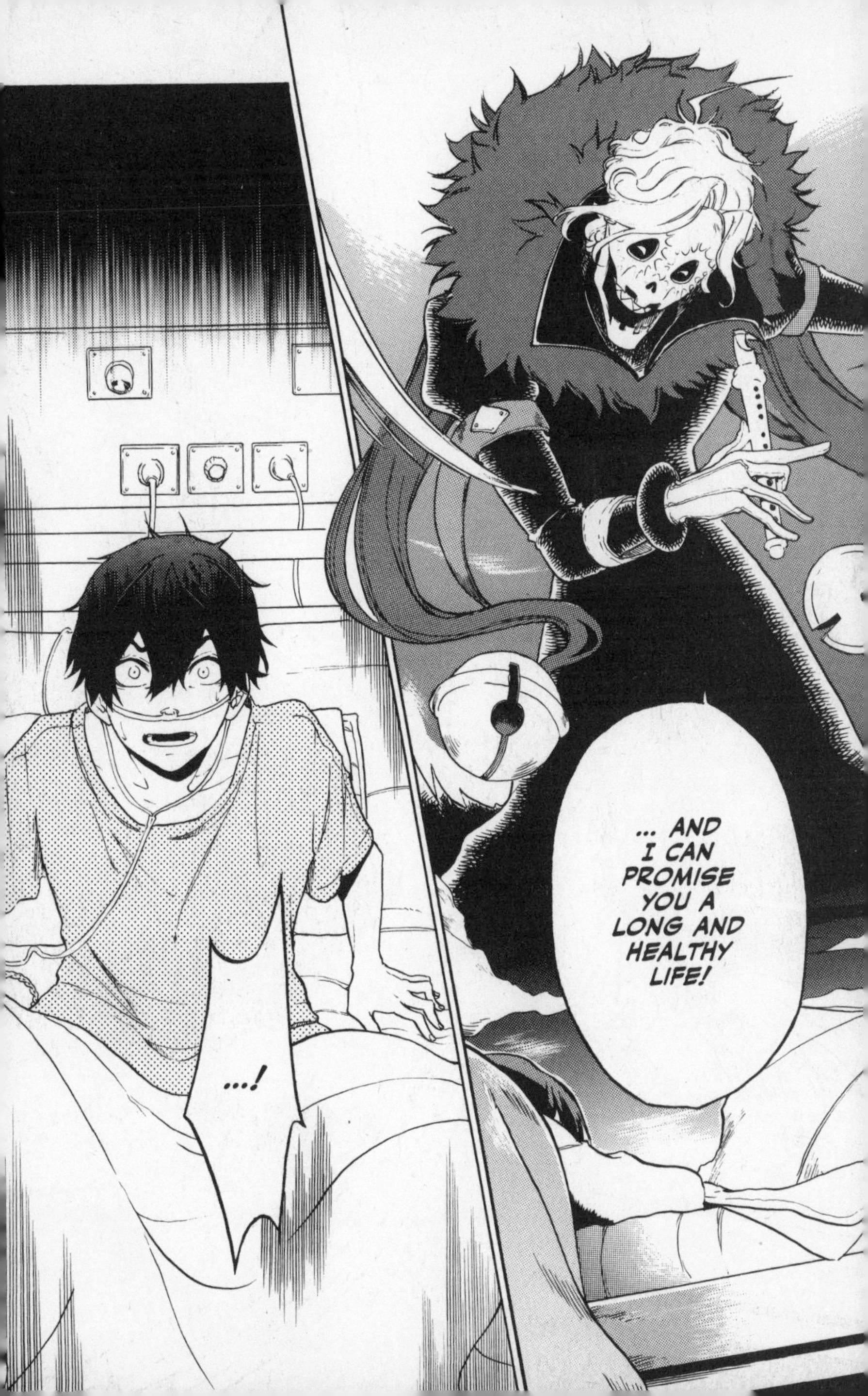
... AND I CAN PROMISE YOU A LONG AND HEALTHY LIFE!
...!

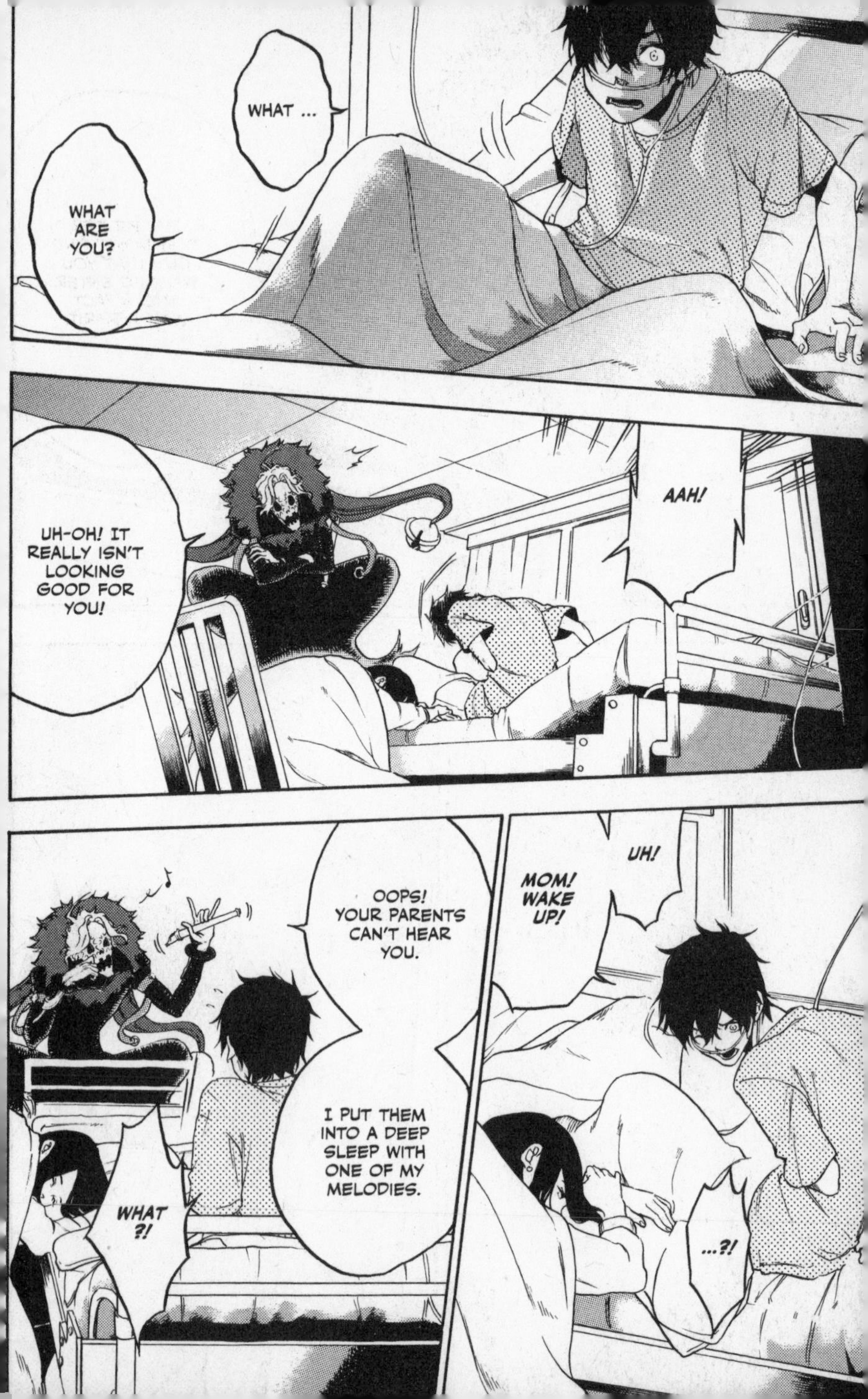
WHAT ...
WHAT ARE YOU?
AAH!
UH-OH! IT REALLY ISN'T LOOKING GOOD FOR YOU!
UH!
MOM! WAKE UP!
...?!
OOPS! YOUR PARENTS CAN'T HEAR YOU.
I PUT THEM INTO A DEEP SLEEP WITH ONE OF MY MELODIES.
WHAT ?!

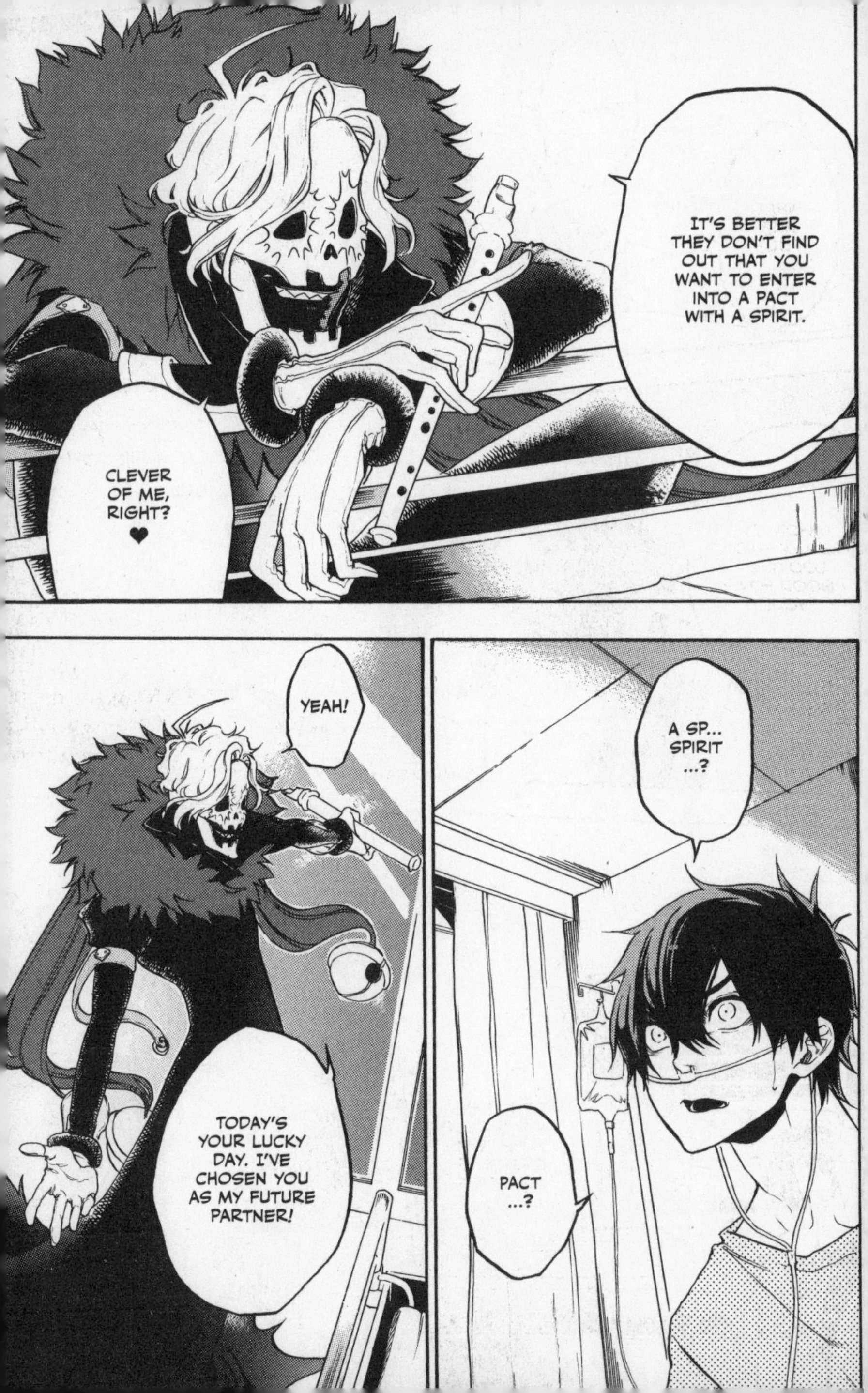
IT'S BETTER THEY DON'T FIND OUT THAT YOU WANT TO ENTER INTO A PACT WITH A SPIRIT.
CLEVER OF ME, RIGHT? ❤
A SP... SPIRIT ...?
PACT ...?
YEAH!
TODAY'S YOUR LUCKY DAY. I'VE CHOSEN YOU AS MY FUTURE PARTNER!

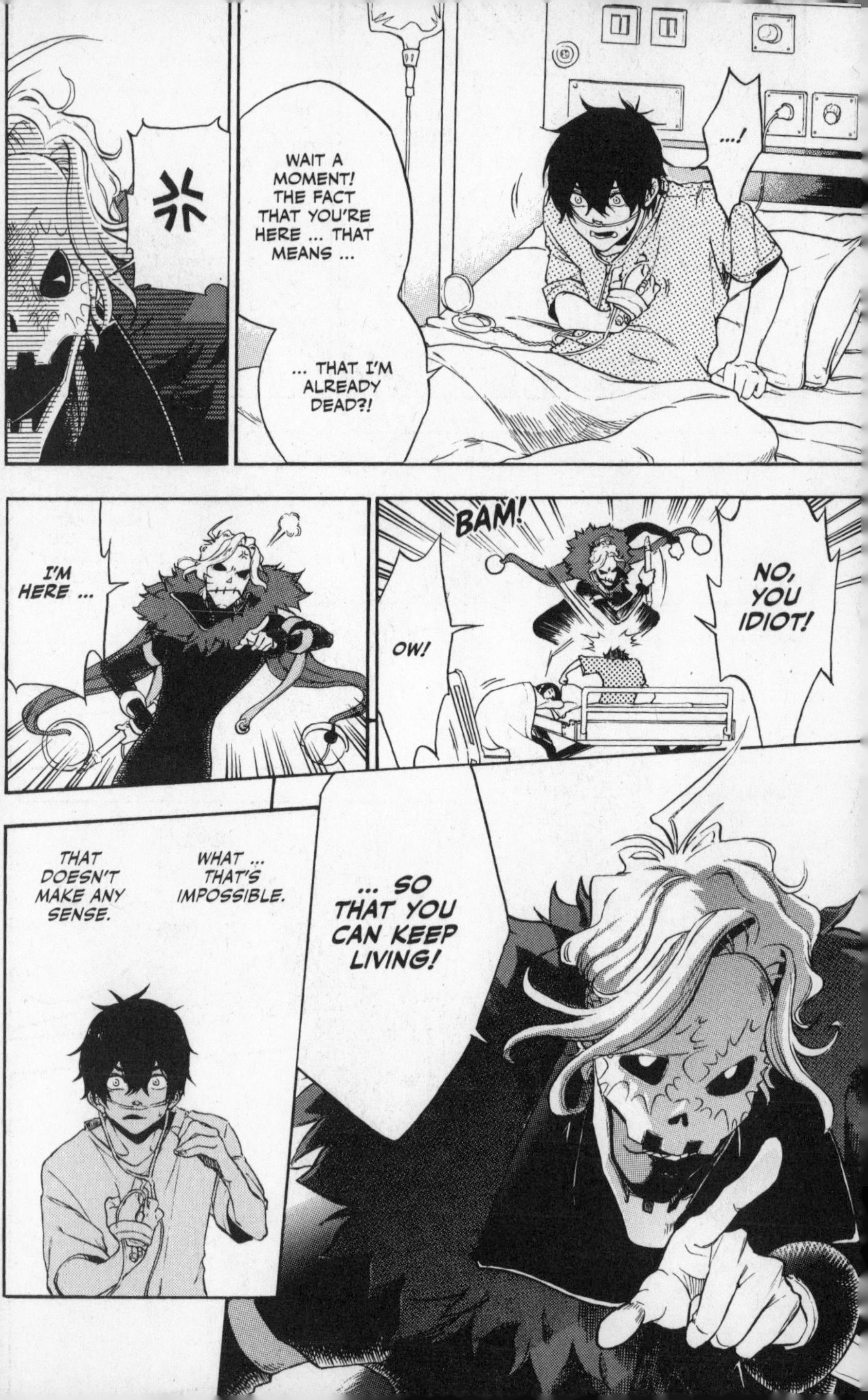
...!
WAIT A MOMENT! THE FACT THAT YOU'RE HERE ... THAT MEANS ...
... THAT I'M ALREADY DEAD?!
NO, YOU IDIOT!
BAM!
OW!
I'M HERE ...
... SO THAT YOU CAN KEEP LIVING!
WHAT ... THAT'S IMPOSSIBLE.
THAT DOESN'T MAKE ANY SENSE.

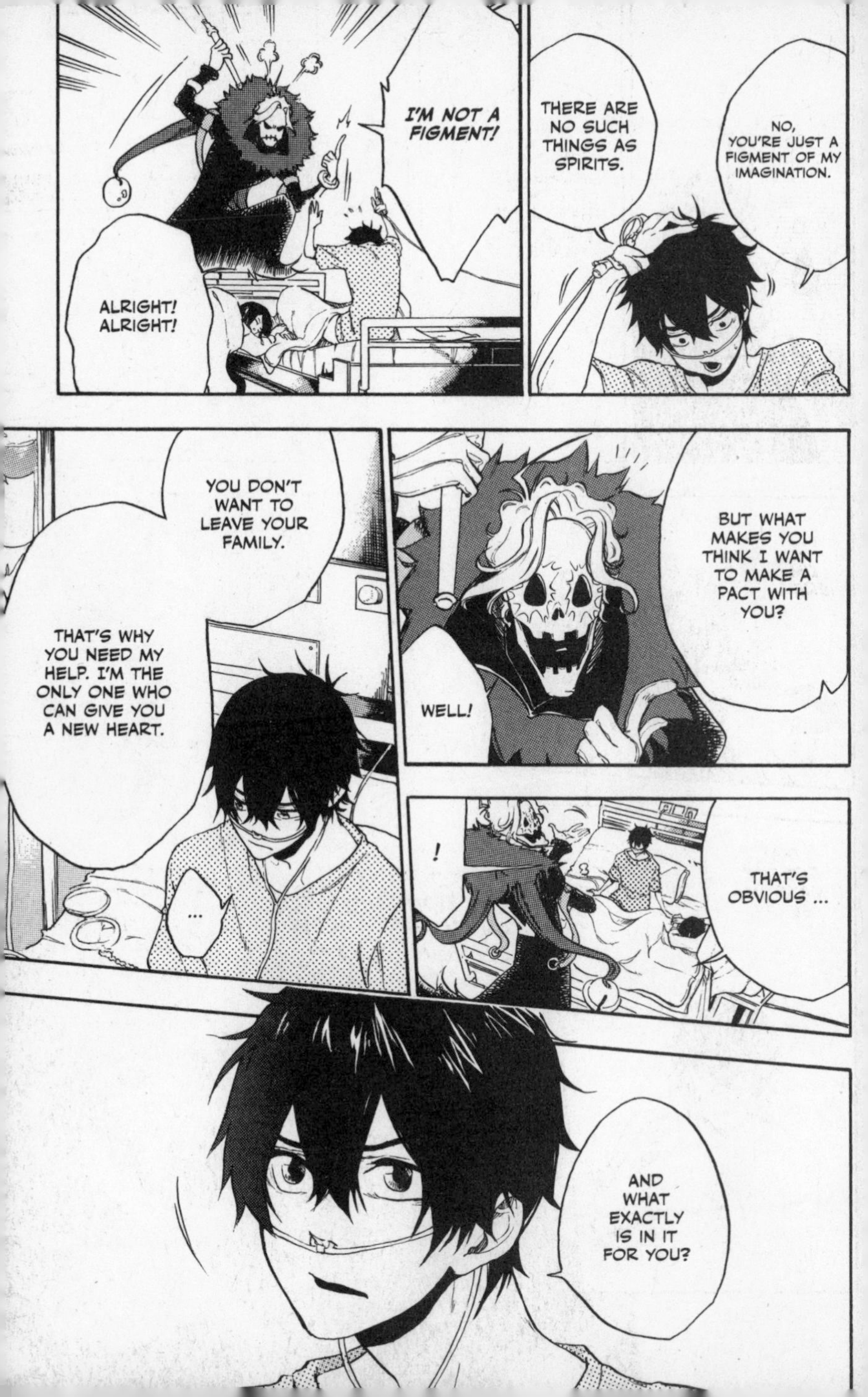
NO, YOU'RE JUST A FIGMENT OF MY IMAGINATION.
THERE ARE NO SUCH THINGS AS SPIRITS.
I'M NOT A FIGMENT!
ALRIGHT! ALRIGHT!
BUT WHAT MAKES YOU THINK I WANT TO MAKE A PACT WITH YOU?
WELL!
THAT'S OBVIOUS ...
!
YOU DON'T WANT TO LEAVE YOUR FAMILY.
THAT'S WHY YOU NEED MY HELP. I'M THE ONLY ONE WHO CAN GIVE YOU A NEW HEART.
...
AND WHAT EXACTLY IS IN IT FOR YOU?

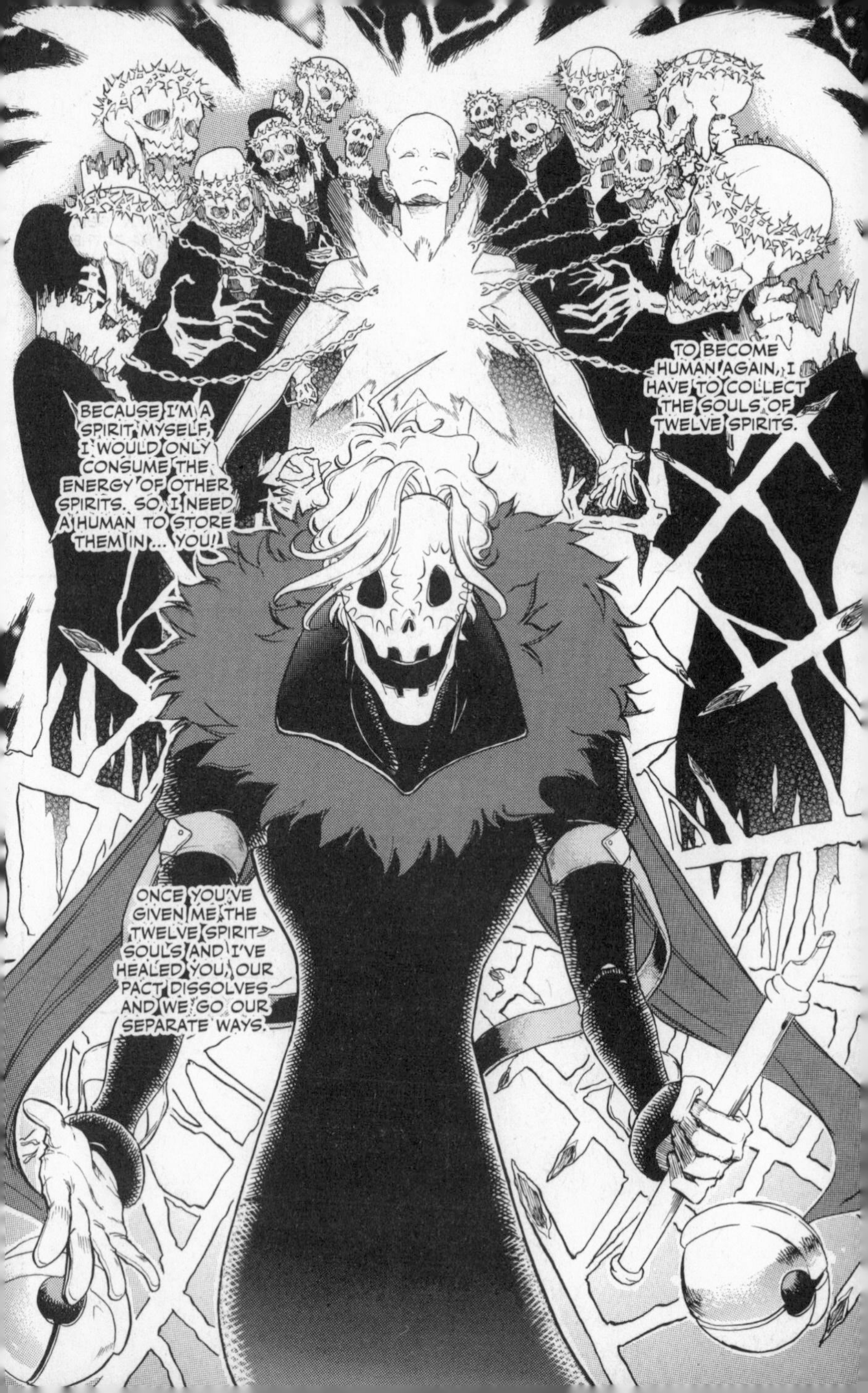
TO BECOME HUMAN AGAIN, I HAVE TO COLLECT THE SOULS OF TWELVE SPIRITS.
BECAUSE I'M A SPIRIT MYSELF, I WOULD ONLY CONSUME THE ENERGY OF OTHER SPIRITS. SO, I NEED A HUMAN TO STORE THEM IN ... YOU!
ONCE YOU'VE GIVEN ME THE TWELVE SPIRIT SOULS AND I'VE HEALED YOU, OUR PACT DISSOLVES AND WE GO OUR SEPARATE WAYS.

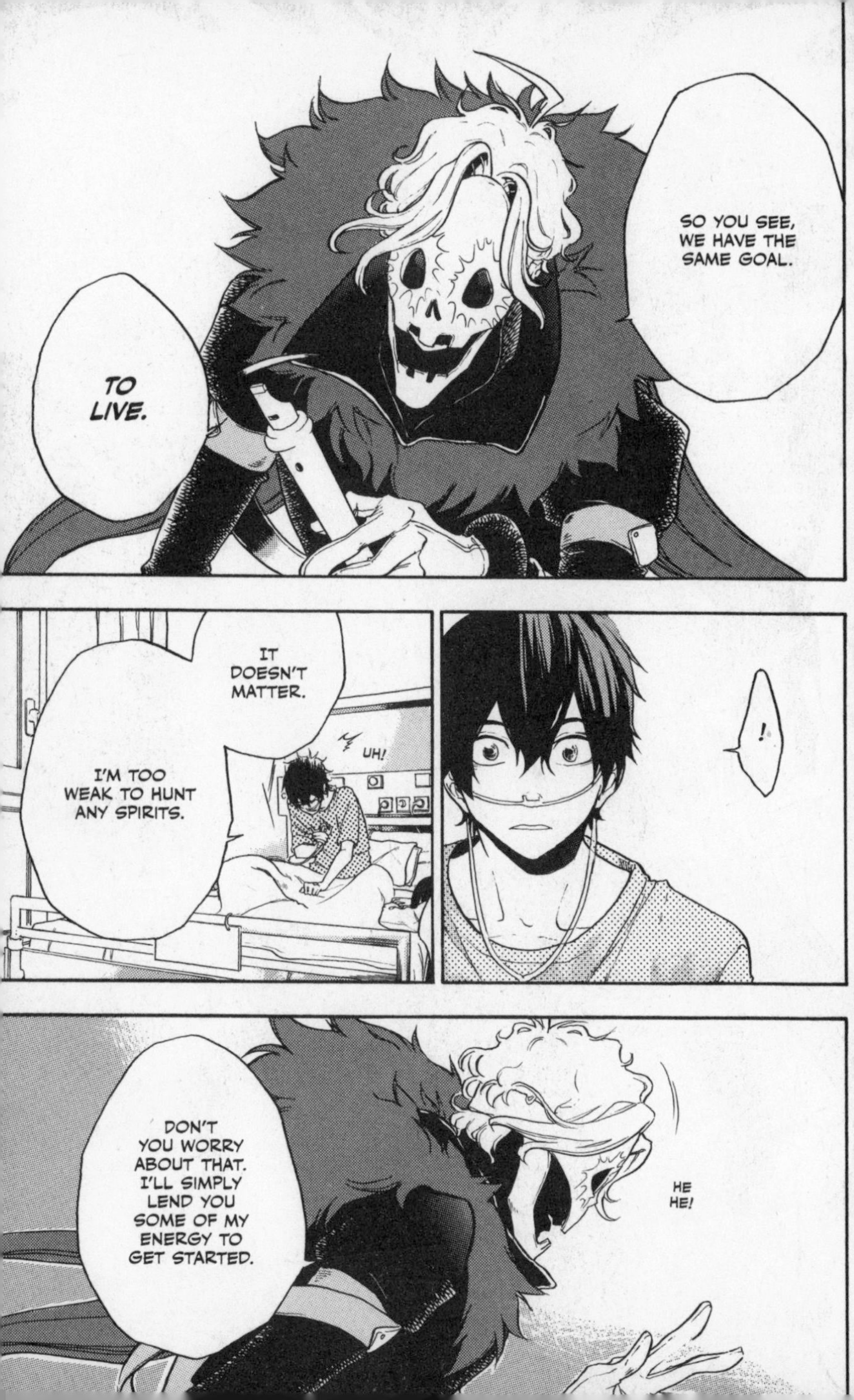
SO YOU SEE, WE HAVE THE SAME GOAL.
TO LIVE.
!
IT DOESN'T MATTER.
UH!
I'M TOO WEAK TO HUNT ANY SPIRITS.
HE HE!
DON'T YOU WORRY ABOUT THAT. I'LL SIMPLY LEND YOU SOME OF MY ENERGY TO GET STARTED.

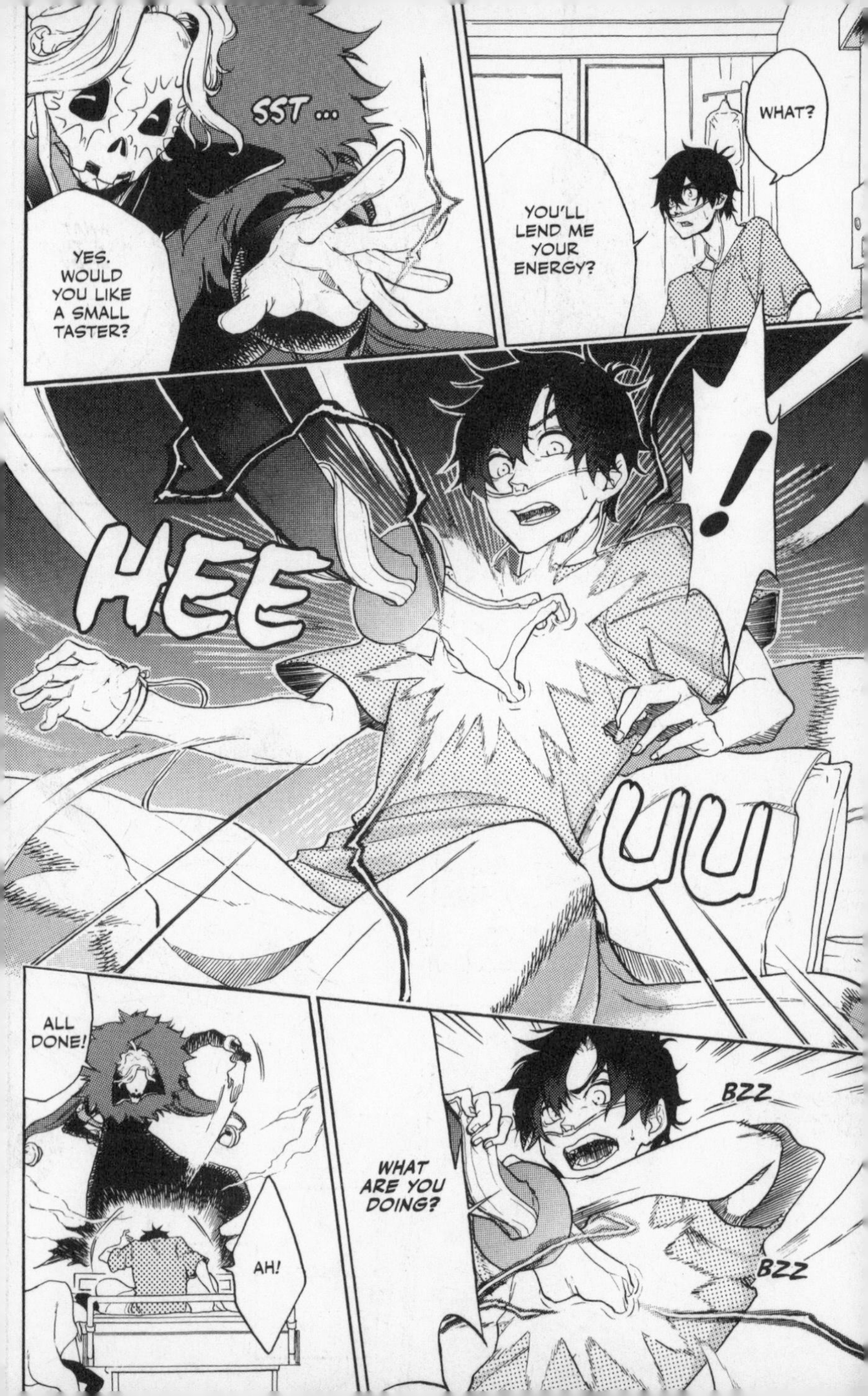
WHAT?
YOU'LL LEND ME YOUR ENERGY?
SST ...
YES. WOULD YOU LIKE A SMALL TASTER?
!
HEE
UU
BZZ
WHAT ARE YOU DOING?
BZZ
ALL DONE!
AH!

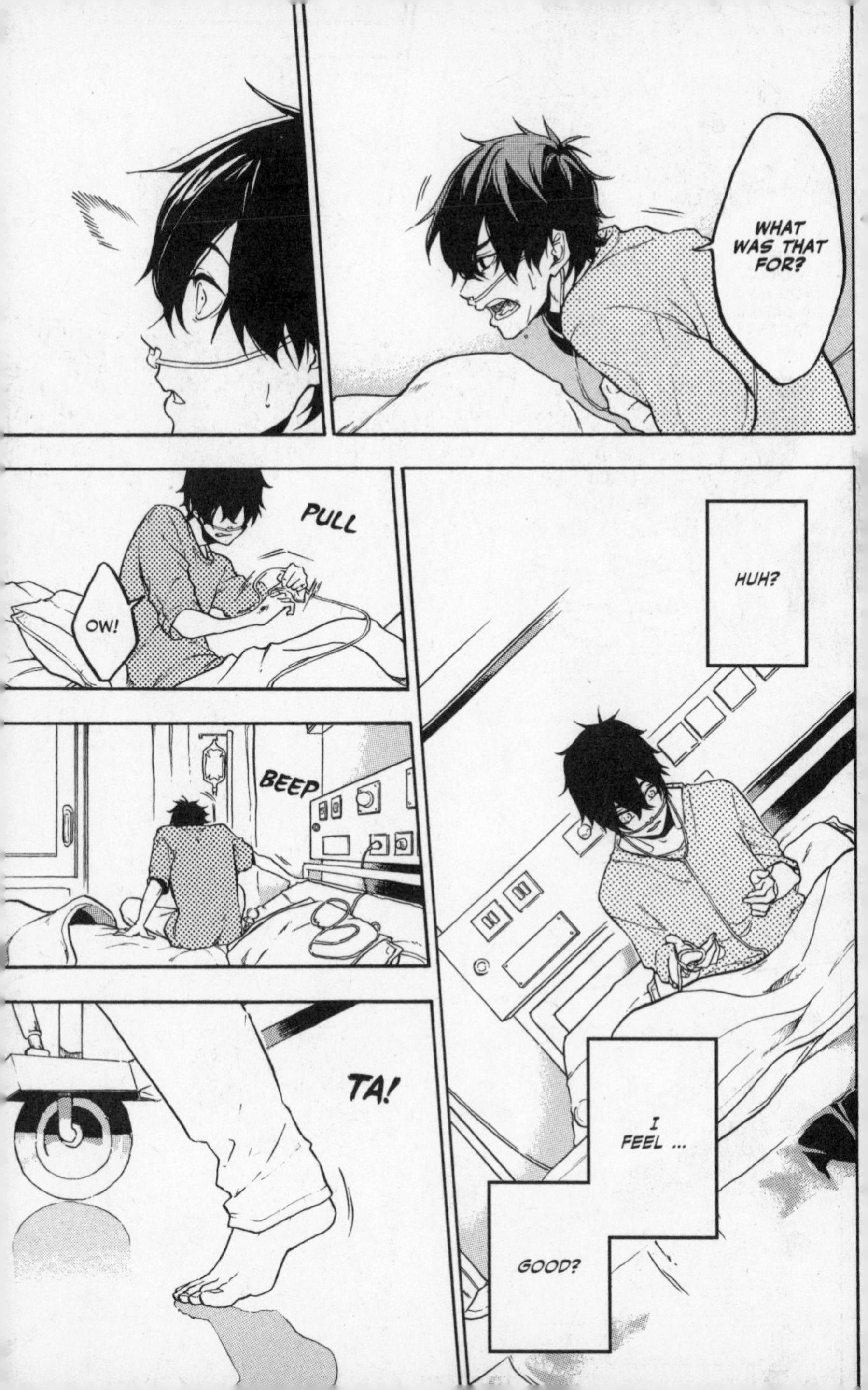
WHAT WAS THAT FOR?
HUH?
I FEEL ...
GOOD?
PULL
OW!
BEEP
TA!

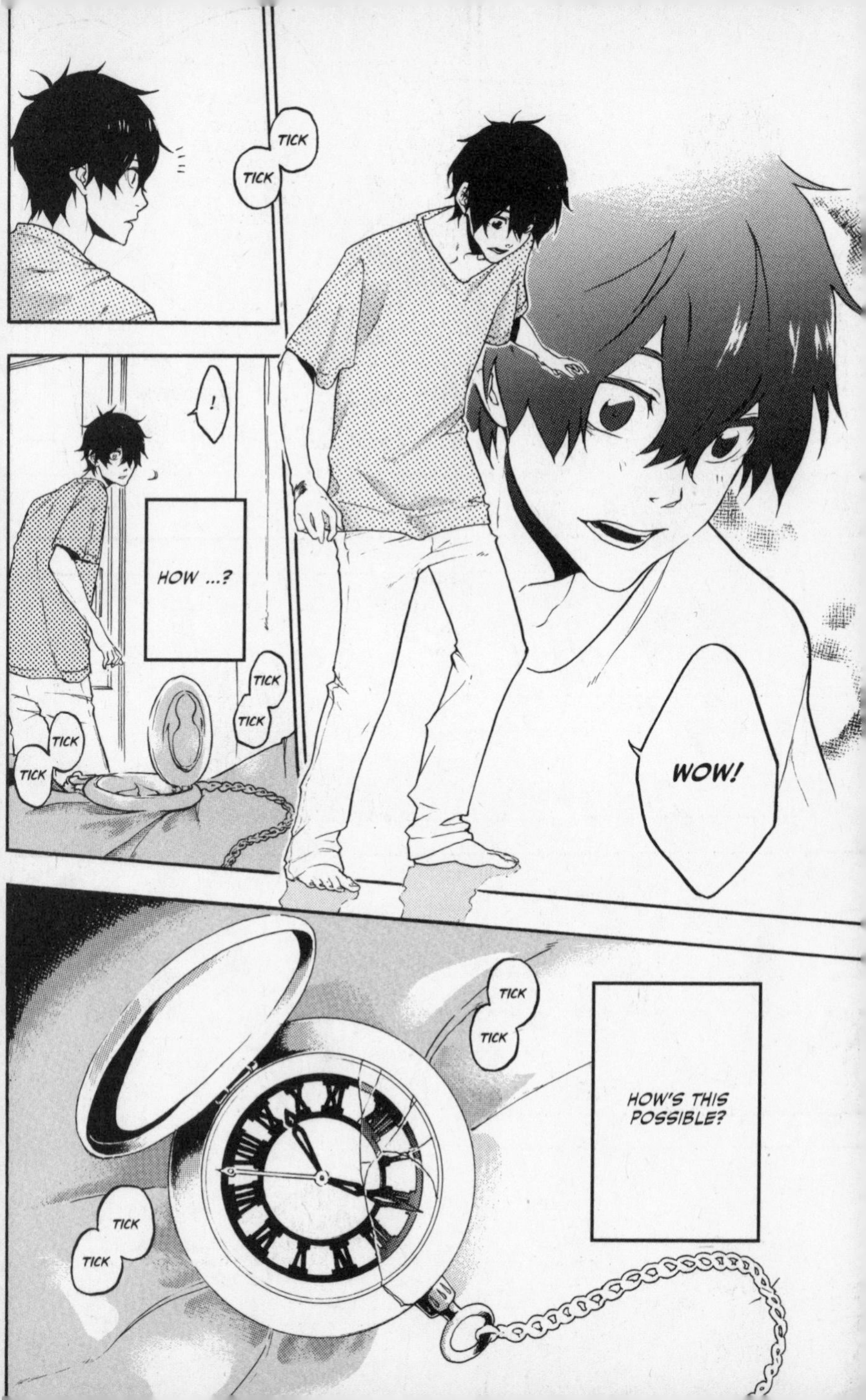
WOW!
TICK
TICK
!
HOW ...?
TICK
TICK
TICK
TICK
TICK
TICK
HOW'S THIS POSSIBLE?
TICK
TICK

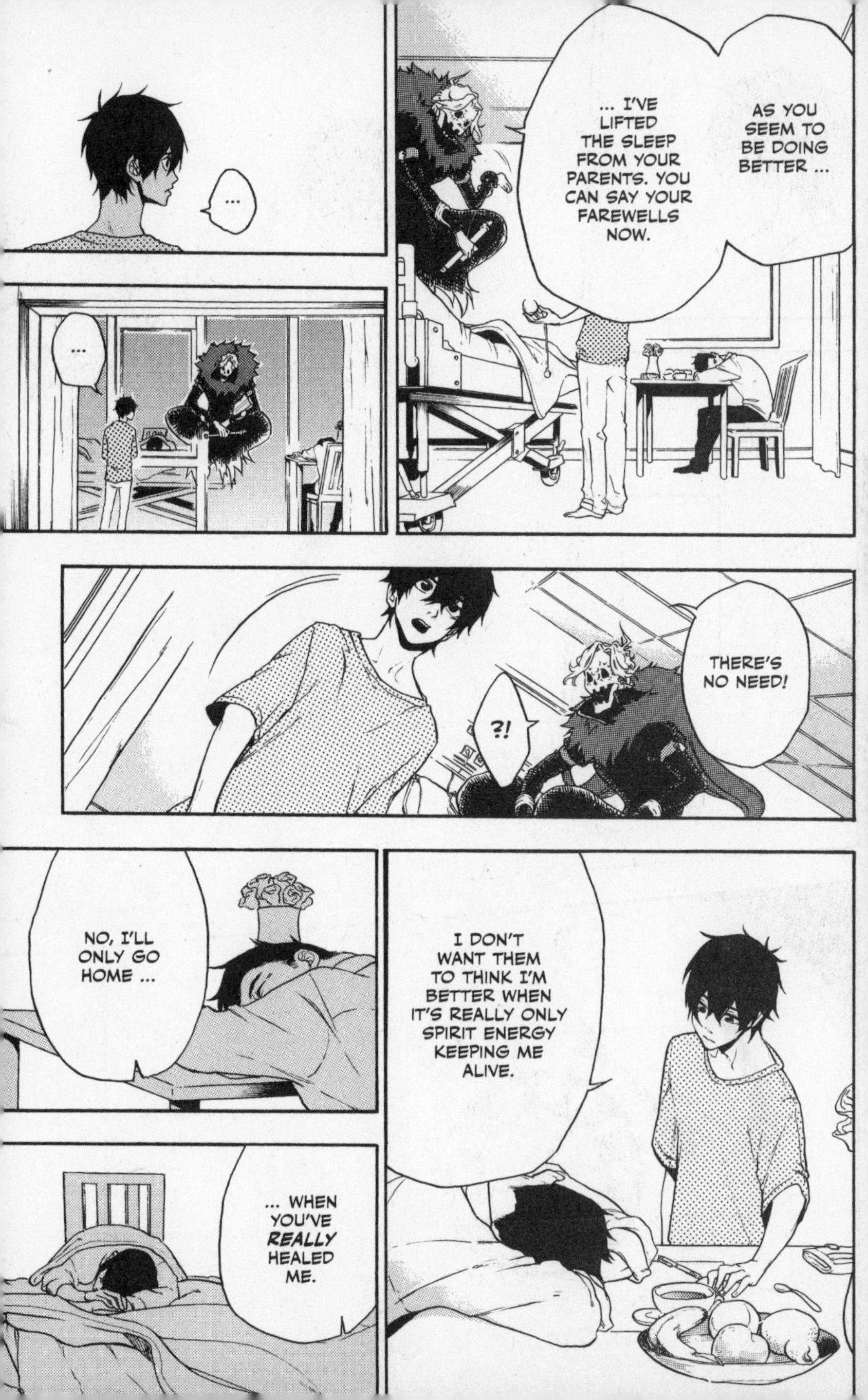
AS YOU SEEM TO BE DOING BETTER ...
... I'VE LIFTED THE SLEEP FROM YOUR PARENTS. YOU CAN SAY YOUR FAREWELLS NOW.
...
...
THERE'S NO NEED!
?!
I DON'T WANT THEM TO THINK I'M BETTER WHEN IT'S REALLY ONLY SPIRIT ENERGY KEEPING ME ALIVE.
NO, I'LL ONLY GO HOME ...
... WHEN YOU'VE *REALLY* HEALED ME.

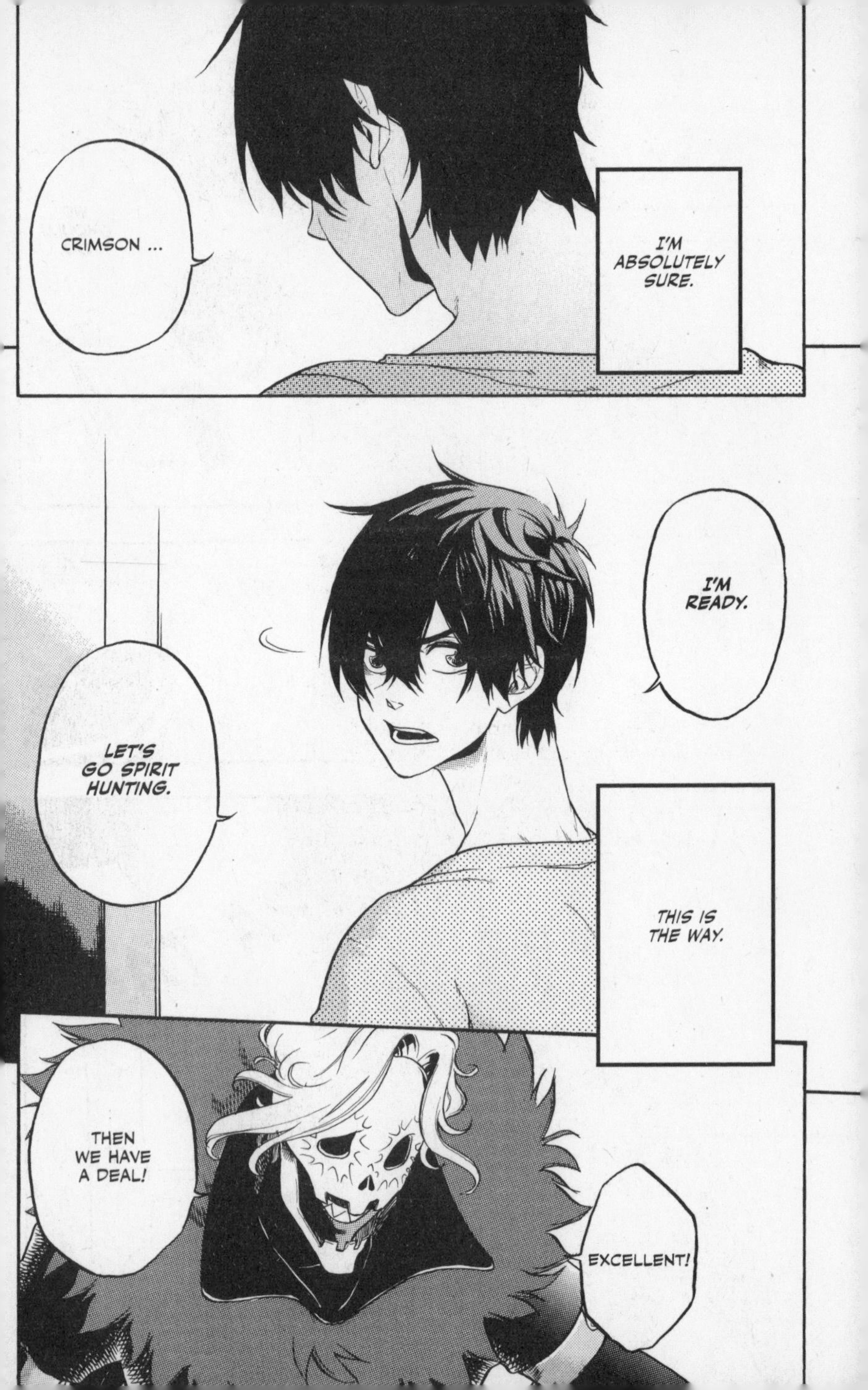
I'M ABSOLUTELY SURE.
CRIMSON ...
I'M READY.
LET'S GO SPIRIT HUNTING.
THIS IS THE WAY.
EXCELLENT!
THEN WE HAVE A DEAL!

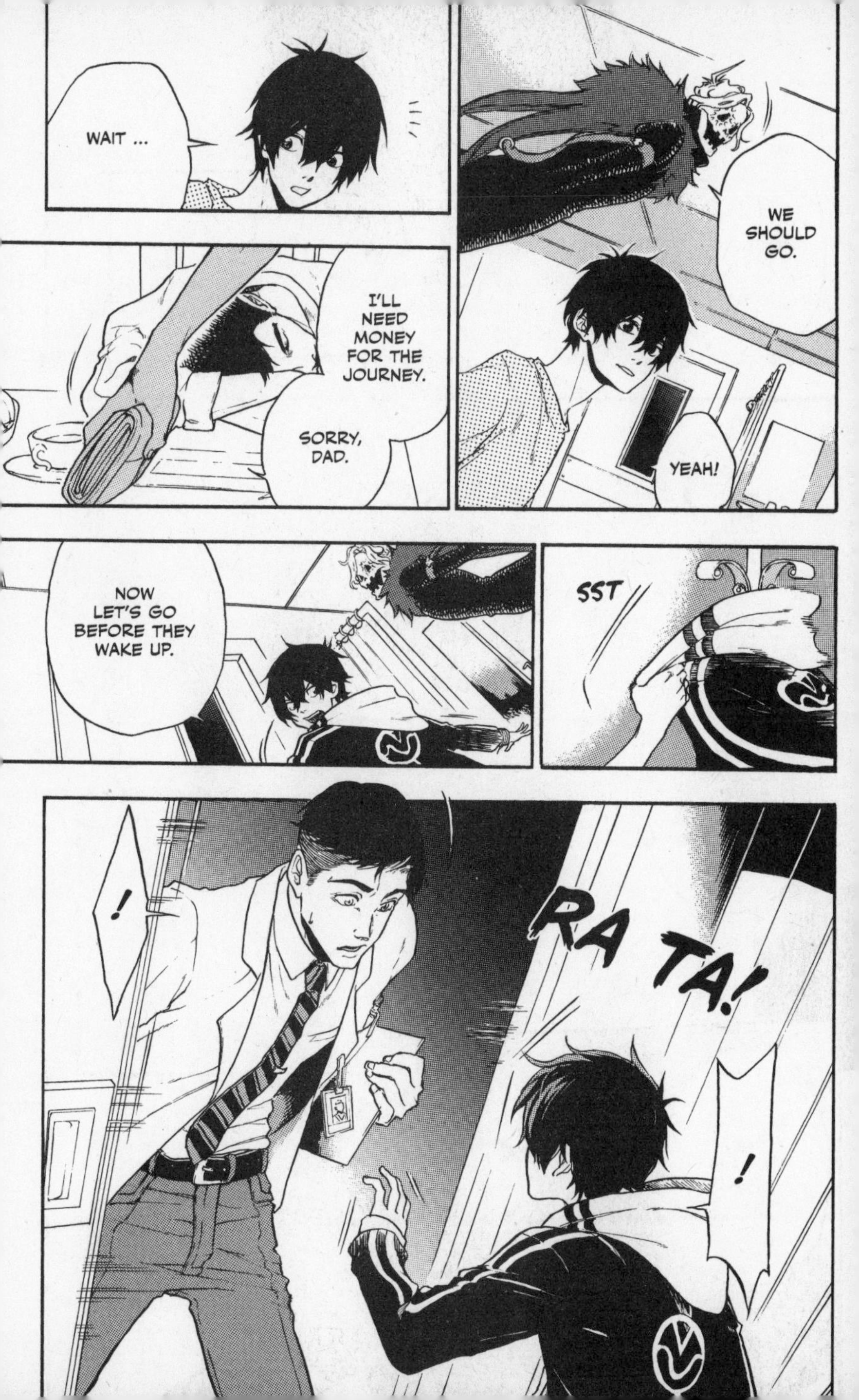
WE SHOULD GO.
YEAH!
WAIT ...
I'LL NEED MONEY FOR THE JOURNEY.
SORRY, DAD.
SST
NOW LET'S GO BEFORE THEY WAKE UP.
RA TA!
!
!

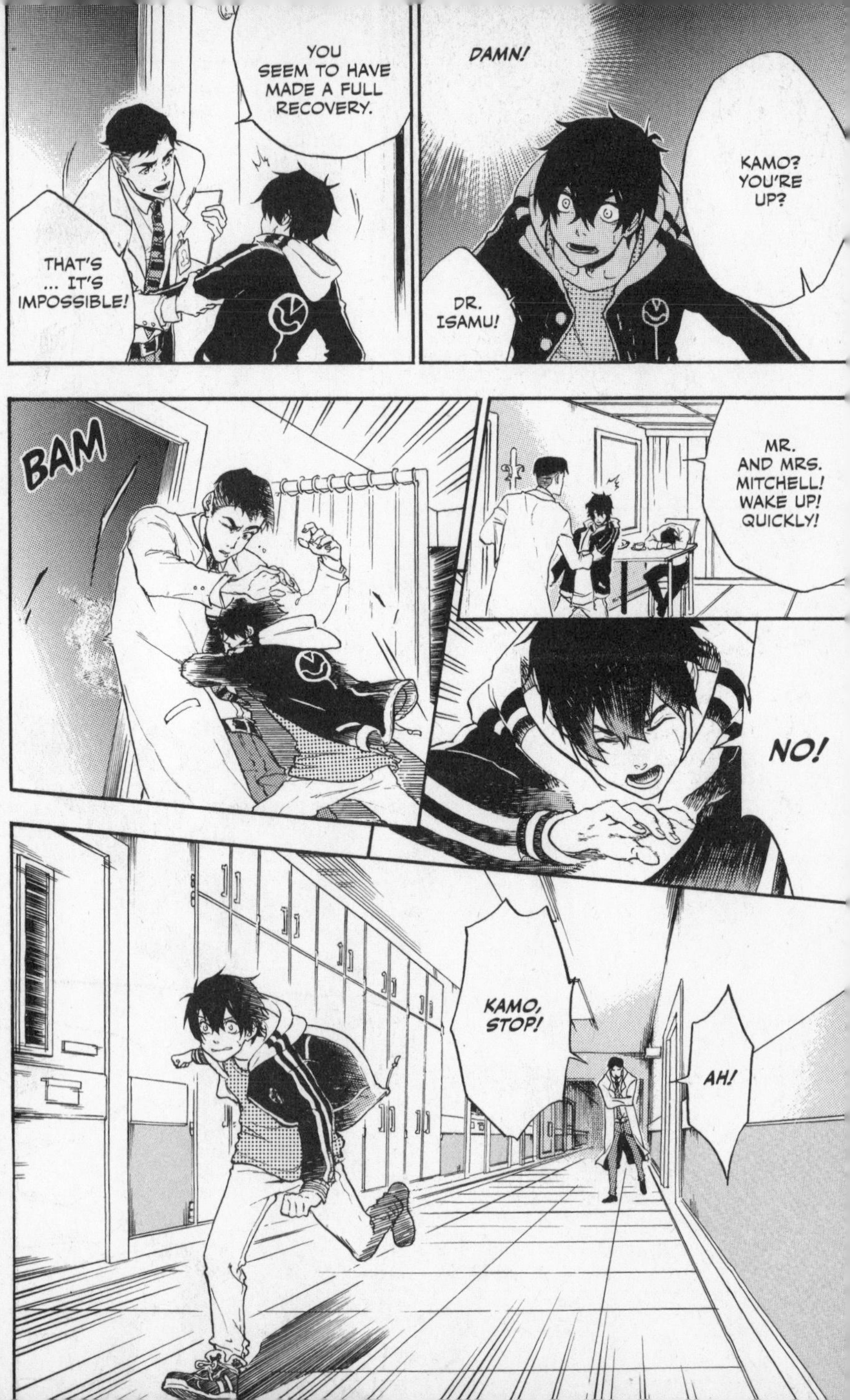

KAMO? YOU'RE UP?
DAMN!
DR. ISAMU!
YOU SEEM TO HAVE MADE A FULL RECOVERY.
THAT'S ... IT'S IMPOSSIBLE!
MR. AND MRS. MITCHELL! WAKE UP! QUICKLY!
NO!
BAM
AH!
KAMO, STOP!

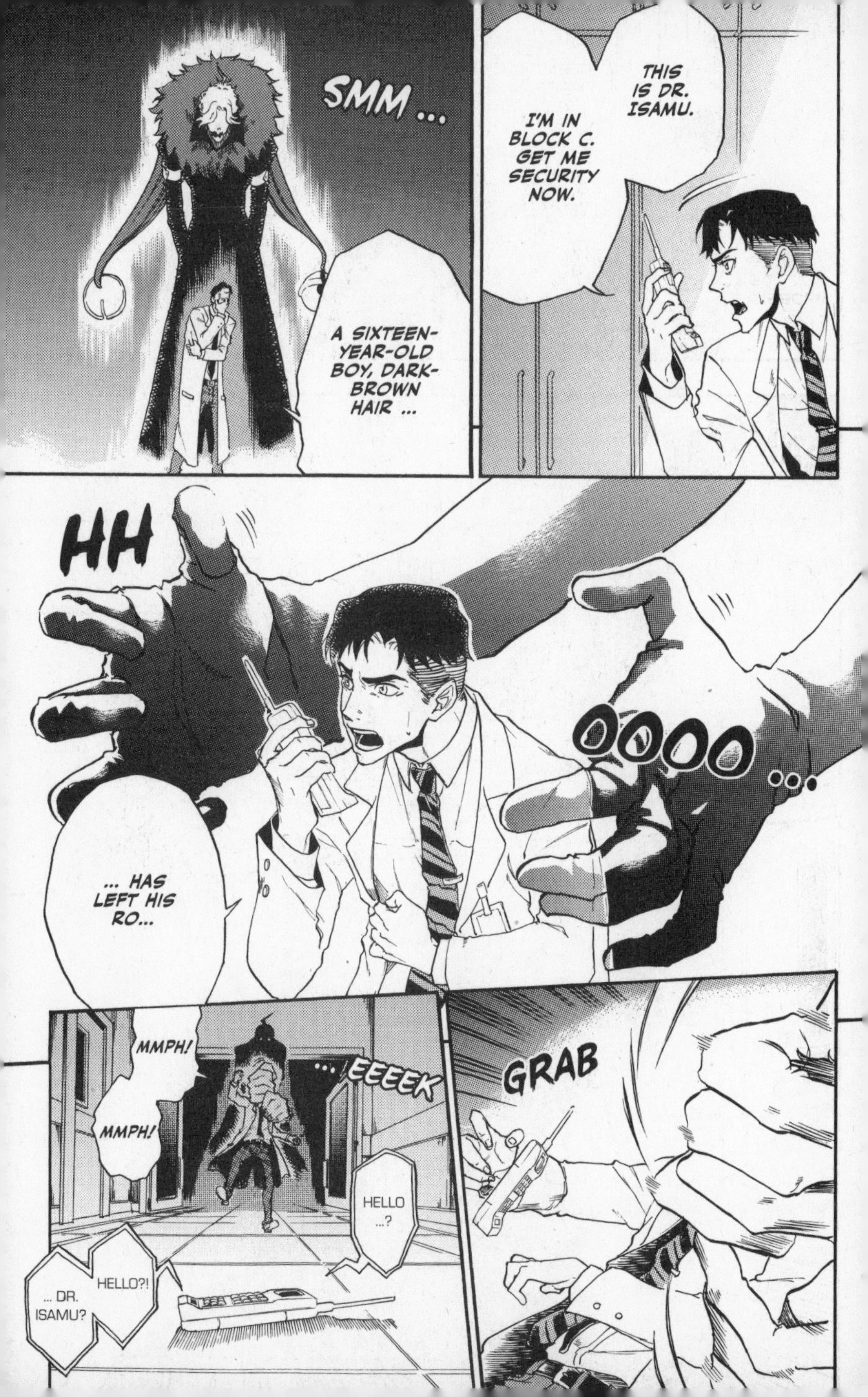
THIS IS DR. ISAMU.
I'M IN BLOCK C. GET ME SECURITY NOW.
SMM ...
A SIXTEEN-YEAR-OLD BOY, DARK-BROWN HAIR ...
HH
OOOO...
... HAS LEFT HIS RO...
GRAB
...EEEEK
MMPH!
MMPH!
HELLO ...?
HELLO?!
... DR. ISAMU?

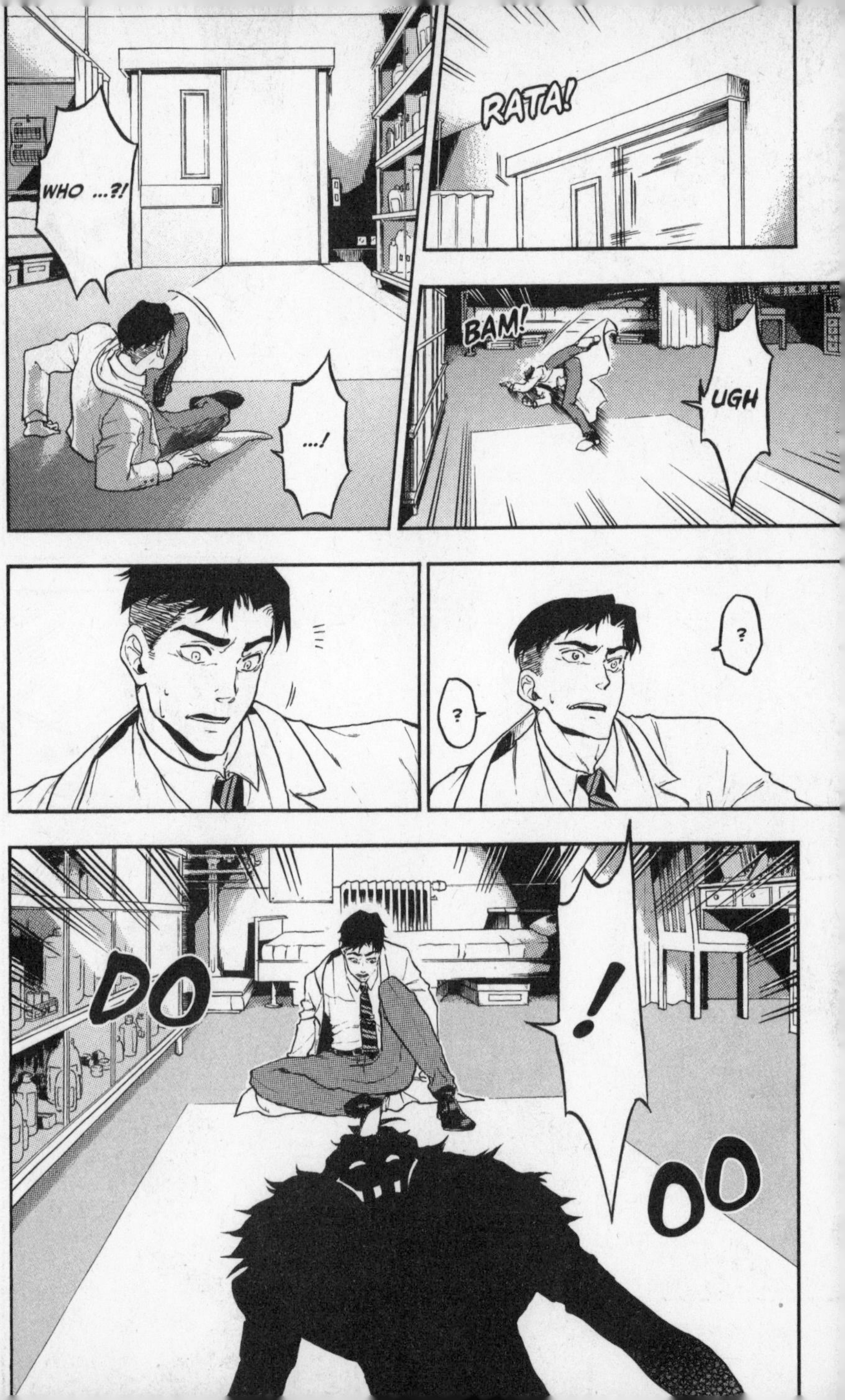

RATA!
BAM!
UGH
WHO ...?!
...!
?
?
DO
!
OO

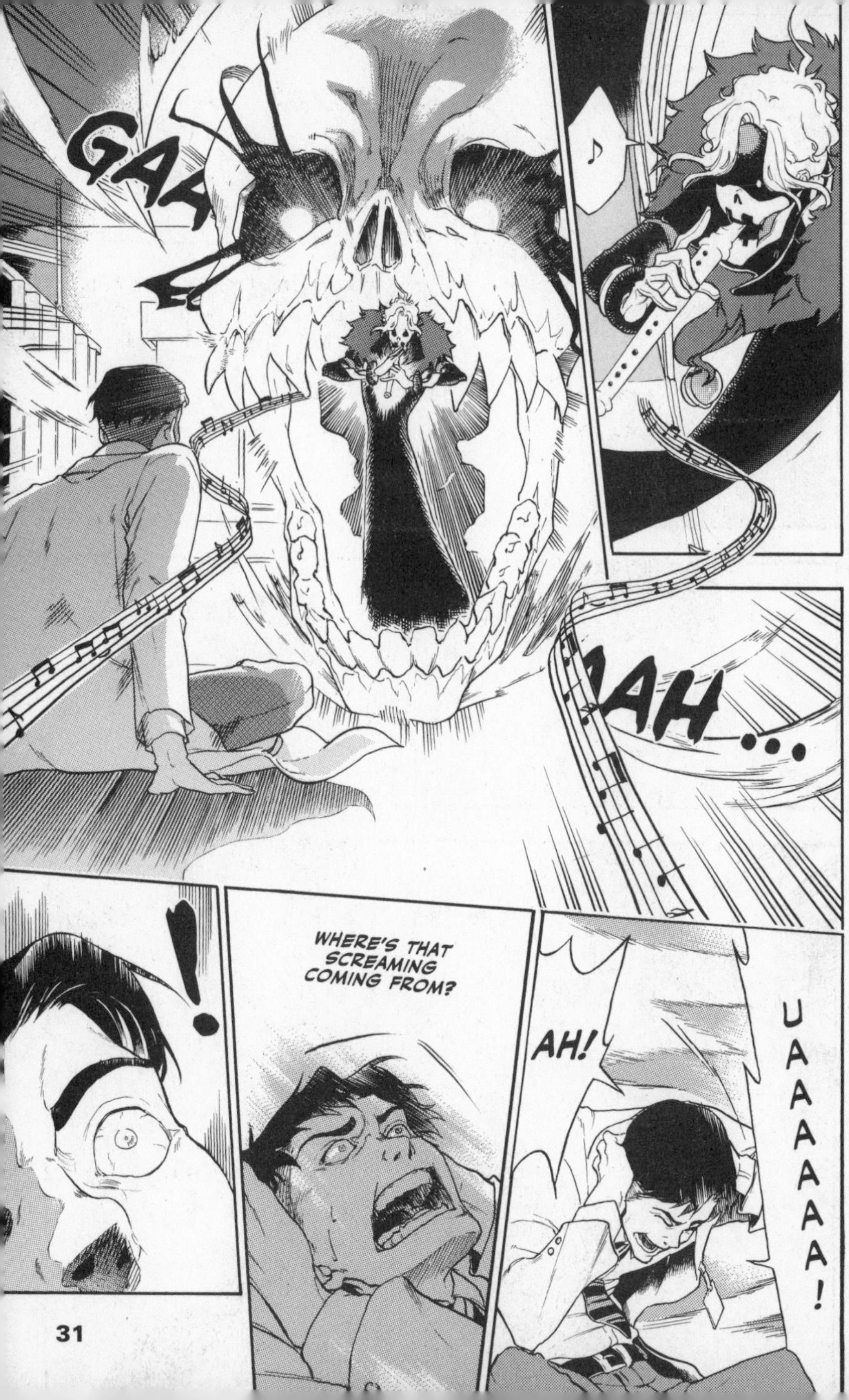
♪
GAA
AAH...
AH!
UAAAAAA!
WHERE'S THAT SCREAMING COMING FROM?
!

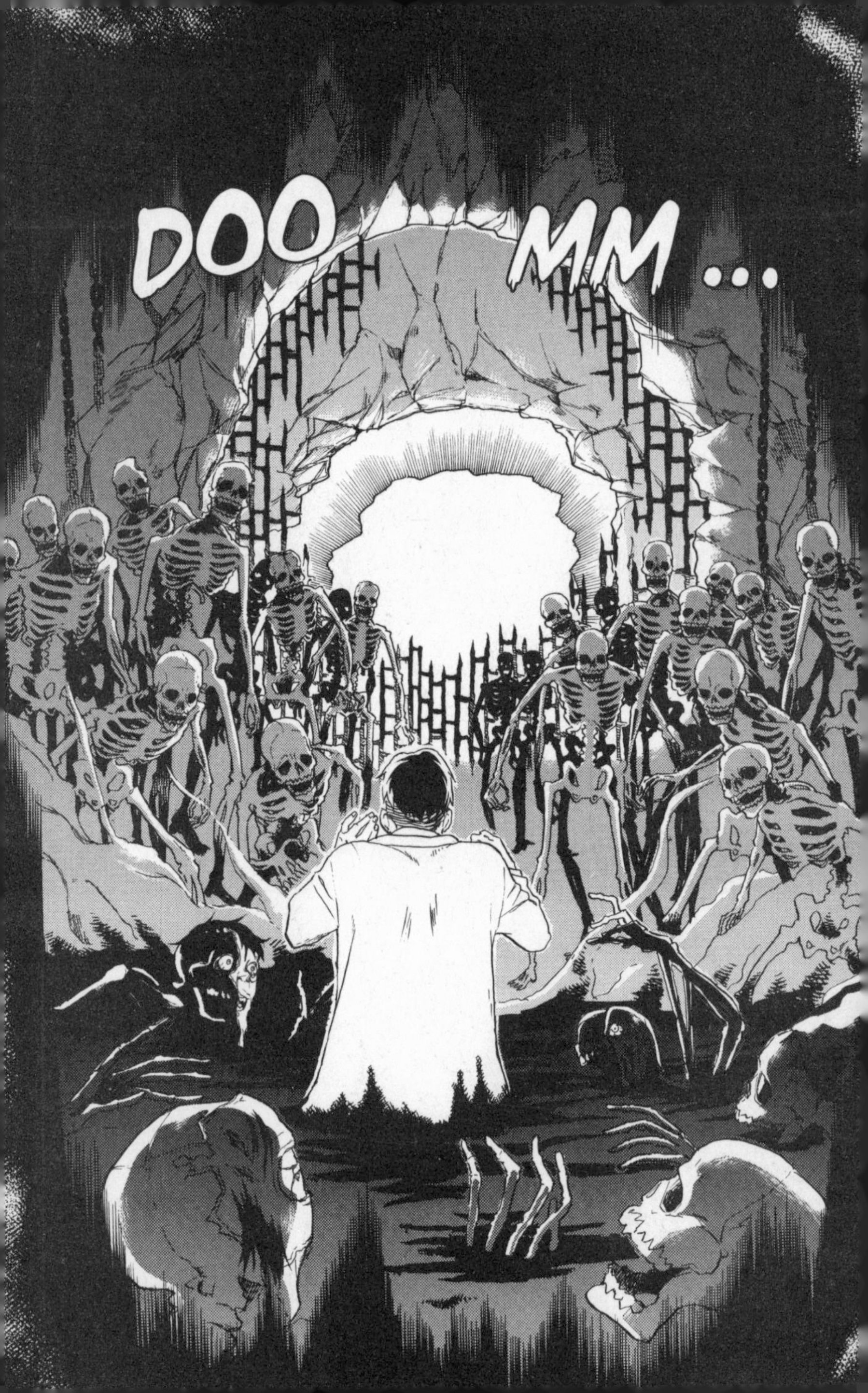
DOO MM...

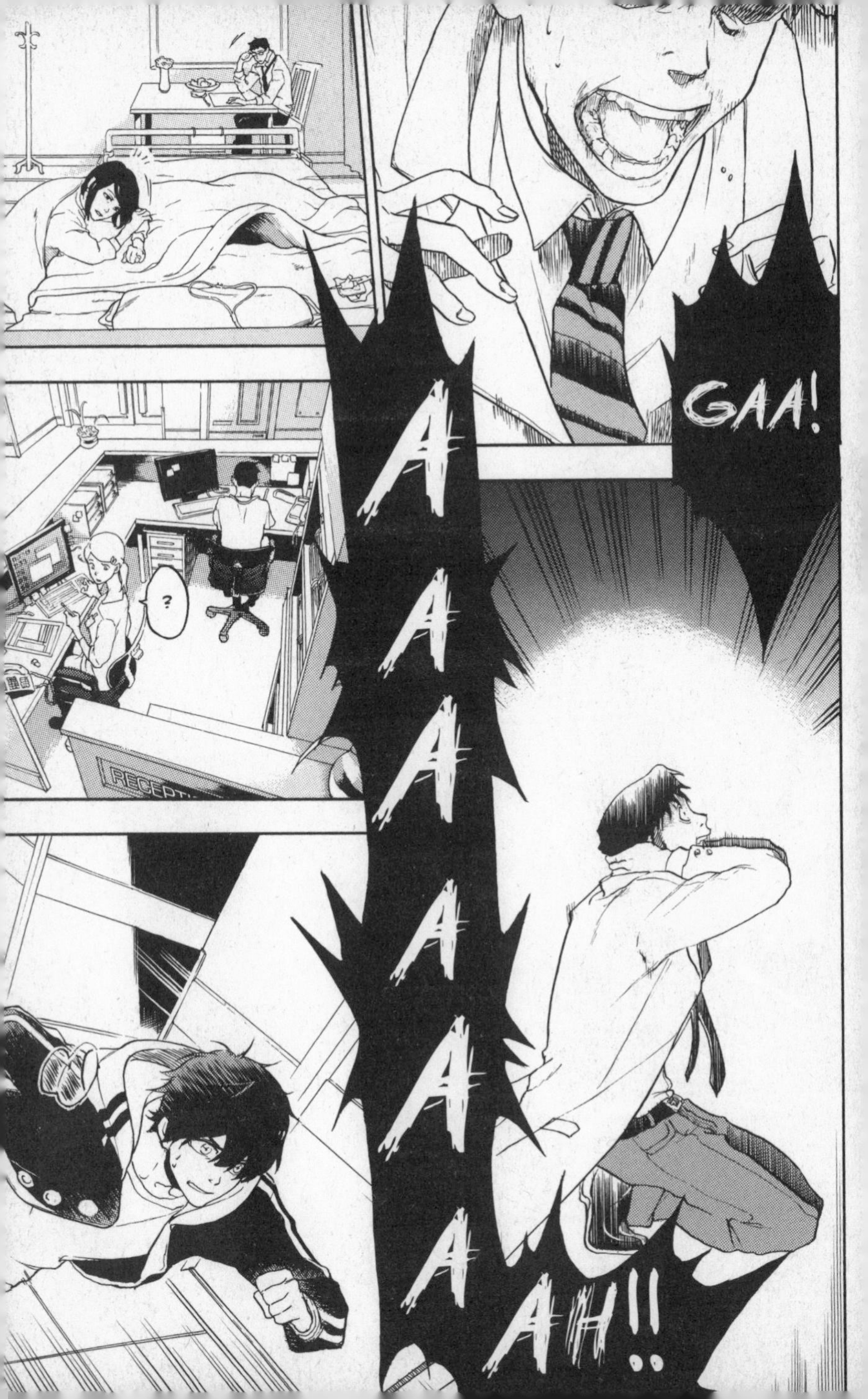
GAA!
AAAAAAAAH!!
?

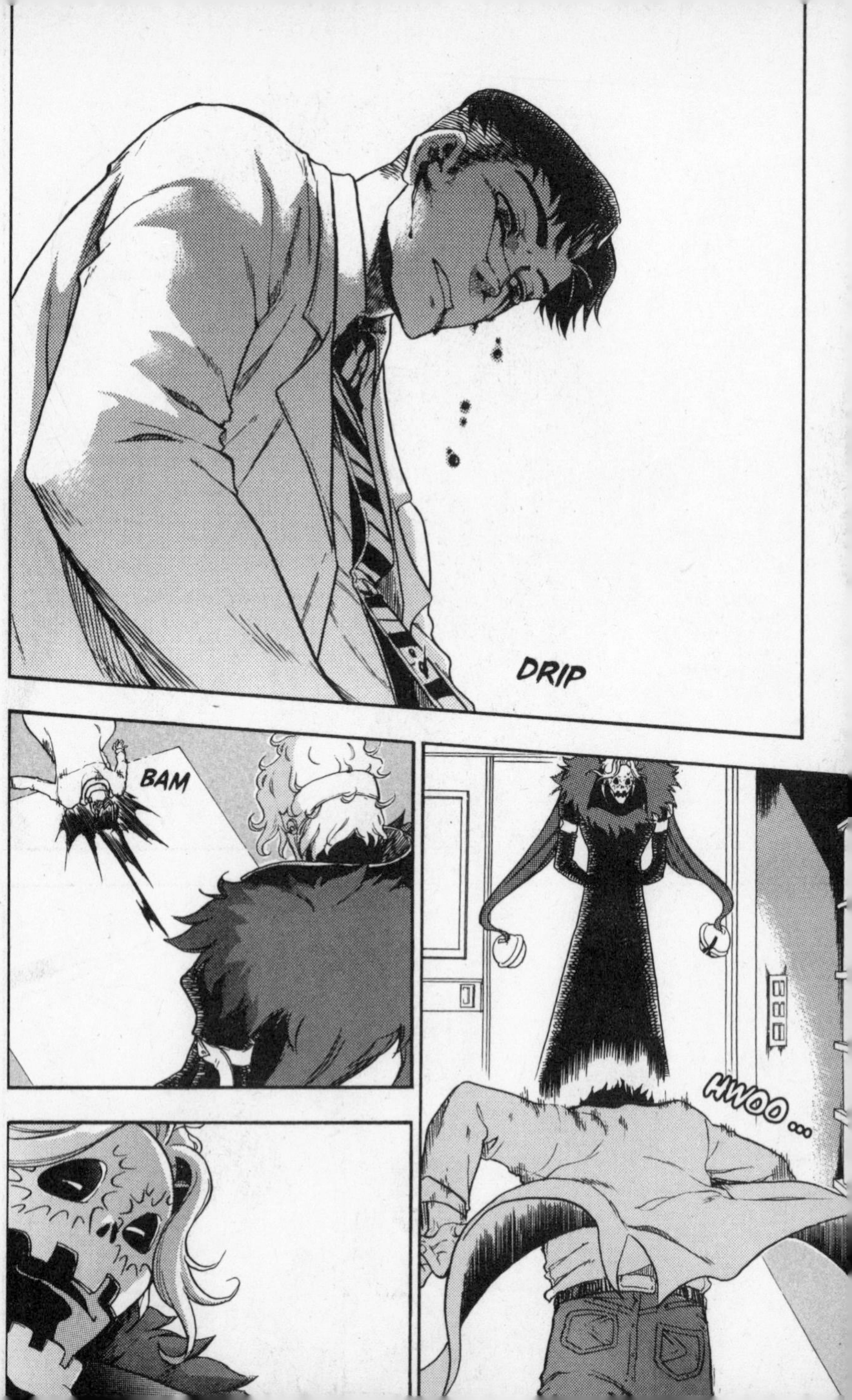
DRIP
HWOO...
BAM

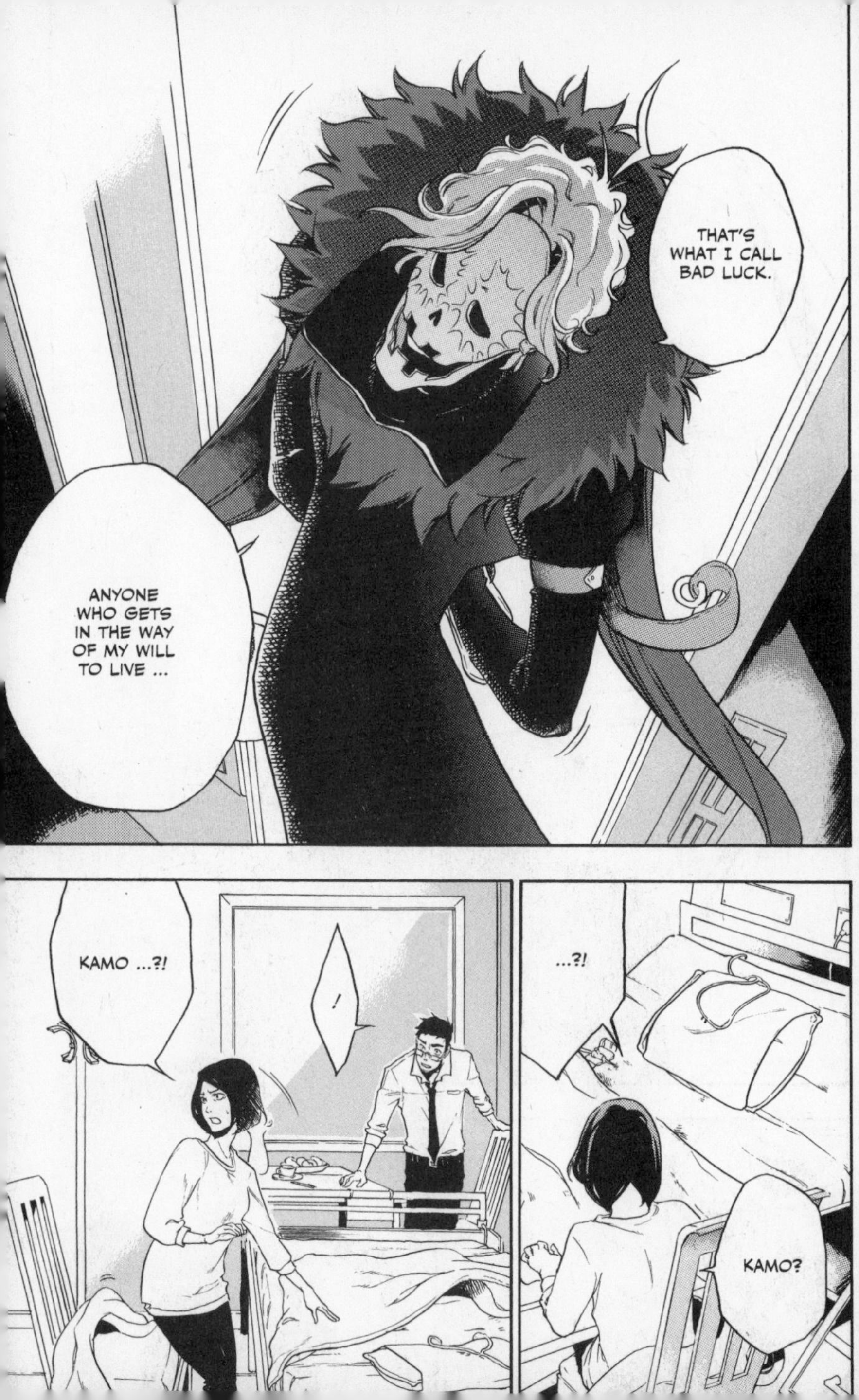
THAT'S WHAT I CALL BAD LUCK.
ANYONE WHO GETS IN THE WAY OF MY WILL TO LIVE ...
...?!
KAMO?
!
KAMO ...?!

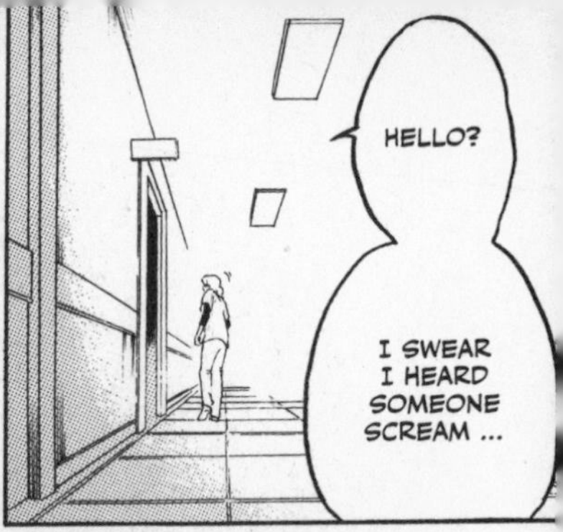
HELLO?
I SWEAR I HEARD SOMEONE SCREAM ...
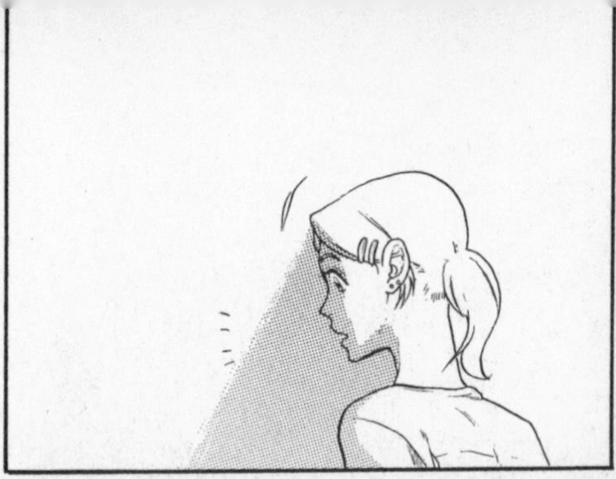
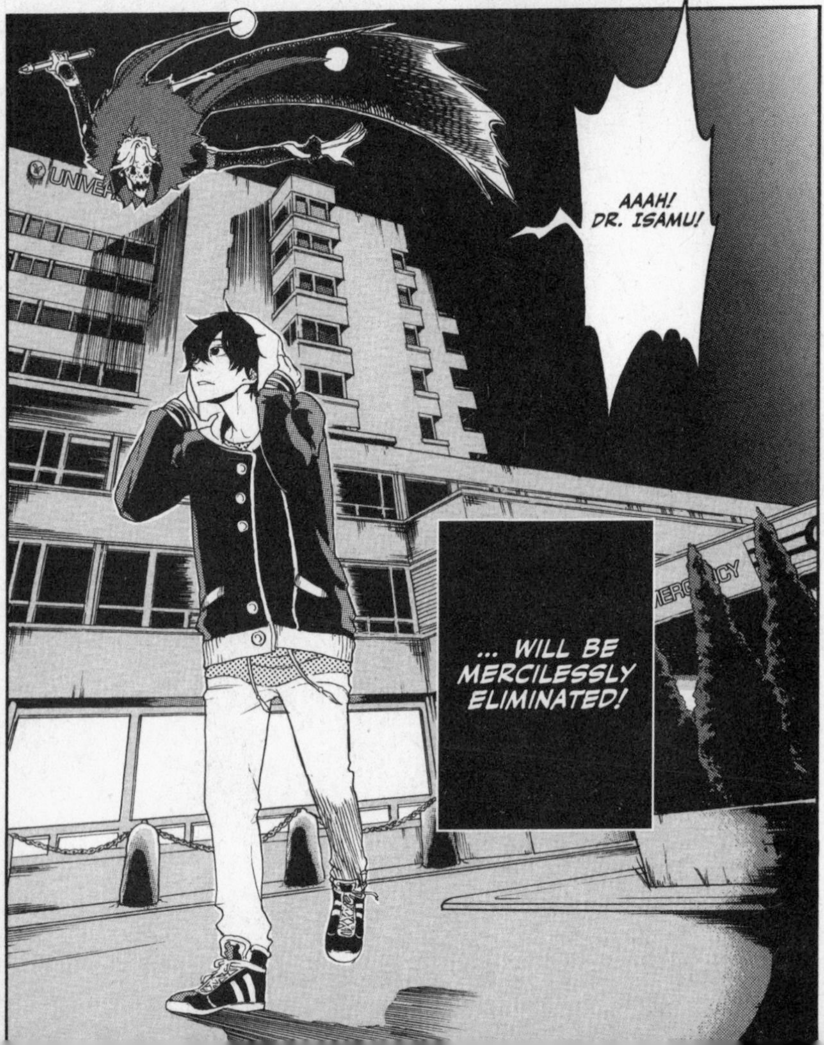
AAAH! DR. ISAMU!
... WILL BE MERCILESSLY ELIMINATED!

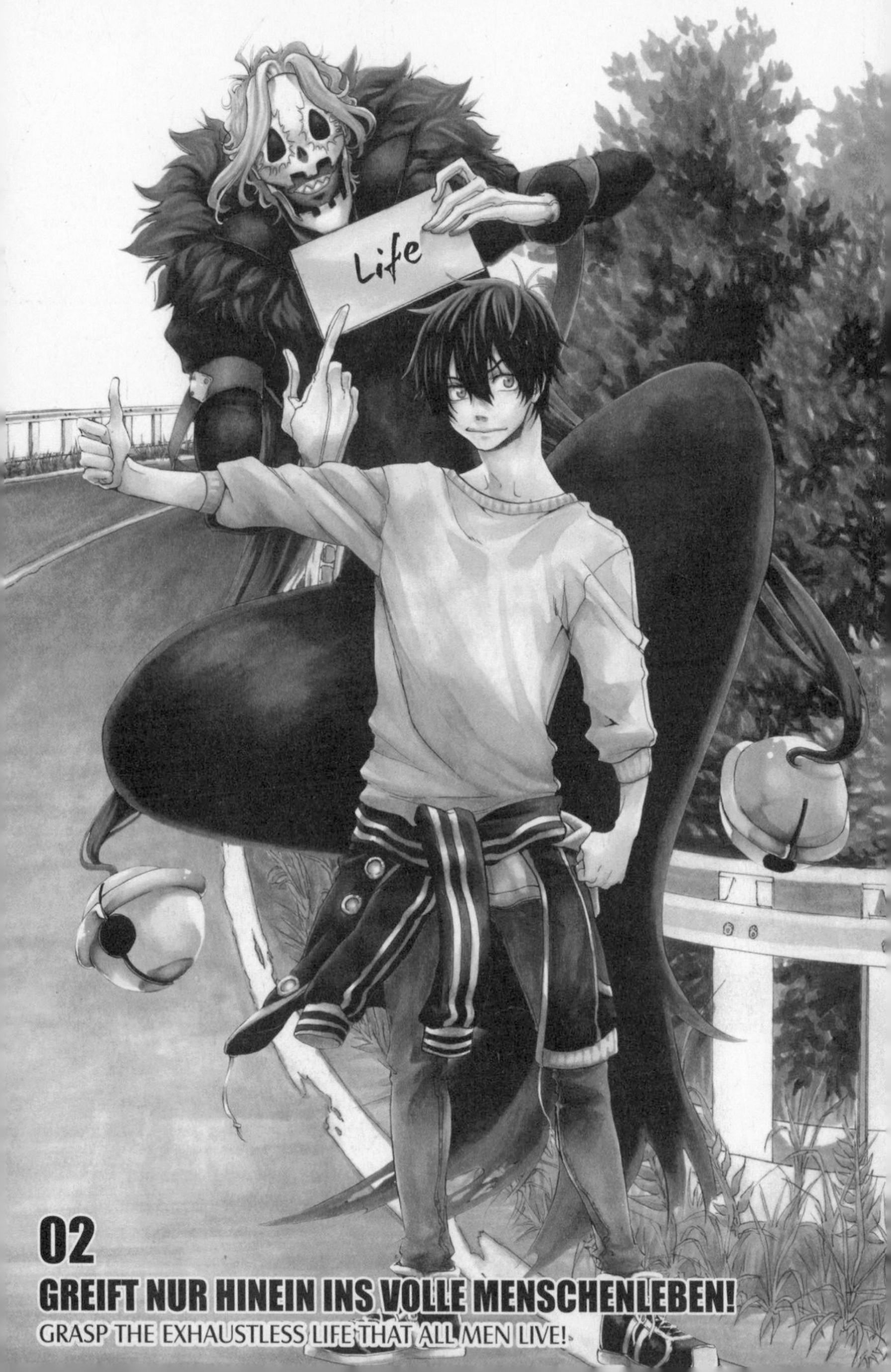
Life

02
GREIFT NUR HINEIN INS VOLLE MENSCHENLEBEN!
GRASP THE EXHAUSTLESS LIFE THAT ALL MEN LIVE!

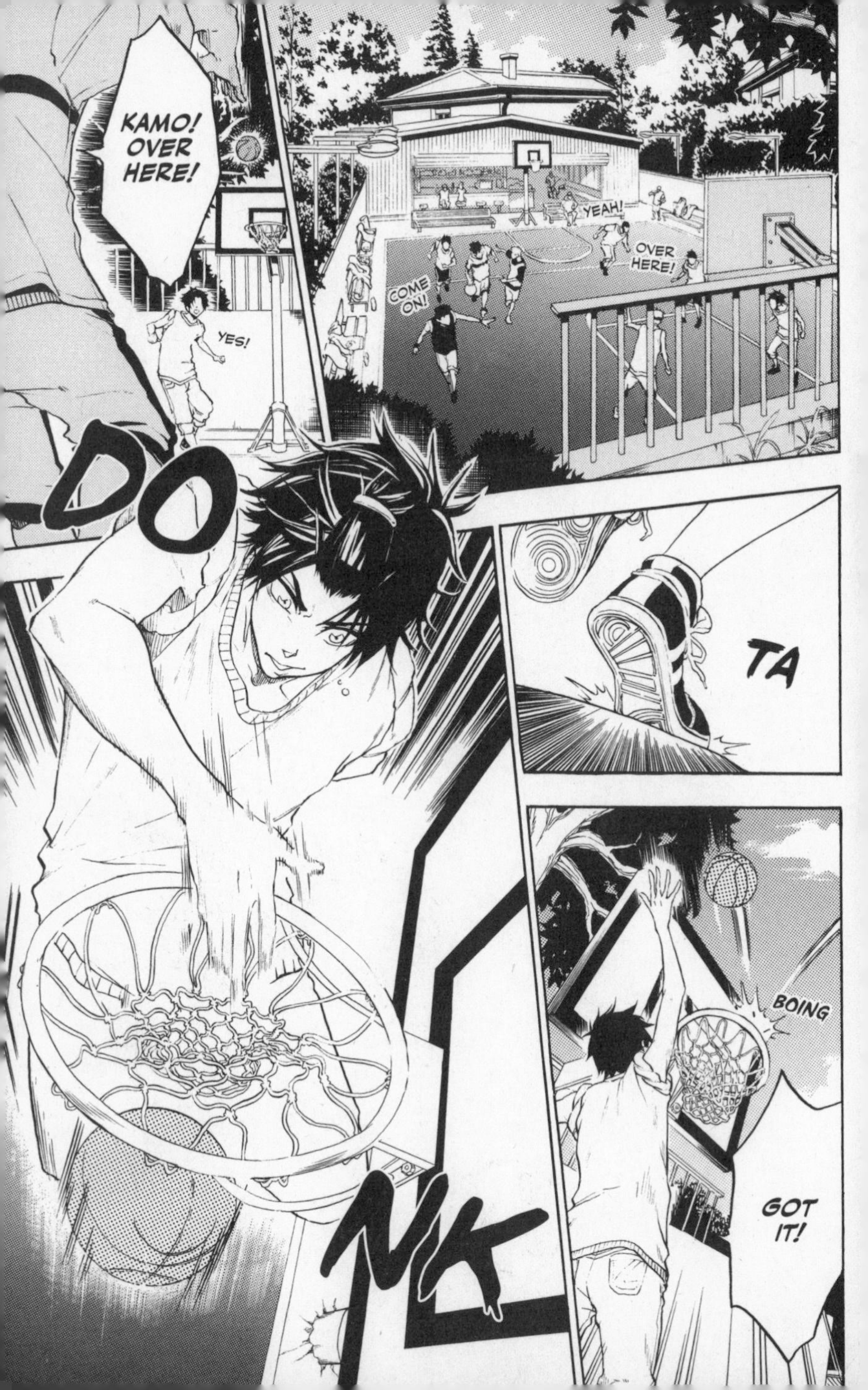
YEAH!
OVER HERE!
COME ON!
KAMO! OVER HERE!
YES!
TA
BOING
GOT IT!
DO
NK

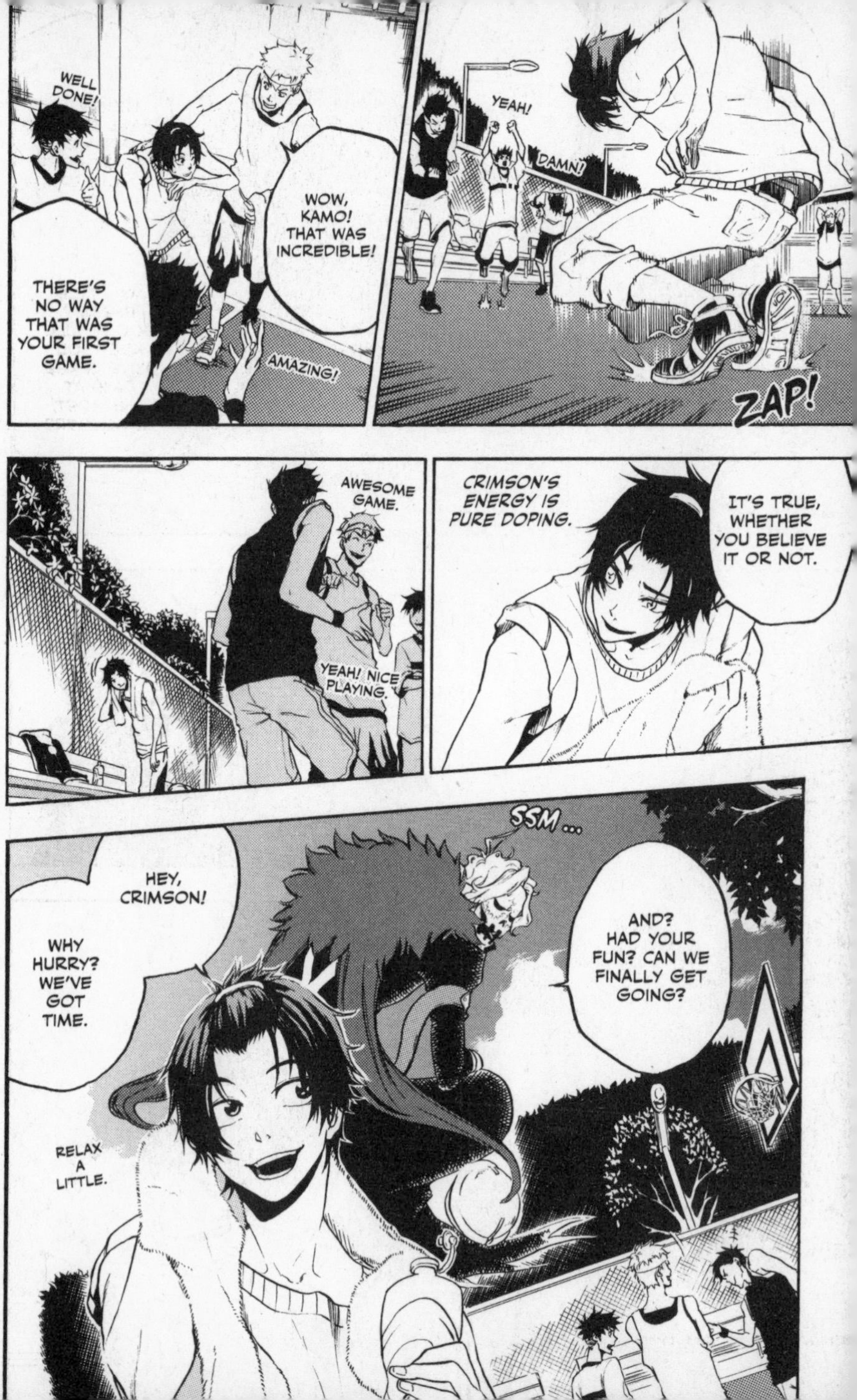
YEAH!
DAMN!
ZAP!
WOW, KAMO! THAT WAS INCREDIBLE!
WELL DONE!
THERE'S NO WAY THAT WAS YOUR FIRST GAME.
AMAZING!
IT'S TRUE, WHETHER YOU BELIEVE IT OR NOT.
CRIMSON'S ENERGY IS PURE DOPING.
AWESOME GAME.
YEAH! NICE PLAYING.
SSM...
AND? HAD YOUR FUN? CAN WE FINALLY GET GOING?
HEY, CRIMSON!
WHY HURRY? WE'VE GOT TIME.
RELAX A LITTLE.

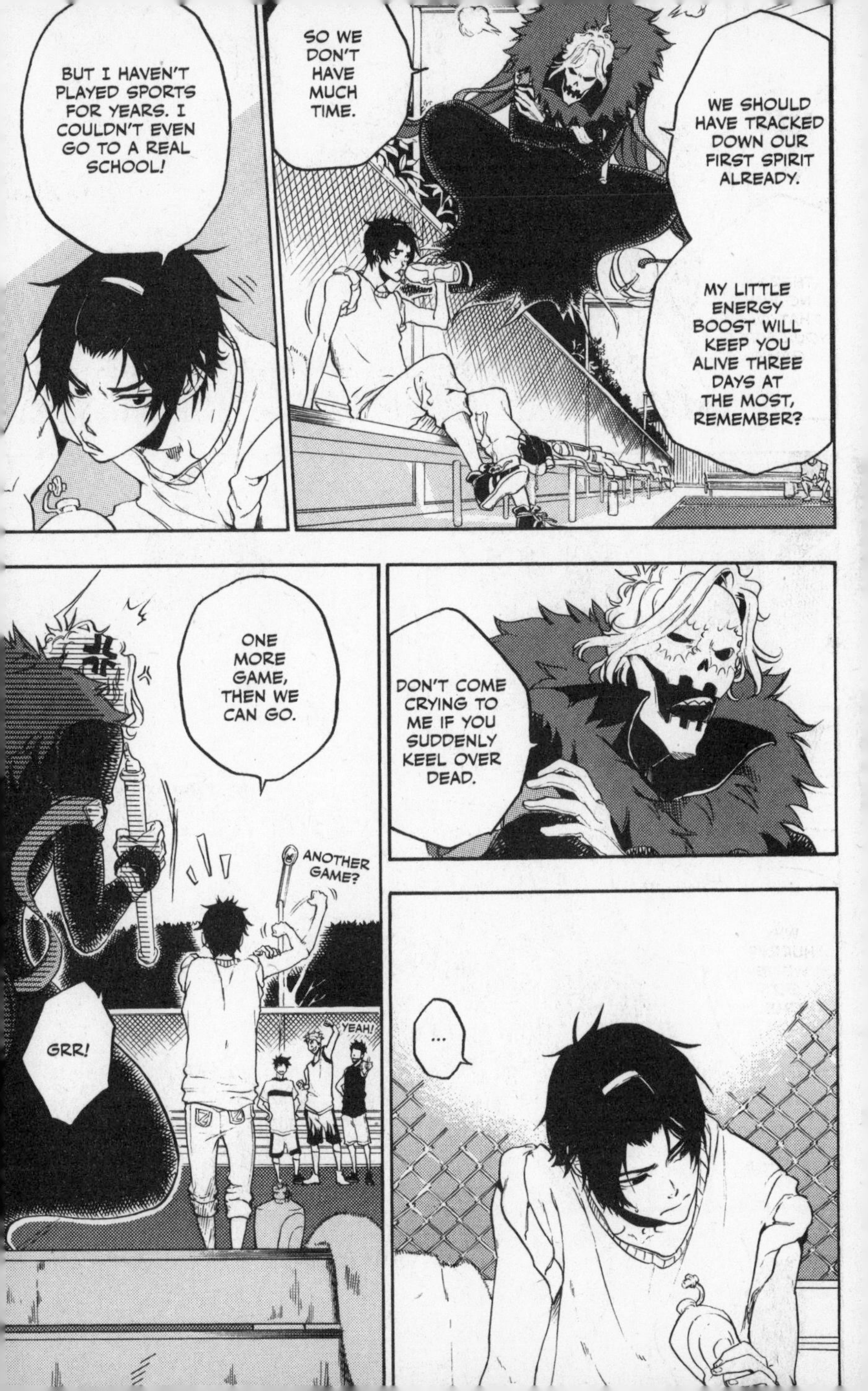
WE SHOULD HAVE TRACKED DOWN OUR FIRST SPIRIT ALREADY.
SO WE DON'T HAVE MUCH TIME.
MY LITTLE ENERGY BOOST WILL KEEP YOU ALIVE THREE DAYS AT THE MOST, REMEMBER?
BUT I HAVEN'T PLAYED SPORTS FOR YEARS. I COULDN'T EVEN GO TO A REAL SCHOOL!
DON'T COME CRYING TO ME IF YOU SUDDENLY KEEL OVER DEAD.
...
ONE MORE GAME, THEN WE CAN GO.
ANOTHER GAME?
YEAH!
GRR!

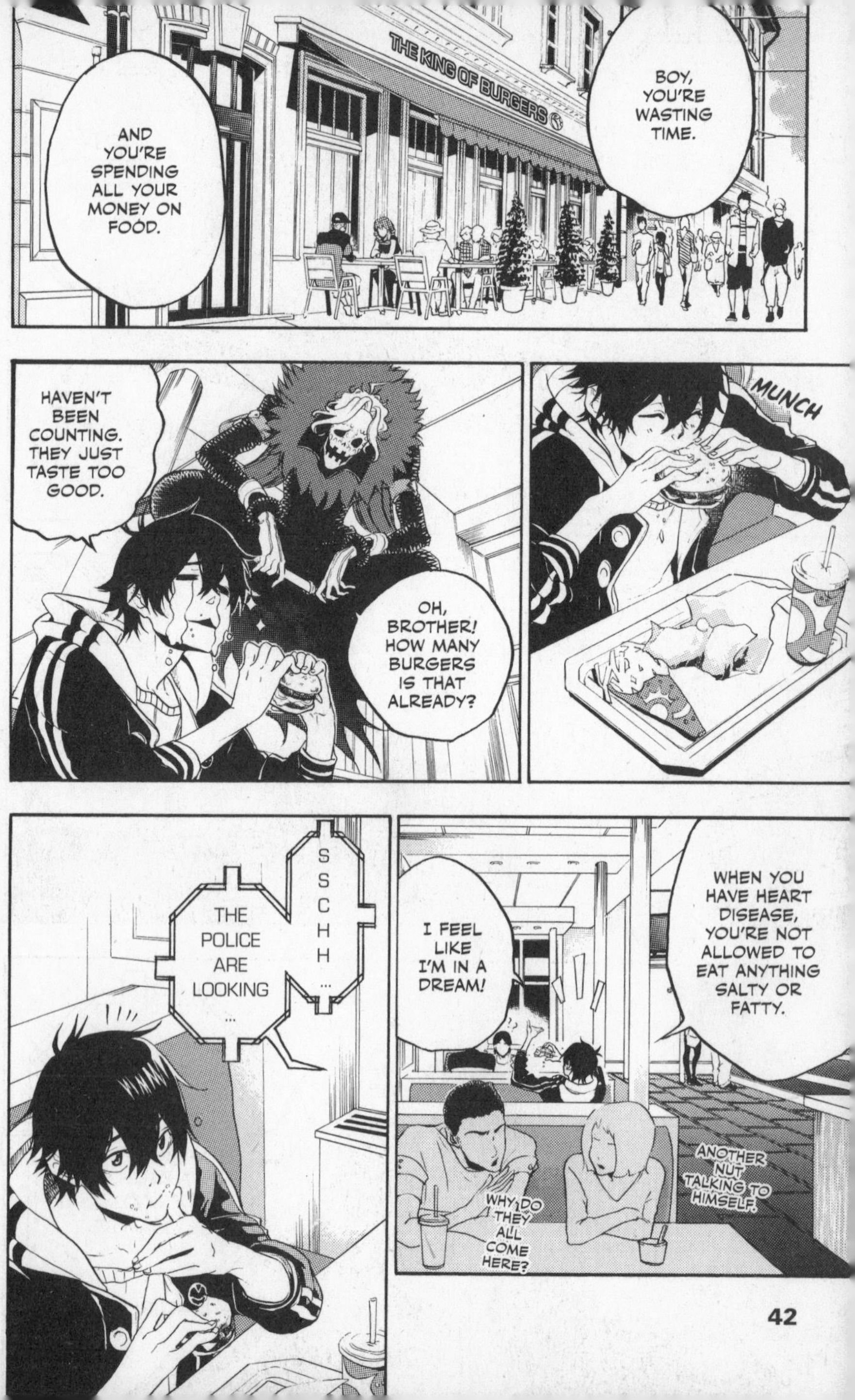
THE KING OF BURGERS
BOY, YOU'RE WASTING TIME.
AND YOU'RE SPENDING ALL YOUR MONEY ON FOOD.
MUNCH
OH, BROTHER! HOW MANY BURGERS IS THAT ALREADY?
HAVEN'T BEEN COUNTING. THEY JUST TASTE TOO GOOD.
WHEN YOU HAVE HEART DISEASE, YOU'RE NOT ALLOWED TO EAT ANYTHING SALTY OR FATTY.
I FEEL LIKE I'M IN A DREAM!
ANOTHER NUT TALKING TO HIMSELF.
WHY DO THEY ALL COME HERE?
SSCHH ...
THE POLICE ARE LOOKING ...

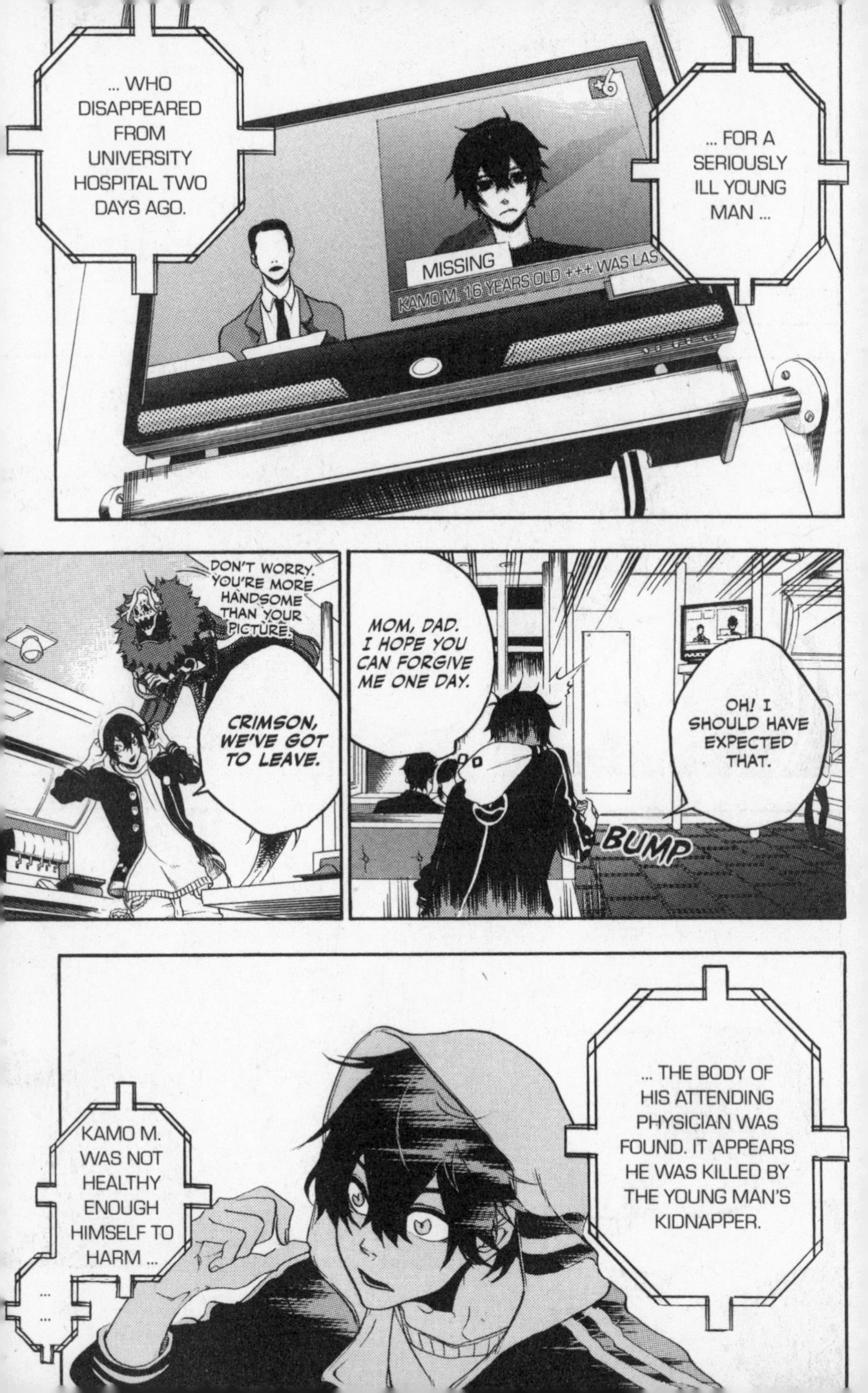
... FOR A SERIOUSLY ILL YOUNG MAN ...
... WHO DISAPPEARED FROM UNIVERSITY HOSPITAL TWO DAYS AGO.
MISSING
KAMO M. 16 YEARS OLD +++ WAS LAS
MOM, DAD. I HOPE YOU CAN FORGIVE ME ONE DAY.
OH! I SHOULD HAVE EXPECTED THAT.
BUMP
DON'T WORRY. YOU'RE MORE HANDSOME THAN YOUR PICTURE.
CRIMSON, WE'VE GOT TO LEAVE.
... THE BODY OF HIS ATTENDING PHYSICIAN WAS FOUND. IT APPEARS HE WAS KILLED BY THE YOUNG MAN'S KIDNAPPER.
KAMO M. WAS NOT HEALTHY ENOUGH HIMSELF TO HARM ...
... ...

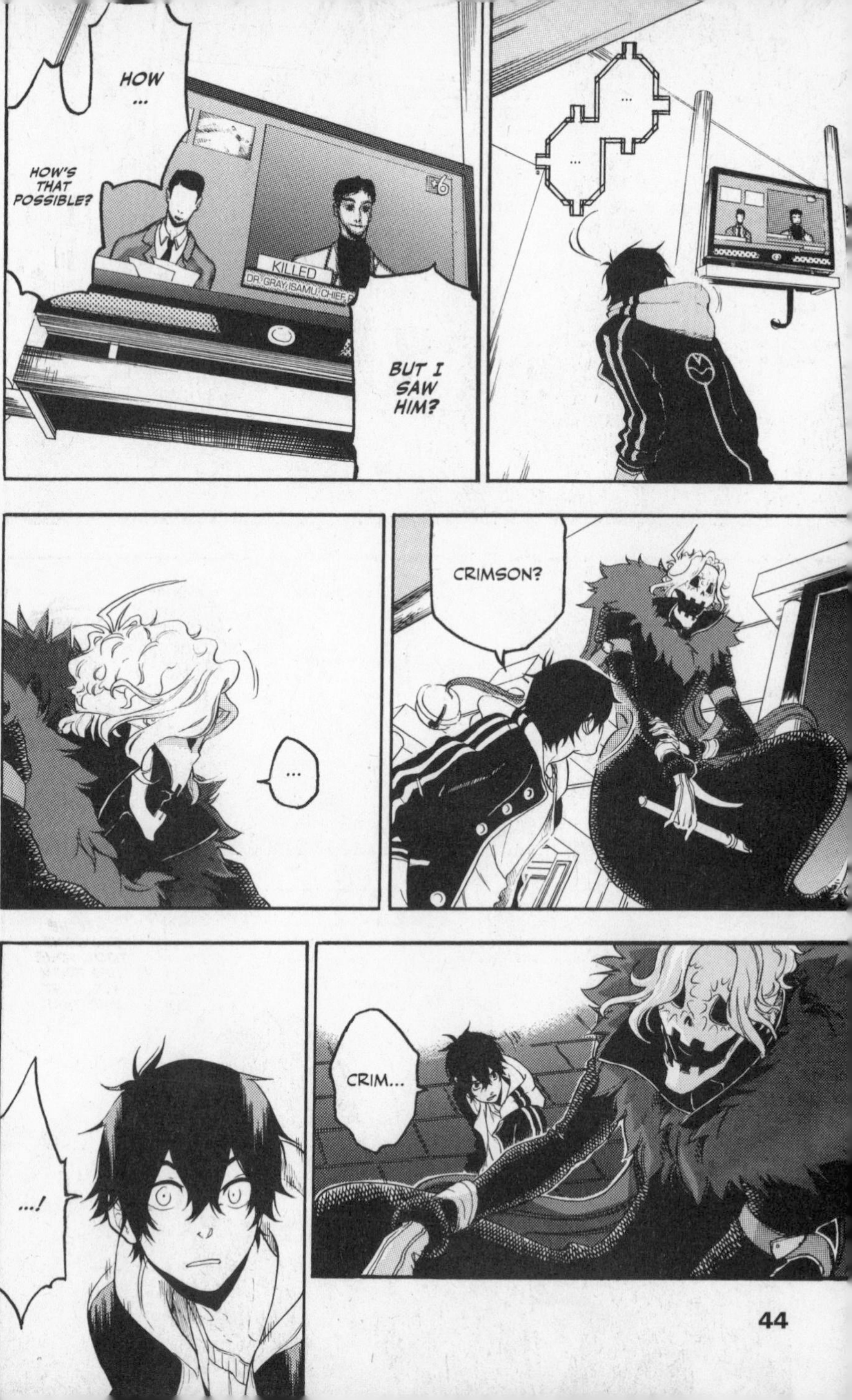
...
...
HOW ...
HOW'S THAT POSSIBLE?
KILLED
DR. GRAY ISAMU, CHIEF
BUT I SAW HIM?
CRIMSON?
...
CRIM...
...!

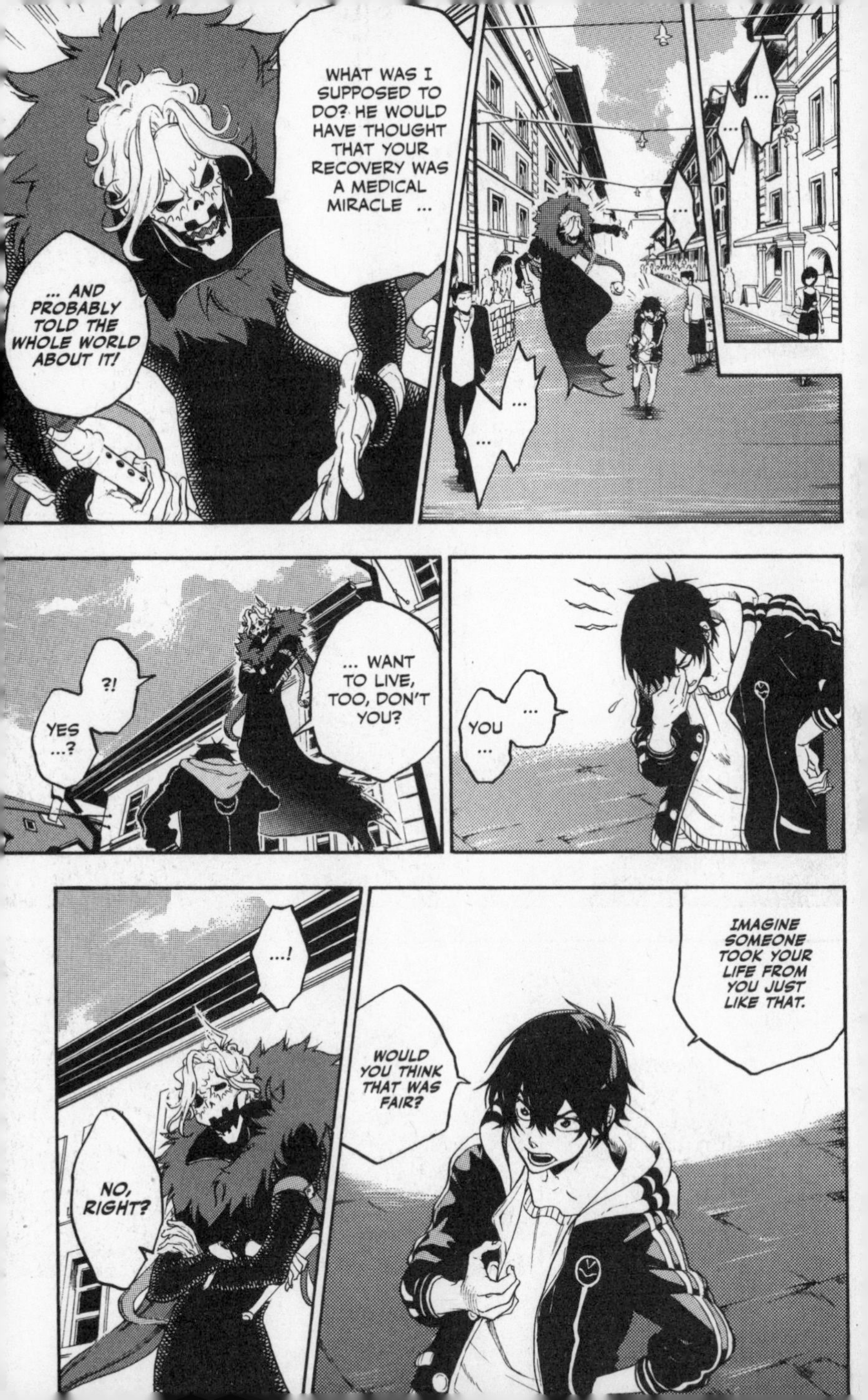
...
...
...
...
...
WHAT WAS I SUPPOSED TO DO? HE WOULD HAVE THOUGHT THAT YOUR RECOVERY WAS A MEDICAL MIRACLE ...
... AND PROBABLY TOLD THE WHOLE WORLD ABOUT IT!
... YOU ...
... WANT TO LIVE, TOO, DON'T YOU?
?! YES ...?
IMAGINE SOMEONE TOOK YOUR LIFE FROM YOU JUST LIKE THAT.
WOULD YOU THINK THAT WAS FAIR?
...!
NO, RIGHT?

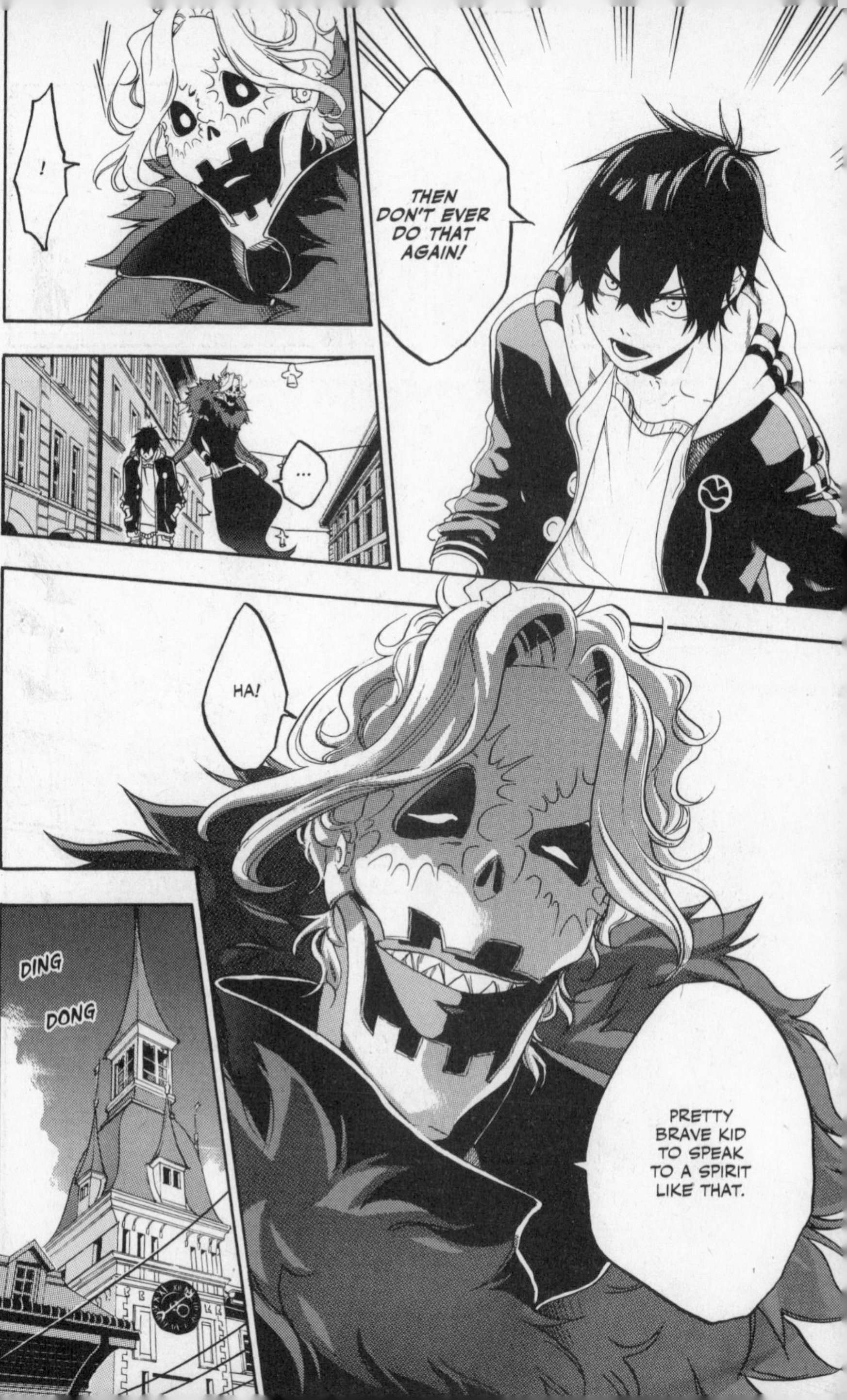
THEN DON'T EVER DO THAT AGAIN!
!
...
HA!
PRETTY BRAVE KID TO SPEAK TO A SPIRIT LIKE THAT.
DING
DONG

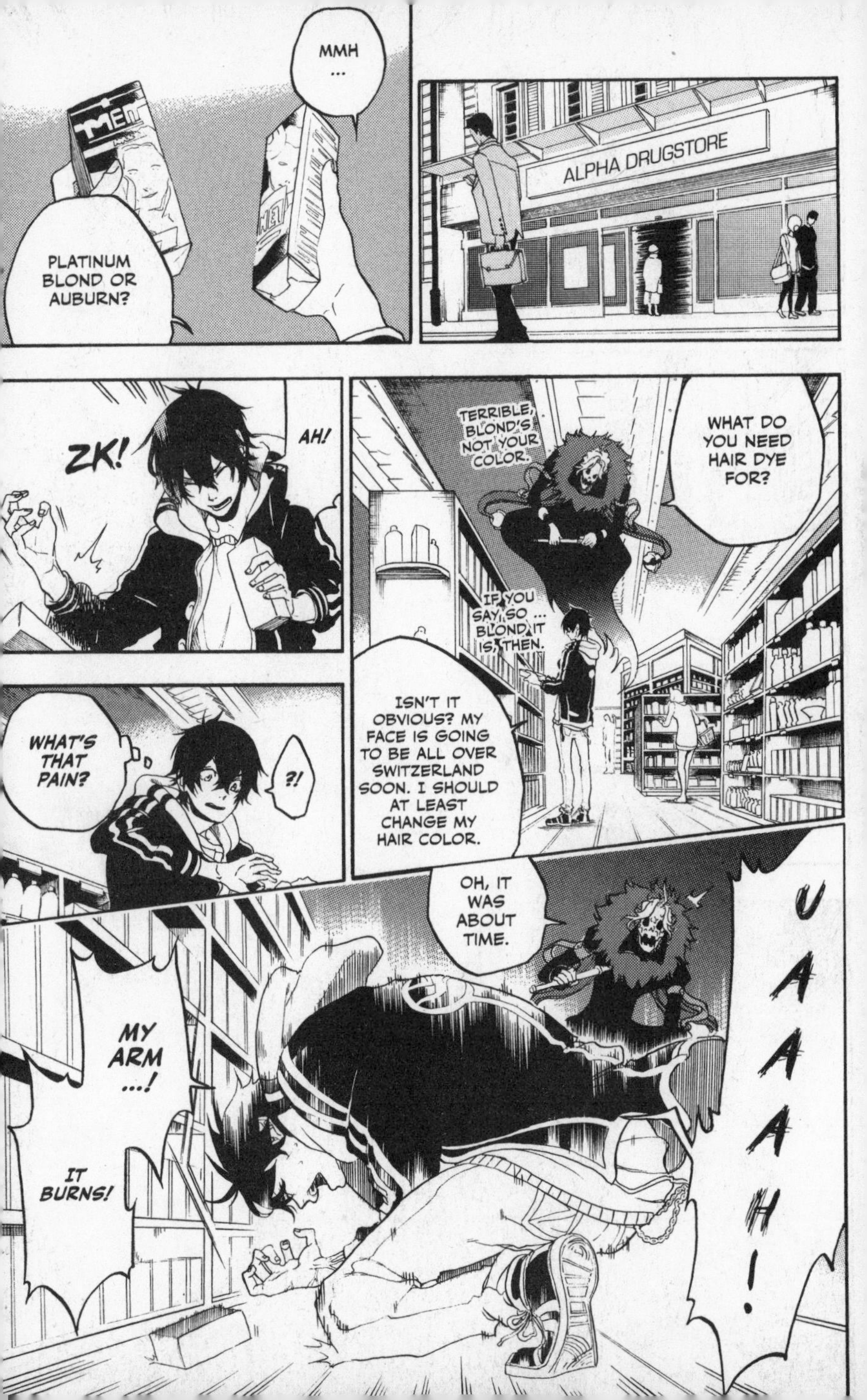
ALPHA DRUGSTORE
MMH ...
PLATINUM BLOND OR AUBURN?
WHAT DO YOU NEED HAIR DYE FOR?
TERRIBLE, BLOND'S NOT YOUR COLOR.
IF YOU SAY SO ... BLOND IT IS, THEN.
ISN'T IT OBVIOUS? MY FACE IS GOING TO BE ALL OVER SWITZERLAND SOON. I SHOULD AT LEAST CHANGE MY HAIR COLOR.
AH!
ZK!
?!
WHAT'S THAT PAIN?
UAAAAH!
OH, IT WAS ABOUT TIME.
MY ARM ...!
IT BURNS!

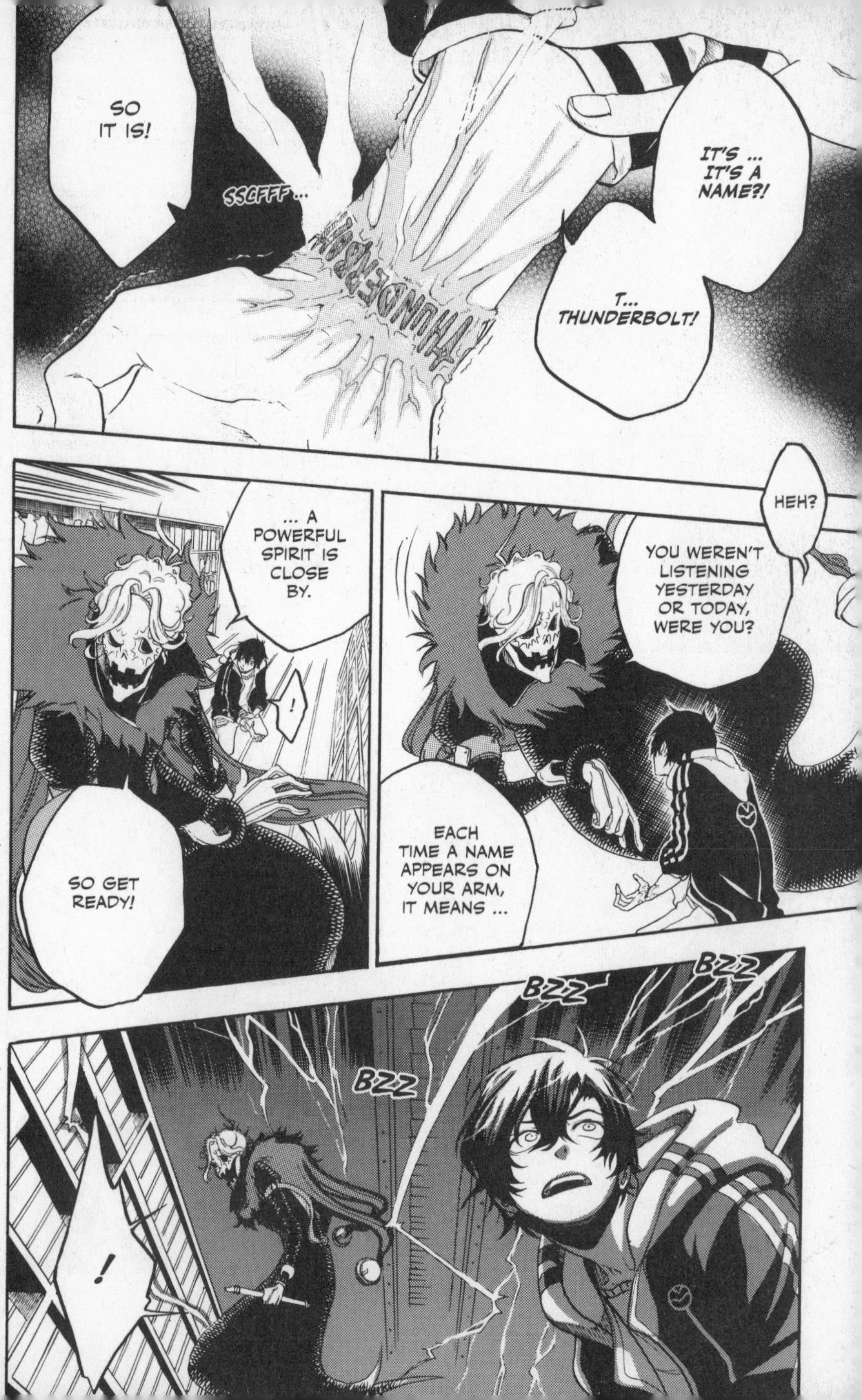

IT'S ... IT'S A NAME?!
T... THUNDERBOLT!
SO IT IS!
SSCFFF ...
THUNDERBOLT
HEH?
YOU WEREN'T LISTENING YESTERDAY OR TODAY, WERE YOU?
EACH TIME A NAME APPEARS ON YOUR ARM, IT MEANS ...
... A POWERFUL SPIRIT IS CLOSE BY.
!
SO GET READY!
BZZ
BZZ
BZZ
!

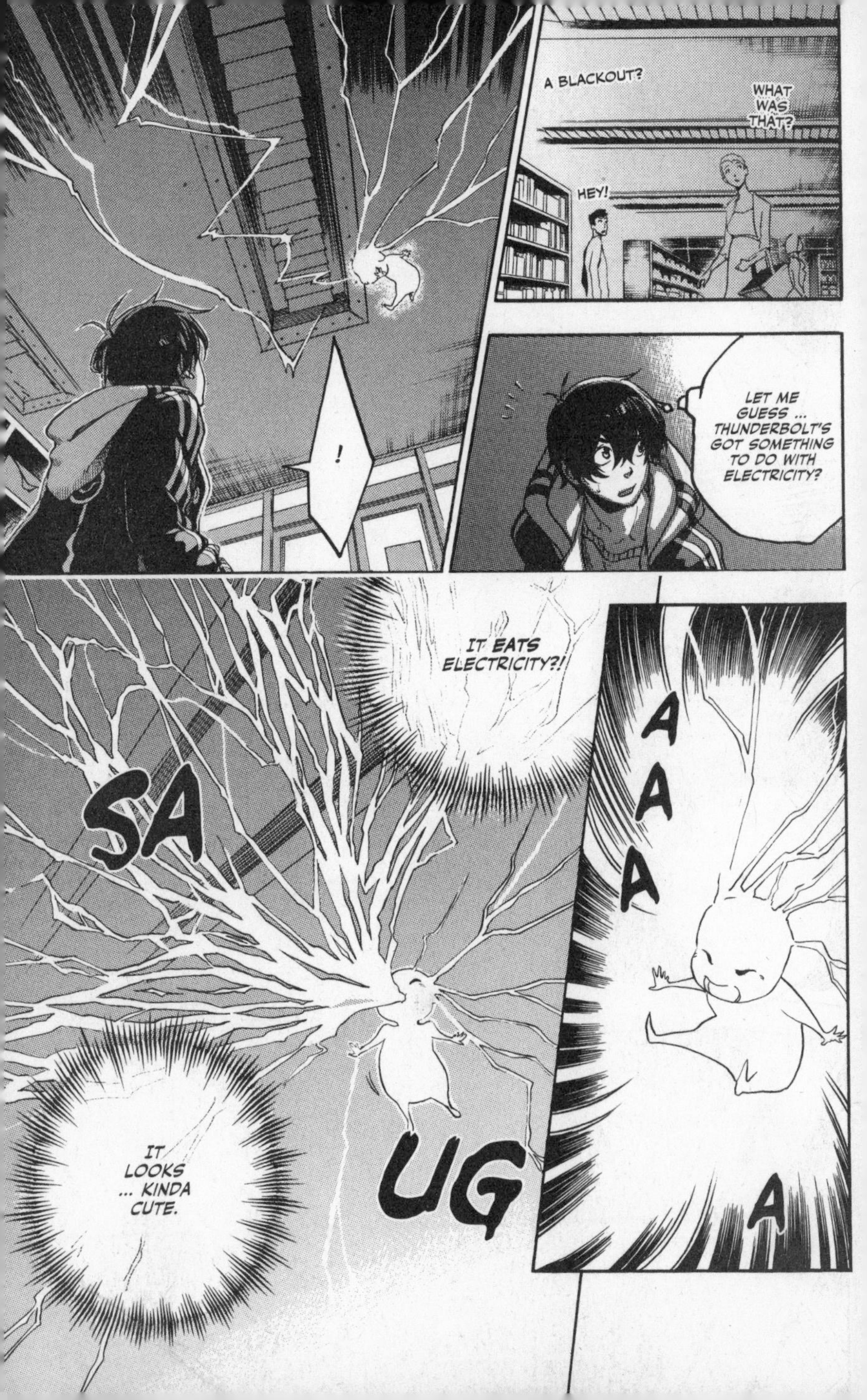
WHAT WAS THAT?
A BLACKOUT?
HEY!
LET ME GUESS ... THUNDERBOLT'S GOT SOMETHING TO DO WITH ELECTRICITY?
!
A
A
A
A
A
IT EATS ELECTRICITY?!
SA
UG
IT LOOKS ... KINDA CUTE.

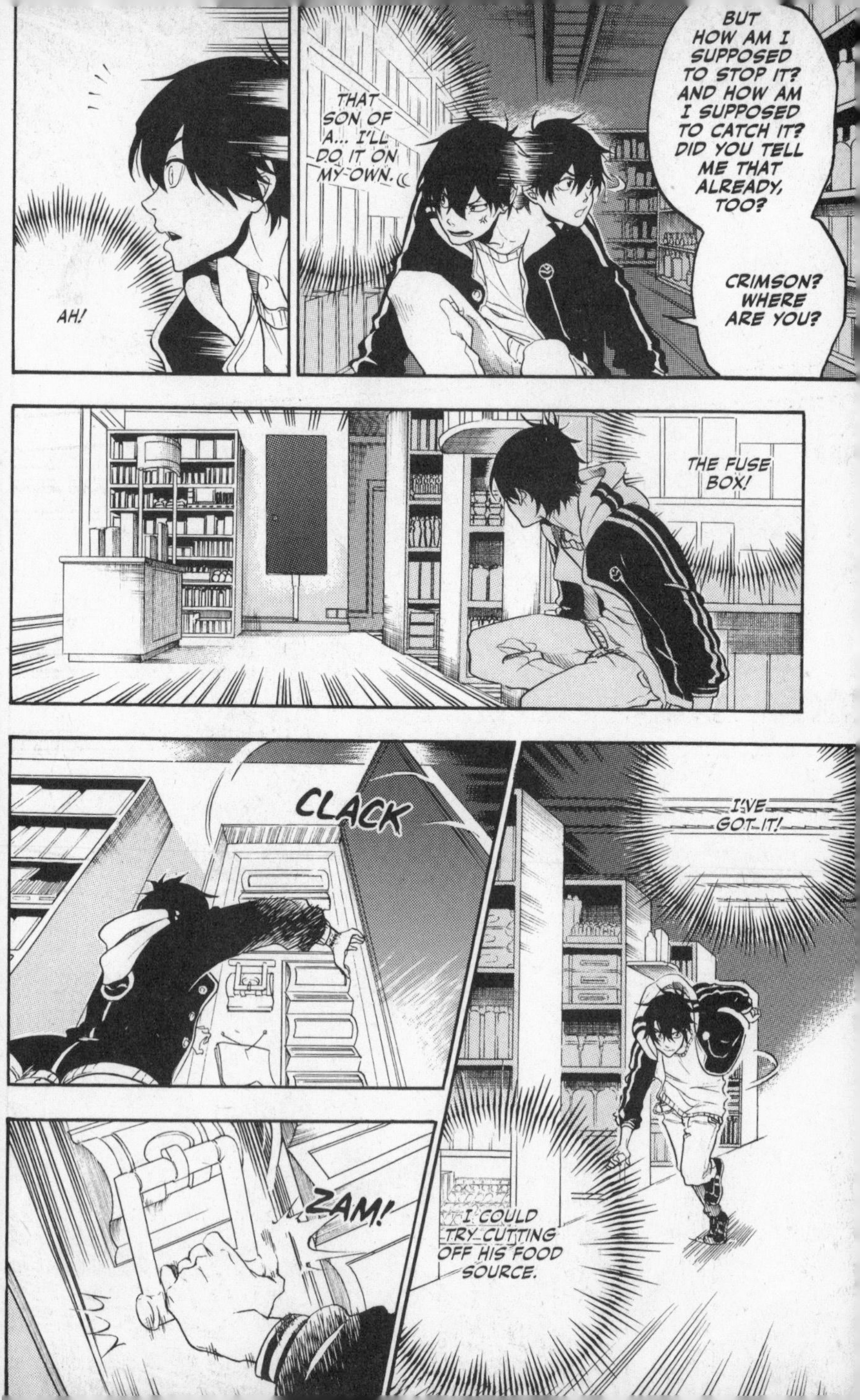
BUT HOW AM I SUPPOSED TO STOP IT? AND HOW AM I SUPPOSED TO CATCH IT? DID YOU TELL ME THAT ALREADY, TOO?
CRIMSON? WHERE ARE YOU?
THAT SON OF A... I'LL DO IT ON MY OWN.
AH!
THE FUSE BOX!
I'VE GOT IT!
I COULD TRY CUTTING OFF HIS FOOD SOURCE.
CLACK
ZAM!

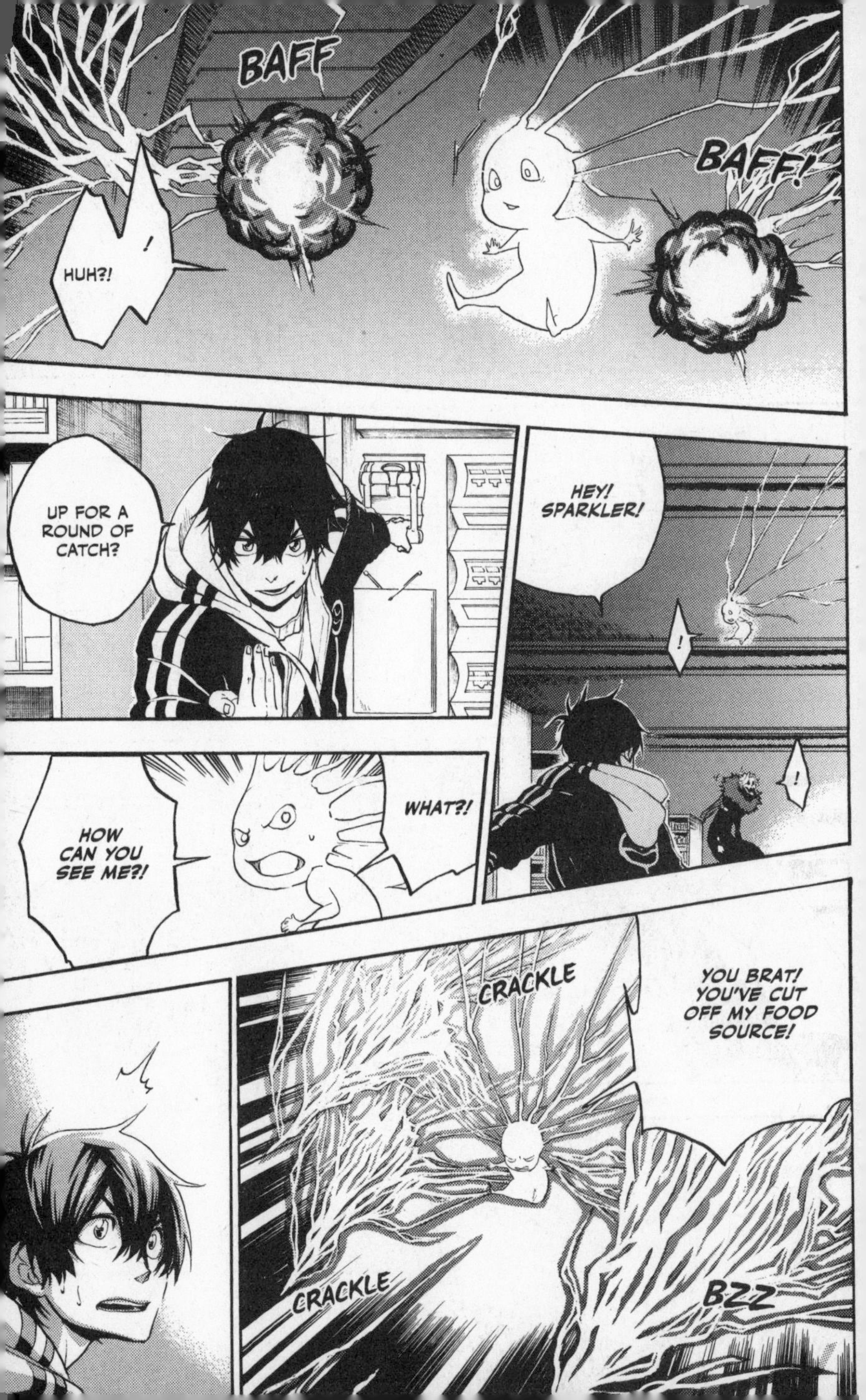
BAFF
BAFF!
!
HUH?!
HEY! SPARKLER!
!
!
UP FOR A ROUND OF CATCH?
WHAT?!
HOW CAN YOU SEE ME?!
YOU BRAT! YOU'VE CUT OFF MY FOOD SOURCE!
CRACKLE
BZZ
CRACKLE

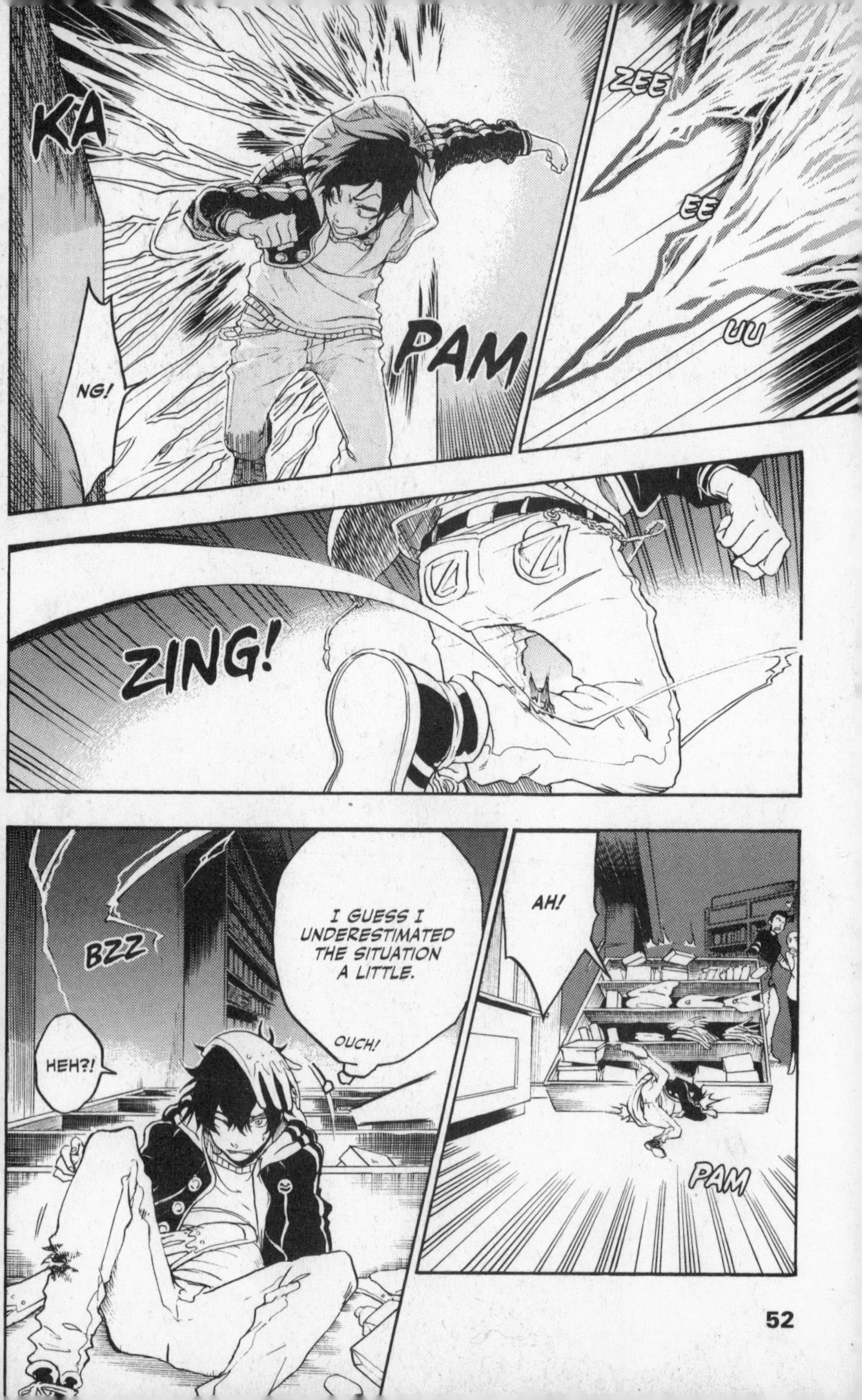
ZEE
EE
UU
KA
PAM
NG!
ZING!
AH!
PAM
I GUESS I UNDERESTIMATED THE SITUATION A LITTLE.
BZZ
OUCH!
HEH?!

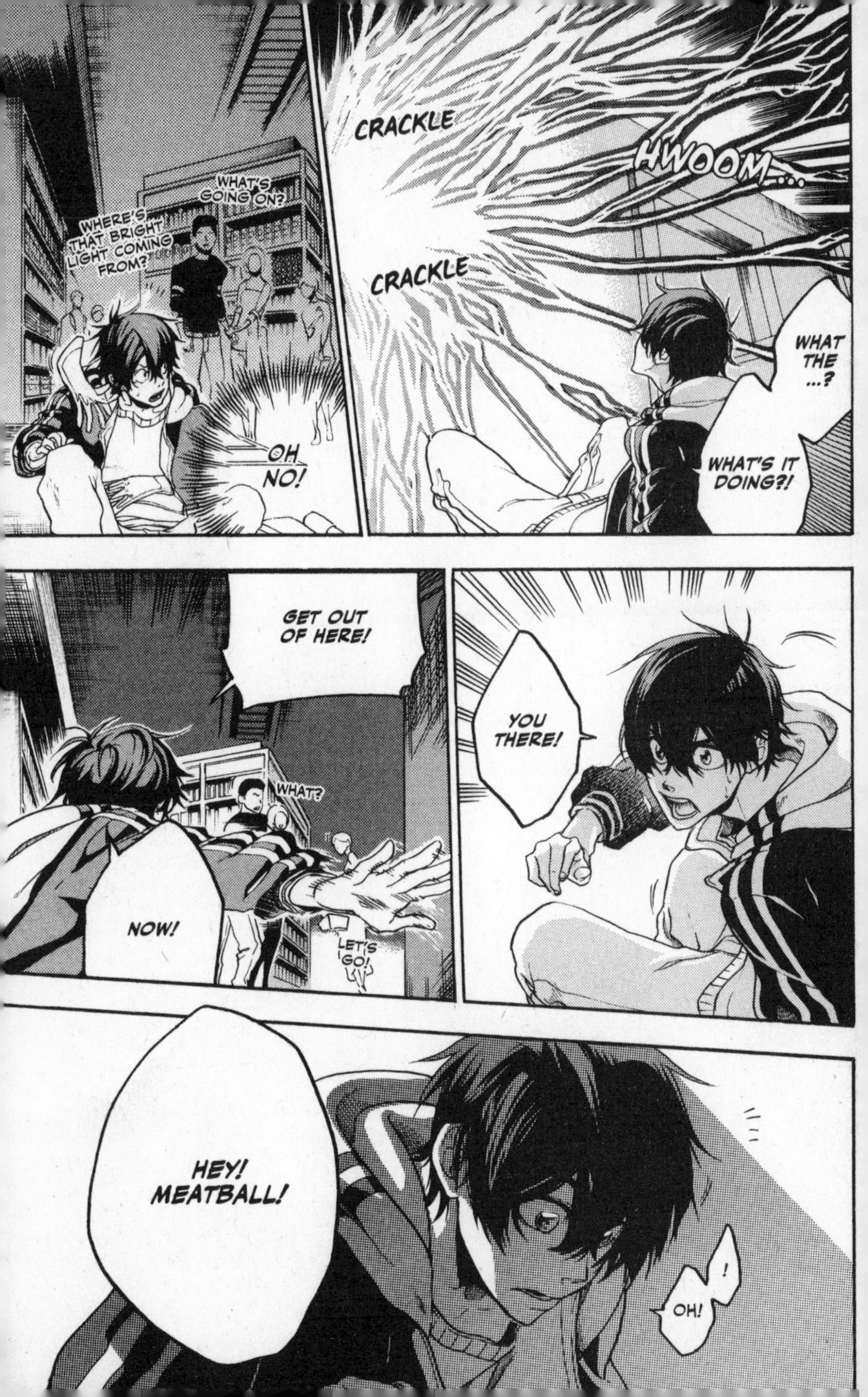
CRACKLE
HWOOM...
CRACKLE
WHAT THE ...?
WHAT'S IT DOING?!
WHAT'S GOING ON?
WHERE'S THAT BRIGHT LIGHT COMING FROM?
OH NO!
YOU THERE!
GET OUT OF HERE!
WHAT?
NOW!
LET'S GO!
!
OH!
HEY! MEATBALL!

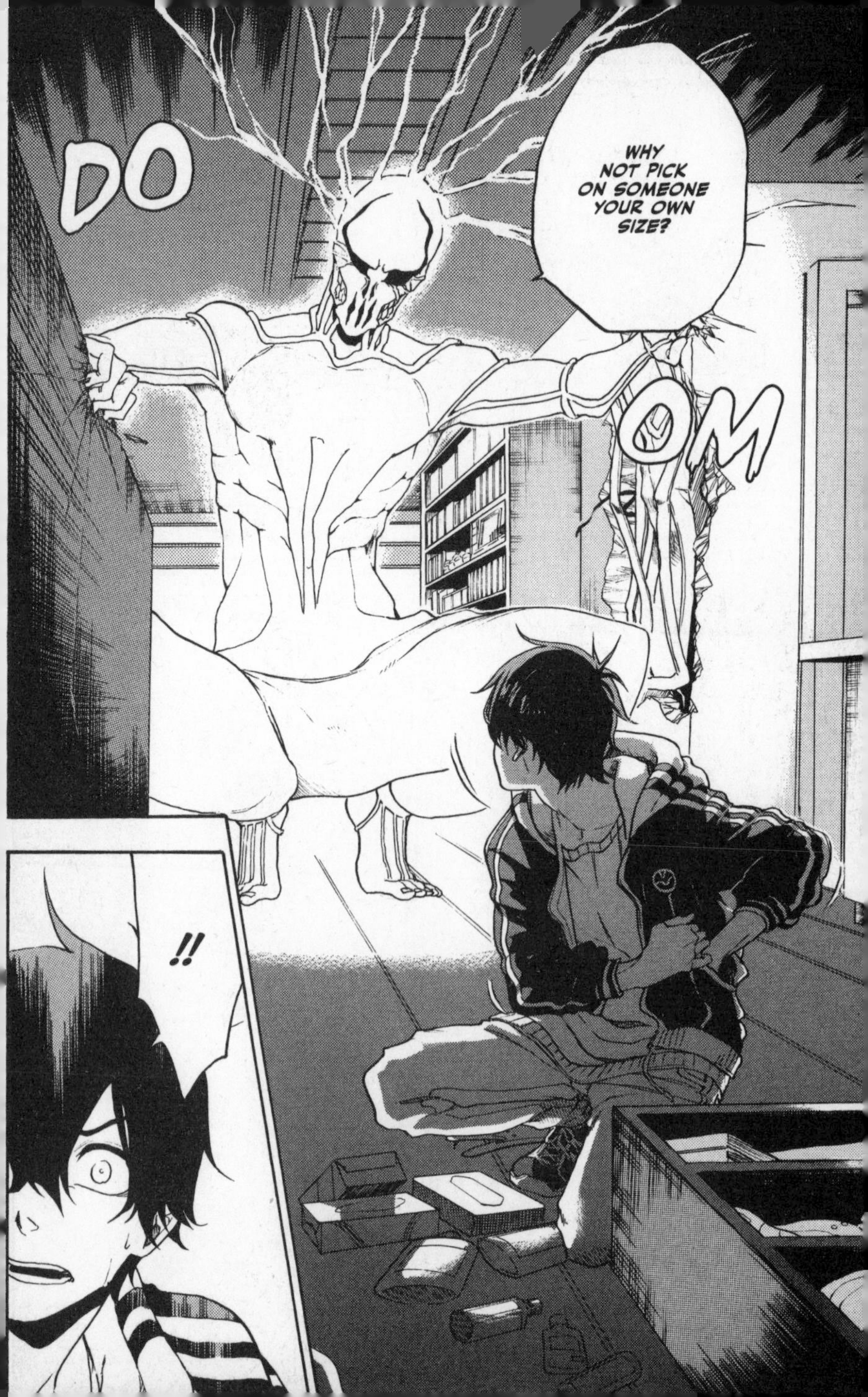
WHY NOT PICK ON SOMEONE YOUR OWN SIZE?
DO
OM
!!

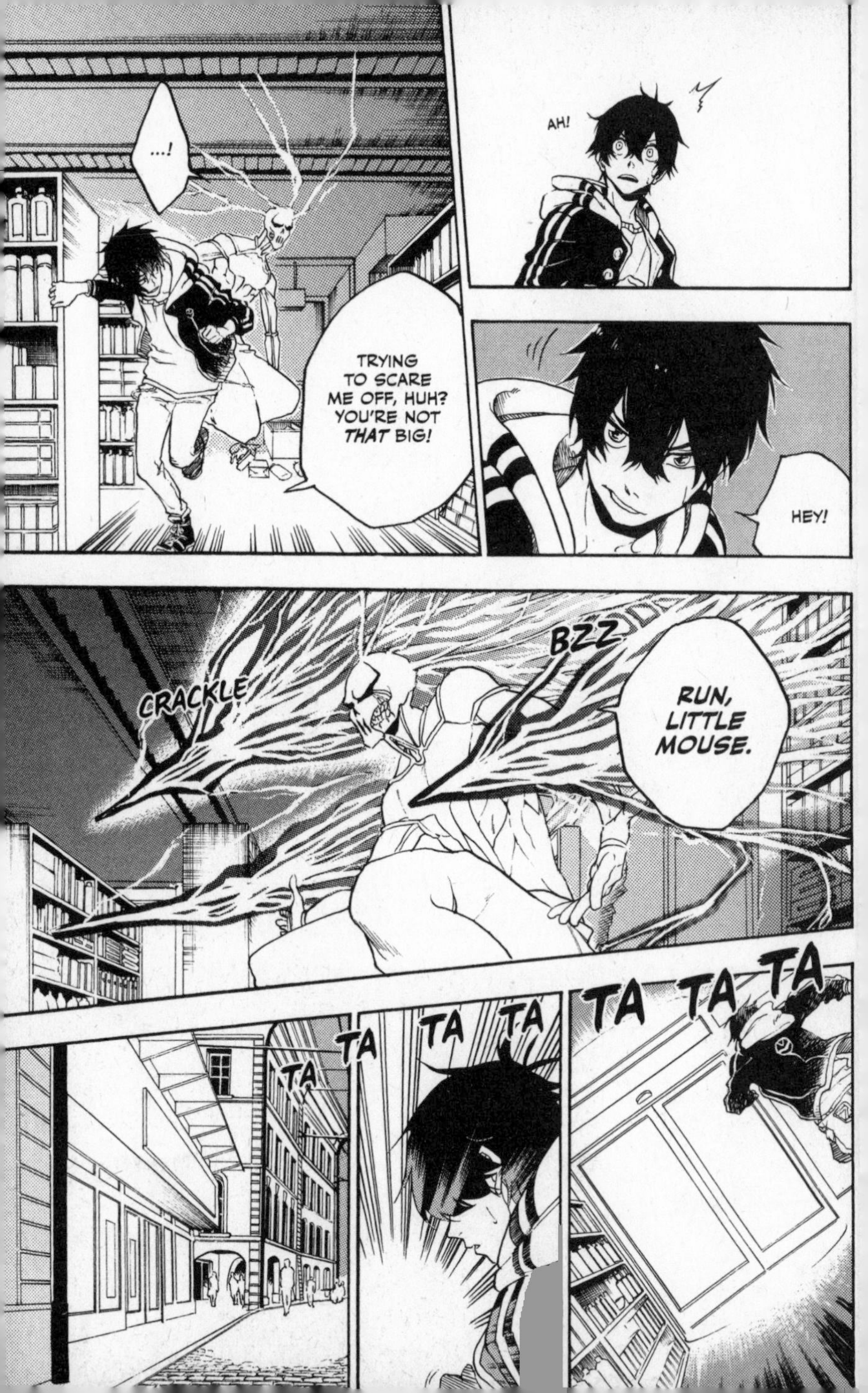
AH!
HEY!
TRYING TO SCARE ME OFF, HUH? YOU'RE NOT *THAT* BIG!
...!
BZZ
RUN, LITTLE MOUSE.
CRACKLE
TA TA TA
TA TA TA
TA TA

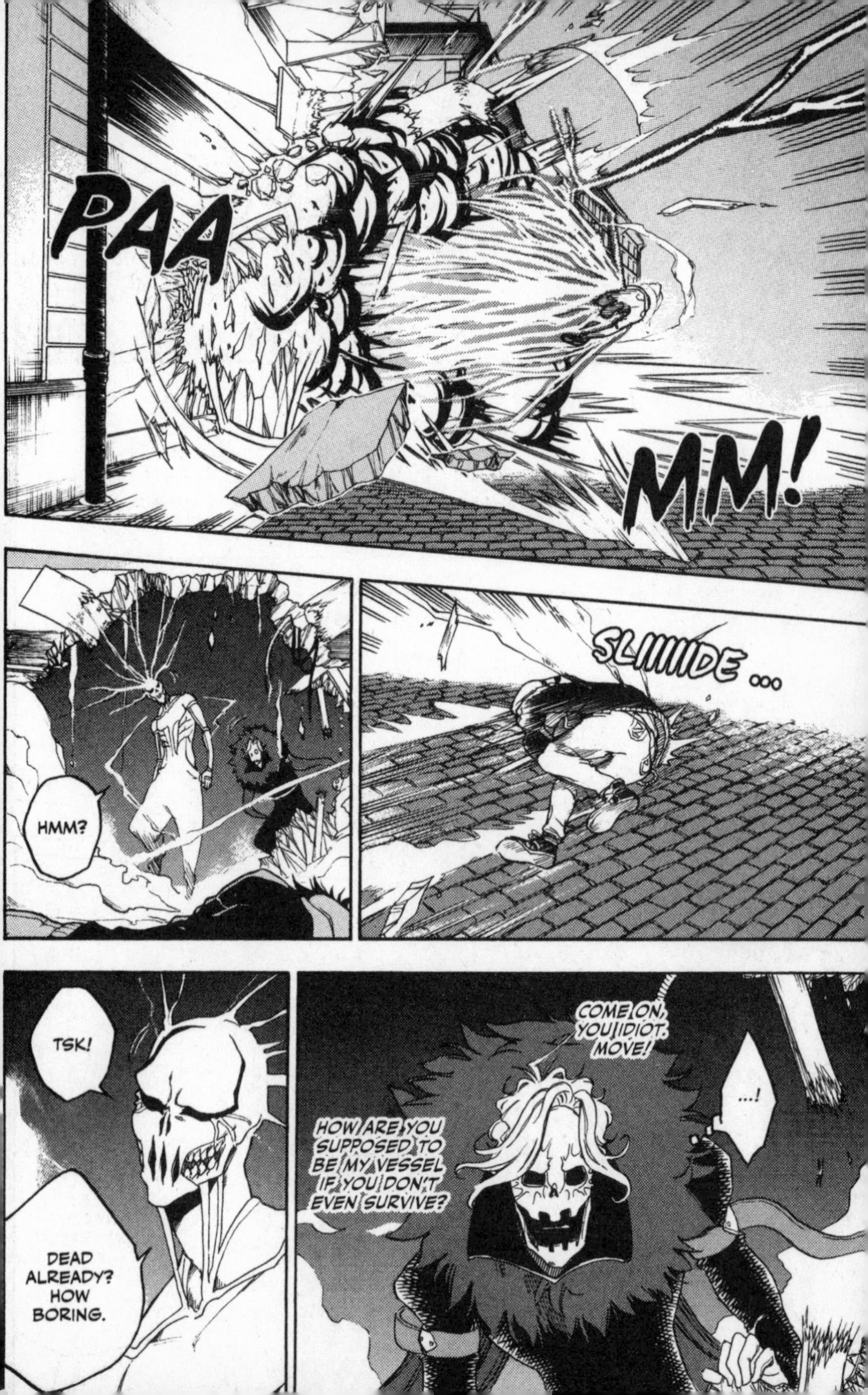
PAAMM!
SLIIIIDE...
HMM?
COME ON, YOU IDIOT. MOVE!
...!
HOW ARE YOU SUPPOSED TO BE MY VESSEL IF YOU DON'T EVEN SURVIVE?
TSK!
DEAD ALREADY? HOW BORING.

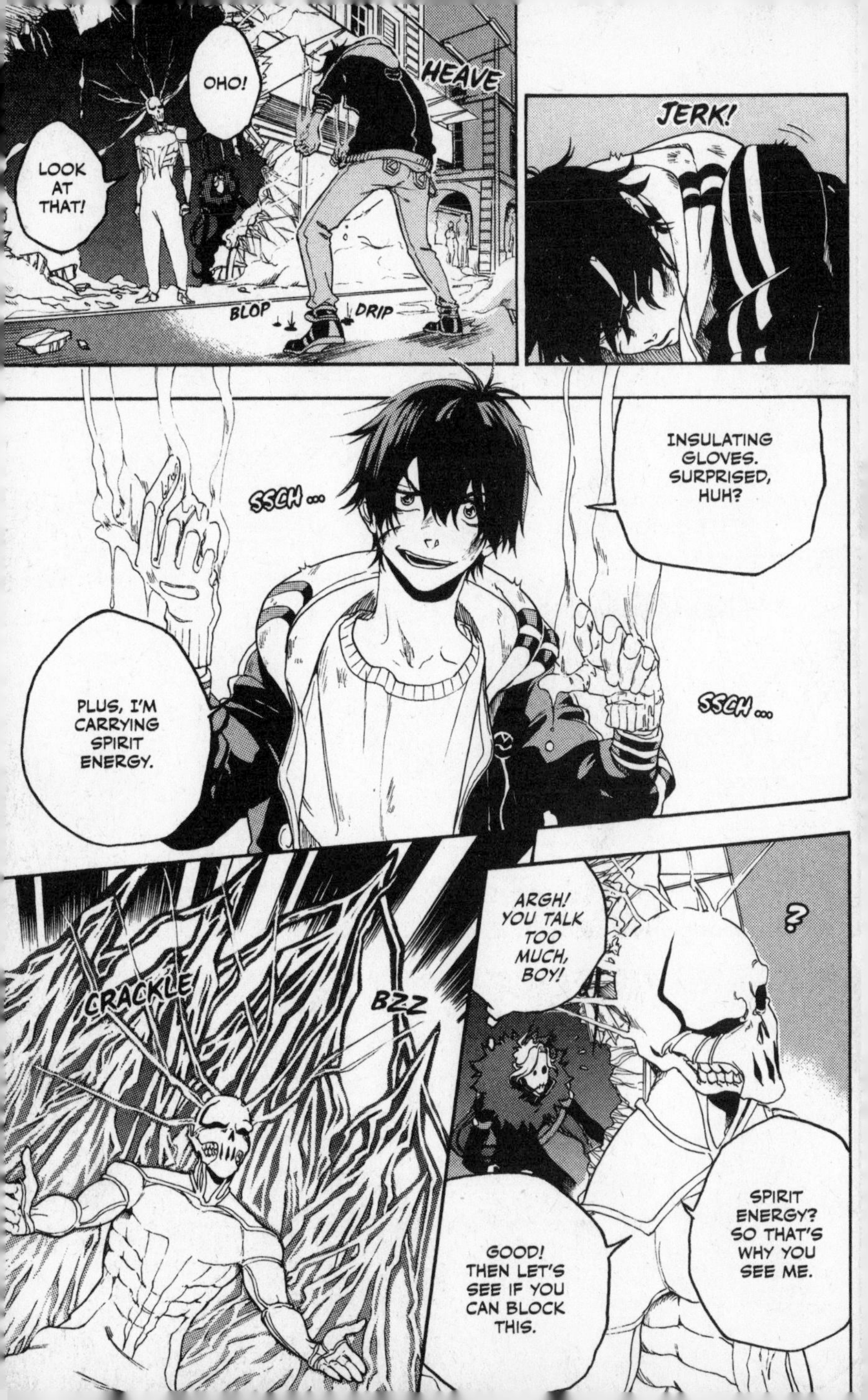
JERK!
HEAVE
OHO!
LOOK AT THAT!
DRIP
BLOP
INSULATING GLOVES. SURPRISED, HUH?
SSCH...
SSCH...
PLUS, I'M CARRYING SPIRIT ENERGY.
?
ARGH! YOU TALK TOO MUCH, BOY!
SPIRIT ENERGY? SO THAT'S WHY YOU SEE ME.
GOOD! THEN LET'S SEE IF YOU CAN BLOCK THIS.
BZZ
CRACKLE

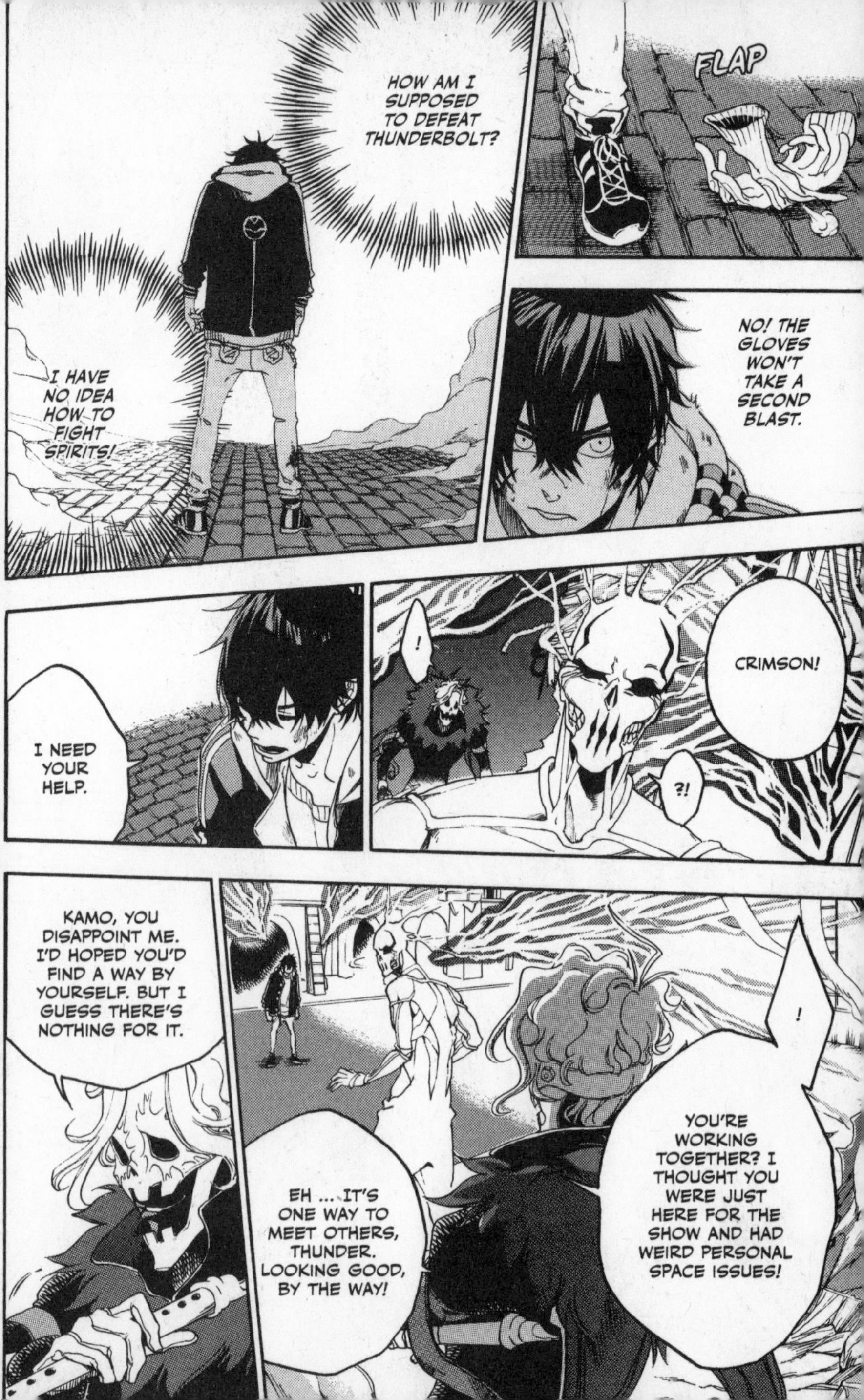
FLAP
NO! THE GLOVES WON'T TAKE A SECOND BLAST.
HOW AM I SUPPOSED TO DEFEAT THUNDERBOLT?
I HAVE NO IDEA HOW TO FIGHT SPIRITS!
CRIMSON!
!
?!
I NEED YOUR HELP.
!
YOU'RE WORKING TOGETHER? I THOUGHT YOU WERE JUST HERE FOR THE SHOW AND HAD WEIRD PERSONAL SPACE ISSUES!
EH ... IT'S ONE WAY TO MEET OTHERS, THUNDER. LOOKING GOOD, BY THE WAY!
KAMO, YOU DISAPPOINT ME. I'D HOPED YOU'D FIND A WAY BY YOURSELF. BUT I GUESS THERE'S NOTHING FOR IT.

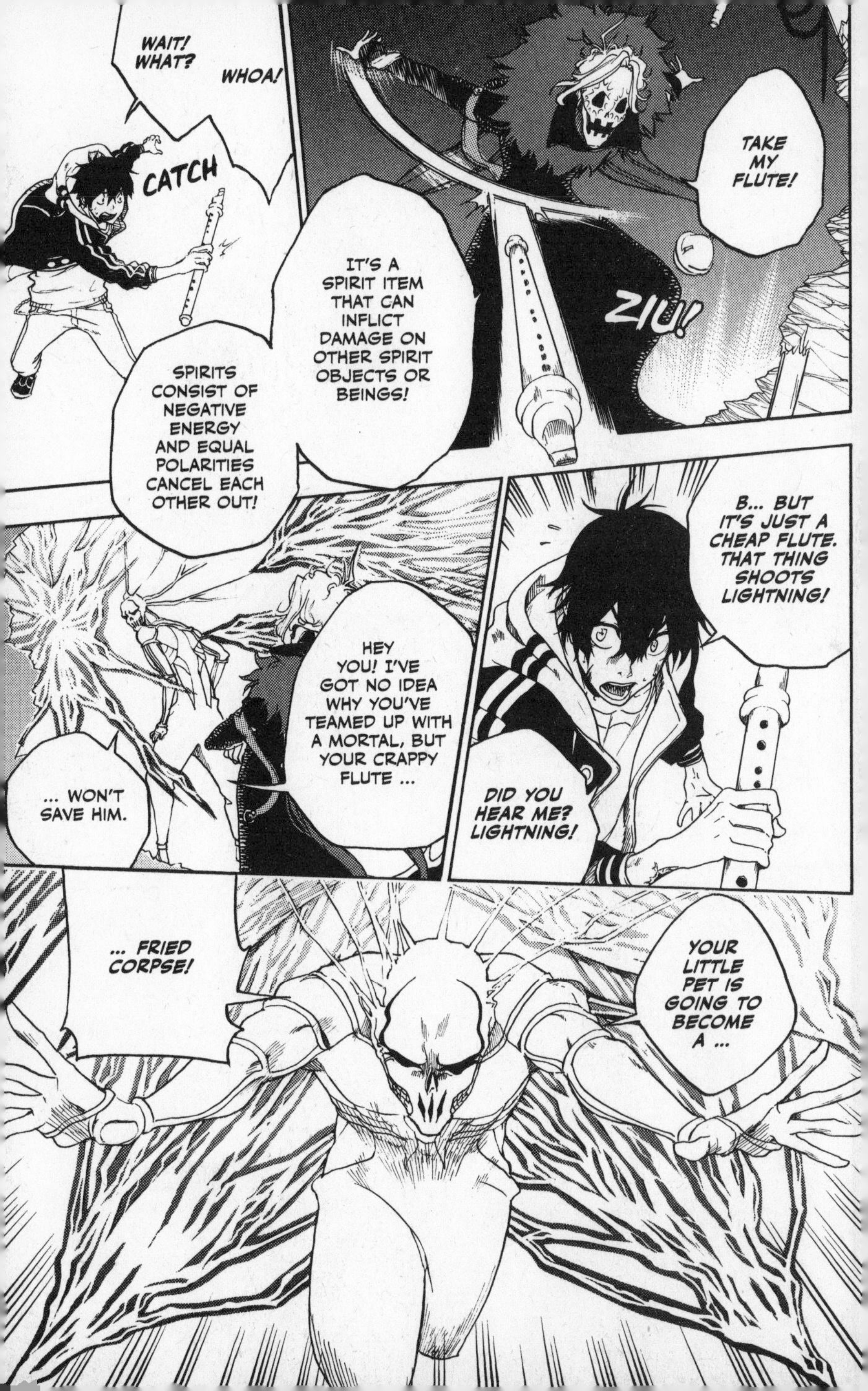
TAKE MY FLUTE!
ZIU!
WAIT! WHAT?
WHOA!
CATCH
IT'S A SPIRIT ITEM THAT CAN INFLICT DAMAGE ON OTHER SPIRIT OBJECTS OR BEINGS!
SPIRITS CONSIST OF NEGATIVE ENERGY AND EQUAL POLARITIES CANCEL EACH OTHER OUT!
B... BUT IT'S JUST A CHEAP FLUTE. THAT THING SHOOTS LIGHTNING!
DID YOU HEAR ME? LIGHTNING!
HEY YOU! I'VE GOT NO IDEA WHY YOU'VE TEAMED UP WITH A MORTAL, BUT YOUR CRAPPY FLUTE ...
... WON'T SAVE HIM.
YOUR LITTLE PET IS GOING TO BECOME A ...
... FRIED CORPSE!

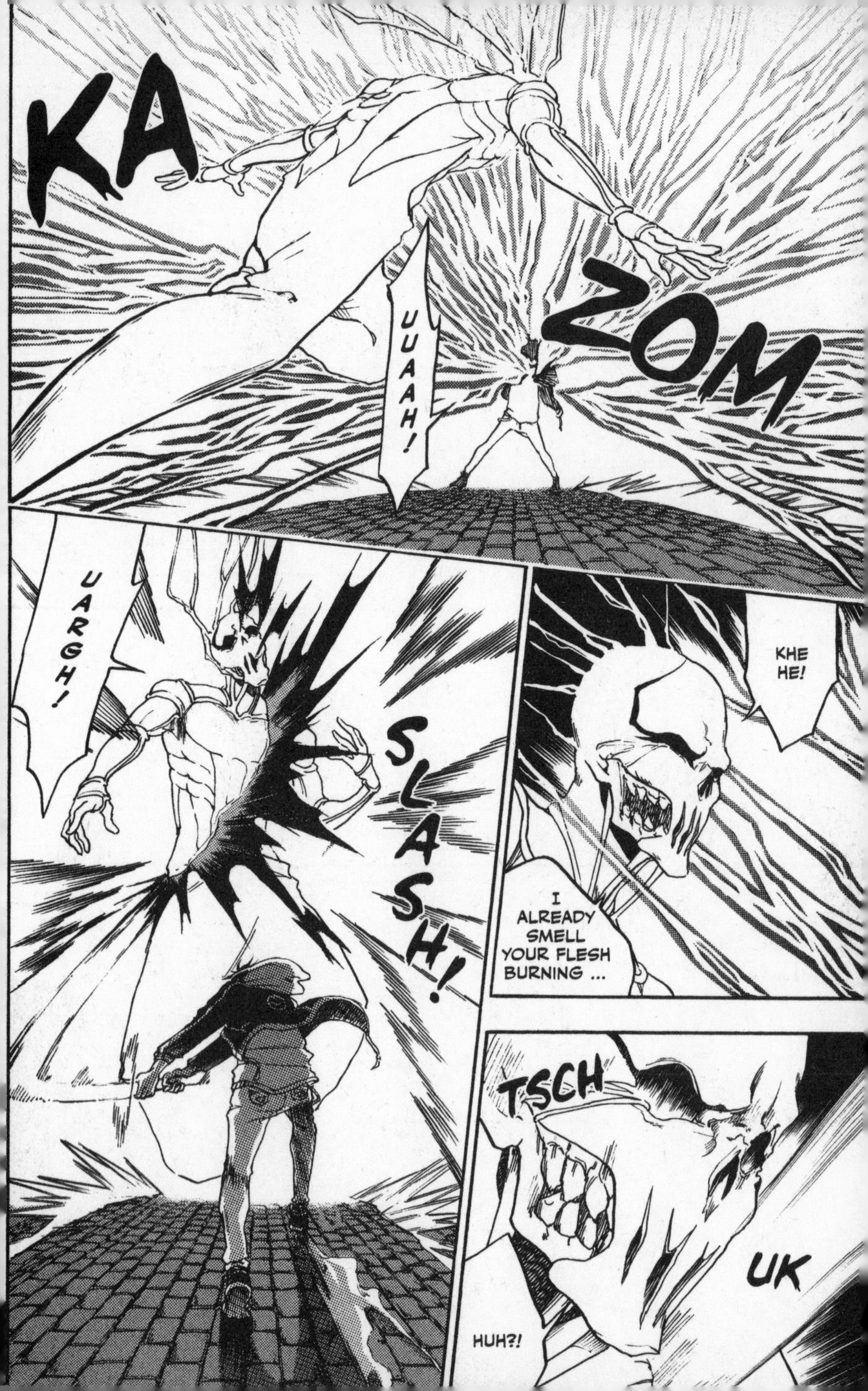
KA
ZOM
UUAAAH!
KHE HE!
I ALREADY SMELL YOUR FLESH BURNING ...
TSCH
UK
HUH?!
UARGH!
SLASH!

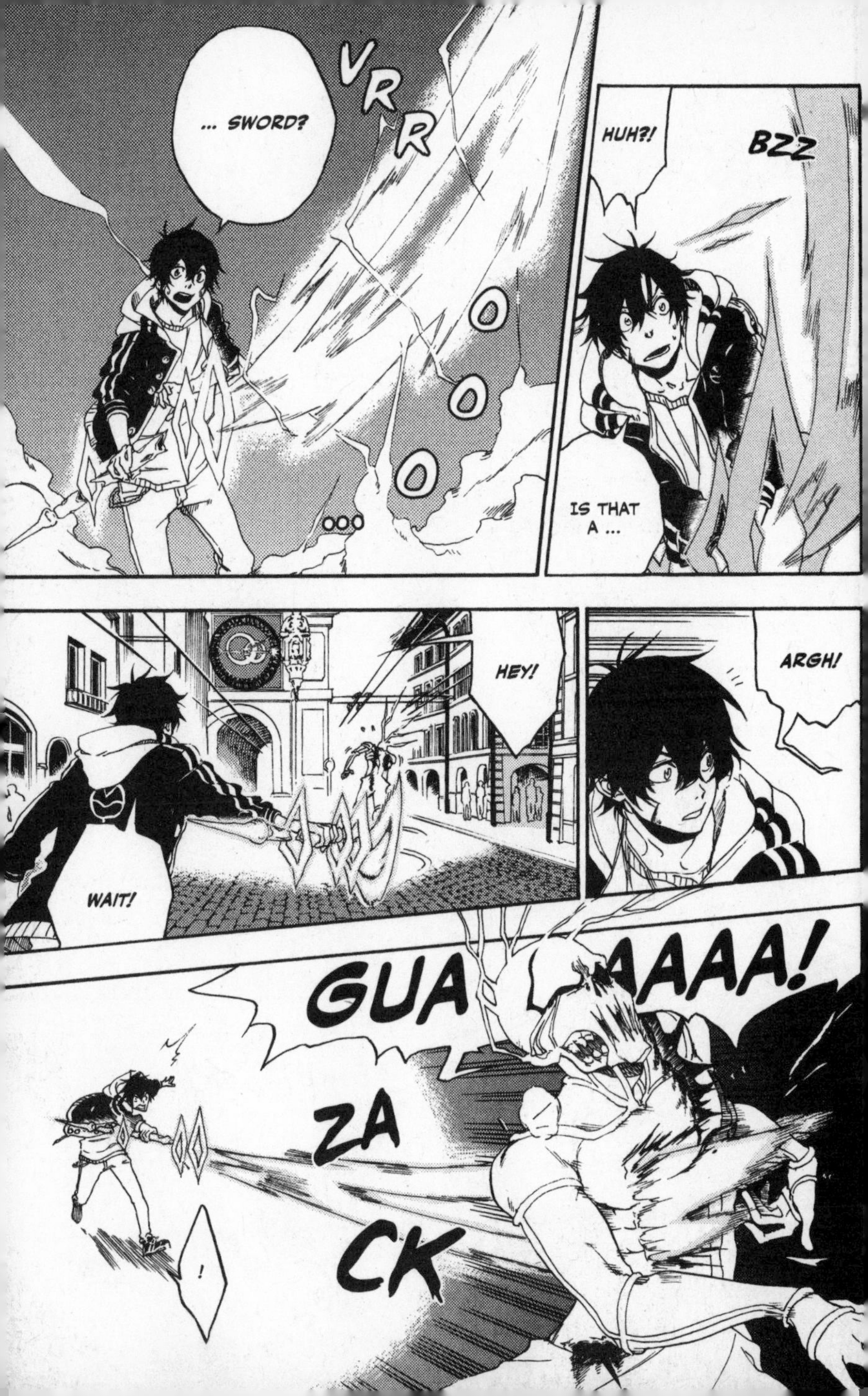
HUH?!
BZZ
IS THAT A ...
... SWORD?
VRR
OOO
OOO
ARGH!
HEY!
WAIT!
GUAAAAA!
ZACK
!

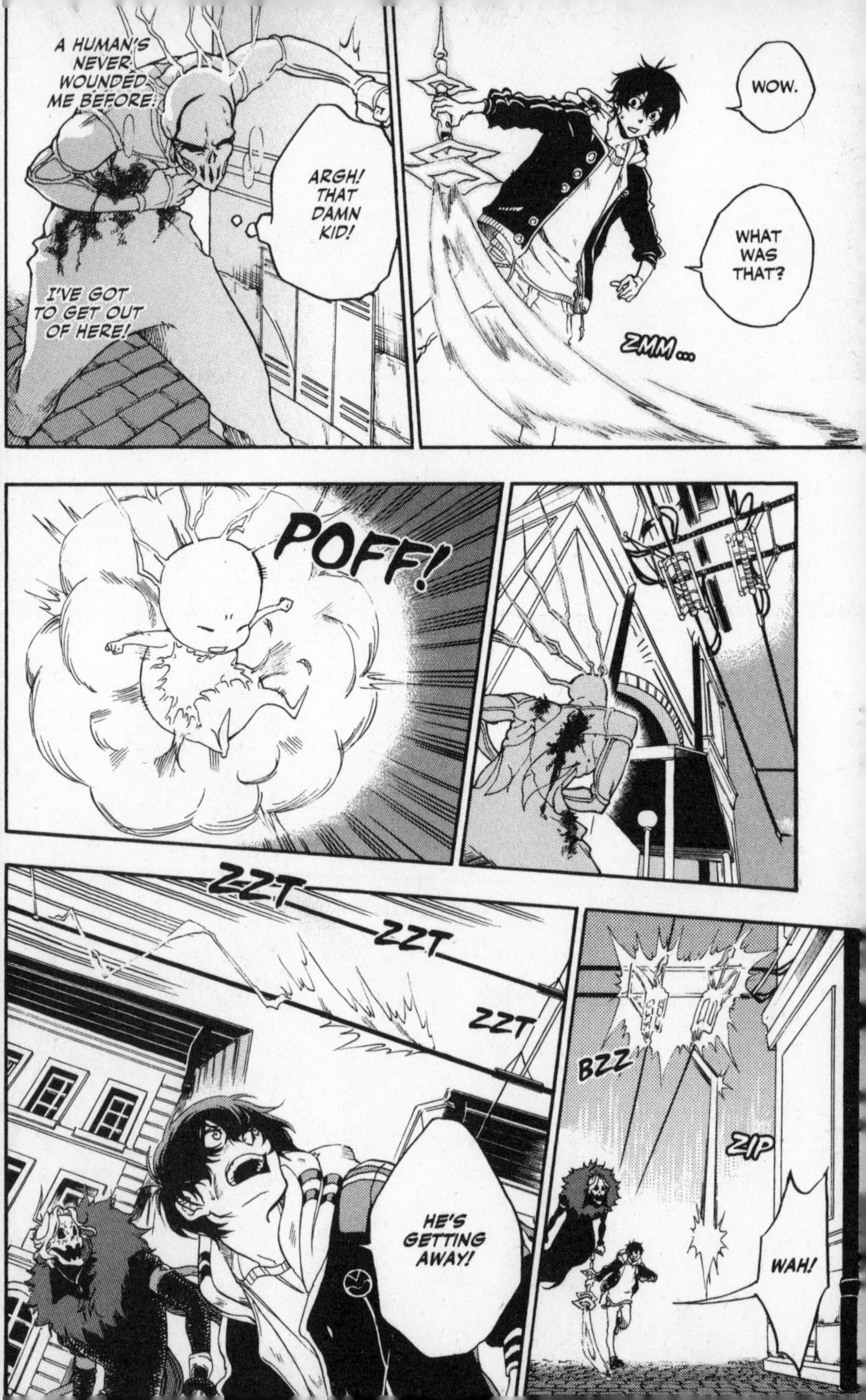
WOW.
WHAT WAS THAT?
ZMM...
A HUMAN'S NEVER WOUNDED ME BEFORE.
ARGH! THAT DAMN KID!
I'VE GOT TO GET OUT OF HERE!
POFF!
BZZ
ZIP
WAH!
Z-Z-T
ZZT
ZZT
HE'S GETTING AWAY!

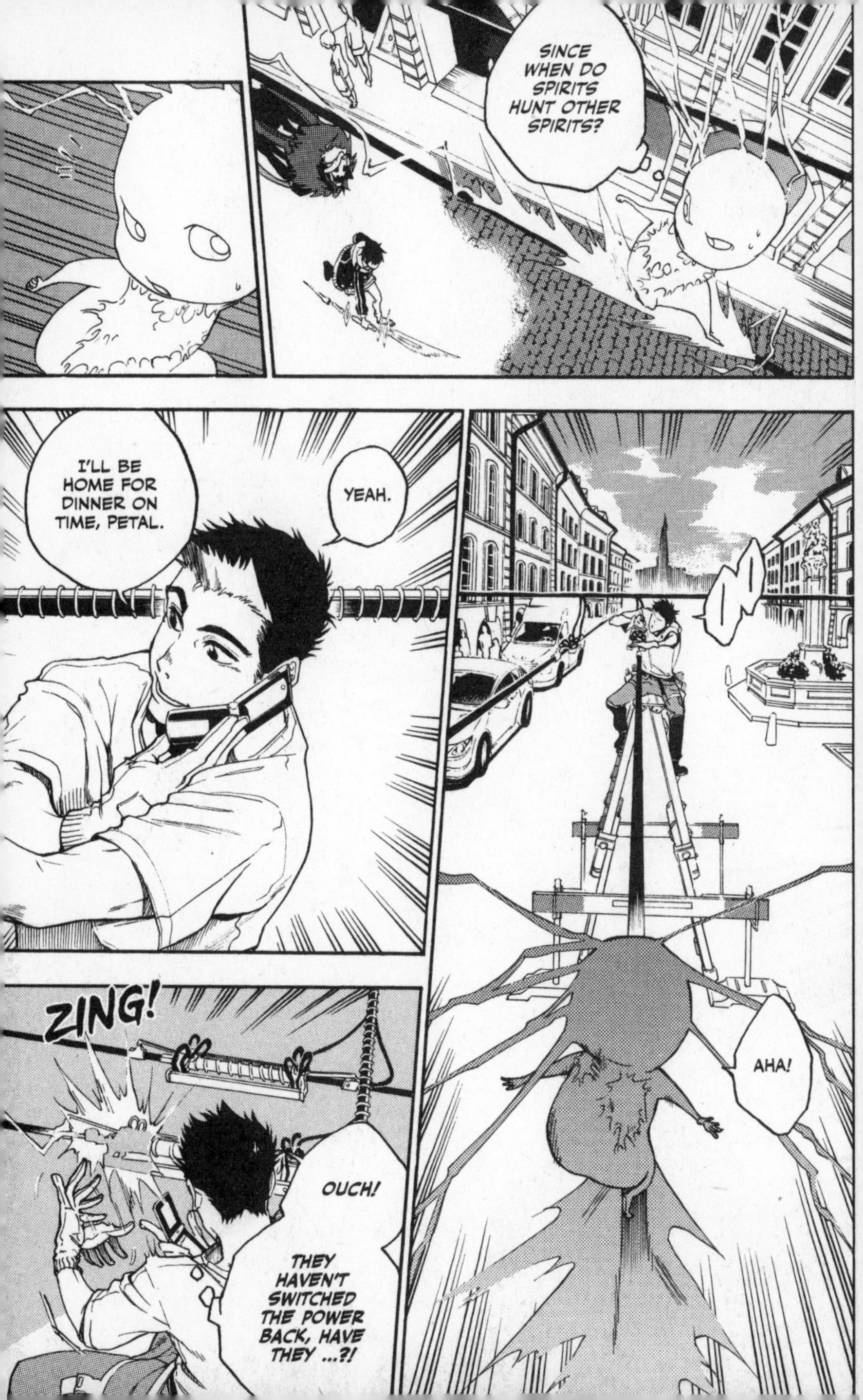
SINCE WHEN DO SPIRITS HUNT OTHER SPIRITS?
AHA!
YEAH.
I'LL BE HOME FOR DINNER ON TIME, PETAL.
ZING!
OUCH!
THEY HAVEN'T SWITCHED THE POWER BACK, HAVE THEY ...?!

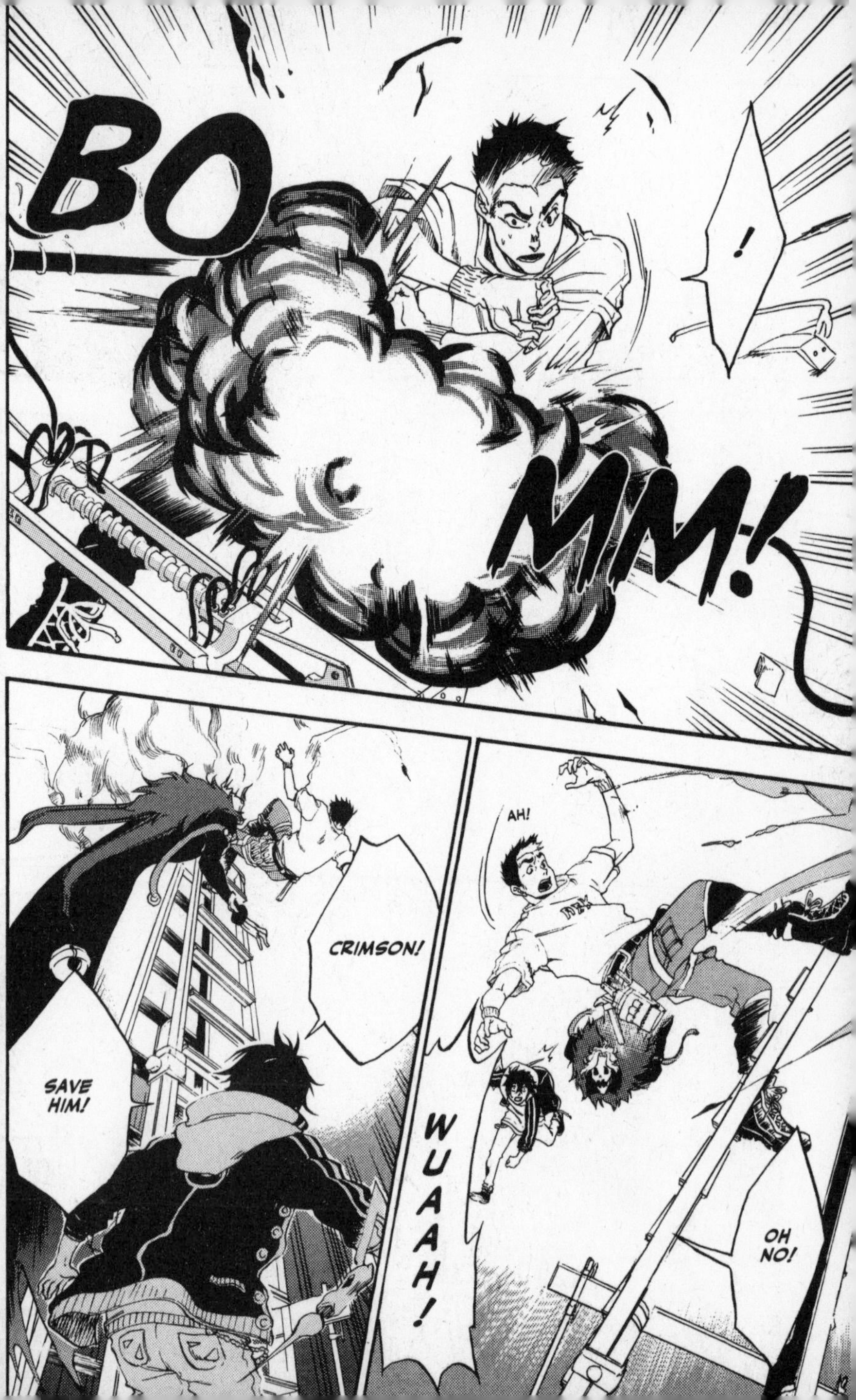
!
BO
MM!
AH!
WUAAH!
OH NO!
CRIMSON!
SAVE HIM!

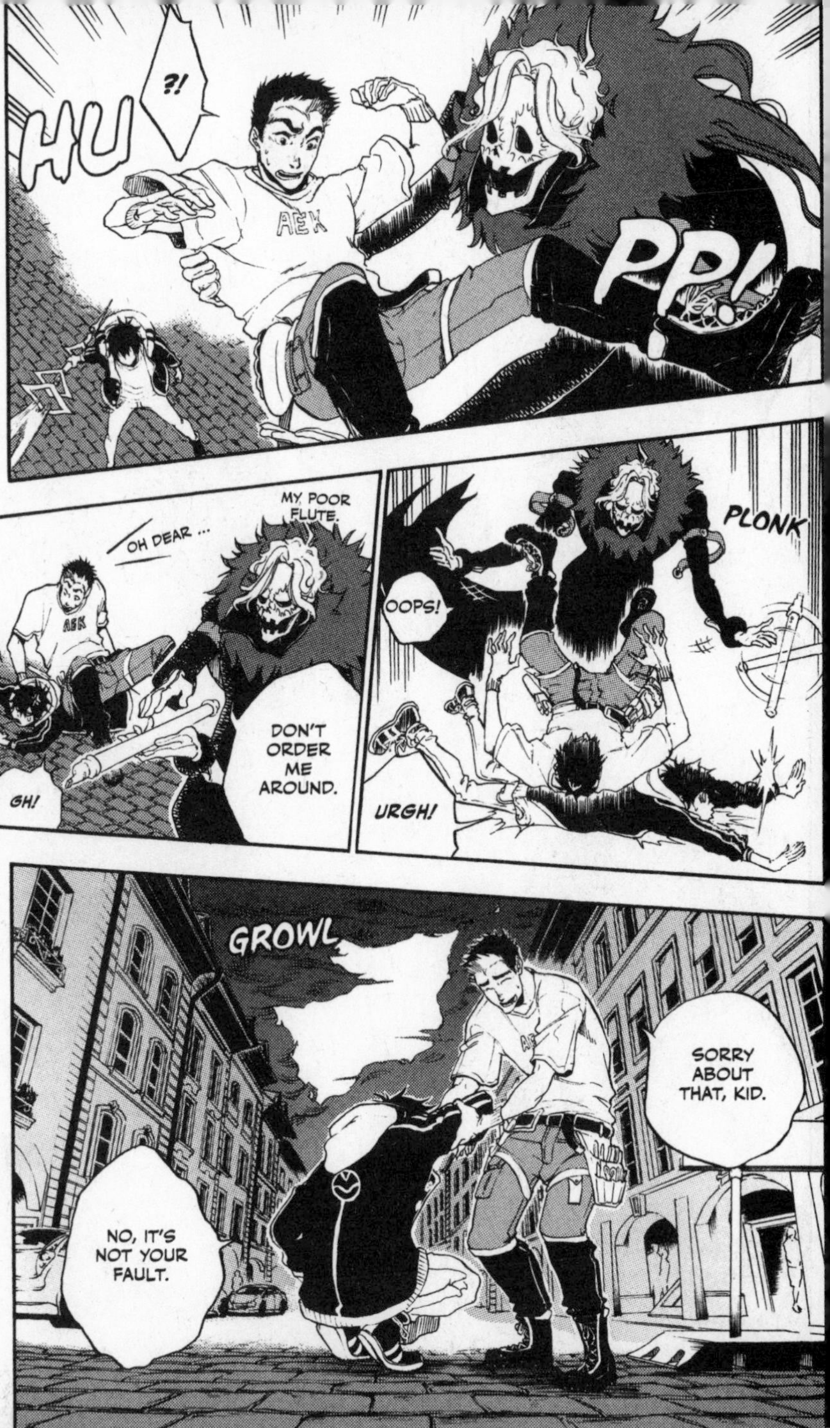
?!
HU
PP!
PLONK
OOPS!
URGH!
MY POOR FLUTE.
OH DEAR ...
DON'T ORDER ME AROUND.
GH!
GROWL
SORRY ABOUT THAT, KID.
NO, IT'S NOT YOUR FAULT.

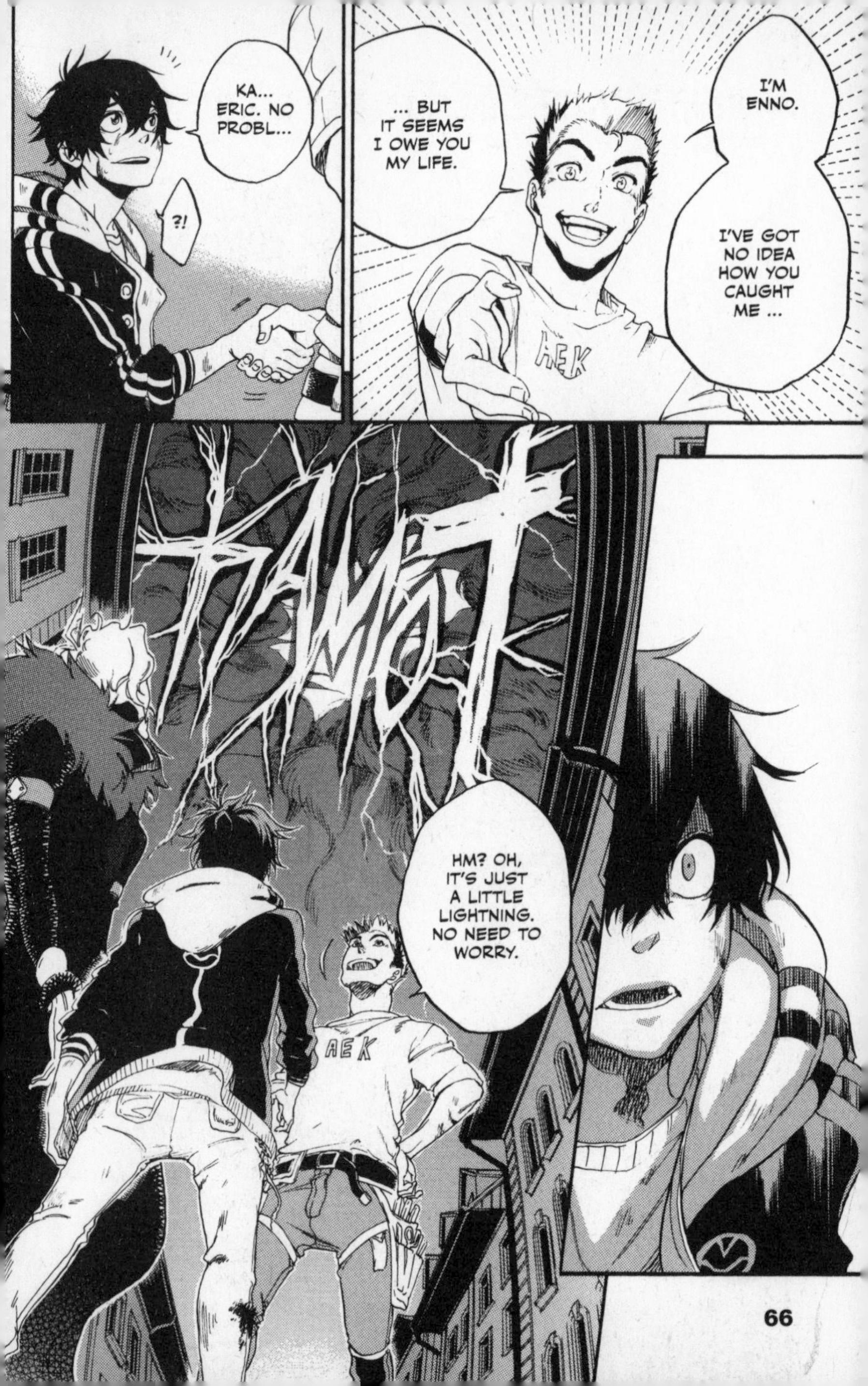
I'M ENNO.
I'VE GOT NO IDEA HOW YOU CAUGHT ME ...
... BUT IT SEEMS I OWE YOU MY LIFE.
KA... ERIC. NO PROBL...
?!
HM? OH, IT'S JUST A LITTLE LIGHTNING. NO NEED TO WORRY.

03

MIT WORTEN LÄSST SICH TREFFLICH STREITEN...

WITH WORDS 'TIS EXCELLENT DISPUTING...

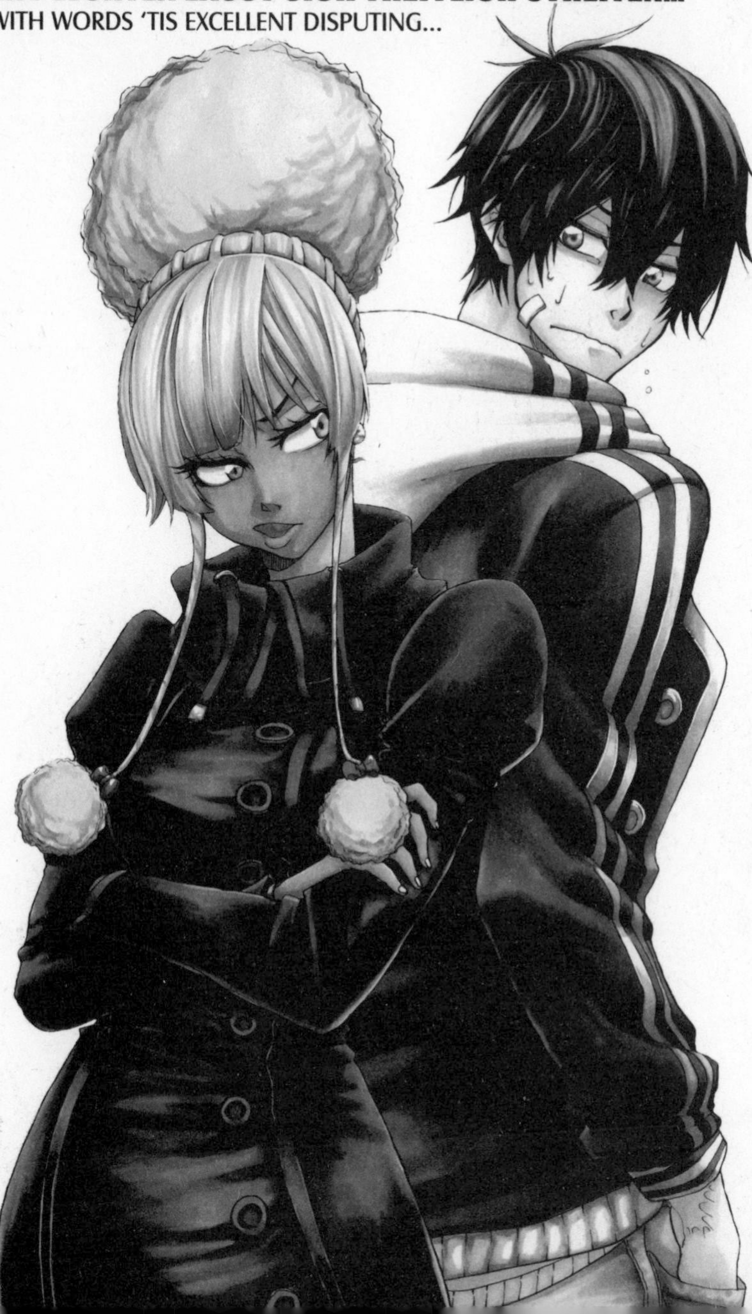

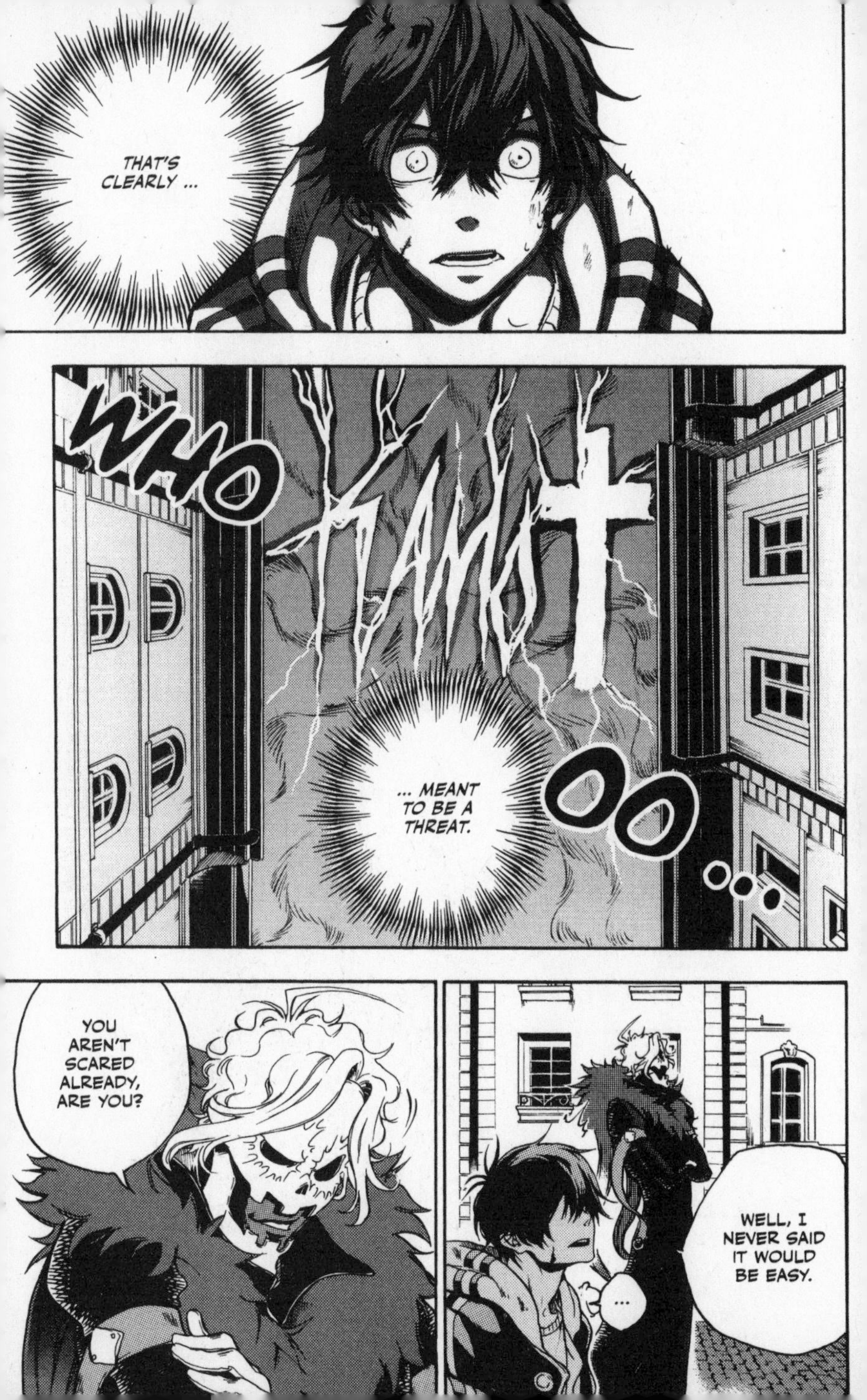
THAT'S CLEARLY ...
WHOOO...
... MEANT TO BE A THREAT.
WELL, I NEVER SAID IT WOULD BE EASY.
...
YOU AREN'T SCARED ALREADY, ARE YOU?

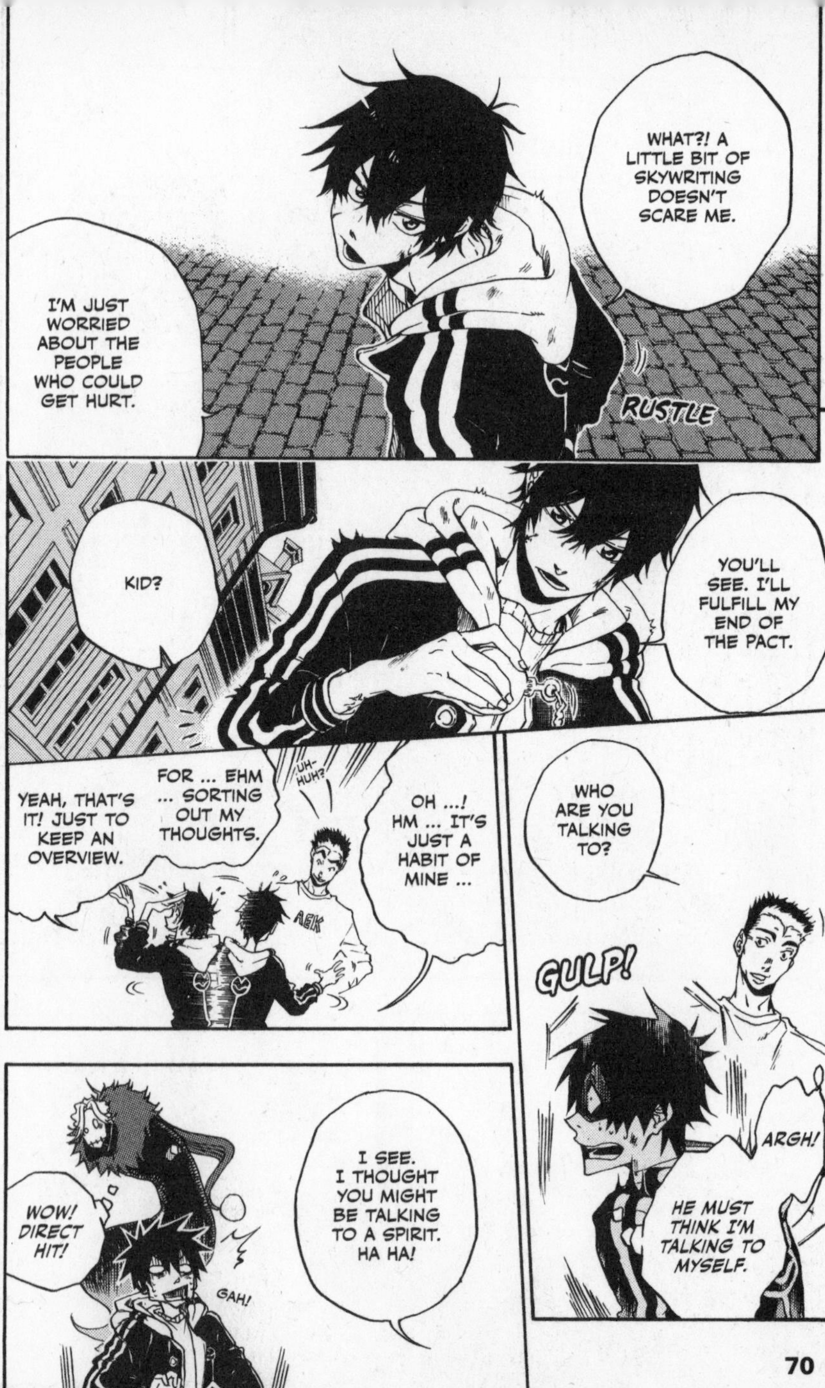
WHAT?! A LITTLE BIT OF SKYWRITING DOESN'T SCARE ME.
RUSTLE
I'M JUST WORRIED ABOUT THE PEOPLE WHO COULD GET HURT.
YOU'LL SEE. I'LL FULFILL MY END OF THE PACT.
KID?
WHO ARE YOU TALKING TO?
GULP!
ARGH!
HE MUST THINK I'M TALKING TO MYSELF.
OH ...! HM ... IT'S JUST A HABIT OF MINE ...
UH-HUH?
FOR ... EHM ... SORTING OUT MY THOUGHTS.
YEAH, THAT'S IT! JUST TO KEEP AN OVERVIEW.
I SEE. I THOUGHT YOU MIGHT BE TALKING TO A SPIRIT. HA HA!
GAH!
WOW! DIRECT HIT!

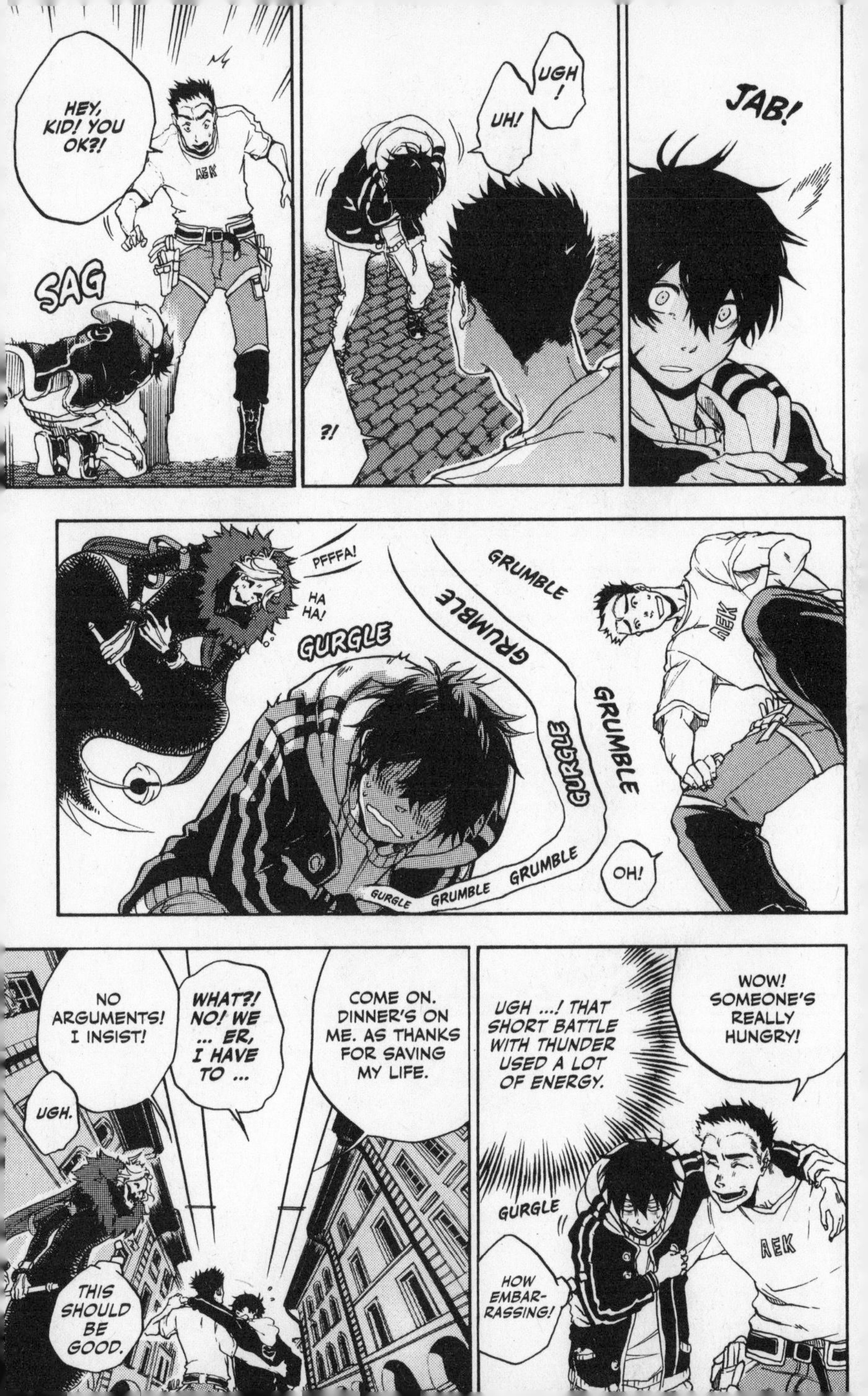
JAB!
UGH !
UH!
?!
HEY, KID! YOU OK?!
SAG
GRUMBLE
GRUMBLE
GRUMBLE
OH!
GURGLE
GRUMBLE
GRUMBLE
GURGLE
PFFFA!
HA HA!
GURGLE
WOW! SOMEONE'S REALLY HUNGRY!
UGH ...! THAT SHORT BATTLE WITH THUNDER USED A LOT OF ENERGY.
GURGLE
HOW EMBAR-RASSING!
COME ON. DINNER'S ON ME. AS THANKS FOR SAVING MY LIFE.
WHAT?! NO! WE ... ER, I HAVE TO ...
NO ARGUMENTS! I INSIST!
UGH.
THIS SHOULD BE GOOD.

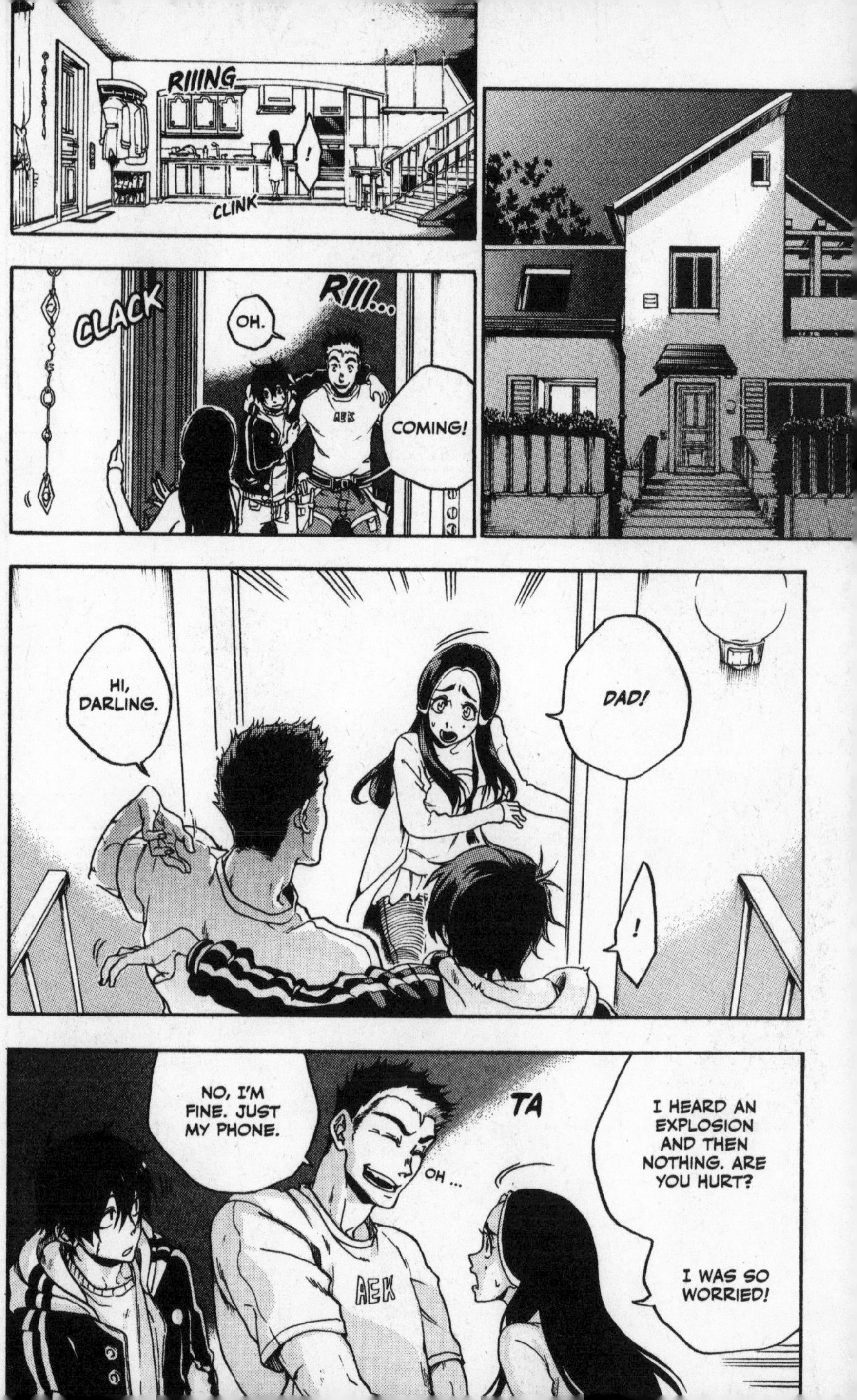
RIIING
!
CLINK
RIII...
OH.
CLACK
COMING!
DAD!
HI, DARLING.
!
I HEARD AN EXPLOSION AND THEN NOTHING. ARE YOU HURT?
I WAS SO WORRIED!
TA
OH ...
NO, I'M FINE. JUST MY PHONE.

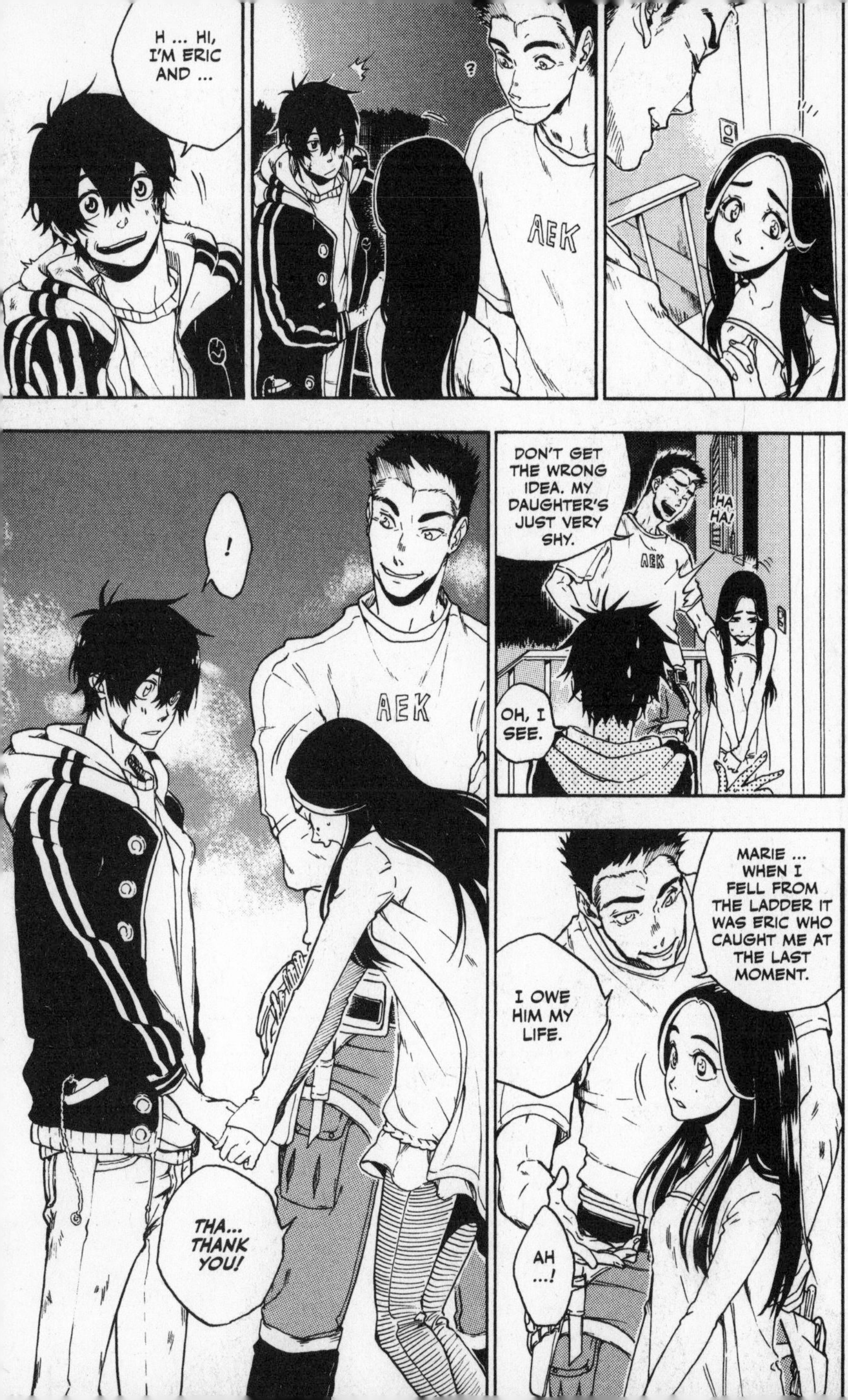
?
H ... HI, I'M ERIC AND ...
DON'T GET THE WRONG IDEA. MY DAUGHTER'S JUST VERY SHY.
HA HA!
OH, I SEE.
MARIE ... WHEN I FELL FROM THE LADDER IT WAS ERIC WHO CAUGHT ME AT THE LAST MOMENT.
I OWE HIM MY LIFE.
AH ...!
!
THA... THANK YOU!

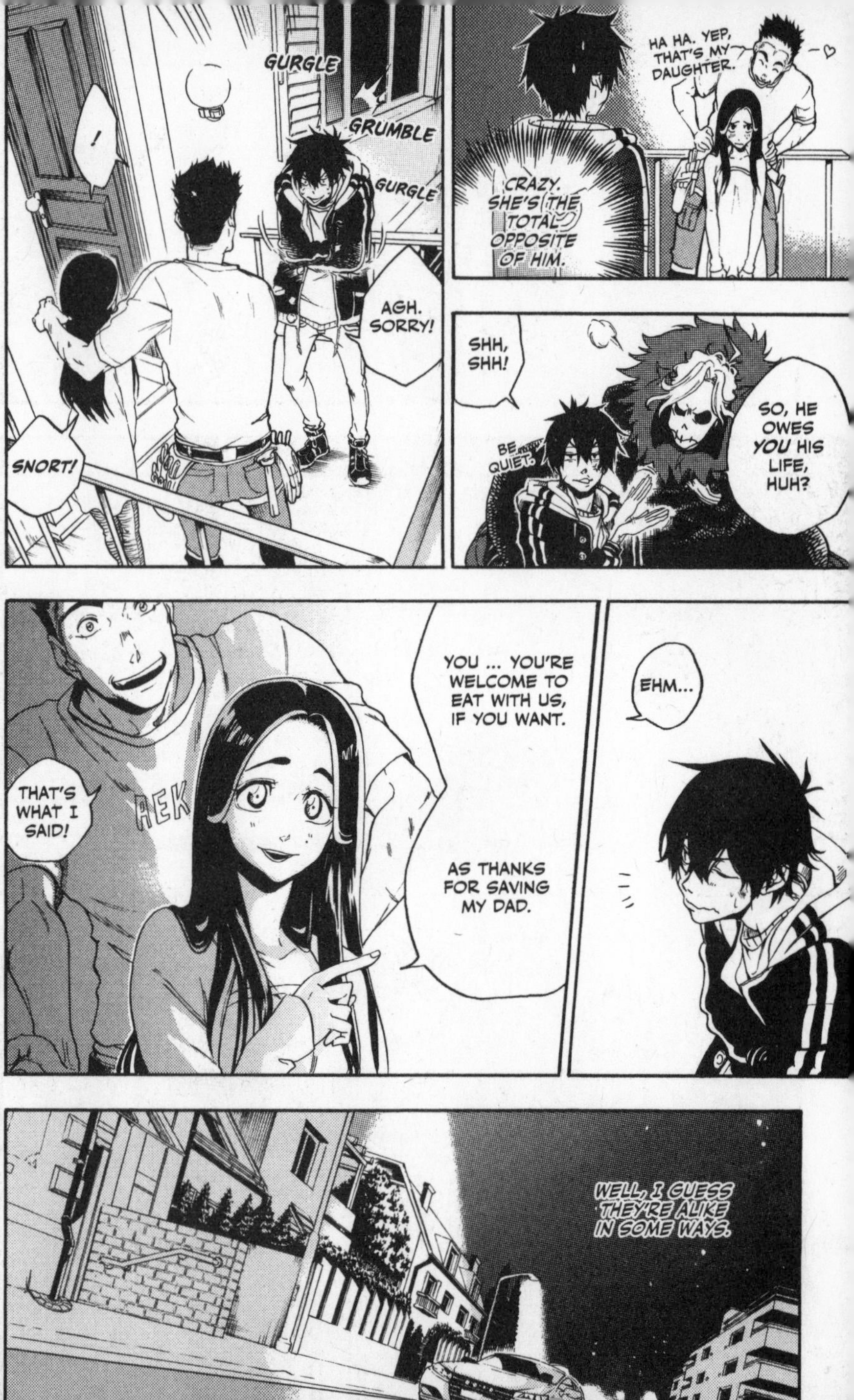
HA HA. YEP, THAT'S MY DAUGHTER.
CRAZY. SHE'S THE TOTAL OPPOSITE OF HIM.
SO, HE OWES *YOU* HIS LIFE, HUH?
SHH, SHH!
BE QUIET.
GURGLE
!
GRUMBLE
GURGLE
AGH. SORRY!
SNORT!
EHM...
YOU ... YOU'RE WELCOME TO EAT WITH US, IF YOU WANT.
AS THANKS FOR SAVING MY DAD.
THAT'S WHAT I SAID!
WELL, I GUESS THEY'RE ALIKE IN SOME WAYS.

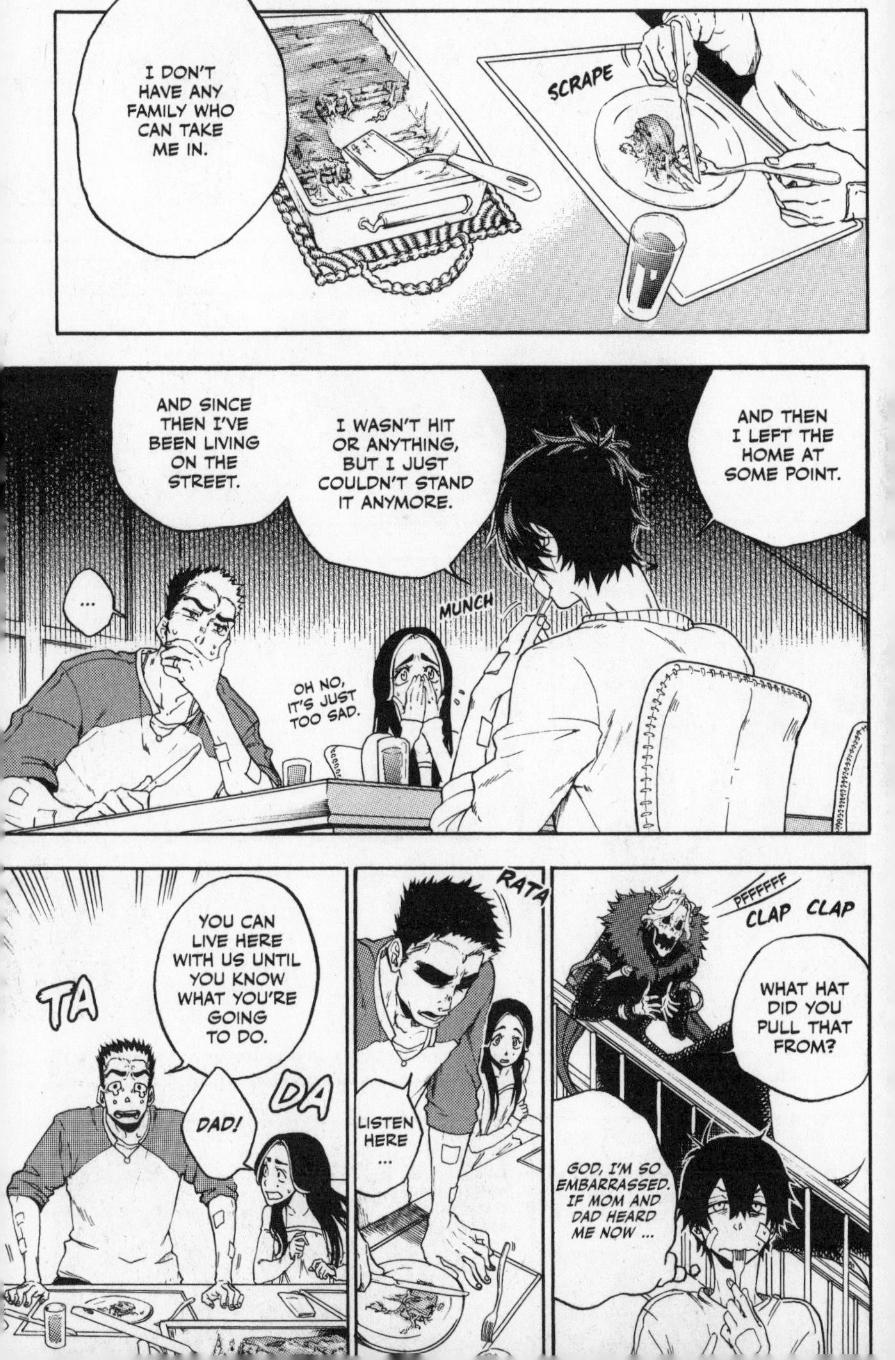
SCRAPE
I DON'T HAVE ANY FAMILY WHO CAN TAKE ME IN.
AND THEN I LEFT THE HOME AT SOME POINT.
I WASN'T HIT OR ANYTHING, BUT I JUST COULDN'T STAND IT ANYMORE.
AND SINCE THEN I'VE BEEN LIVING ON THE STREET.
MUNCH
...
OH NO, IT'S JUST TOO SAD.
PFFFFFF
CLAP CLAP
WHAT HAT DID YOU PULL THAT FROM?
GOD, I'M SO EMBARRASSED. IF MOM AND DAD HEARD ME NOW ...
RATA
LISTEN HERE ...
YOU CAN LIVE HERE WITH US UNTIL YOU KNOW WHAT YOU'RE GOING TO DO.
TA
DA
DAD!

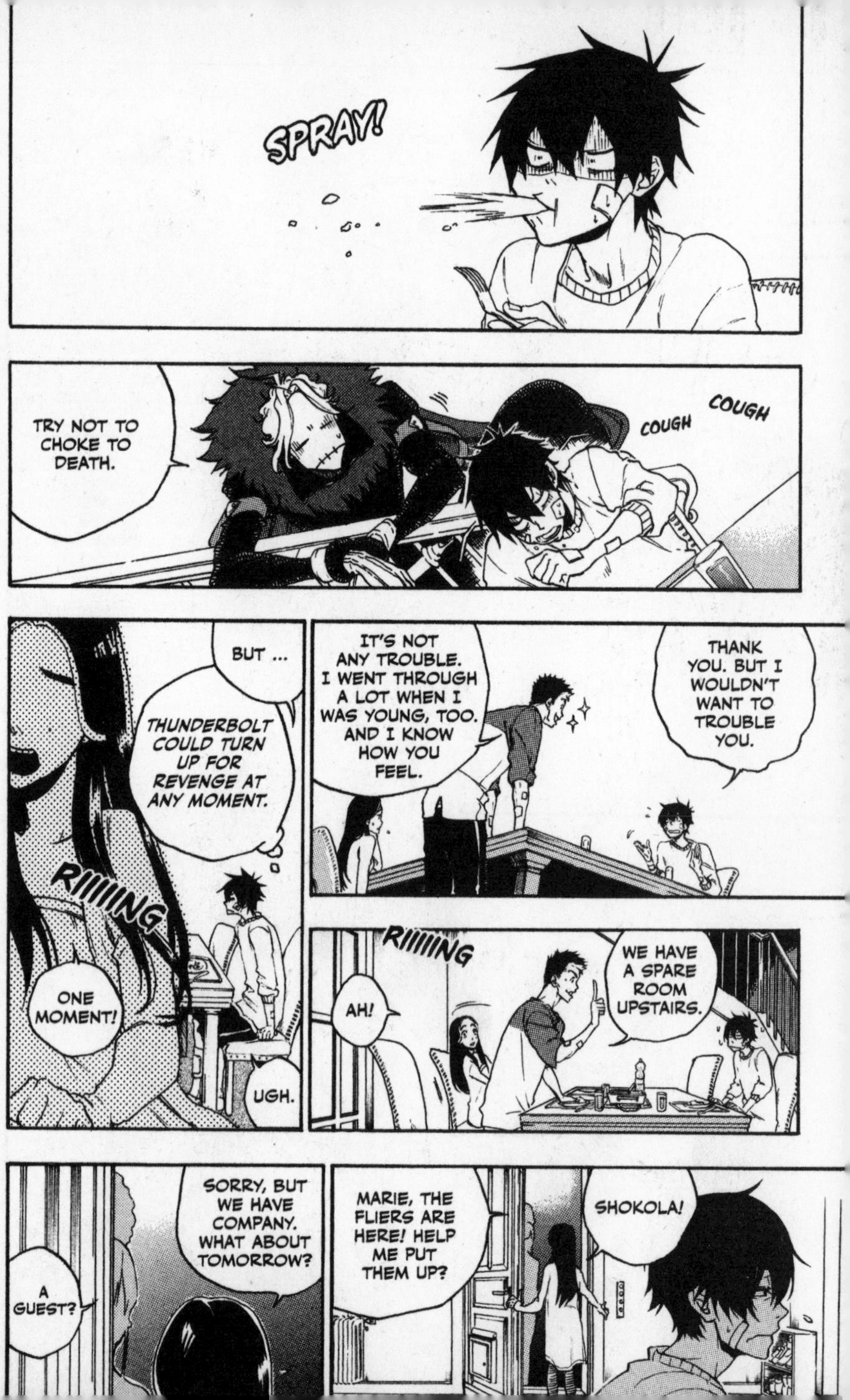
SPRAY!
COUGH
COUGH
TRY NOT TO CHOKE TO DEATH.
THANK YOU. BUT I WOULDN'T WANT TO TROUBLE YOU.
IT'S NOT ANY TROUBLE. I WENT THROUGH A LOT WHEN I WAS YOUNG, TOO. AND I KNOW HOW YOU FEEL.
WE HAVE A SPARE ROOM UPSTAIRS.
RIIIIING
AH!
BUT ...
THUNDERBOLT COULD TURN UP FOR REVENGE AT ANY MOMENT.
RIIIIING
ONE MOMENT!
UGH.
SHOKOLA!
MARIE, THE FLIERS ARE HERE! HELP ME PUT THEM UP?
SORRY, BUT WE HAVE COMPANY. WHAT ABOUT TOMORROW?
A GUEST?

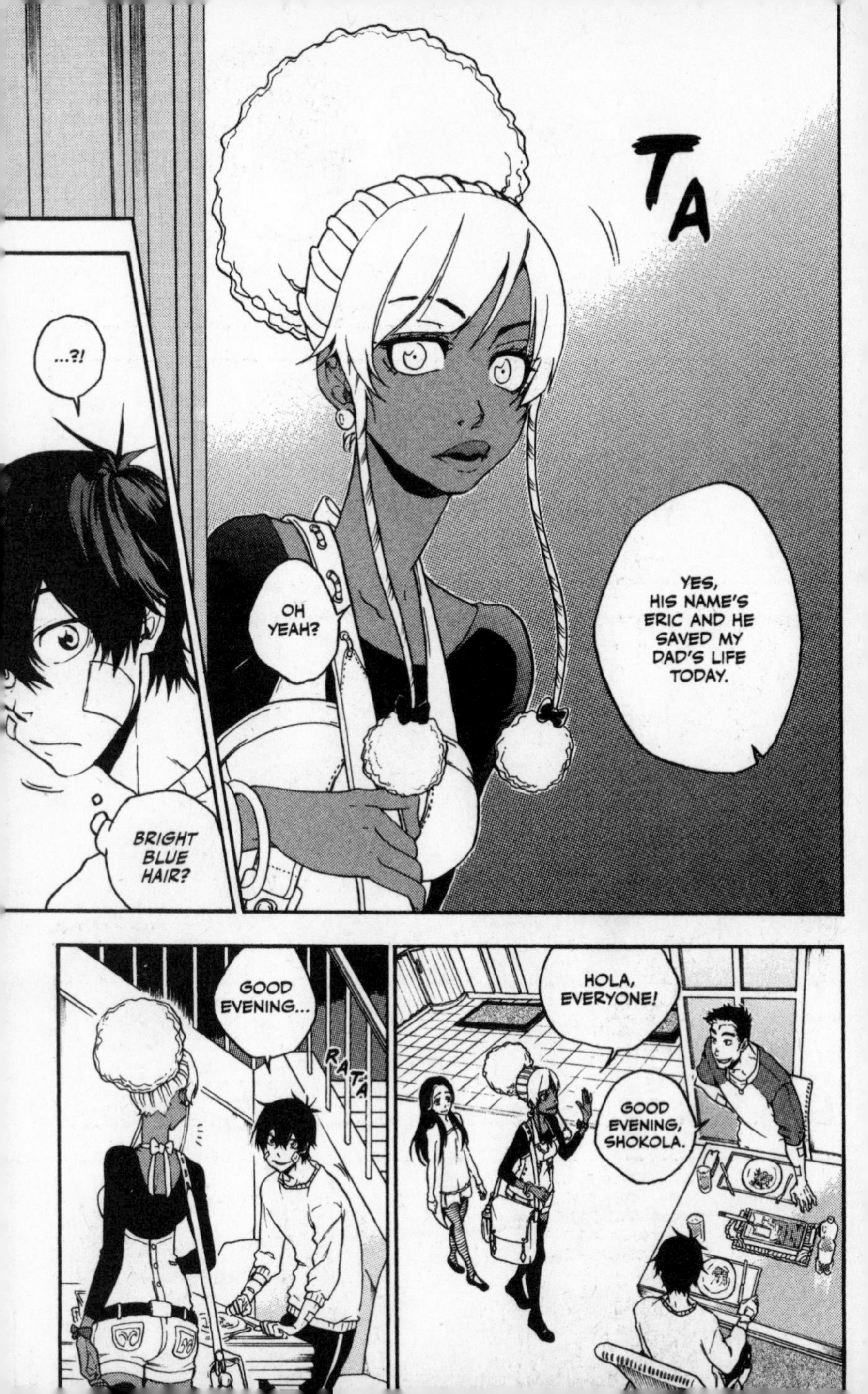
TA
YES, HIS NAME'S ERIC AND HE SAVED MY DAD'S LIFE TODAY.
OH YEAH?
...?!
BRIGHT BLUE HAIR?
HOLA, EVERYONE!
GOOD EVENING, SHOKOLA.
GOOD EVENING...
RATA

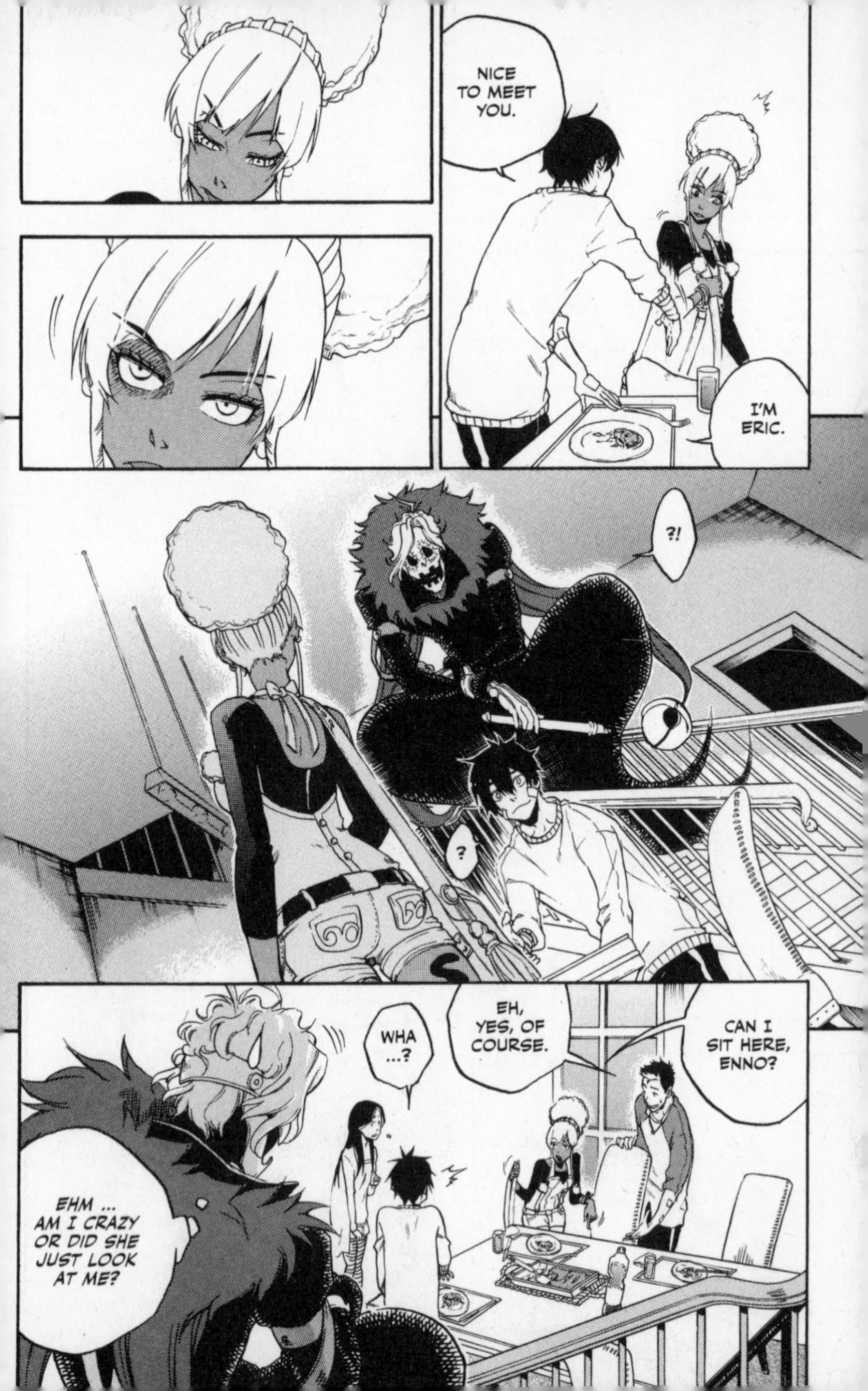
NICE TO MEET YOU.
I'M ERIC.
?!
?
CAN I SIT HERE, ENNO?
EH, YES, OF COURSE.
WHA ...?
EHM ... AM I CRAZY OR DID SHE JUST LOOK AT ME?

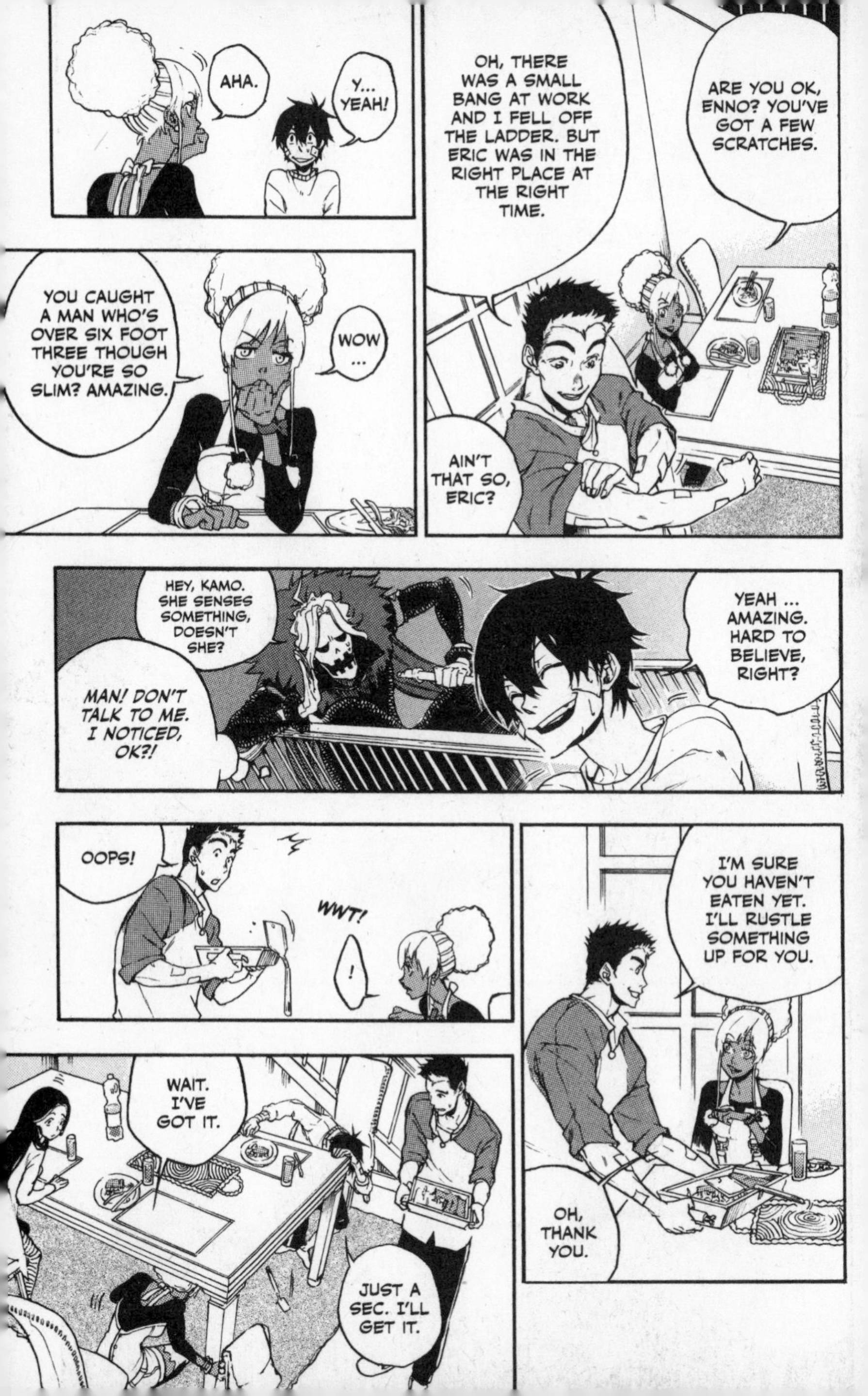
ARE YOU OK, ENNO? YOU'VE GOT A FEW SCRATCHES.
OH, THERE WAS A SMALL BANG AT WORK AND I FELL OFF THE LADDER. BUT ERIC WAS IN THE RIGHT PLACE AT THE RIGHT TIME.
AIN'T THAT SO, ERIC?
Y... YEAH!
AHA.
WOW ...
YOU CAUGHT A MAN WHO'S OVER SIX FOOT THREE THOUGH YOU'RE SO SLIM? AMAZING.
YEAH ... AMAZING. HARD TO BELIEVE, RIGHT?
HEY, KAMO. SHE SENSES SOMETHING, DOESN'T SHE?
MAN! DON'T TALK TO ME. I NOTICED, OK?!
I'M SURE YOU HAVEN'T EATEN YET. I'LL RUSTLE SOMETHING UP FOR YOU.
OH, THANK YOU.
OOPS!
WWT!
!
WAIT. I'VE GOT IT.
JUST A SEC. I'LL GET IT.

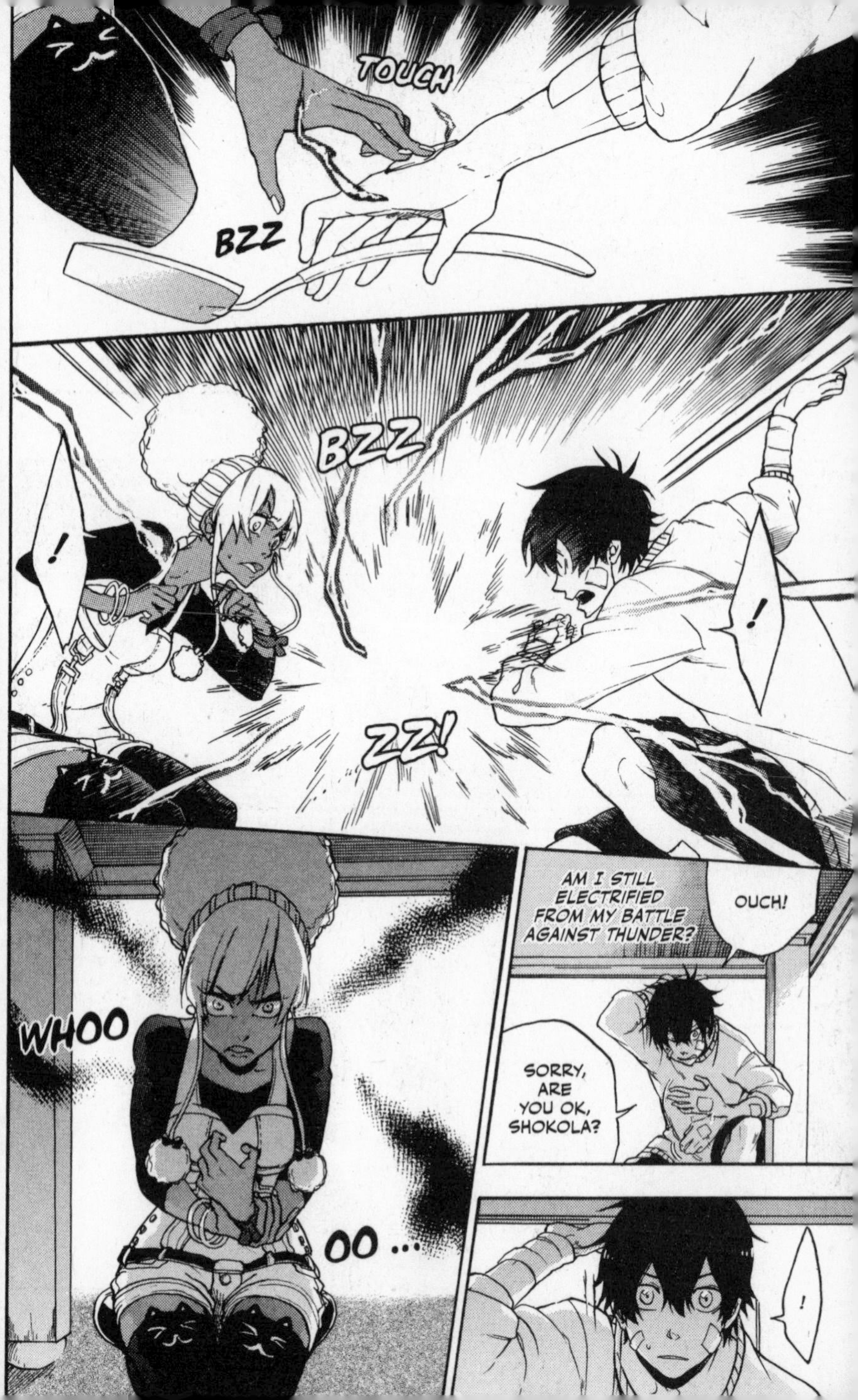
TOUCH
BZZ
BZZ
!
!
ZZ!
OUCH!
AM I STILL ELECTRIFIED FROM MY BATTLE AGAINST THUNDER?
SORRY, ARE YOU OK, SHOKOLA?
!
WHOO
OO...

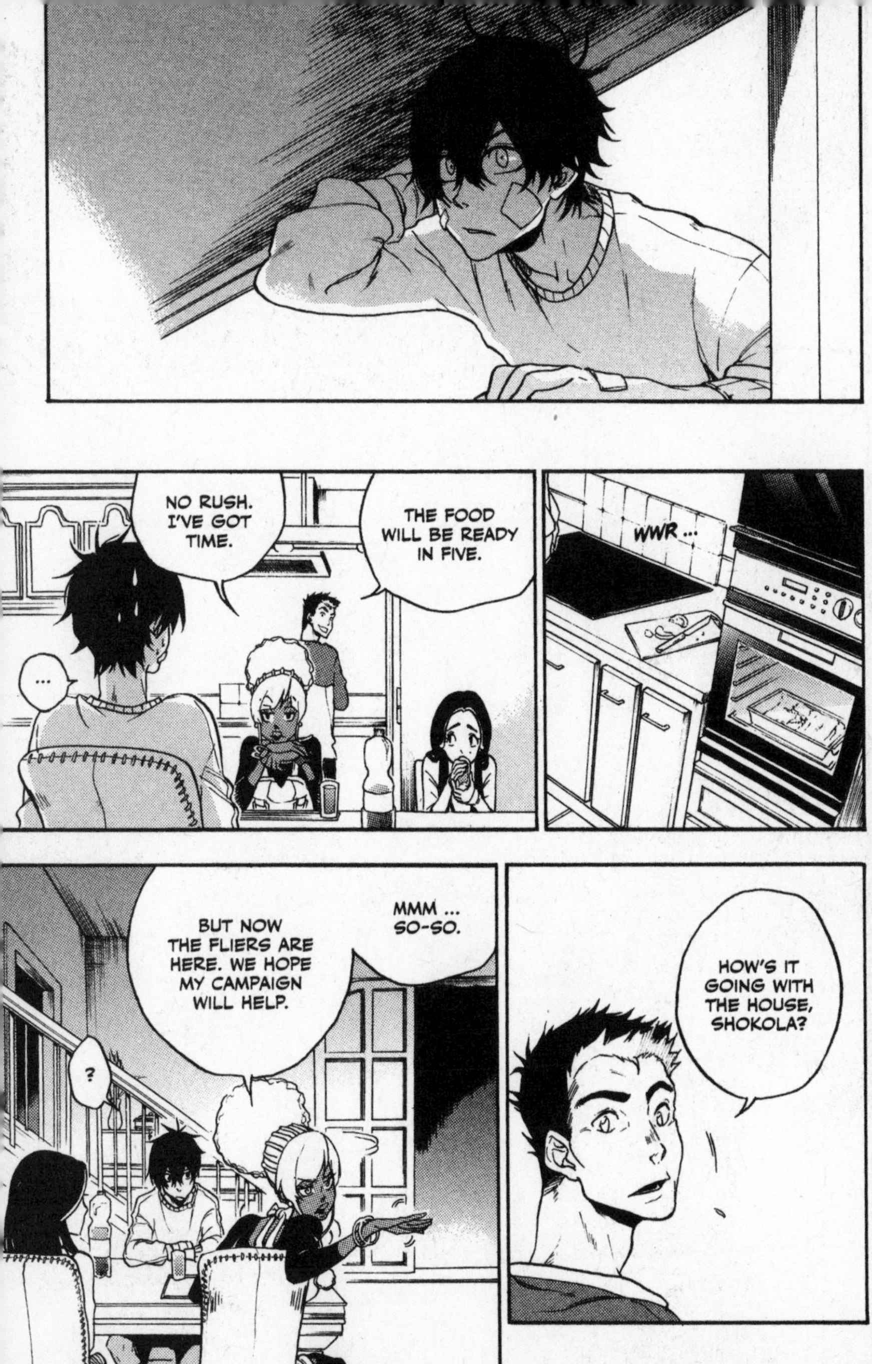
WWR ...
THE FOOD WILL BE READY IN FIVE.
NO RUSH. I'VE GOT TIME.
...
HOW'S IT GOING WITH THE HOUSE, SHOKOLA?
MMM ... SO-SO.
BUT NOW THE FLIERS ARE HERE. WE HOPE MY CAMPAIGN WILL HELP.
?

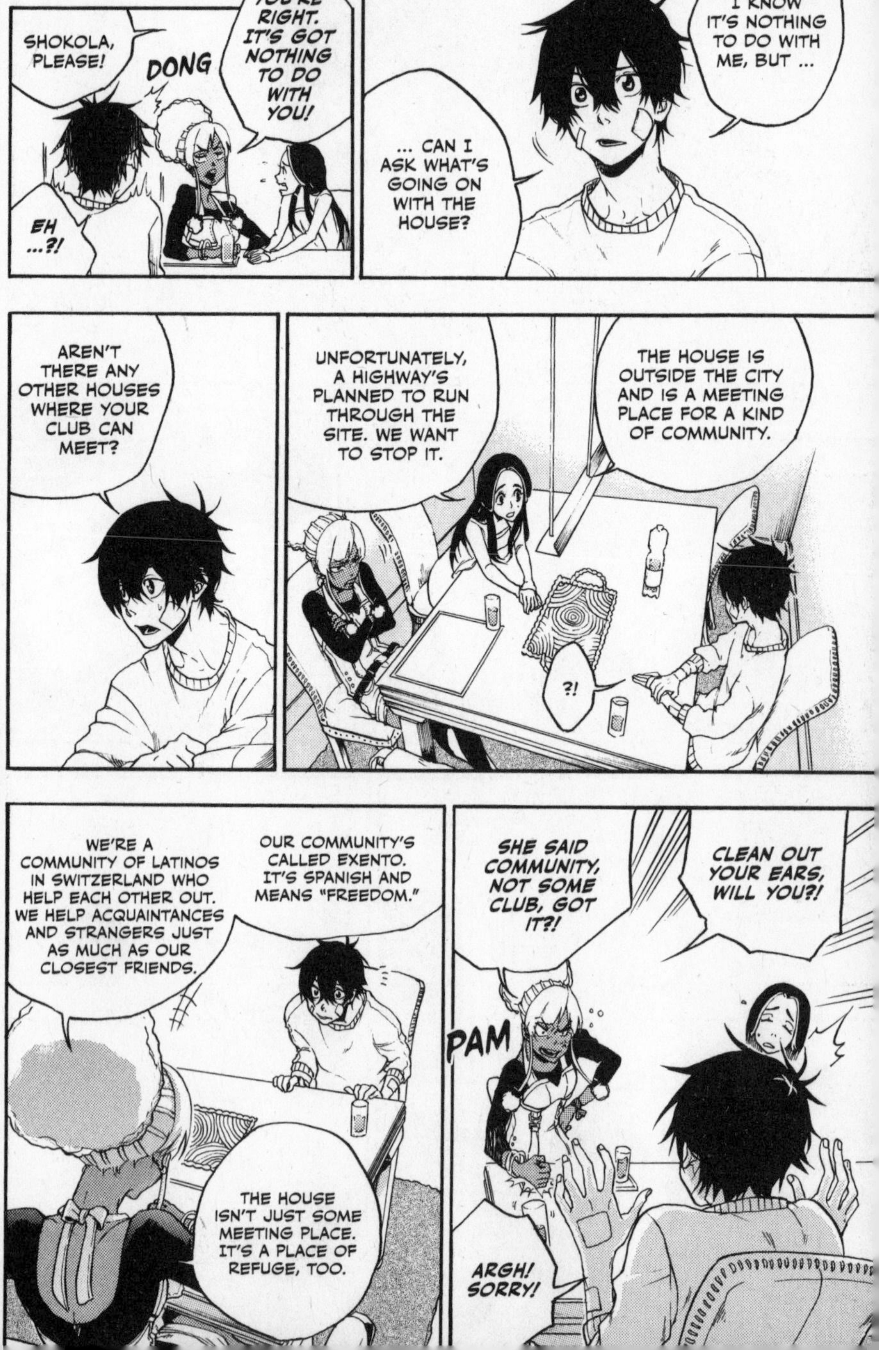
I KNOW IT'S NOTHING TO DO WITH ME, BUT ...
... CAN I ASK WHAT'S GOING ON WITH THE HOUSE?
YOU'RE RIGHT. IT'S GOT NOTHING TO DO WITH YOU!
DONG
SHOKOLA, PLEASE!
EH ...?!
THE HOUSE IS OUTSIDE THE CITY AND IS A MEETING PLACE FOR A KIND OF COMMUNITY.
UNFORTUNATELY, A HIGHWAY'S PLANNED TO RUN THROUGH THE SITE. WE WANT TO STOP IT.
?!
AREN'T THERE ANY OTHER HOUSES WHERE YOUR CLUB CAN MEET?
CLEAN OUT YOUR EARS, WILL YOU?!
SHE SAID COMMUNITY, NOT SOME CLUB, GOT IT?!
PAM
ARGH! SORRY!
OUR COMMUNITY'S CALLED EXENTO. IT'S SPANISH AND MEANS "FREEDOM."
WE'RE A COMMUNITY OF LATINOS IN SWITZERLAND WHO HELP EACH OTHER OUT. WE HELP ACQUAINTANCES AND STRANGERS JUST AS MUCH AS OUR CLOSEST FRIENDS.
THE HOUSE ISN'T JUST SOME MEETING PLACE. IT'S A PLACE OF REFUGE, TOO.

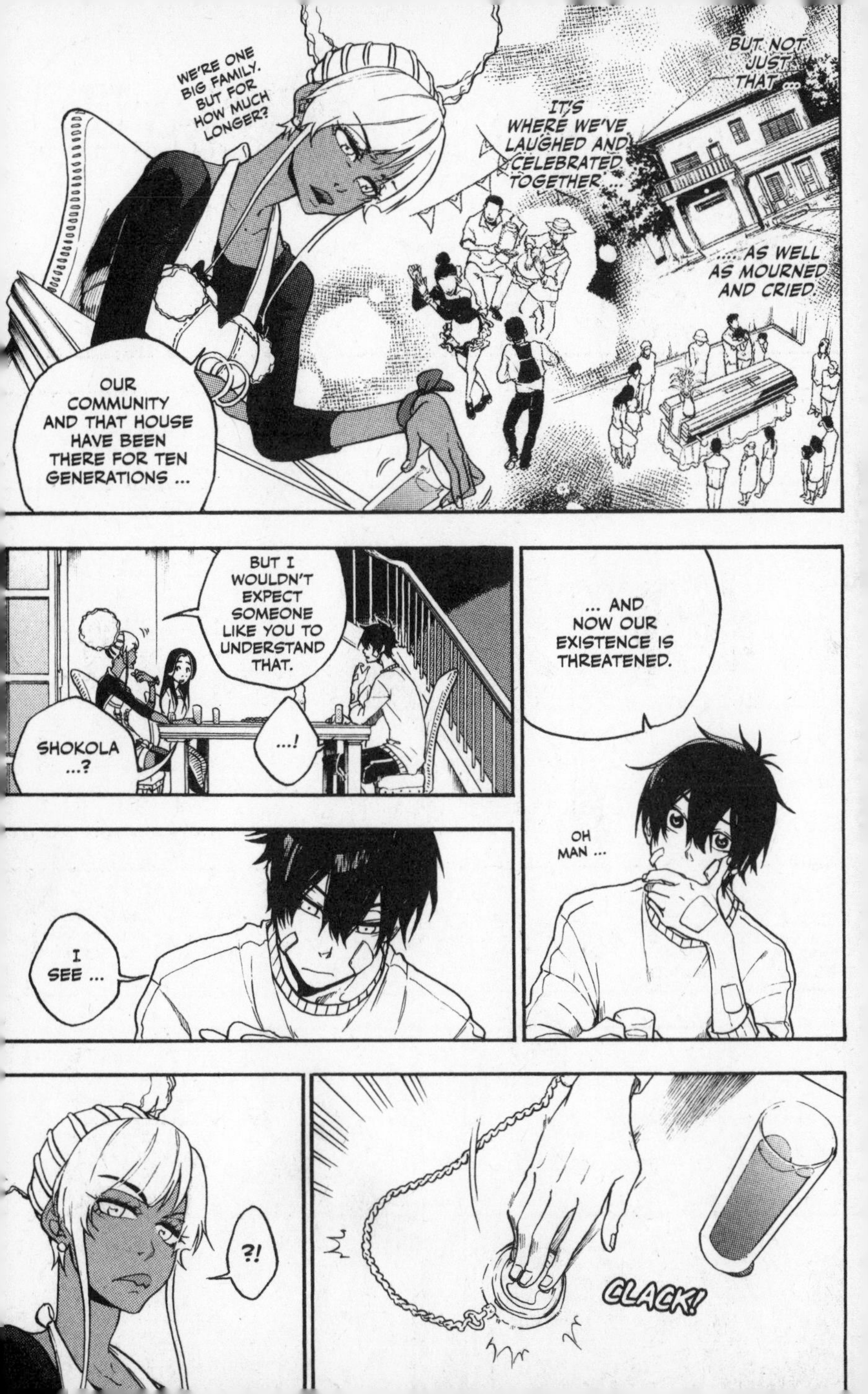
BUT NOT JUST THAT ...
IT'S WHERE WE'VE LAUGHED AND CELEBRATED TOGETHER ...
WE'RE ONE BIG FAMILY. BUT FOR HOW MUCH LONGER?
... AS WELL AS MOURNED AND CRIED.
OUR COMMUNITY AND THAT HOUSE HAVE BEEN THERE FOR TEN GENERATIONS ...
... AND NOW OUR EXISTENCE IS THREATENED.
OH MAN ...
BUT I WOULDN'T EXPECT SOMEONE LIKE YOU TO UNDERSTAND THAT.
...!
SHOKOLA ...?
I SEE ...
CLACK!
?!

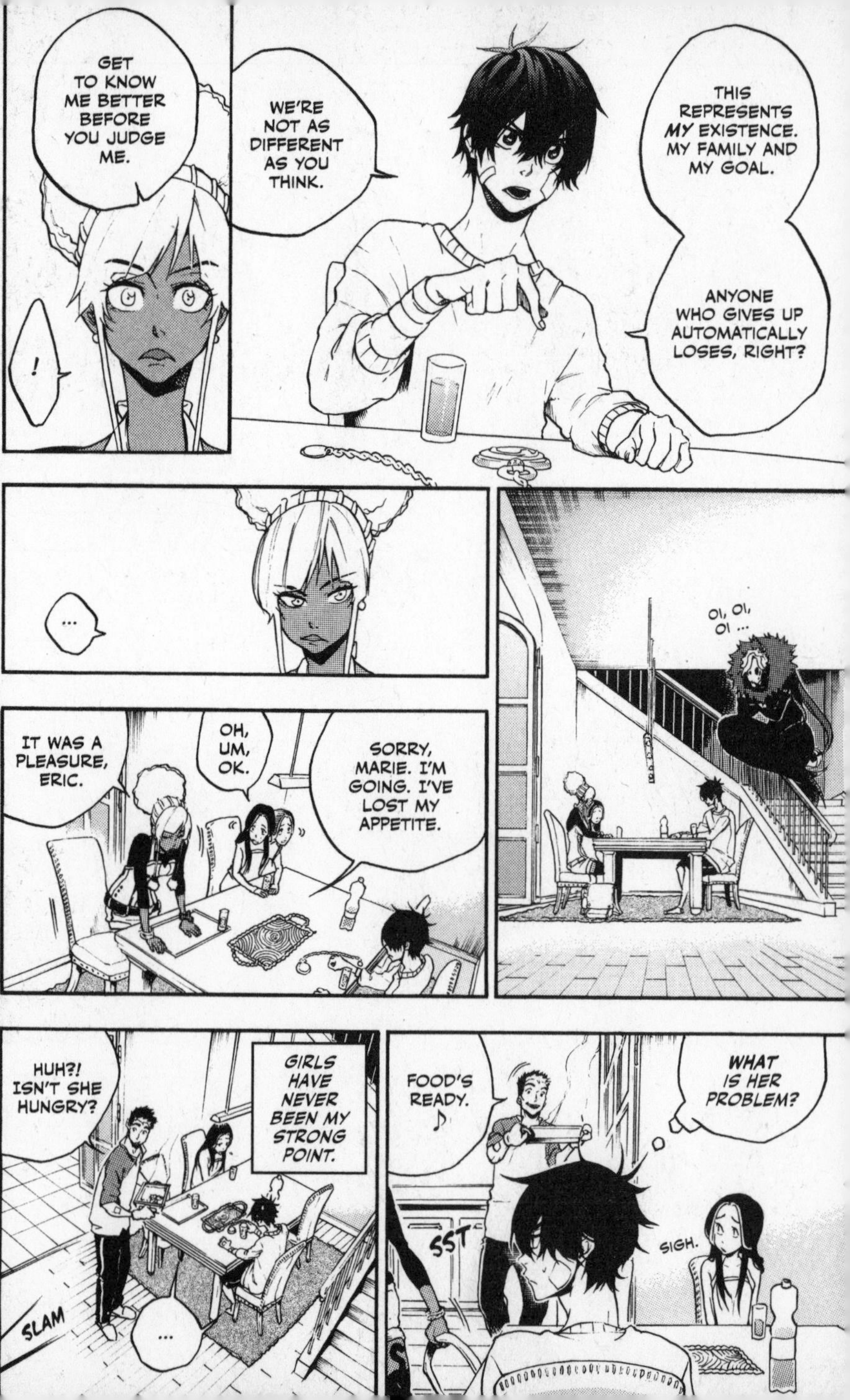

THIS REPRESENTS MY EXISTENCE. MY FAMILY AND MY GOAL.
ANYONE WHO GIVES UP AUTOMATICALLY LOSES, RIGHT?
WE'RE NOT AS DIFFERENT AS YOU THINK.
GET TO KNOW ME BETTER BEFORE YOU JUDGE ME.
!
OI, OI, OI ...
...
SORRY, MARIE. I'M GOING. I'VE LOST MY APPETITE.
OH, UM, OK.
IT WAS A PLEASURE, ERIC.
WHAT IS HER PROBLEM?
FOOD'S READY. ♪
SST
SIGH.
GIRLS HAVE NEVER BEEN MY STRONG POINT.
HUH?! ISN'T SHE HUNGRY?
SLAM
...

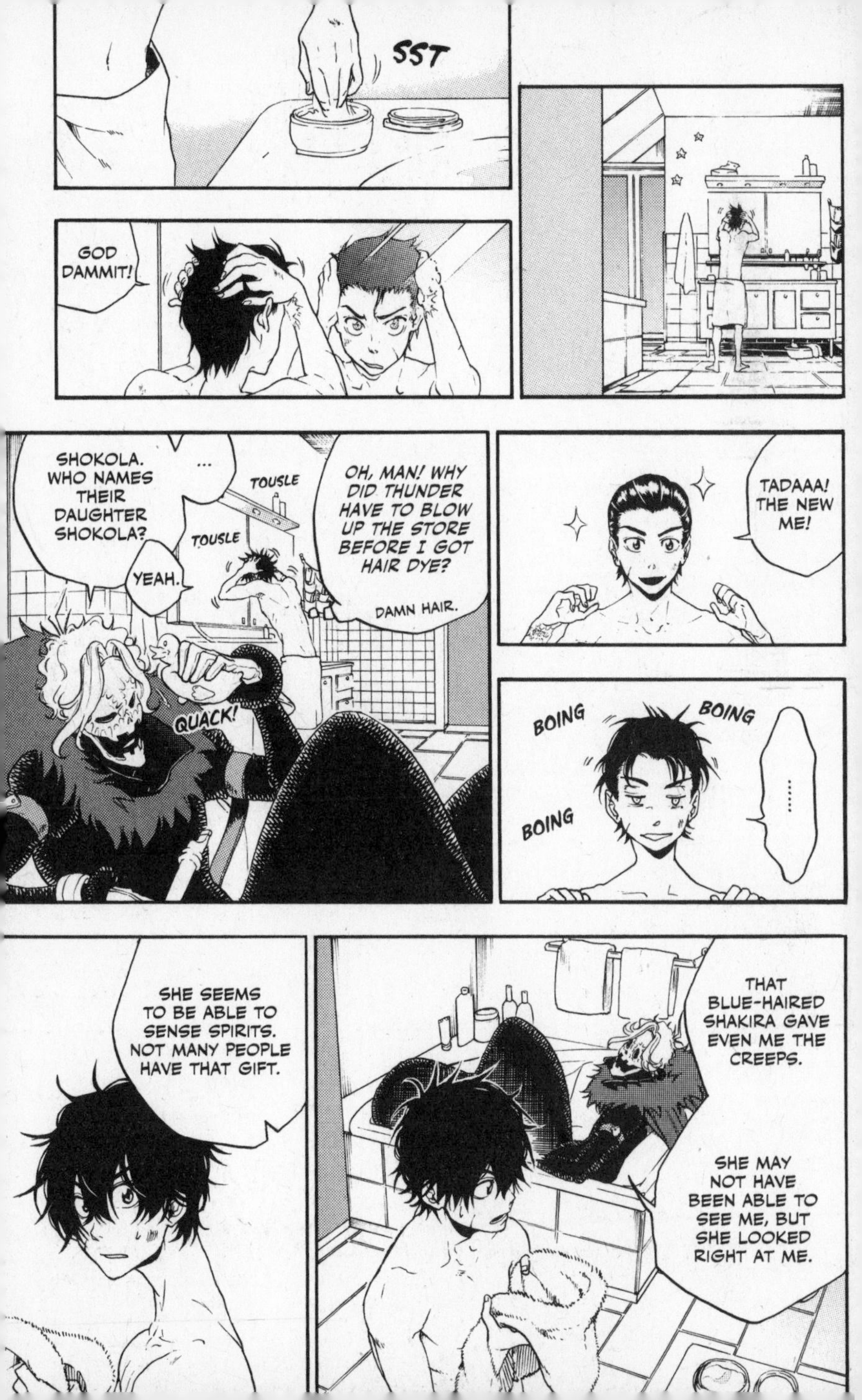
SST
GOD DAMMIT!
TADAAA! THE NEW ME!
BOING
BOING
BOING
......
OH, MAN! WHY DID THUNDER HAVE TO BLOW UP THE STORE BEFORE I GOT HAIR DYE?
TOUSLE
SHOKOLA. WHO NAMES THEIR DAUGHTER SHOKOLA?
...
TOUSLE
YEAH.
DAMN HAIR.
QUACK!
THAT BLUE-HAIRED SHAKIRA GAVE EVEN ME THE CREEPS.
SHE MAY NOT HAVE BEEN ABLE TO SEE ME, BUT SHE LOOKED RIGHT AT ME.
SHE SEEMS TO BE ABLE TO SENSE SPIRITS. NOT MANY PEOPLE HAVE THAT GIFT.

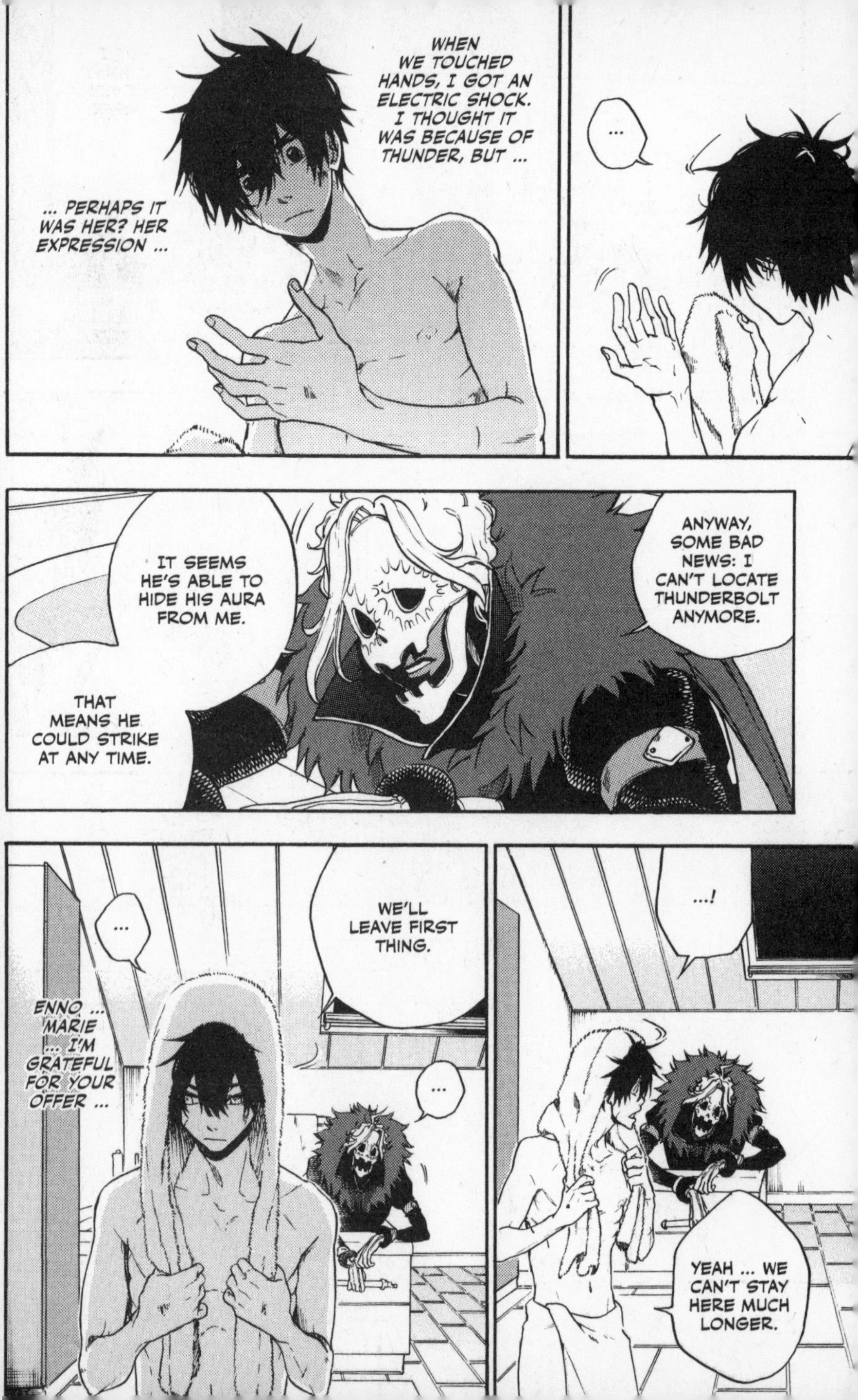
...
WHEN WE TOUCHED HANDS, I GOT AN ELECTRIC SHOCK. I THOUGHT IT WAS BECAUSE OF THUNDER, BUT ...
... PERHAPS IT WAS HER? HER EXPRESSION ...
ANYWAY, SOME BAD NEWS: I CAN'T LOCATE THUNDERBOLT ANYMORE.
IT SEEMS HE'S ABLE TO HIDE HIS AURA FROM ME.
THAT MEANS HE COULD STRIKE AT ANY TIME.
...!
YEAH ... WE CAN'T STAY HERE MUCH LONGER.
WE'LL LEAVE FIRST THING.
...
ENNO ... MARIE ... I'M GRATEFUL FOR YOUR OFFER ...
...

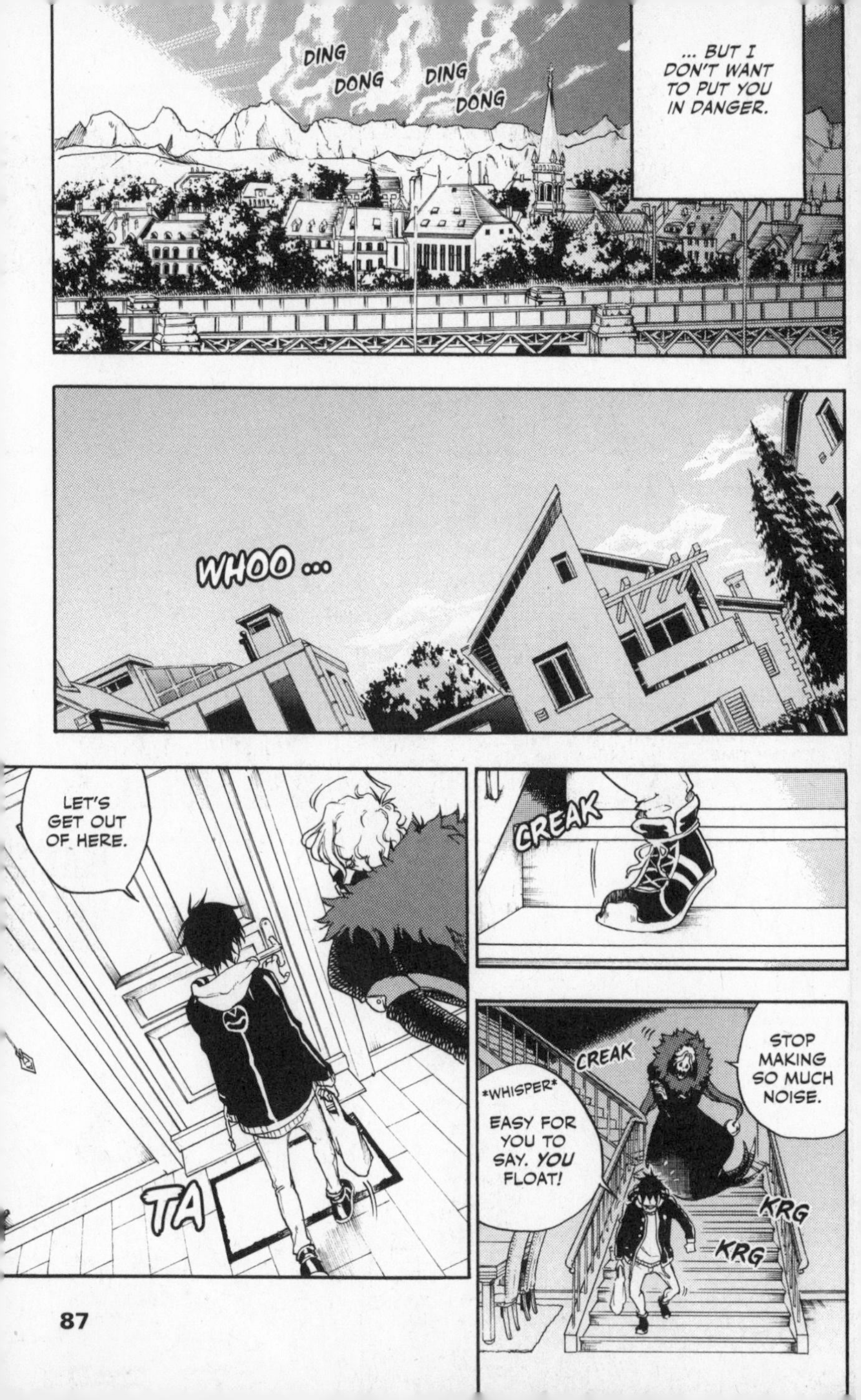
... BUT I DON'T WANT TO PUT YOU IN DANGER.
DING
DONG
DING
DONG
WHOO ...
CREAK
STOP MAKING SO MUCH NOISE.
CREAK
WHISPER EASY FOR YOU TO SAY. *YOU* FLOAT!
KRG
KRG
LET'S GET OUT OF HERE.
TA

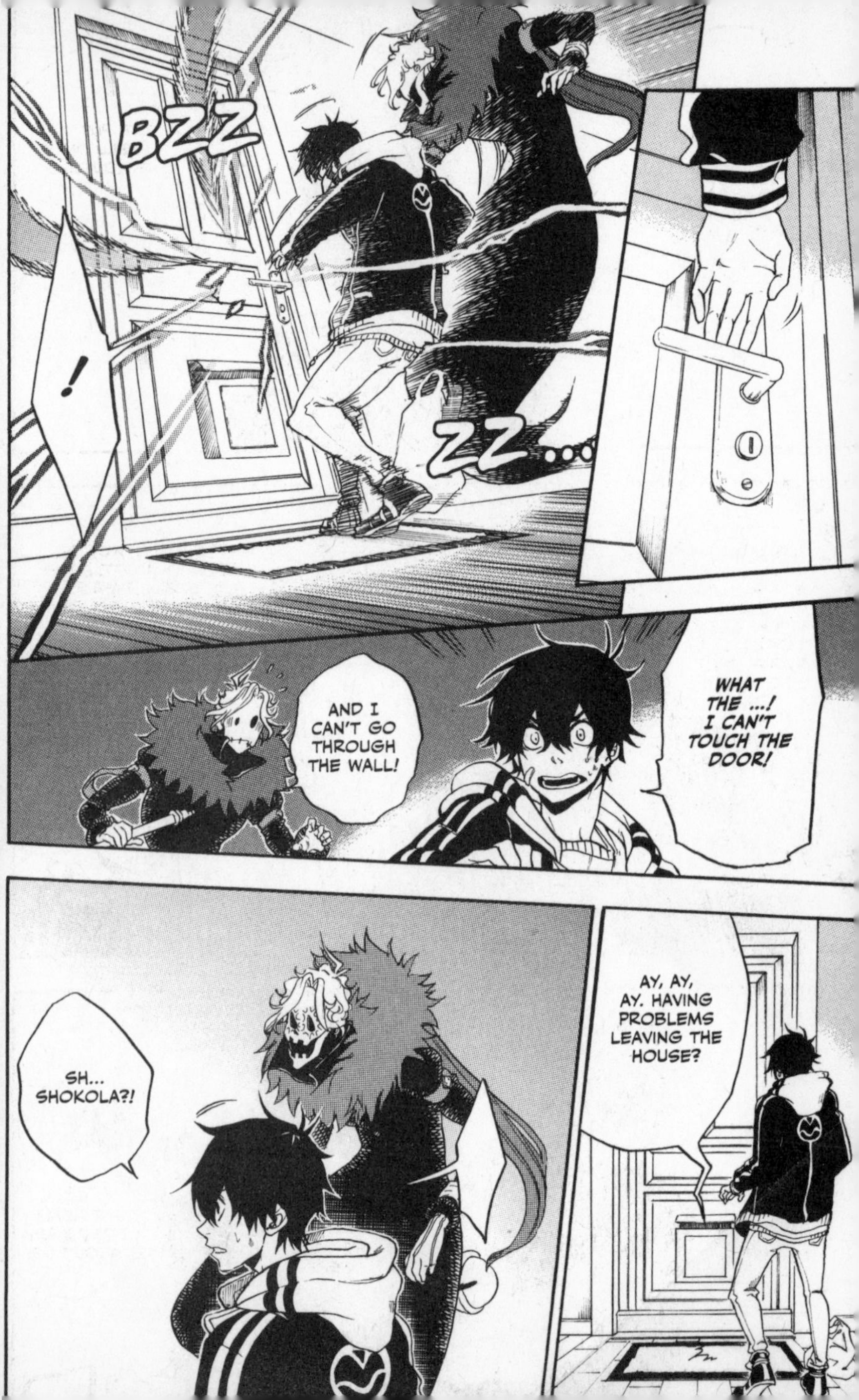
BZZ
!
ZZ
WHAT THE ...! I CAN'T TOUCH THE DOOR!
AND I CAN'T GO THROUGH THE WALL!
AY, AY, AY. HAVING PROBLEMS LEAVING THE HOUSE?
SH... SHOKOLA?!

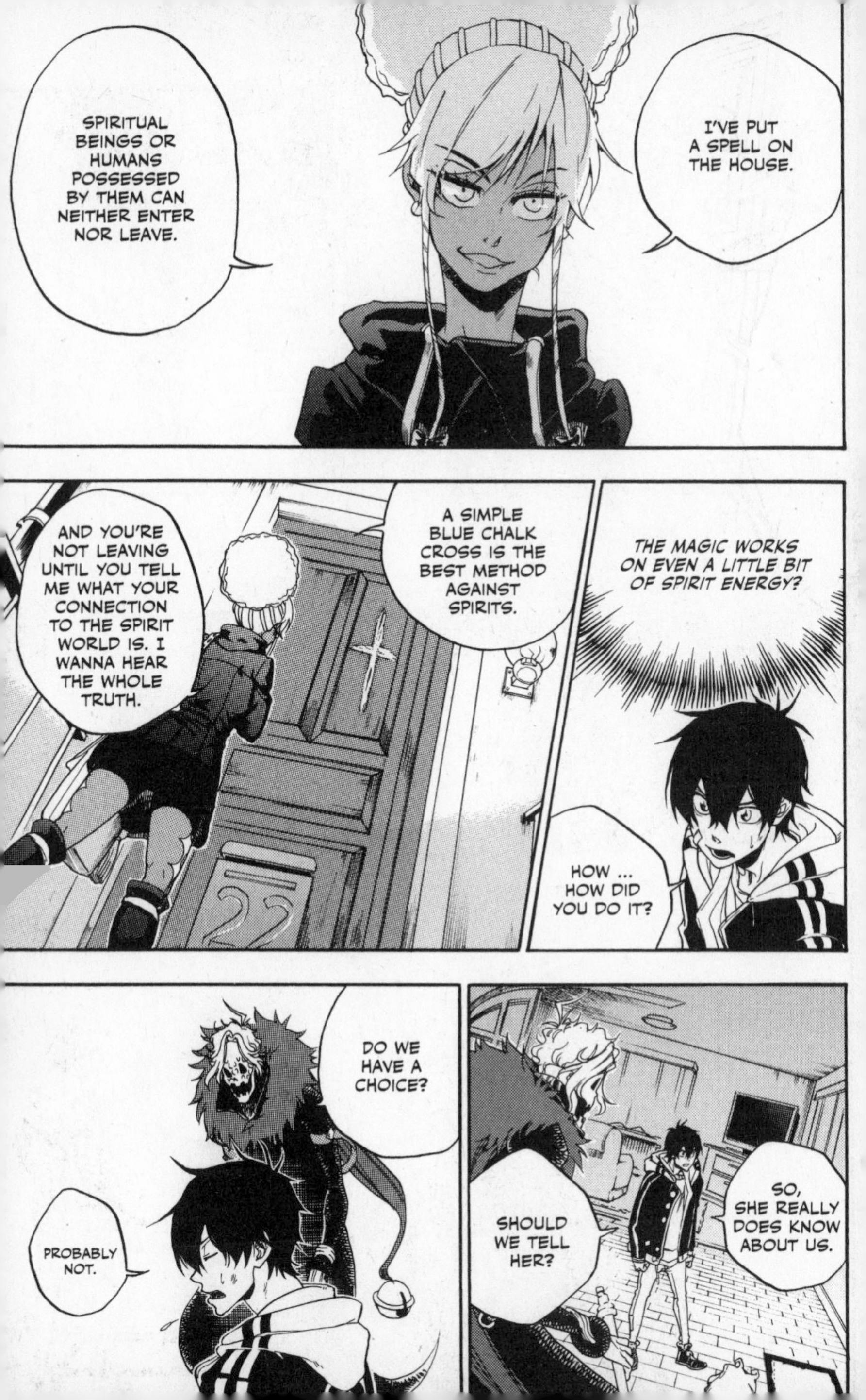
I'VE PUT A SPELL ON THE HOUSE.
SPIRITUAL BEINGS OR HUMANS POSSESSED BY THEM CAN NEITHER ENTER NOR LEAVE.
THE MAGIC WORKS ON EVEN A LITTLE BIT OF SPIRIT ENERGY?
HOW ... HOW DID YOU DO IT?
A SIMPLE BLUE CHALK CROSS IS THE BEST METHOD AGAINST SPIRITS.
AND YOU'RE NOT LEAVING UNTIL YOU TELL ME WHAT YOUR CONNECTION TO THE SPIRIT WORLD IS. I WANNA HEAR THE WHOLE TRUTH.
SO, SHE REALLY DOES KNOW ABOUT US.
SHOULD WE TELL HER?
DO WE HAVE A CHOICE?
PROBABLY NOT.

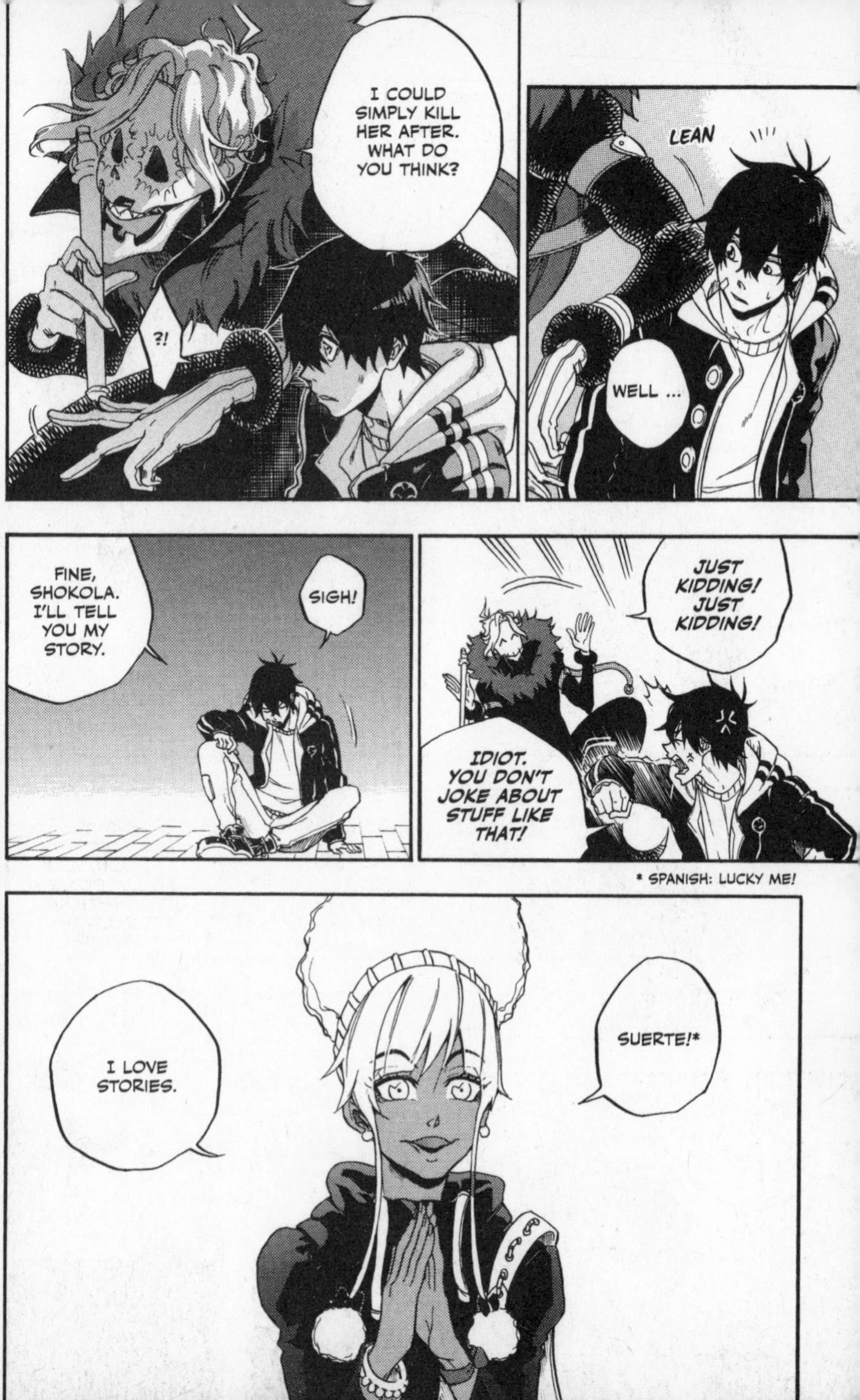
LEAN
WELL ...
I COULD SIMPLY KILL HER AFTER. WHAT DO YOU THINK?
?!
JUST KIDDING! JUST KIDDING!
IDIOT. YOU DON'T JOKE ABOUT STUFF LIKE THAT!
SIGH!
FINE, SHOKOLA. I'LL TELL YOU MY STORY.
* SPANISH: LUCKY ME!
SUERTE!*
I LOVE STORIES.

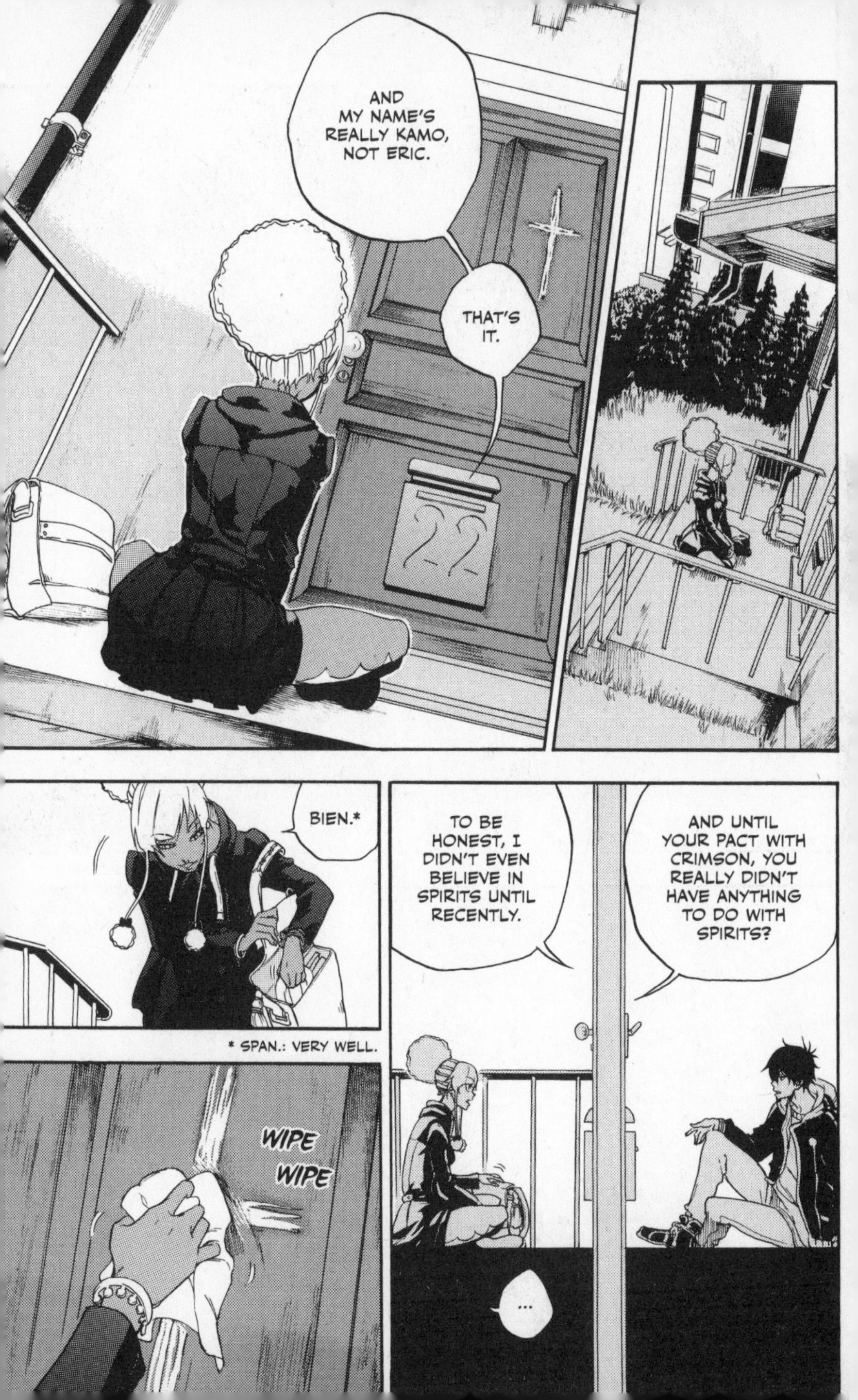
AND MY NAME'S REALLY KAMO, NOT ERIC.
THAT'S IT.
AND UNTIL YOUR PACT WITH CRIMSON, YOU REALLY DIDN'T HAVE ANYTHING TO DO WITH SPIRITS?
TO BE HONEST, I DIDN'T EVEN BELIEVE IN SPIRITS UNTIL RECENTLY.
...
BIEN.*
* SPAN.: VERY WELL.
WIPE
WIPE

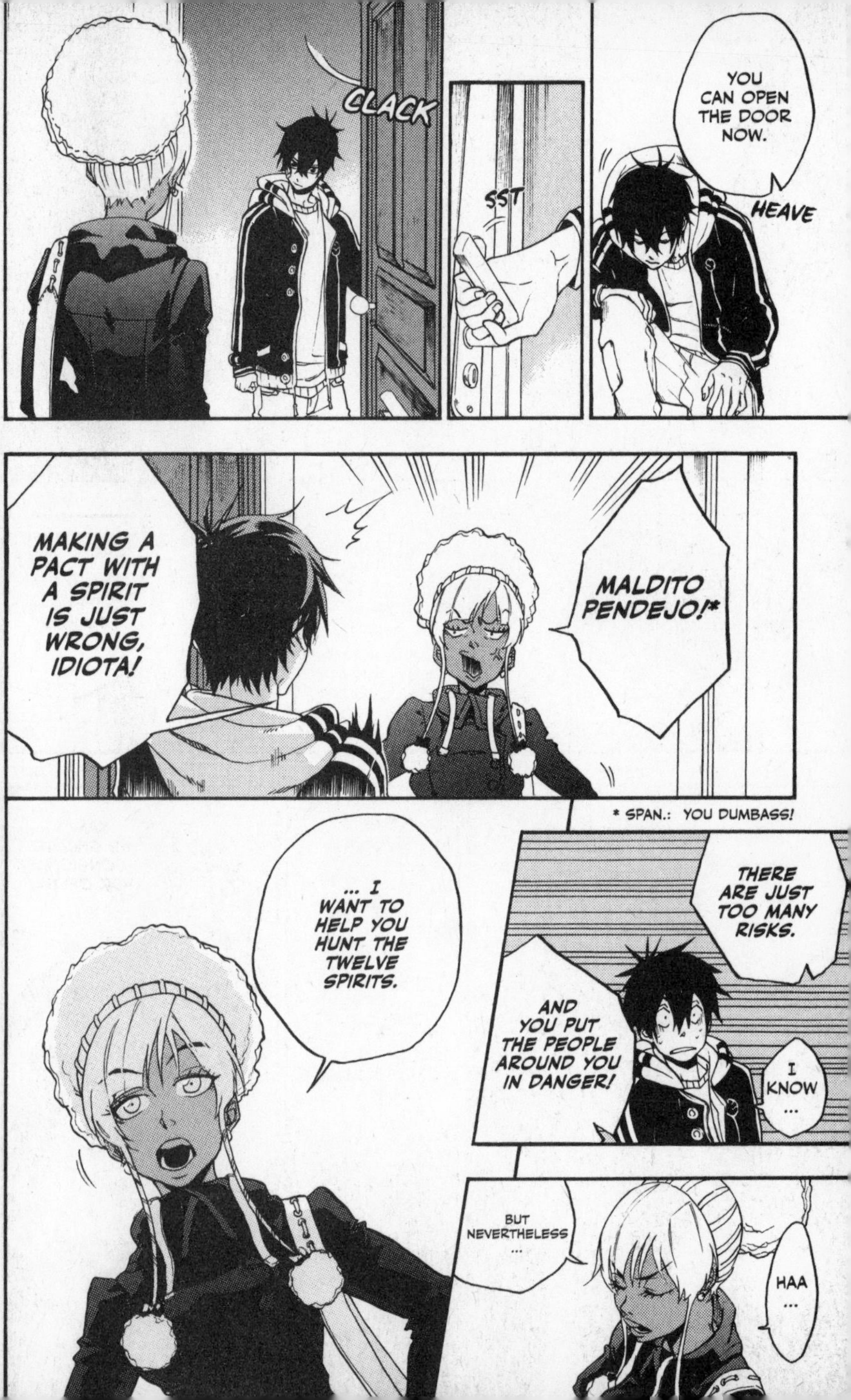
YOU CAN OPEN THE DOOR NOW.
HEAVE
SST
CLACK
MALDITO PENDEJO!*
MAKING A PACT WITH A SPIRIT IS JUST WRONG, IDIOTA!
* SPAN.: YOU DUMBASS!
THERE ARE JUST TOO MANY RISKS.
AND YOU PUT THE PEOPLE AROUND YOU IN DANGER!
I KNOW ...
HAA ...
BUT NEVERTHELESS ...
... I WANT TO HELP YOU HUNT THE TWELVE SPIRITS.

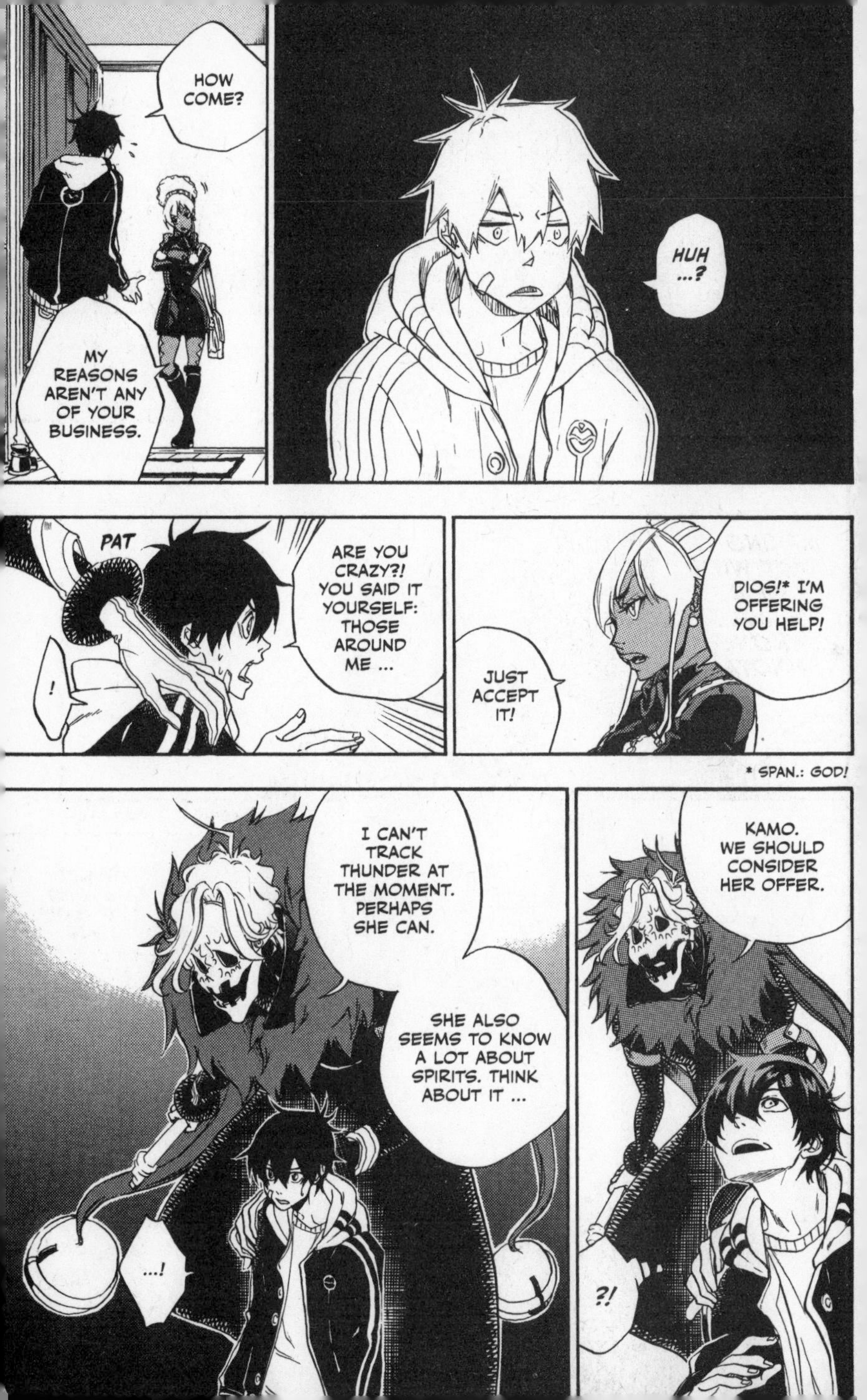
HUH ...?
HOW COME?
MY REASONS AREN'T ANY OF YOUR BUSINESS.
DIOS!* I'M OFFERING YOU HELP!
JUST ACCEPT IT!
PAT
ARE YOU CRAZY?! YOU SAID IT YOURSELF: THOSE AROUND ME ...
!
KAMO. WE SHOULD CONSIDER HER OFFER.
?!
I CAN'T TRACK THUNDER AT THE MOMENT. PERHAPS SHE CAN.
SHE ALSO SEEMS TO KNOW A LOT ABOUT SPIRITS. THINK ABOUT IT ...
...!

* SPAN.: GOD!

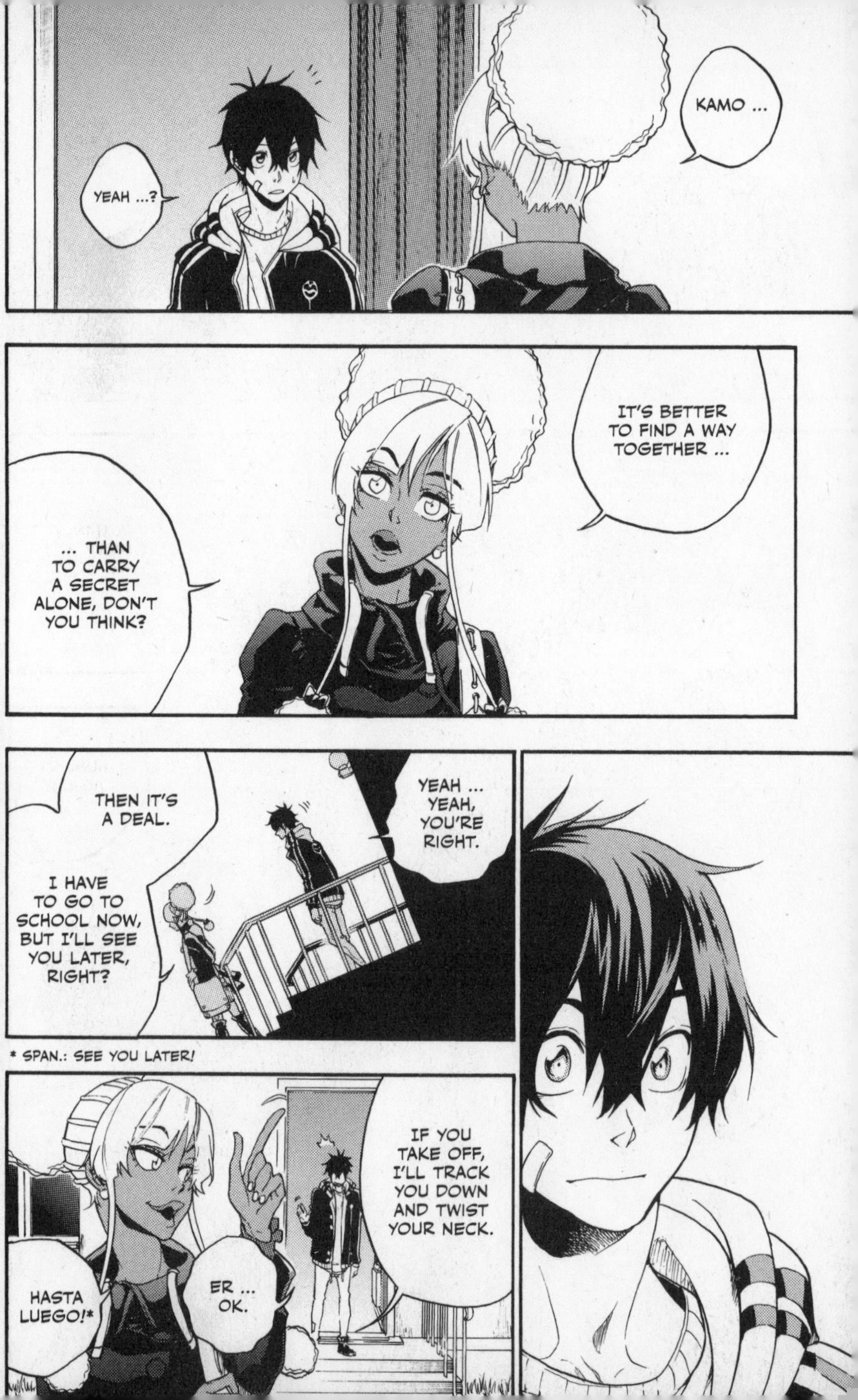
KAMO ...
YEAH ...?
IT'S BETTER TO FIND A WAY TOGETHER ...
... THAN TO CARRY A SECRET ALONE, DON'T YOU THINK?
YEAH ... YEAH, YOU'RE RIGHT.
THEN IT'S A DEAL.
I HAVE TO GO TO SCHOOL NOW, BUT I'LL SEE YOU LATER, RIGHT?
IF YOU TAKE OFF, I'LL TRACK YOU DOWN AND TWIST YOUR NECK.
ER ... OK.
HASTA LUEGO!*

* SPAN.: SEE YOU LATER!

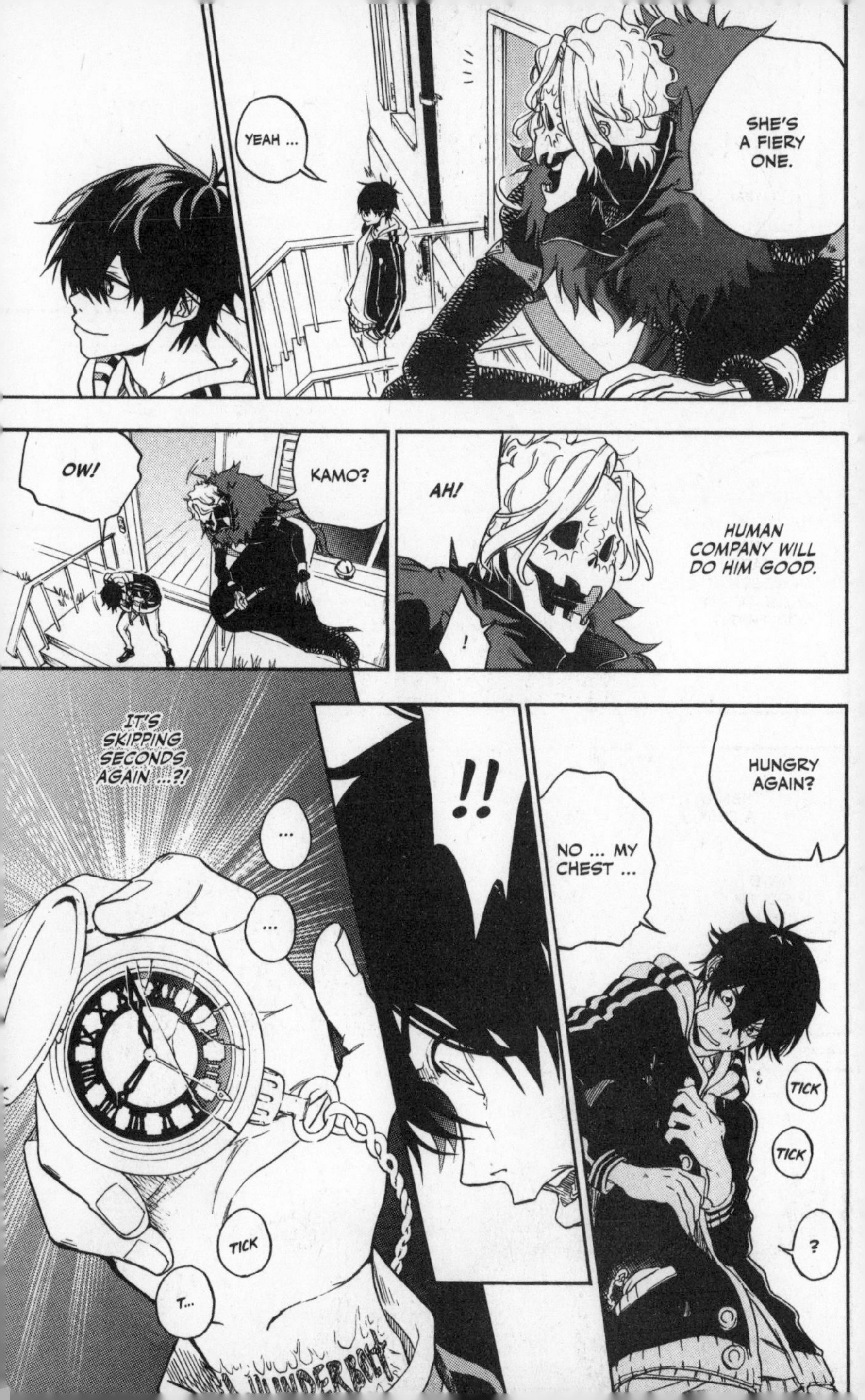
SHE'S A FIERY ONE.
YEAH ...
HUMAN COMPANY WILL DO HIM GOOD.
AH!
!
KAMO?
OW!
HUNGRY AGAIN?
NO ... MY CHEST ...
TICK
TICK
?
!!
IT'S SKIPPING SECONDS AGAIN ...?!
...
...
TICK
T...

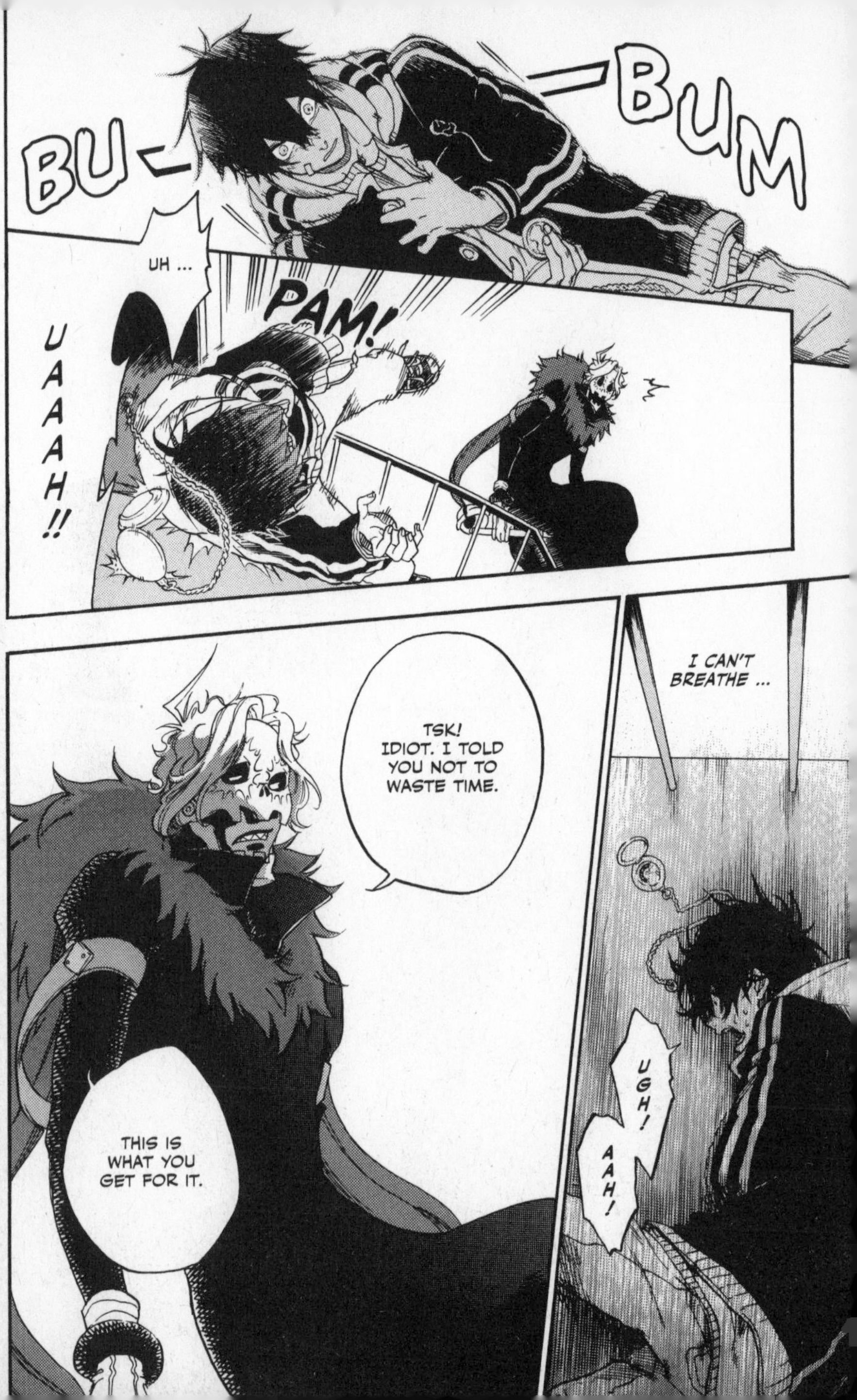
BU— —BUM
UH ...
PAM!
UAAAAH!!
I CAN'T BREATHE ...
UGH! AAH!
TSK! IDIOT. I TOLD YOU NOT TO WASTE TIME.
THIS IS WHAT YOU GET FOR IT.

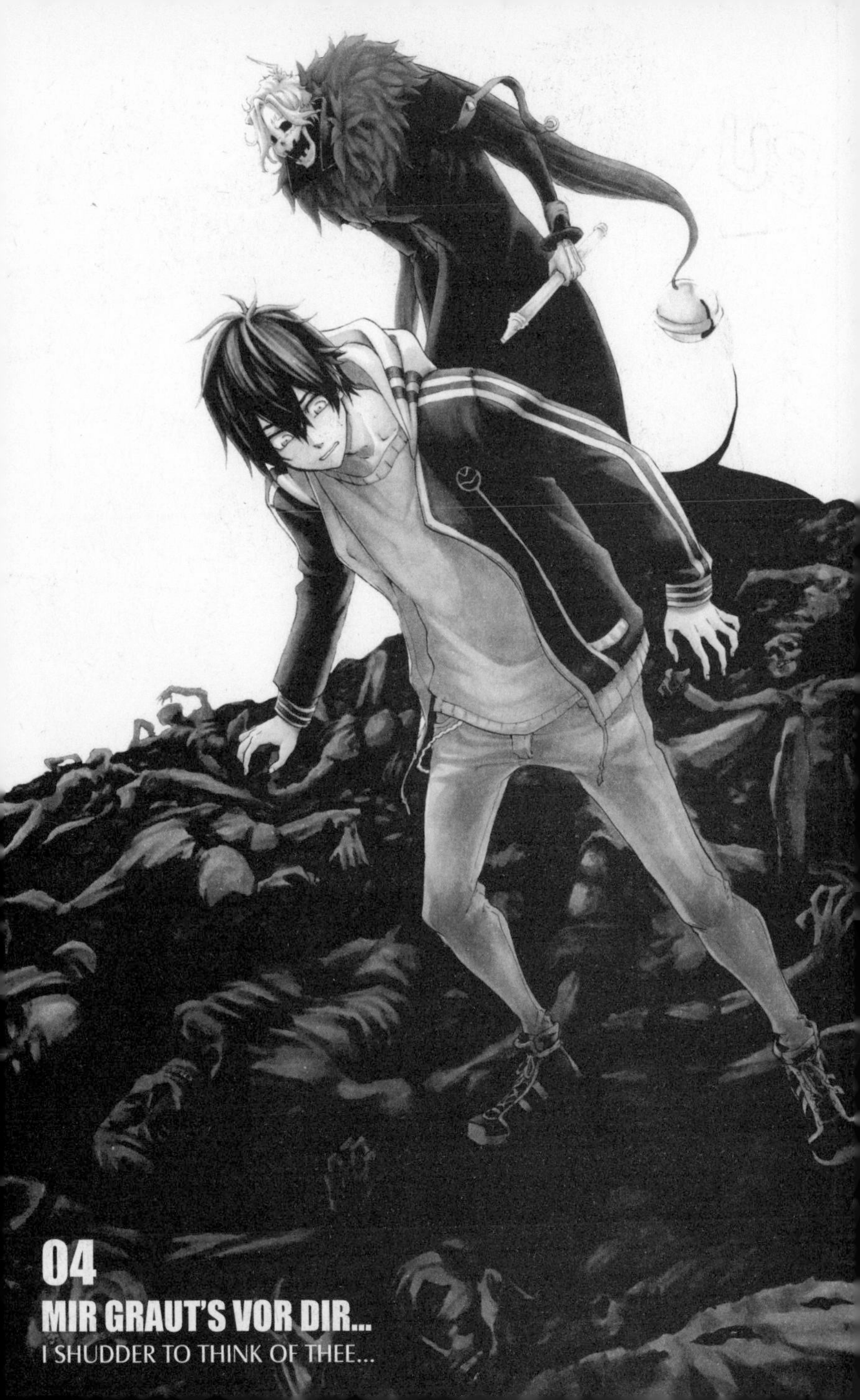

04

MIR GRAUT'S VOR DIR...

I SHUDDER TO THINK OF THEE...

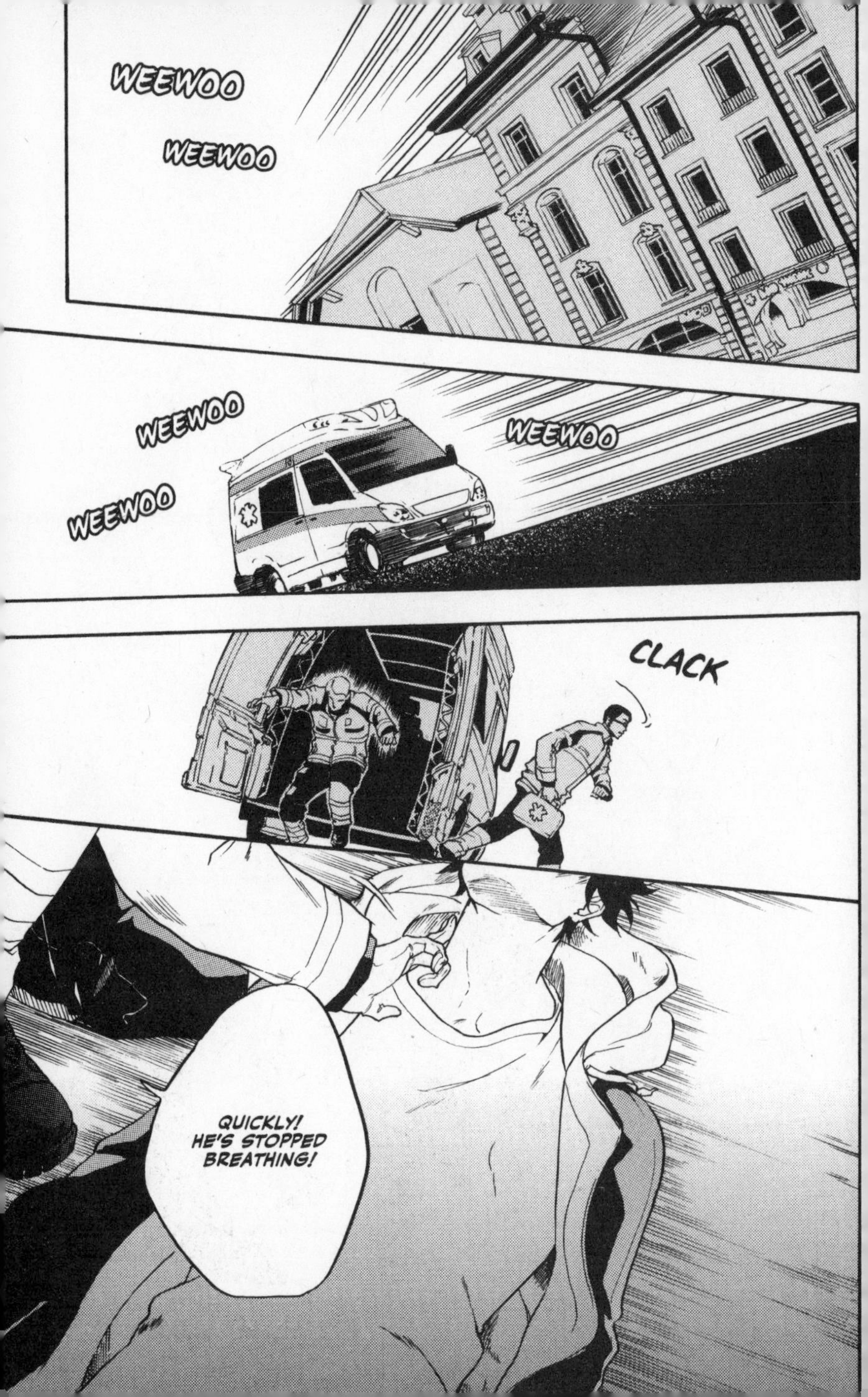
WEEWOO
WEEWOO
WEEWOO
WEEWOO
WEEWOO
CLACK
QUICKLY! HE'S STOPPED BREATHING!

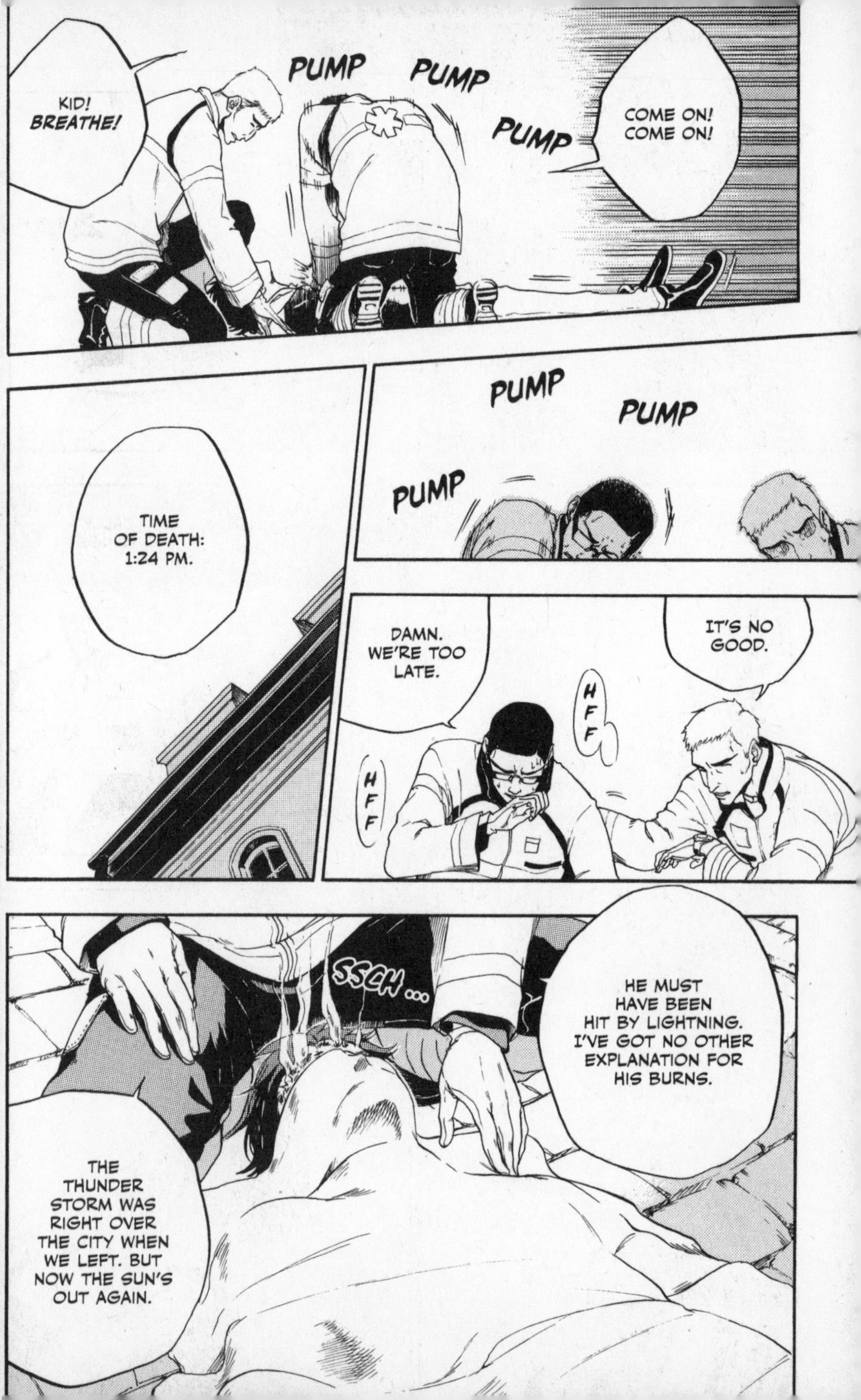
COME ON! COME ON!
PUMP
PUMP
PUMP
KID! BREATHE!
PUMP
PUMP
PUMP
IT'S NO GOOD.
HFF
DAMN. WE'RE TOO LATE.
HFF
TIME OF DEATH: 1:24 PM.
HE MUST HAVE BEEN HIT BY LIGHTNING. I'VE GOT NO OTHER EXPLANATION FOR HIS BURNS.
SSCH...
THE THUNDER STORM WAS RIGHT OVER THE CITY WHEN WE LEFT. BUT NOW THE SUN'S OUT AGAIN.

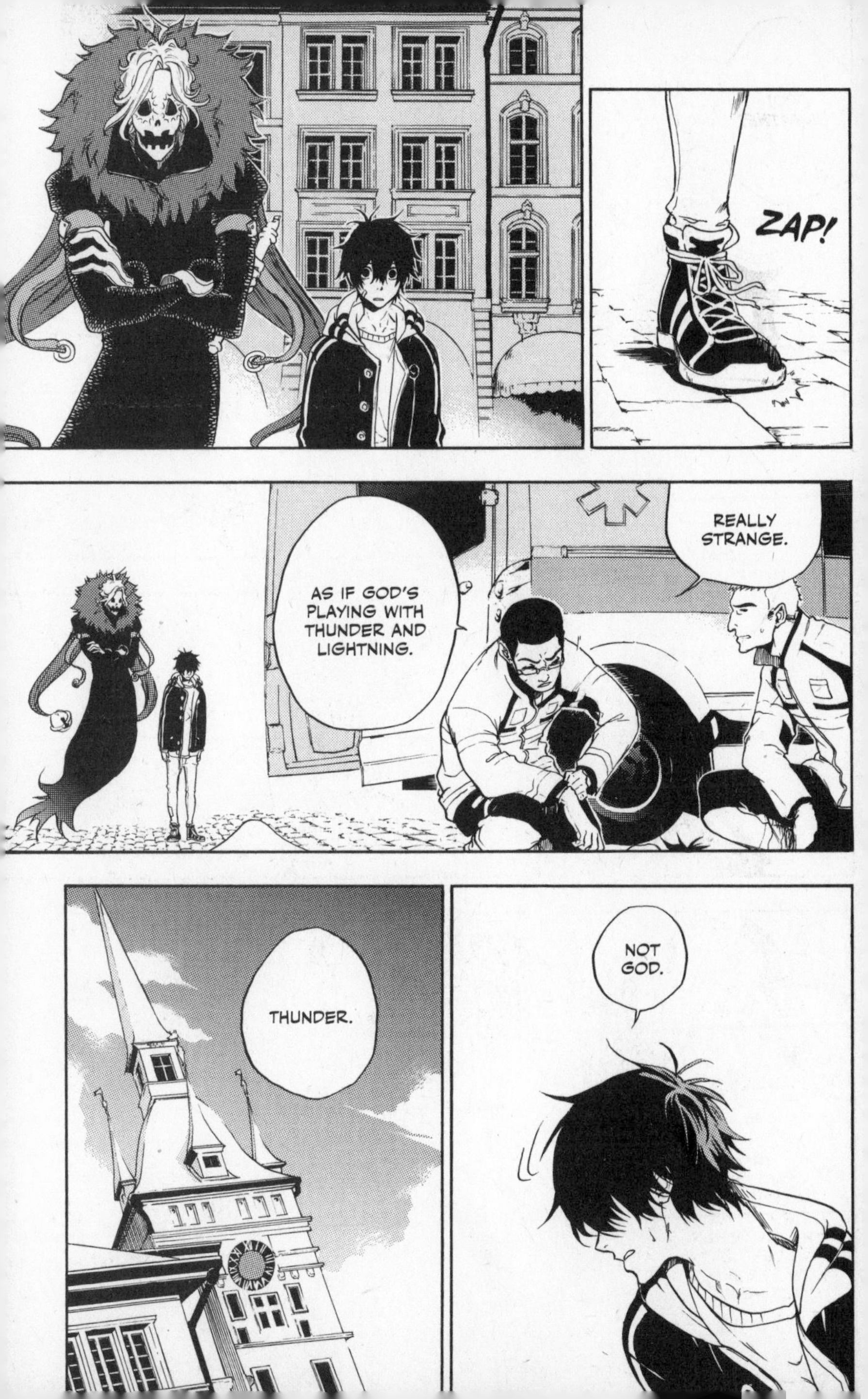
ZAP!
REALLY STRANGE.
AS IF GOD'S PLAYING WITH THUNDER AND LIGHTNING.
NOT GOD.
THUNDER.

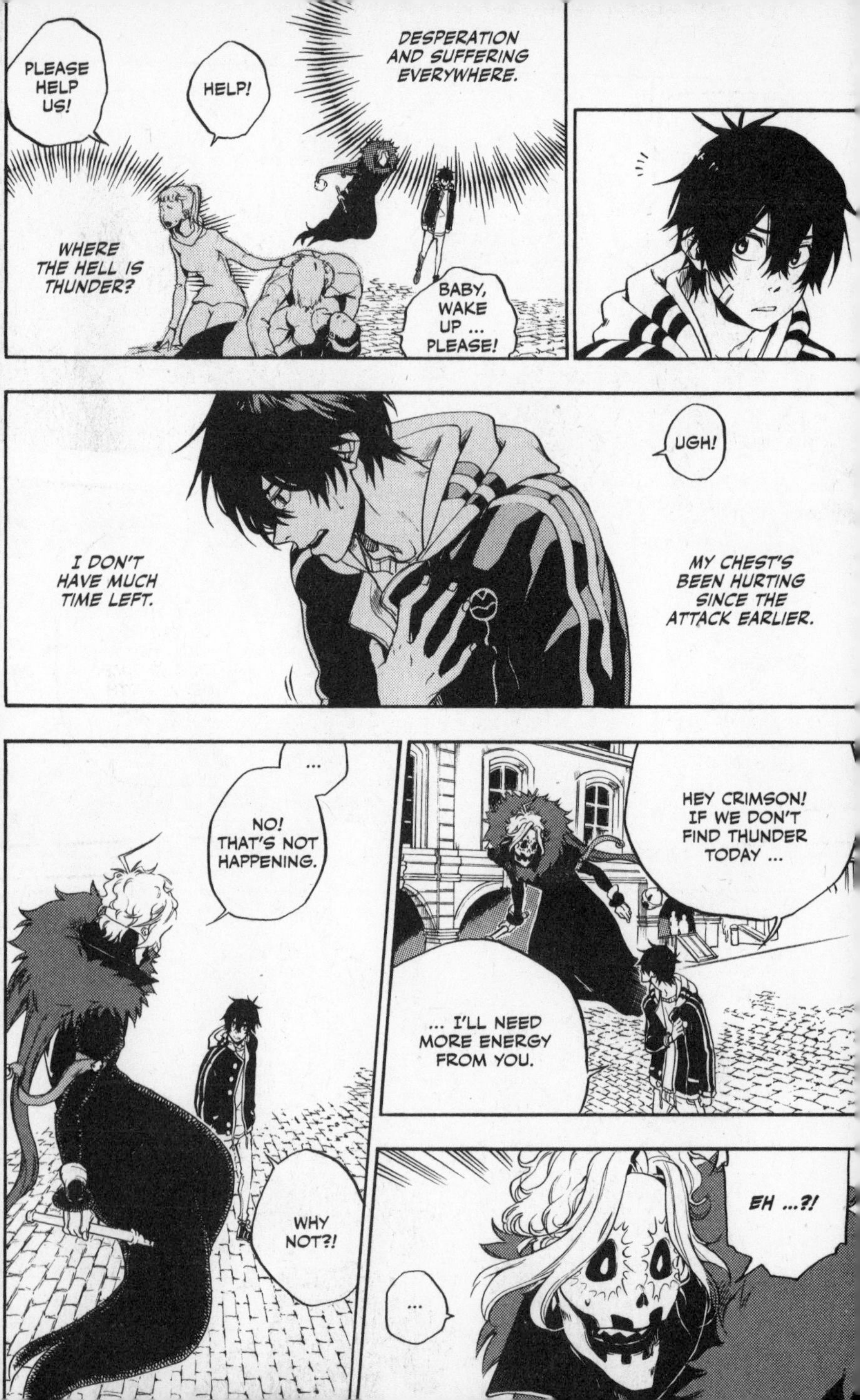
DESPERATION AND SUFFERING EVERYWHERE.
HELP!
PLEASE HELP US!
BABY, WAKE UP ... PLEASE!
WHERE THE HELL IS THUNDER?
UGH!
MY CHEST'S BEEN HURTING SINCE THE ATTACK EARLIER.
I DON'T HAVE MUCH TIME LEFT.
HEY CRIMSON! IF WE DON'T FIND THUNDER TODAY ...
... I'LL NEED MORE ENERGY FROM YOU.
EH ...?!
...
...
NO! THAT'S NOT HAPPENING.
WHY NOT?!

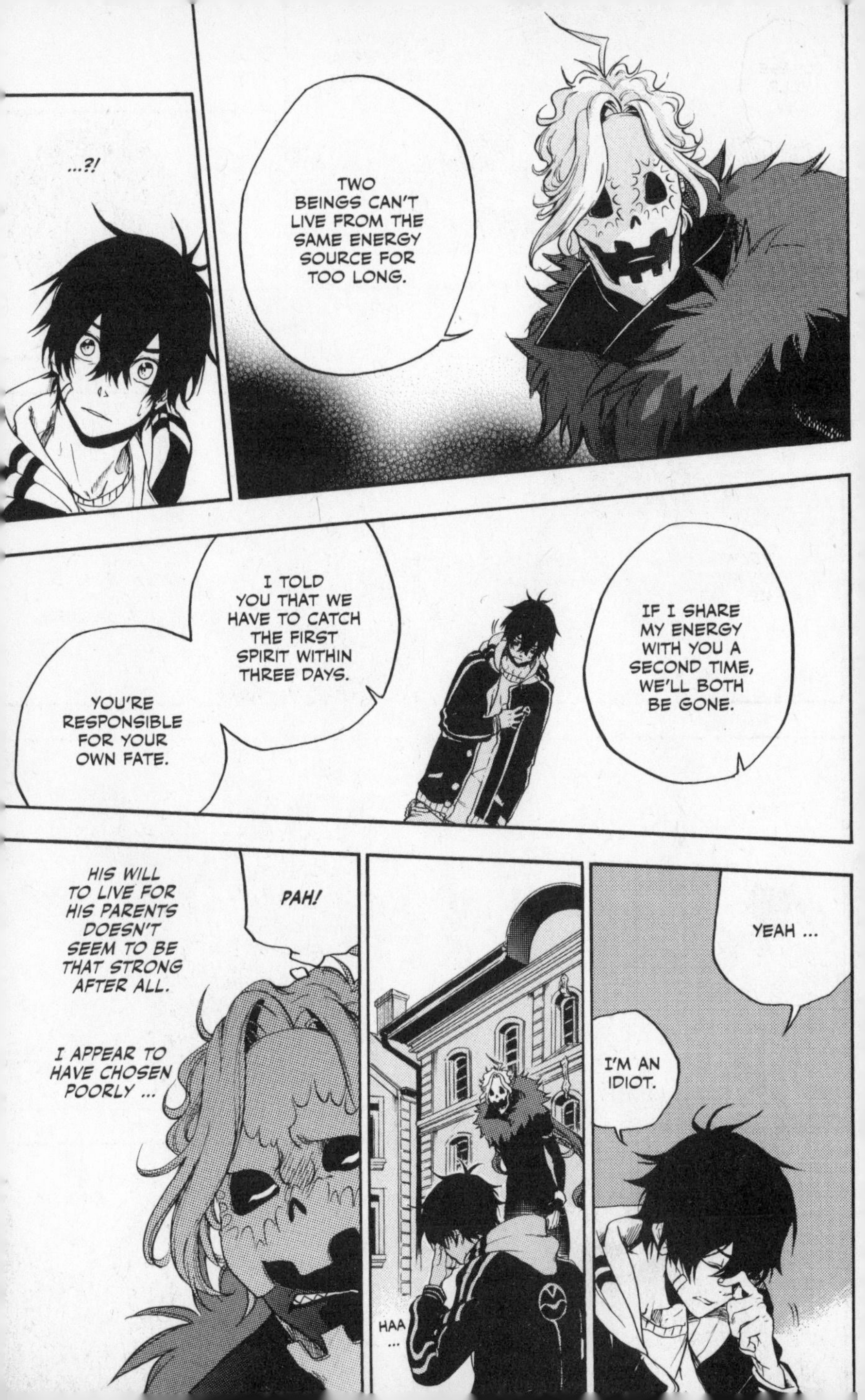

TWO BEINGS CAN'T LIVE FROM THE SAME ENERGY SOURCE FOR TOO LONG.
...?!
IF I SHARE MY ENERGY WITH YOU A SECOND TIME, WE'LL BOTH BE GONE.
I TOLD YOU THAT WE HAVE TO CATCH THE FIRST SPIRIT WITHIN THREE DAYS.
YOU'RE RESPONSIBLE FOR YOUR OWN FATE.
YEAH ...
I'M AN IDIOT.
HAA ...
PAH!
HIS WILL TO LIVE FOR HIS PARENTS DOESN'T SEEM TO BE THAT STRONG AFTER ALL.
I APPEAR TO HAVE CHOSEN POORLY ...

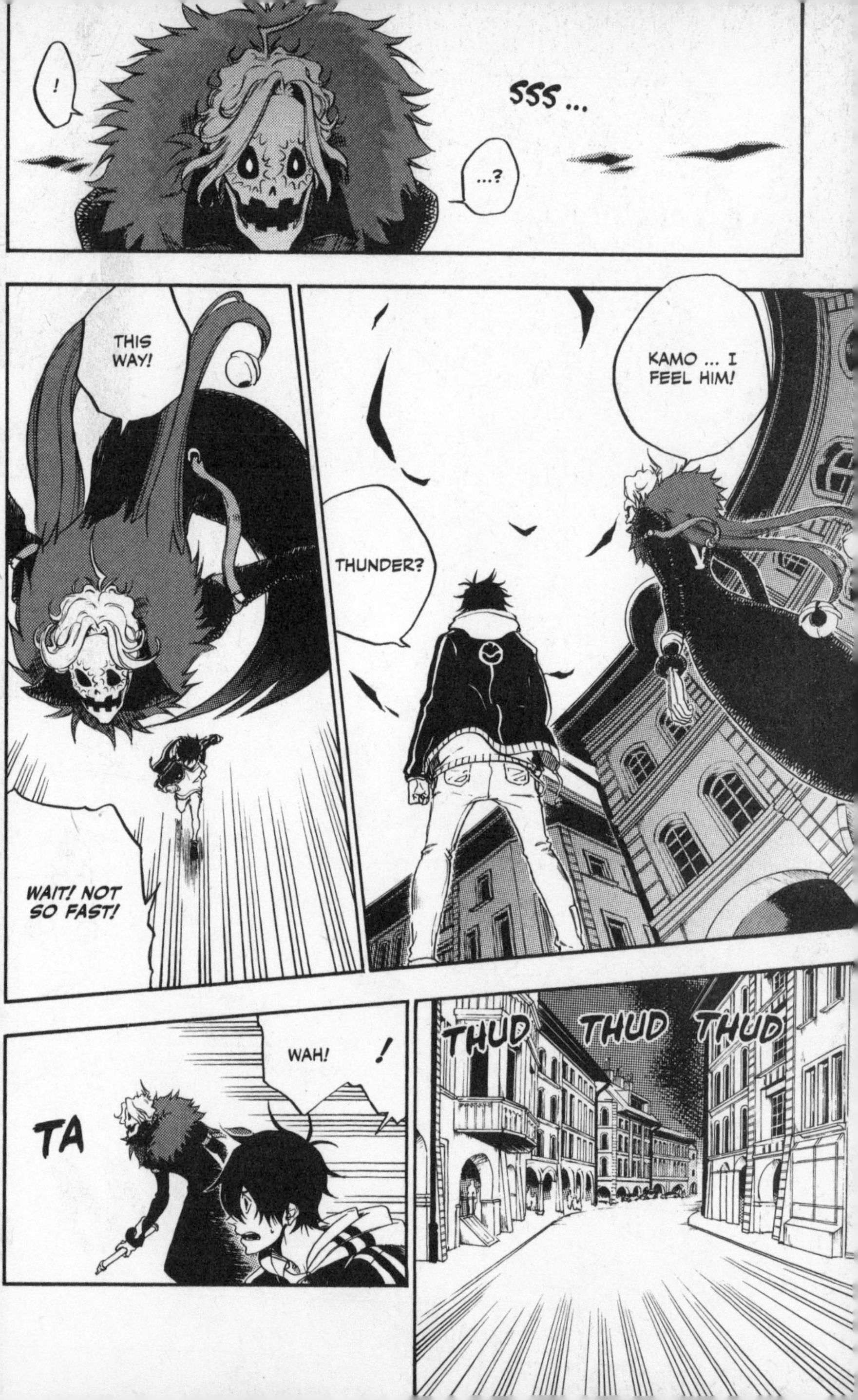
SSS ...
!
...?
KAMO ... I FEEL HIM!
THUNDER?
THIS WAY!
WAIT! NOT SO FAST!
THUD THUD THUD
!
WAH!
TA

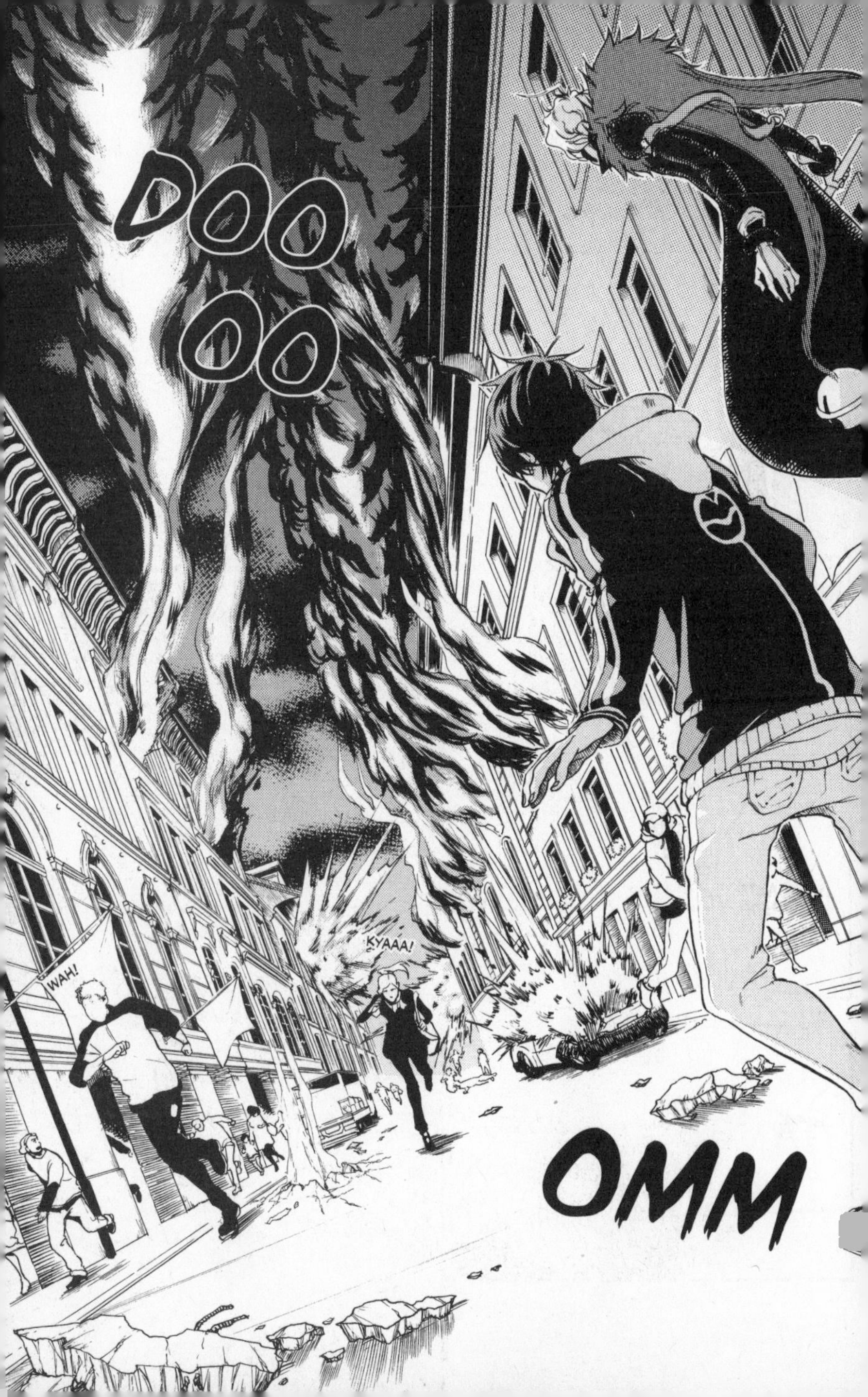
DOOOO
KYAAA!
WAH!
OMM

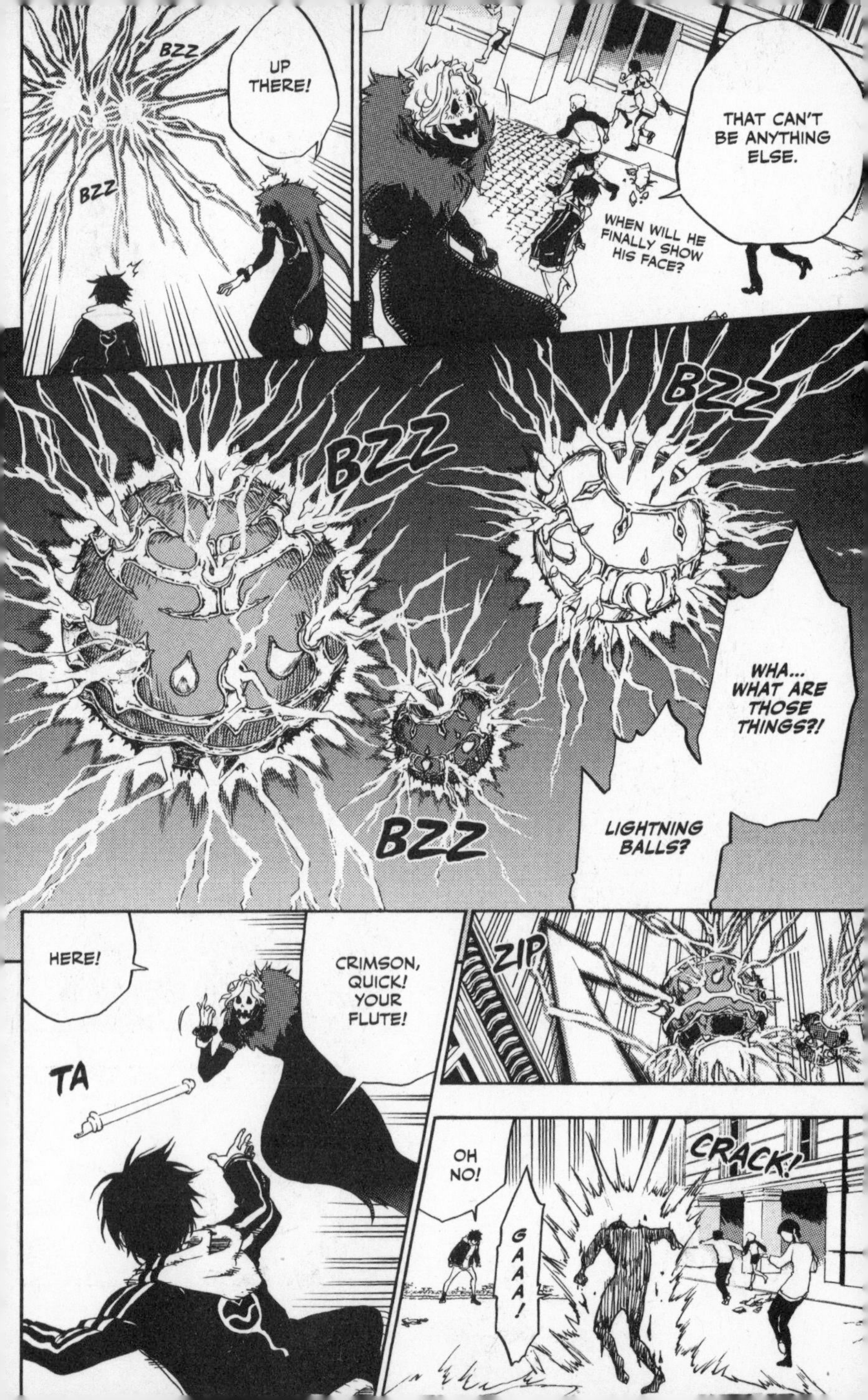
THAT CAN'T BE ANYTHING ELSE.
WHEN WILL HE FINALLY SHOW HIS FACE?
BZZ
UP THERE!
BZZ
BZZ
WHA... WHAT ARE THOSE THINGS?!
LIGHTNING BALLS?
BZZ
BZZ
ZIP
CRACK!
OH NO!
GAAA!
CRIMSON, QUICK! YOUR FLUTE!
HERE!
TA

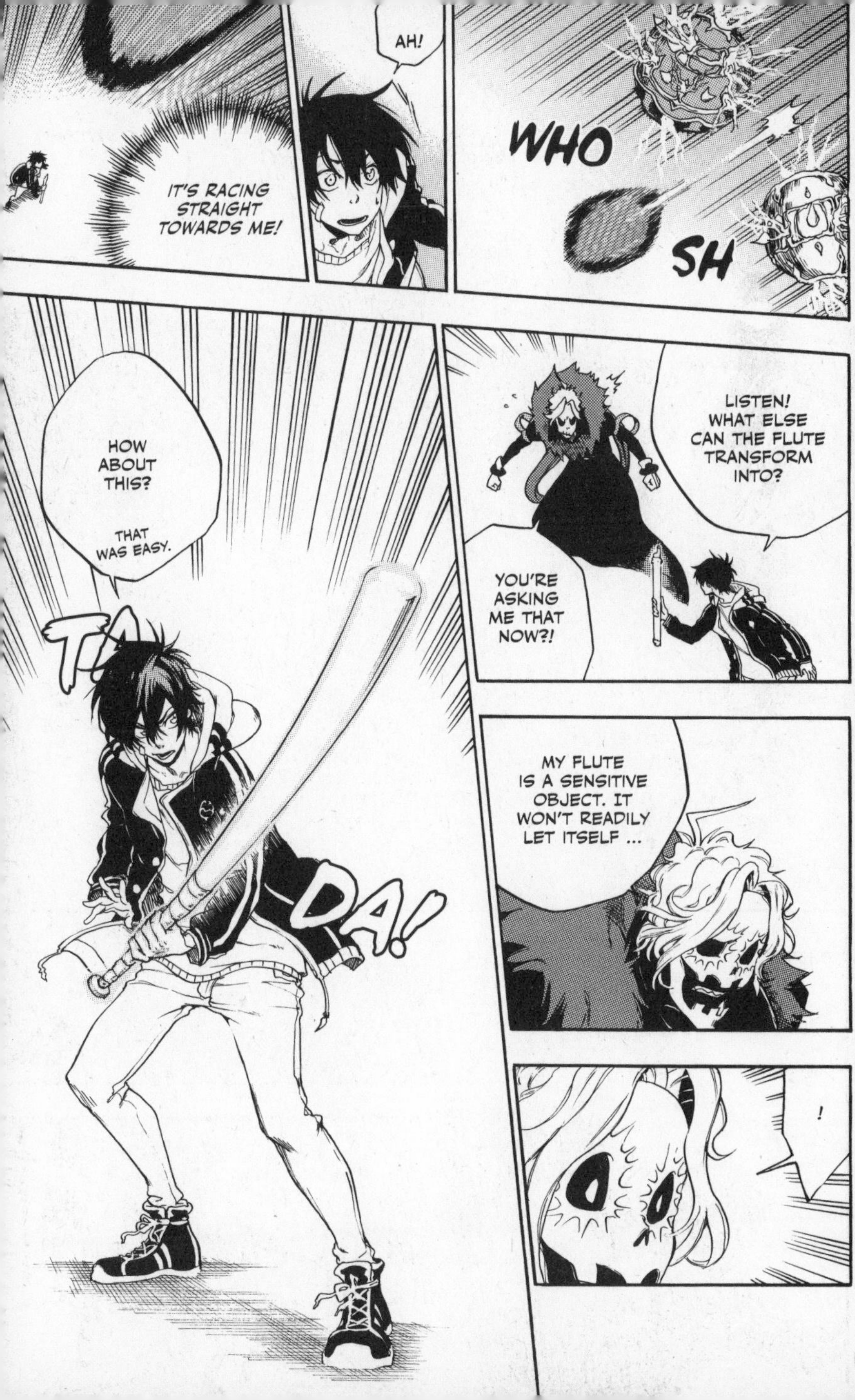
WHO
SH
AH!
IT'S RACING STRAIGHT TOWARDS ME!
LISTEN! WHAT ELSE CAN THE FLUTE TRANSFORM INTO?
YOU'RE ASKING ME THAT NOW?!
MY FLUTE IS A SENSITIVE OBJECT. IT WON'T READILY LET ITSELF ...
!
HOW ABOUT THIS?
THAT WAS EASY.
TA
DA!

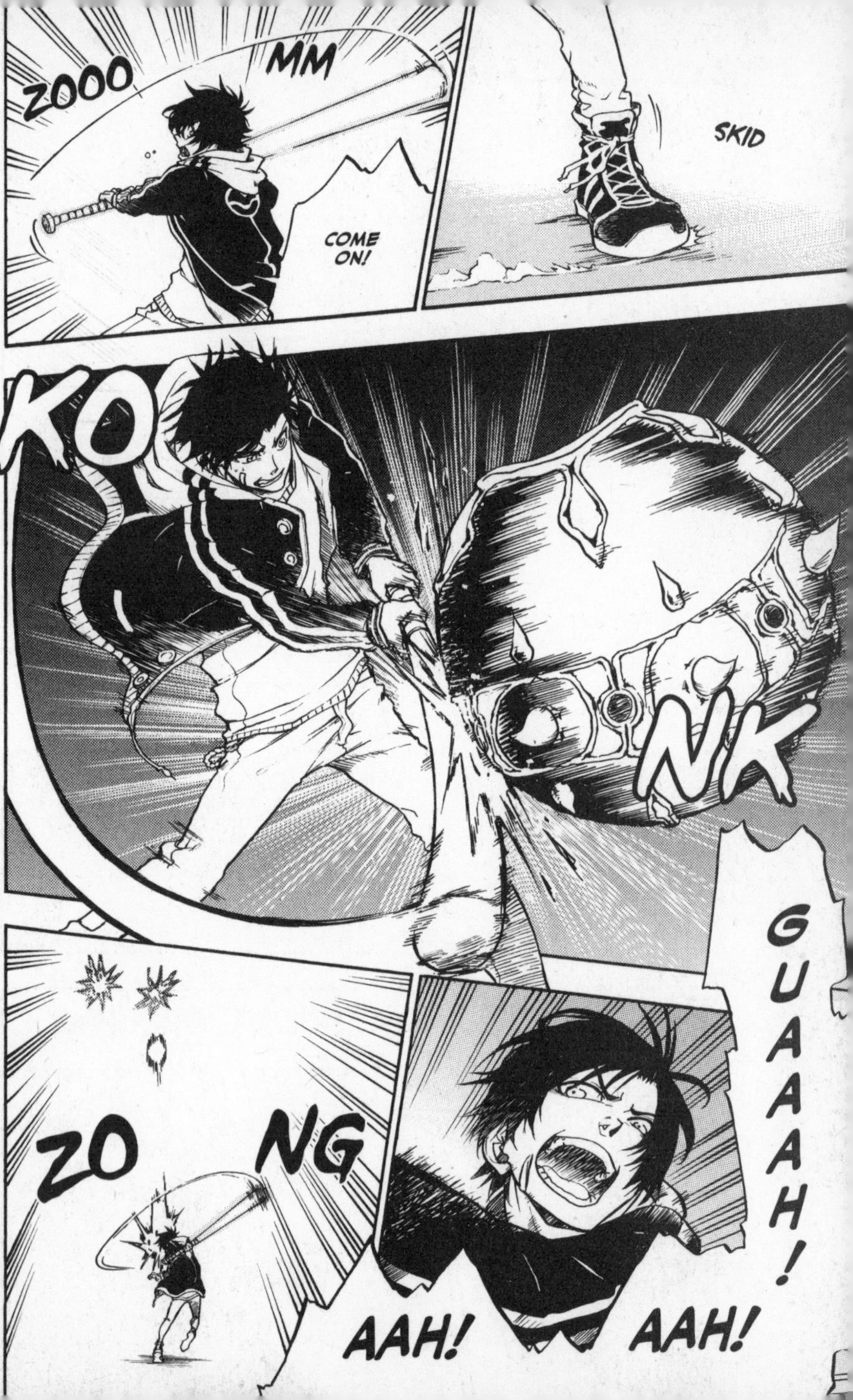

SKID
ZOOOMM
COME ON!
KONK
GUAAAAH!
AAH!
AAH!
ZONG

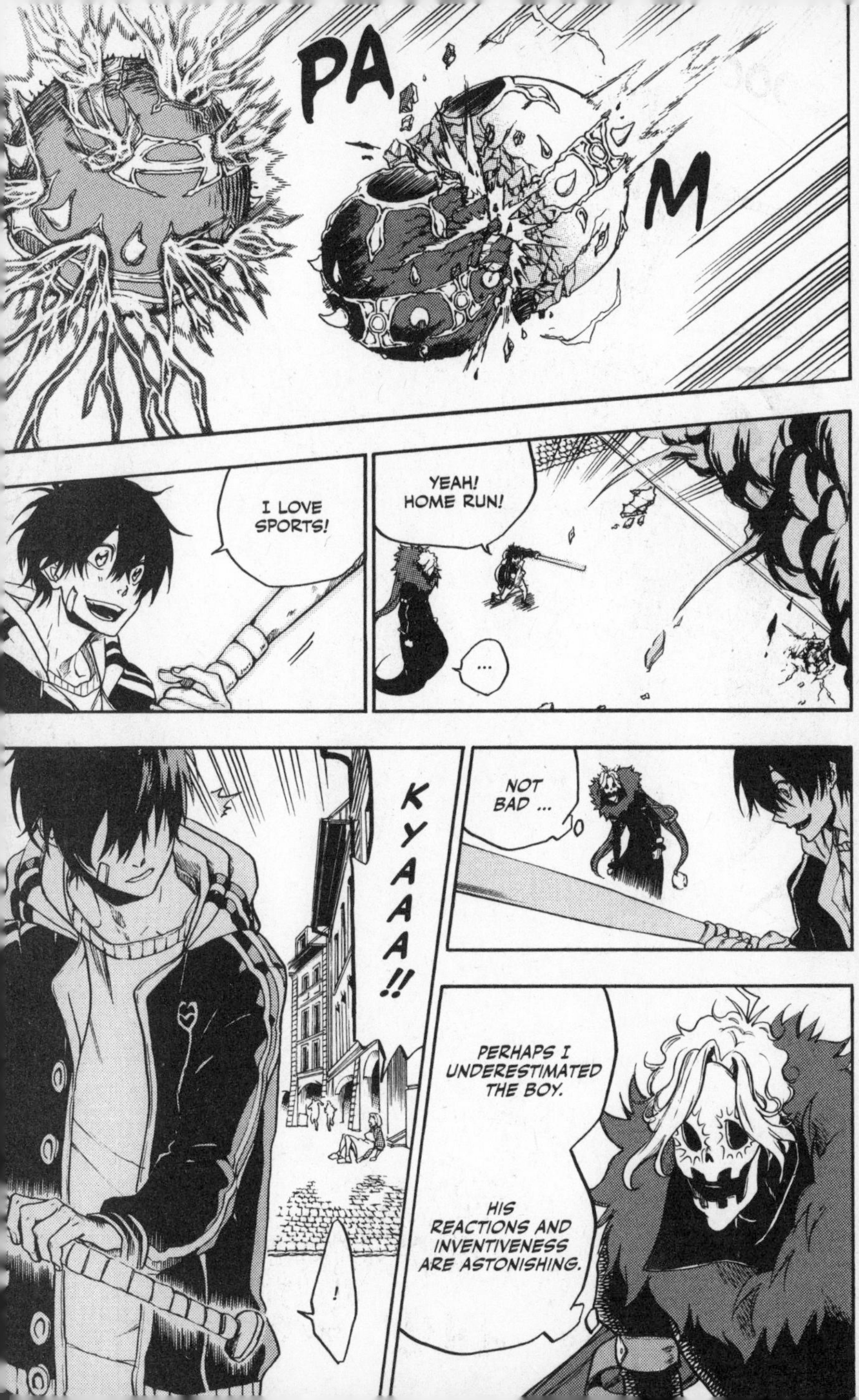
PA
M
YEAH! HOME RUN!
...
I LOVE SPORTS!
NOT BAD ...
PERHAPS I UNDERESTIMATED THE BOY.
HIS REACTIONS AND INVENTIVENESS ARE ASTONISHING.
KYAAAA!!
!

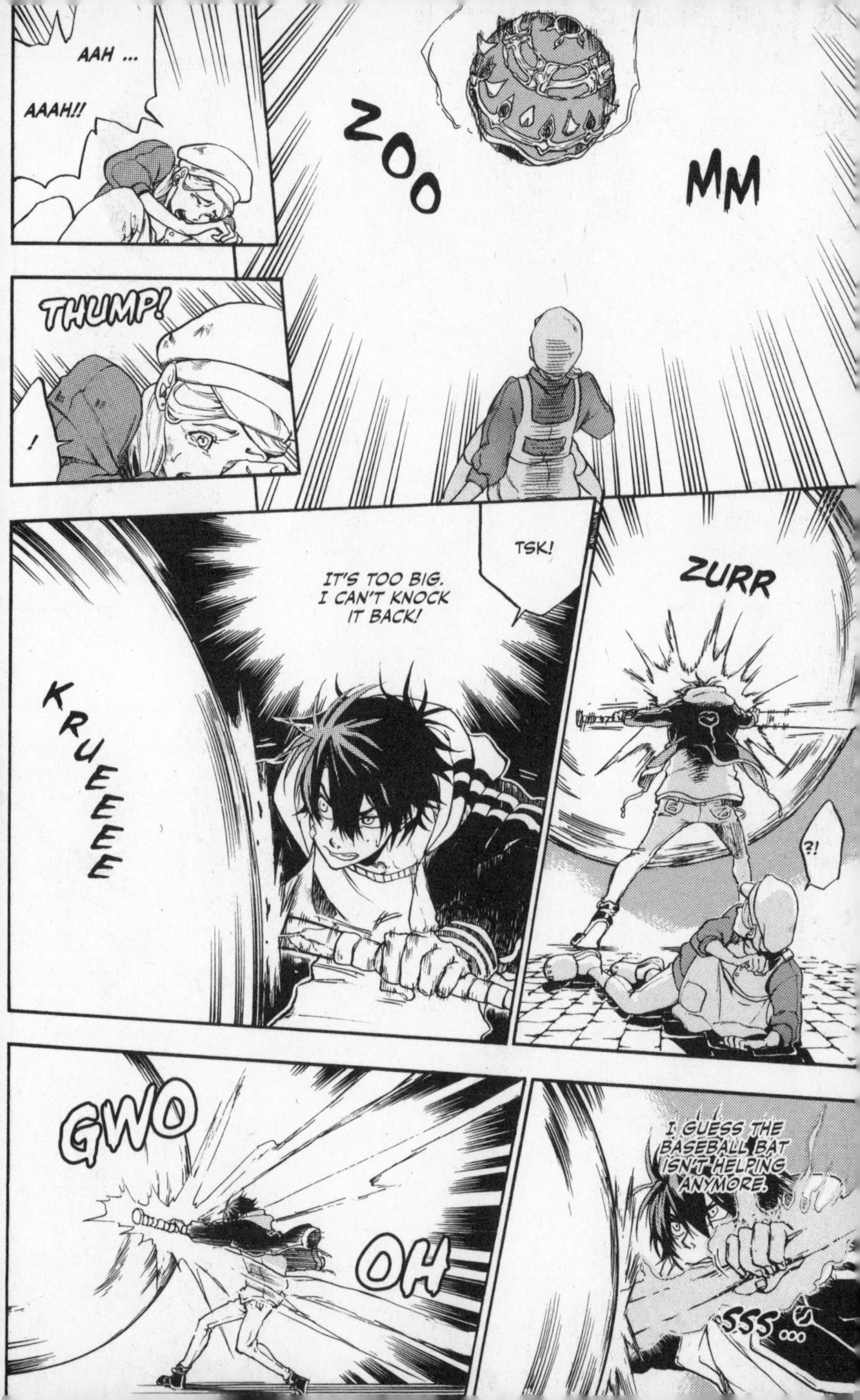

ZOO
MM
AAH ...
AAAH!!
THUMP!
!
ZURR
?!
TSK!
IT'S TOO BIG. I CAN'T KNOCK IT BACK!
KRUEEEE
I GUESS THE BASEBALL BAT ISN'T HELPING ANYMORE.
SSS ...
GWO
OH

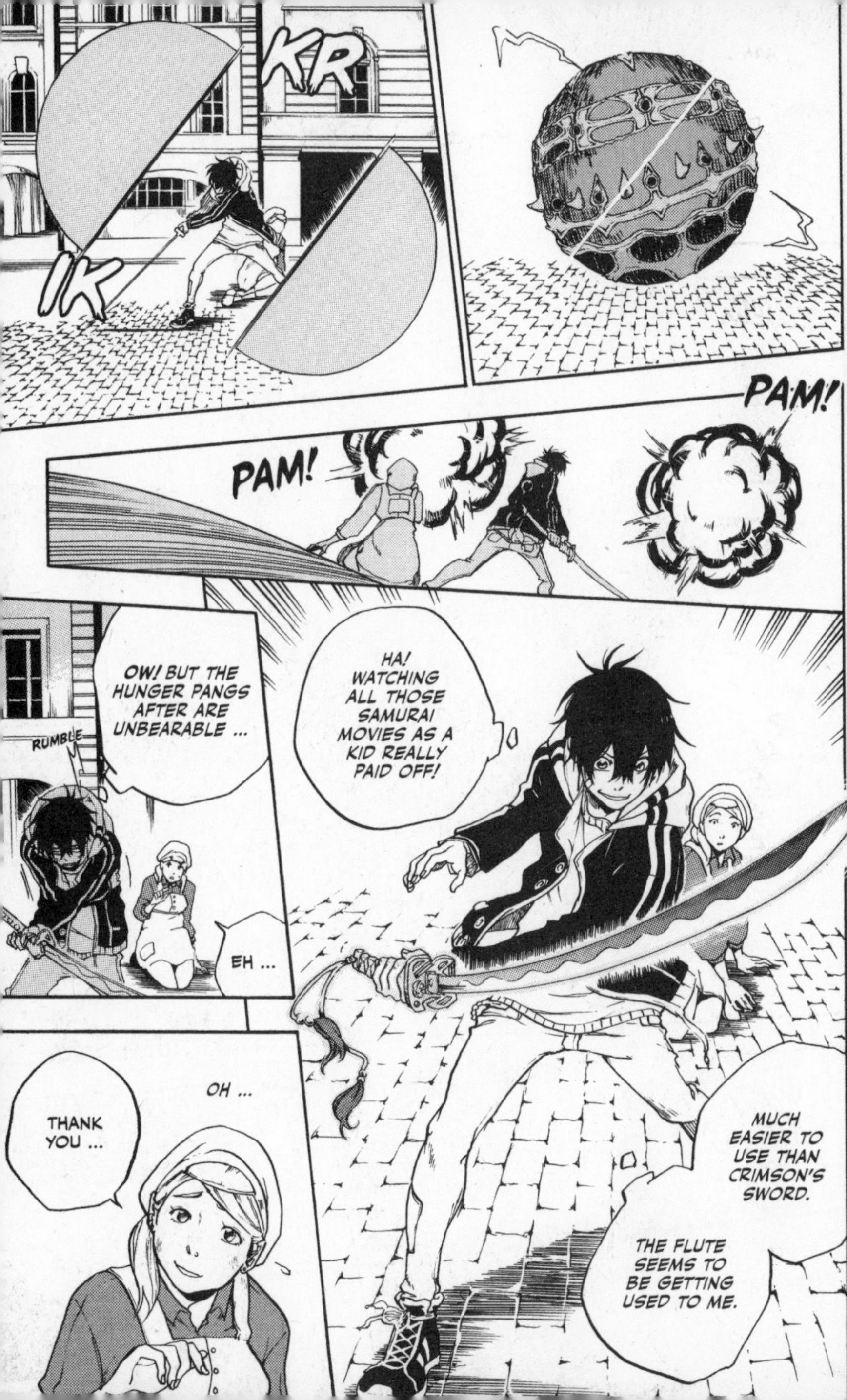
KR
IK
PAM!
PAM!
HA! WATCHING ALL THOSE SAMURAI MOVIES AS A KID REALLY PAID OFF!
MUCH EASIER TO USE THAN CRIMSON'S SWORD.
THE FLUTE SEEMS TO BE GETTING USED TO ME.
OW! BUT THE HUNGER PANGS AFTER ARE UNBEARABLE ...
RUMBLE
EH ...
OH ...
THANK YOU ...

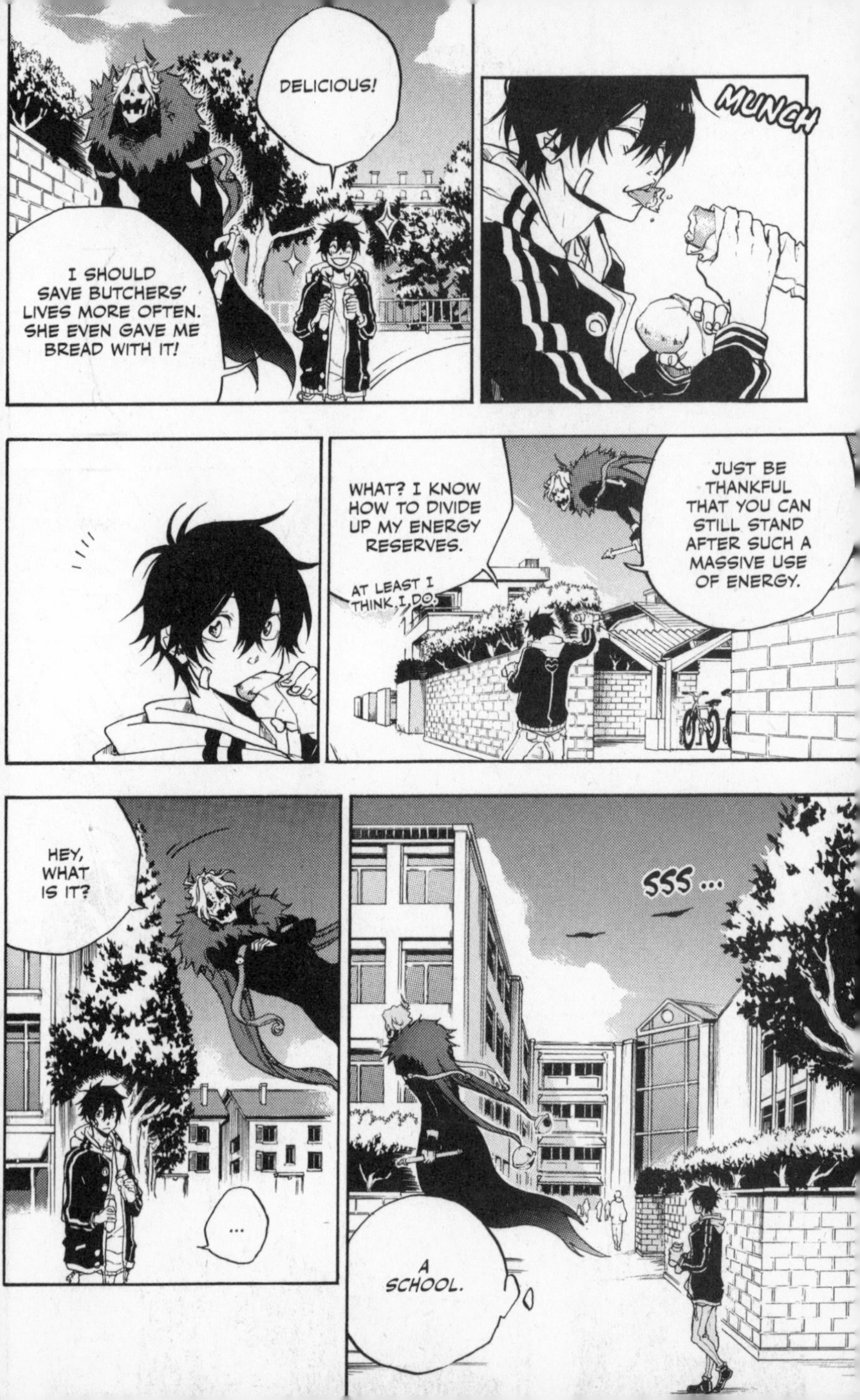
MUNCH
DELICIOUS!
I SHOULD SAVE BUTCHERS' LIVES MORE OFTEN. SHE EVEN GAVE ME BREAD WITH IT!
JUST BE THANKFUL THAT YOU CAN STILL STAND AFTER SUCH A MASSIVE USE OF ENERGY.
WHAT? I KNOW HOW TO DIVIDE UP MY ENERGY RESERVES.
AT LEAST I THINK I DO.
SSS...
A SCHOOL.
HEY, WHAT IS IT?
...

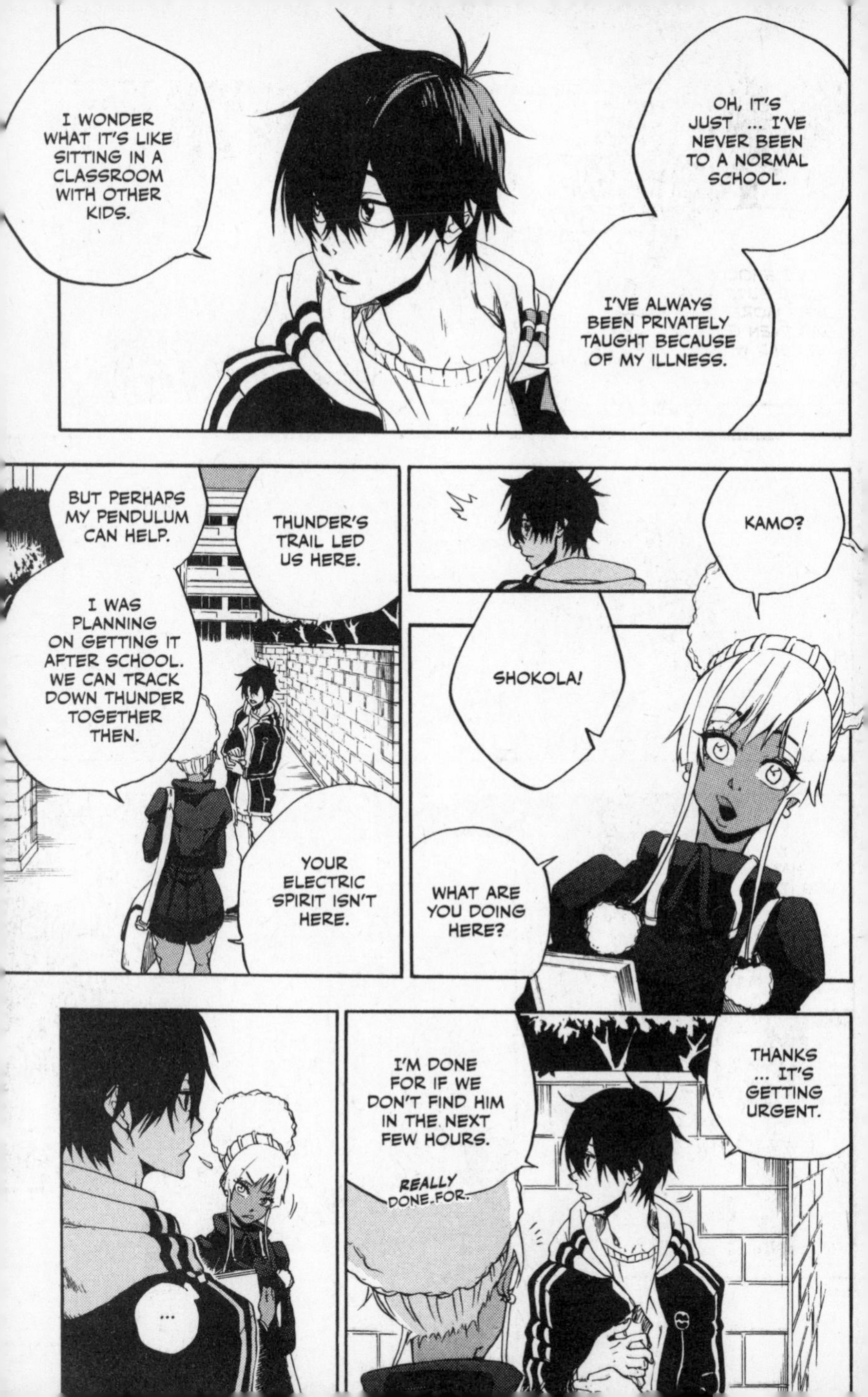
OH, IT'S JUST ... I'VE NEVER BEEN TO A NORMAL SCHOOL.
I'VE ALWAYS BEEN PRIVATELY TAUGHT BECAUSE OF MY ILLNESS.
I WONDER WHAT IT'S LIKE SITTING IN A CLASSROOM WITH OTHER KIDS.
KAMO?
SHOKOLA!
WHAT ARE YOU DOING HERE?
THUNDER'S TRAIL LED US HERE.
YOUR ELECTRIC SPIRIT ISN'T HERE.
BUT PERHAPS MY PENDULUM CAN HELP.
I WAS PLANNING ON GETTING IT AFTER SCHOOL. WE CAN TRACK DOWN THUNDER TOGETHER THEN.
THANKS ... IT'S GETTING URGENT.
I'M DONE FOR IF WE DON'T FIND HIM IN THE NEXT FEW HOURS.
REALLY DONE FOR.
...

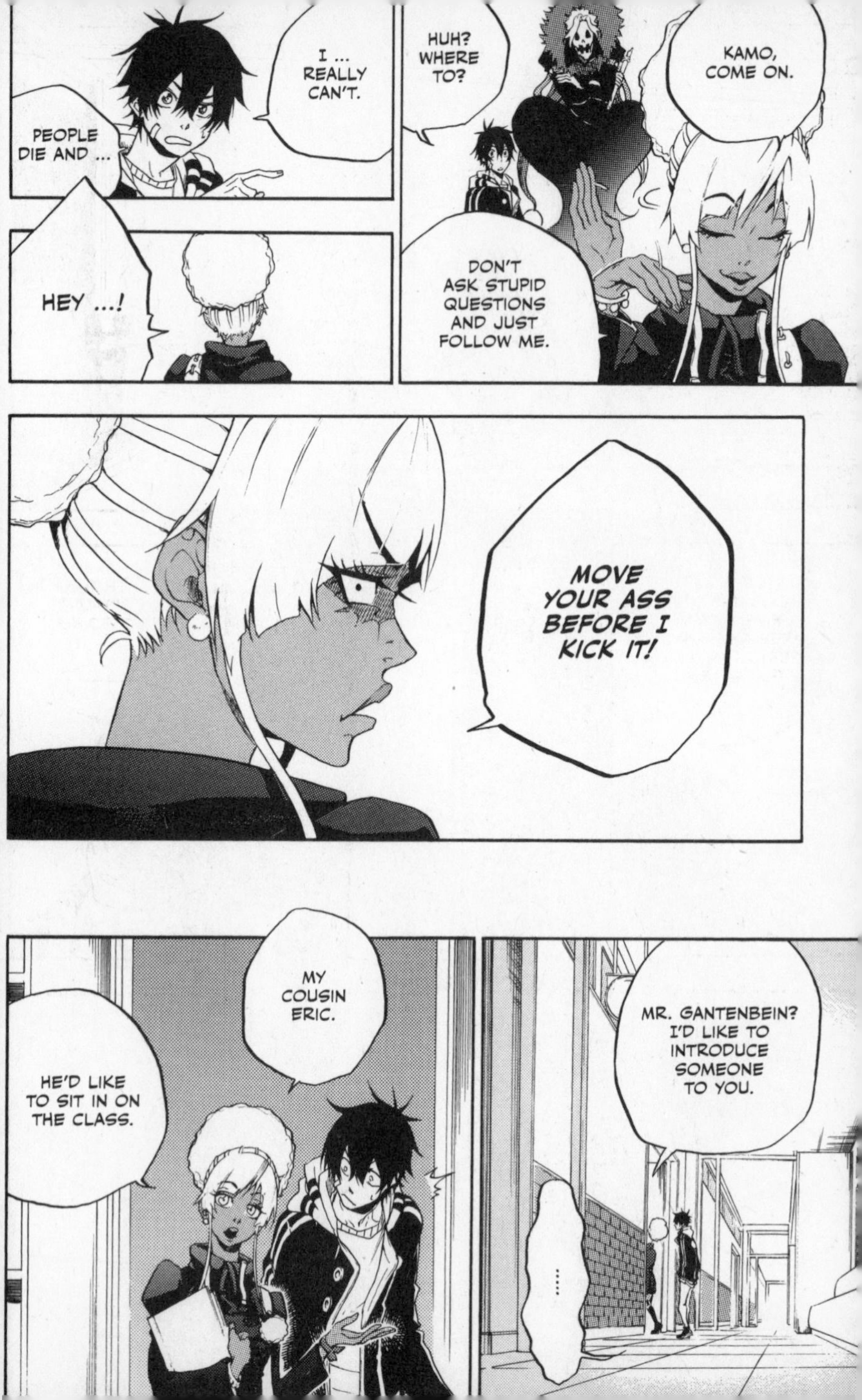
KAMO, COME ON.
HUH? WHERE TO?
DON'T ASK STUPID QUESTIONS AND JUST FOLLOW ME.
I ... REALLY CAN'T.
PEOPLE DIE AND ...
HEY ...!
MOVE YOUR ASS BEFORE I KICK IT!
MR. GANTENBEIN? I'D LIKE TO INTRODUCE SOMEONE TO YOU.
......
MY COUSIN ERIC.
HE'D LIKE TO SIT IN ON THE CLASS.

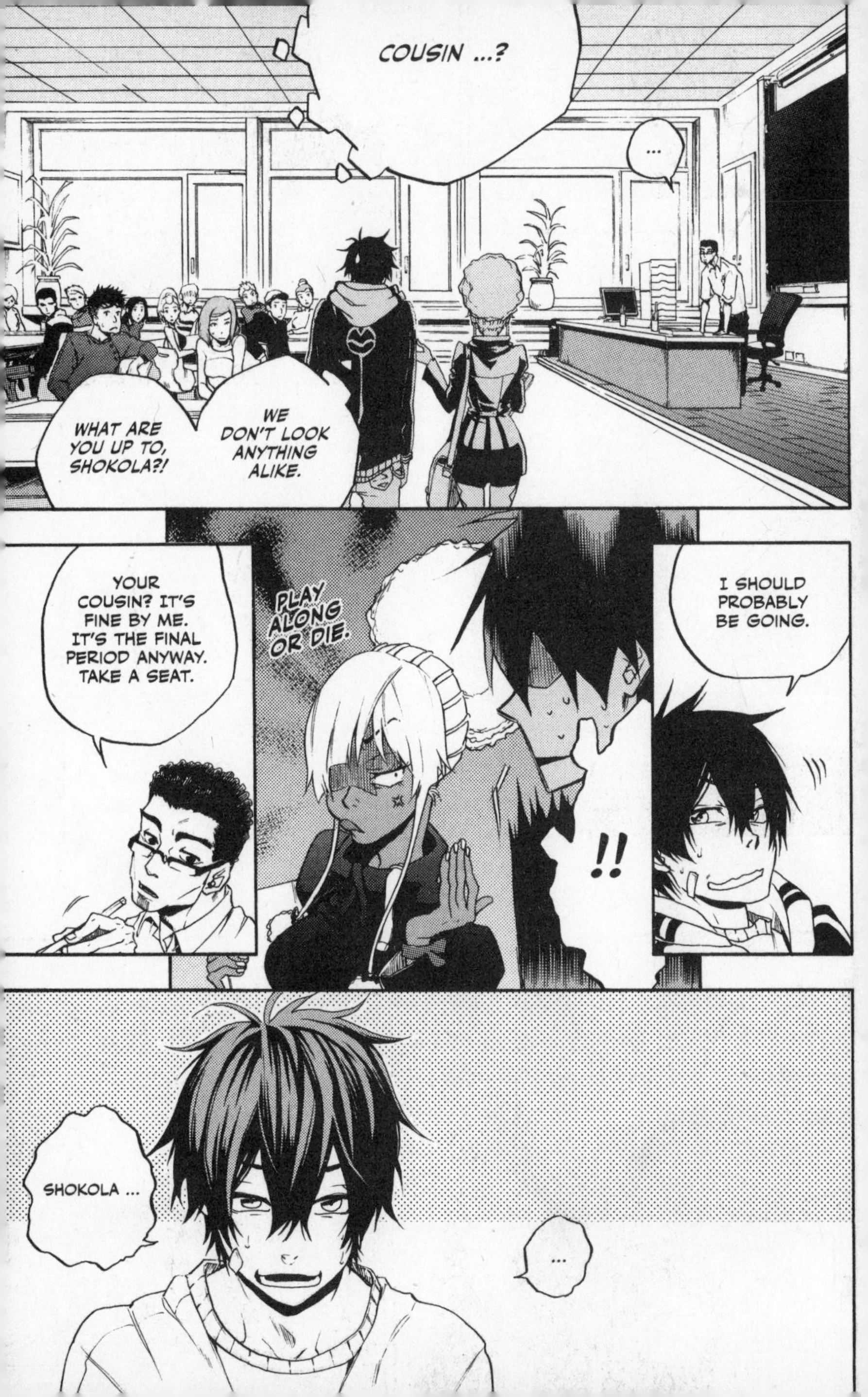
COUSIN ...?
...
WE DON'T LOOK ANYTHING ALIKE.
WHAT ARE YOU UP TO, SHOKOLA?!
I SHOULD PROBABLY BE GOING.
!!
PLAY ALONG OR DIE.
YOUR COUSIN? IT'S FINE BY ME. IT'S THE FINAL PERIOD ANYWAY. TAKE A SEAT.
SHOKOLA ...
...

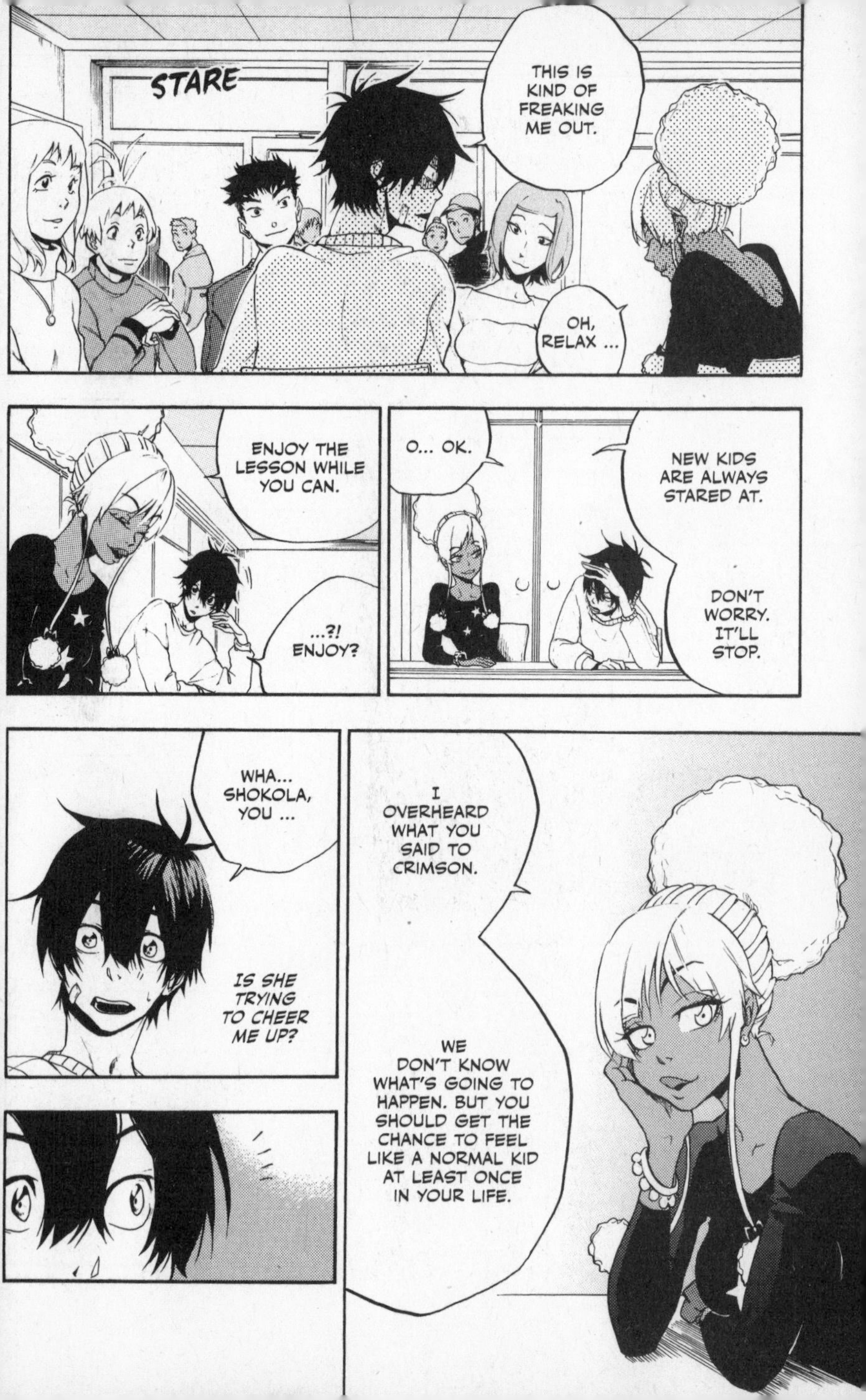
THIS IS KIND OF FREAKING ME OUT.
OH, RELAX ...
STARE
NEW KIDS ARE ALWAYS STARED AT.
DON'T WORRY. IT'LL STOP.
O... OK.
ENJOY THE LESSON WHILE YOU CAN.
...?! ENJOY?
I OVERHEARD WHAT YOU SAID TO CRIMSON.
WE DON'T KNOW WHAT'S GOING TO HAPPEN. BUT YOU SHOULD GET THE CHANCE TO FEEL LIKE A NORMAL KID AT LEAST ONCE IN YOUR LIFE.
WHA... SHOKOLA, YOU ...
IS SHE TRYING TO CHEER ME UP?

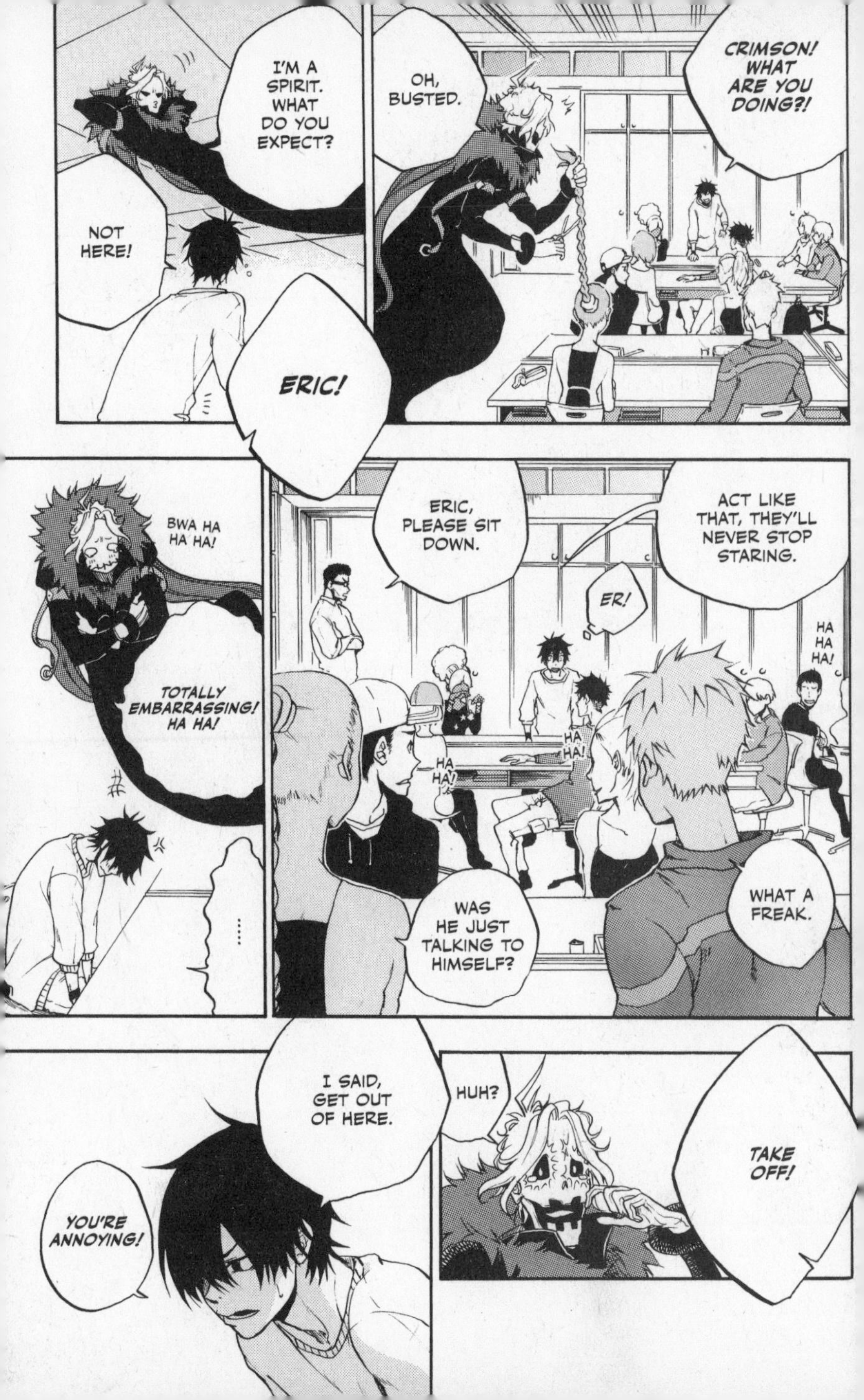

CRIMSON! WHAT ARE YOU DOING?!
OH, BUSTED.
I'M A SPIRIT. WHAT DO YOU EXPECT?
NOT HERE!
ERIC!
ACT LIKE THAT, THEY'LL NEVER STOP STARING.
ERIC, PLEASE SIT DOWN.
ER!
HA HA HA!
HA HA!
HA HA!
WHAT A FREAK.
WAS HE JUST TALKING TO HIMSELF?
BWA HA HA HA!
TOTALLY EMBARRASSING! HA HA!
……
TAKE OFF!
HUH?
I SAID, GET OUT OF HERE.
YOU'RE ANNOYING!

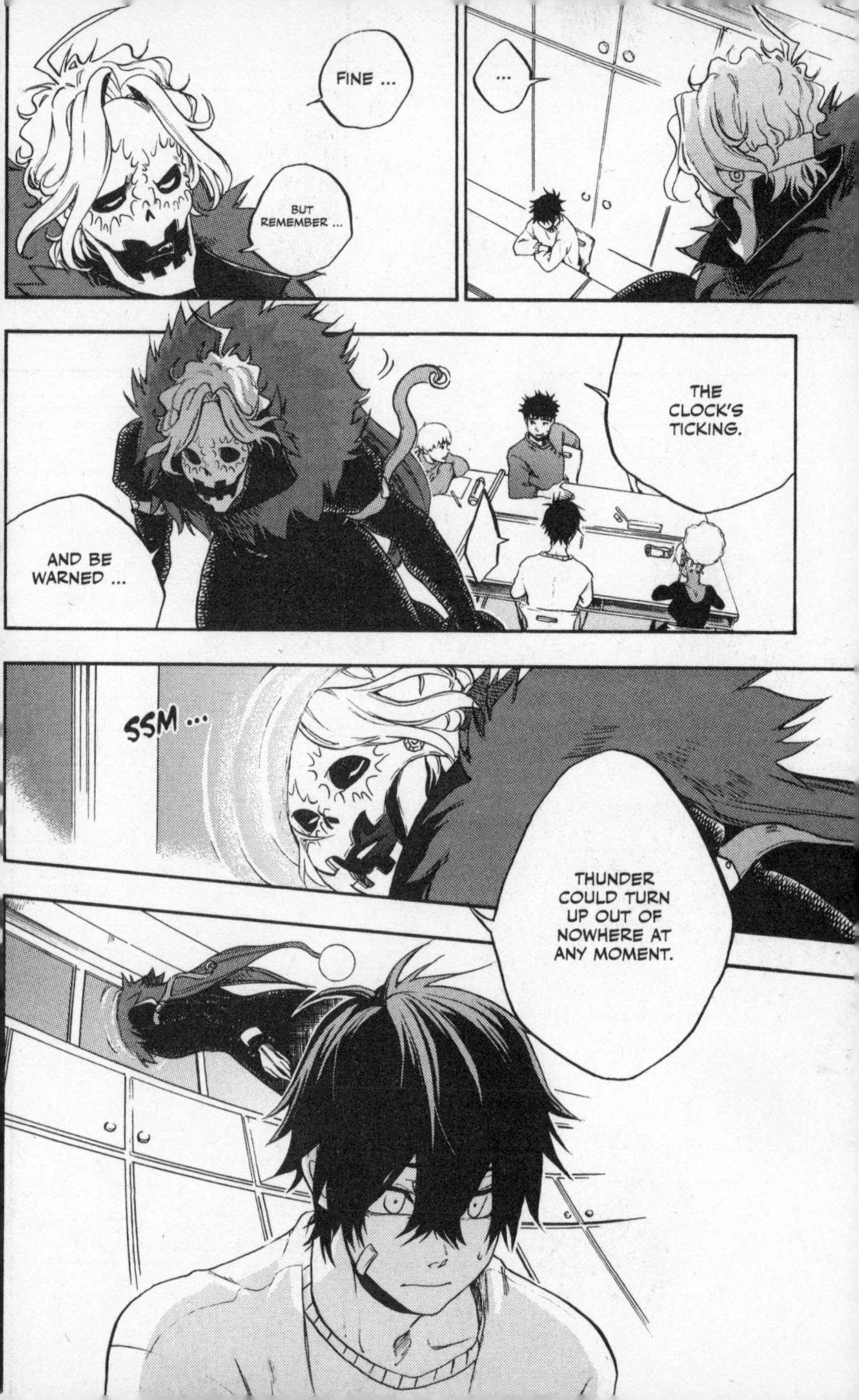
...
FINE ...
BUT REMEMBER ...
THE CLOCK'S TICKING.
AND BE WARNED ...
THUNDER COULD TURN UP OUT OF NOWHERE AT ANY MOMENT.
SSM ...

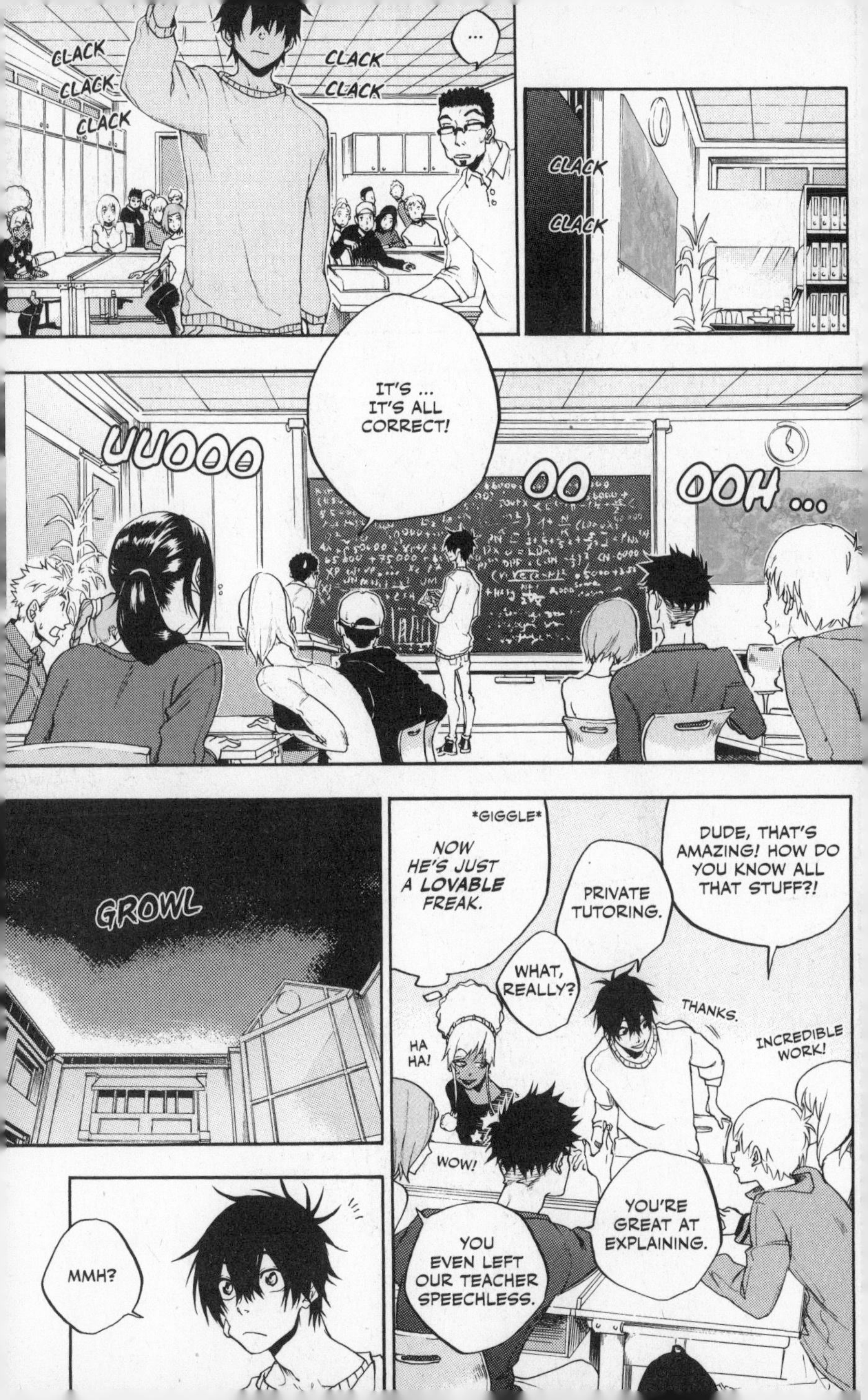
CLACK
CLACK
...
CLACK
CLACK
CLACK
CLACK
CLACK
IT'S ... IT'S ALL CORRECT!
UUOOO
OO
OOH ...
DUDE, THAT'S AMAZING! HOW DO YOU KNOW ALL THAT STUFF?!
PRIVATE TUTORING.
GIGGLE
NOW HE'S JUST A LOVABLE FREAK.
WHAT, REALLY?
THANKS.
INCREDIBLE WORK!
HA HA!
YOU'RE GREAT AT EXPLAINING.
WOW!
YOU EVEN LEFT OUR TEACHER SPEECHLESS.
GROWL
MMH?

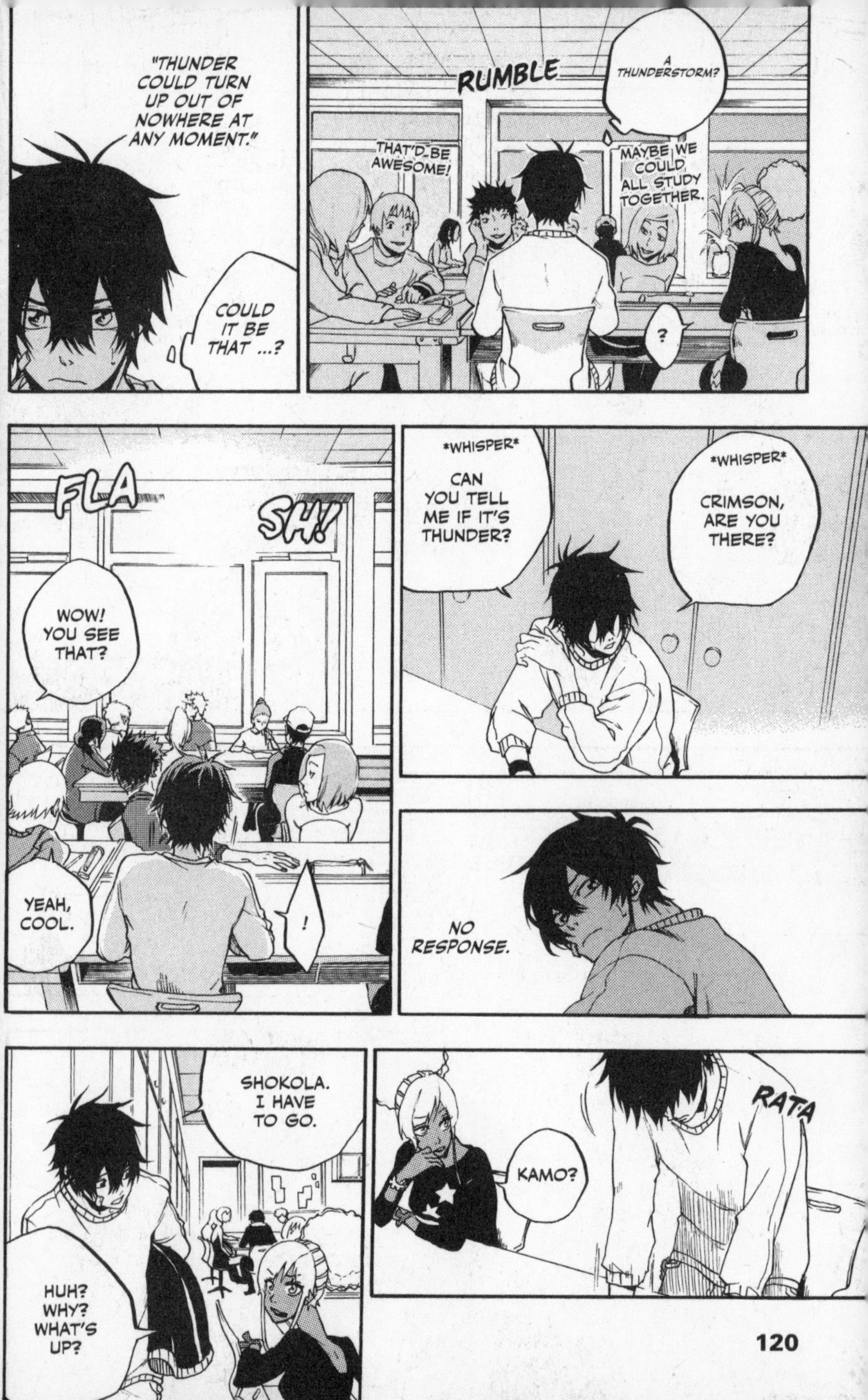
RUMBLE
A THUNDERSTORM?
MAYBE WE COULD ALL STUDY TOGETHER.
THAT'D BE AWESOME!
?
"THUNDER COULD TURN UP OUT OF NOWHERE AT ANY MOMENT."
COULD IT BE THAT ...?
WHISPER CRIMSON, ARE YOU THERE?
WHISPER CAN YOU TELL ME IF IT'S THUNDER?
NO RESPONSE.
FLASH!
WOW! YOU SEE THAT?
!
YEAH, COOL.
RATA
KAMO?
SHOKOLA. I HAVE TO GO.
HUH? WHY? WHAT'S UP?

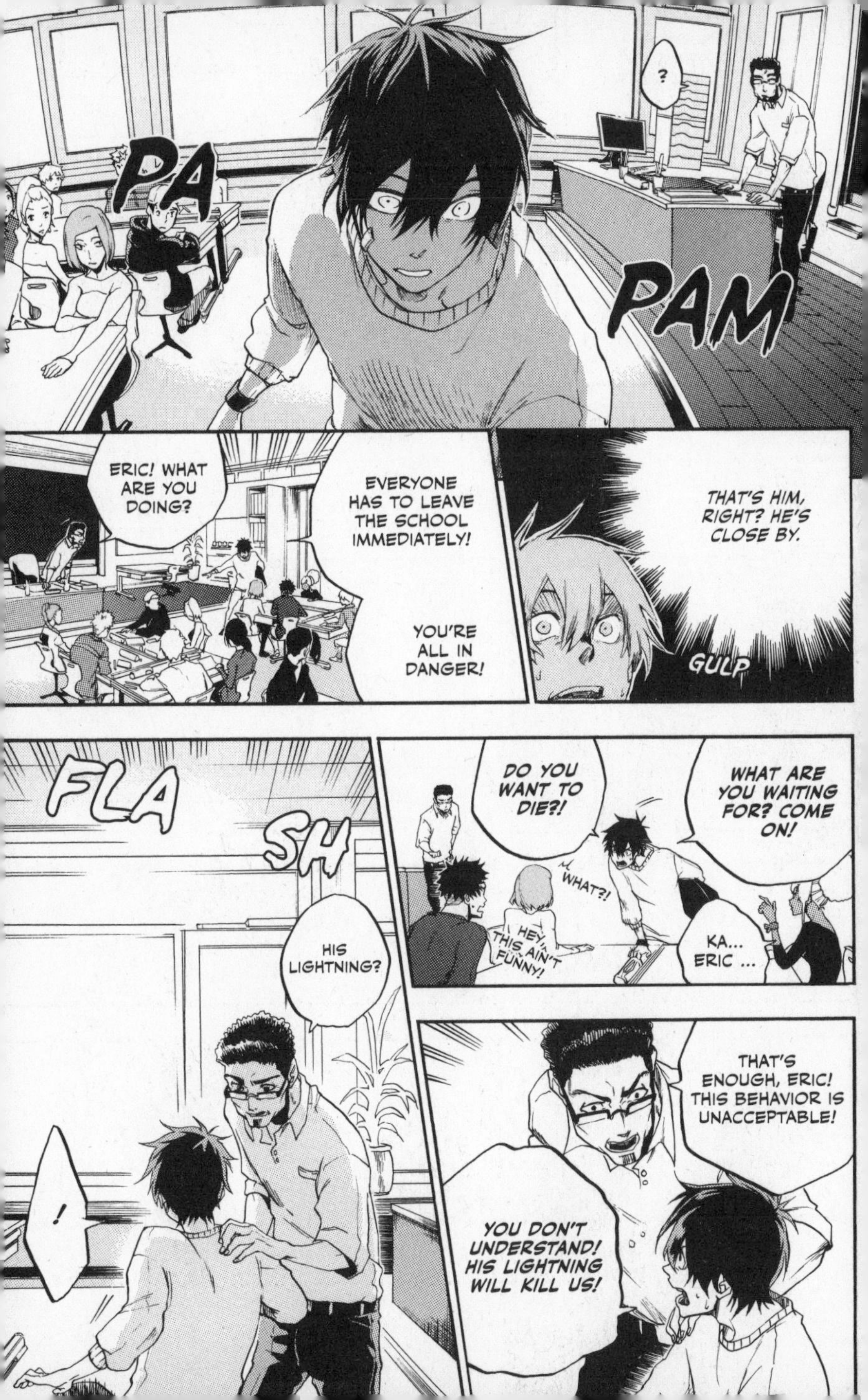
?
PA
PAM
THAT'S HIM, RIGHT? HE'S CLOSE BY.
GULP
ERIC! WHAT ARE YOU DOING?
EVERYONE HAS TO LEAVE THE SCHOOL IMMEDIATELY!
YOU'RE ALL IN DANGER!
WHAT ARE YOU WAITING FOR? COME ON!
DO YOU WANT TO DIE?!
WHAT?!
HEY, THIS AIN'T FUNNY!
KA... ERIC ...
THAT'S ENOUGH, ERIC! THIS BEHAVIOR IS UNACCEPTABLE!
YOU DON'T UNDERSTAND! HIS LIGHTNING WILL KILL US!
FLA
SH
HIS LIGHTNING?
!

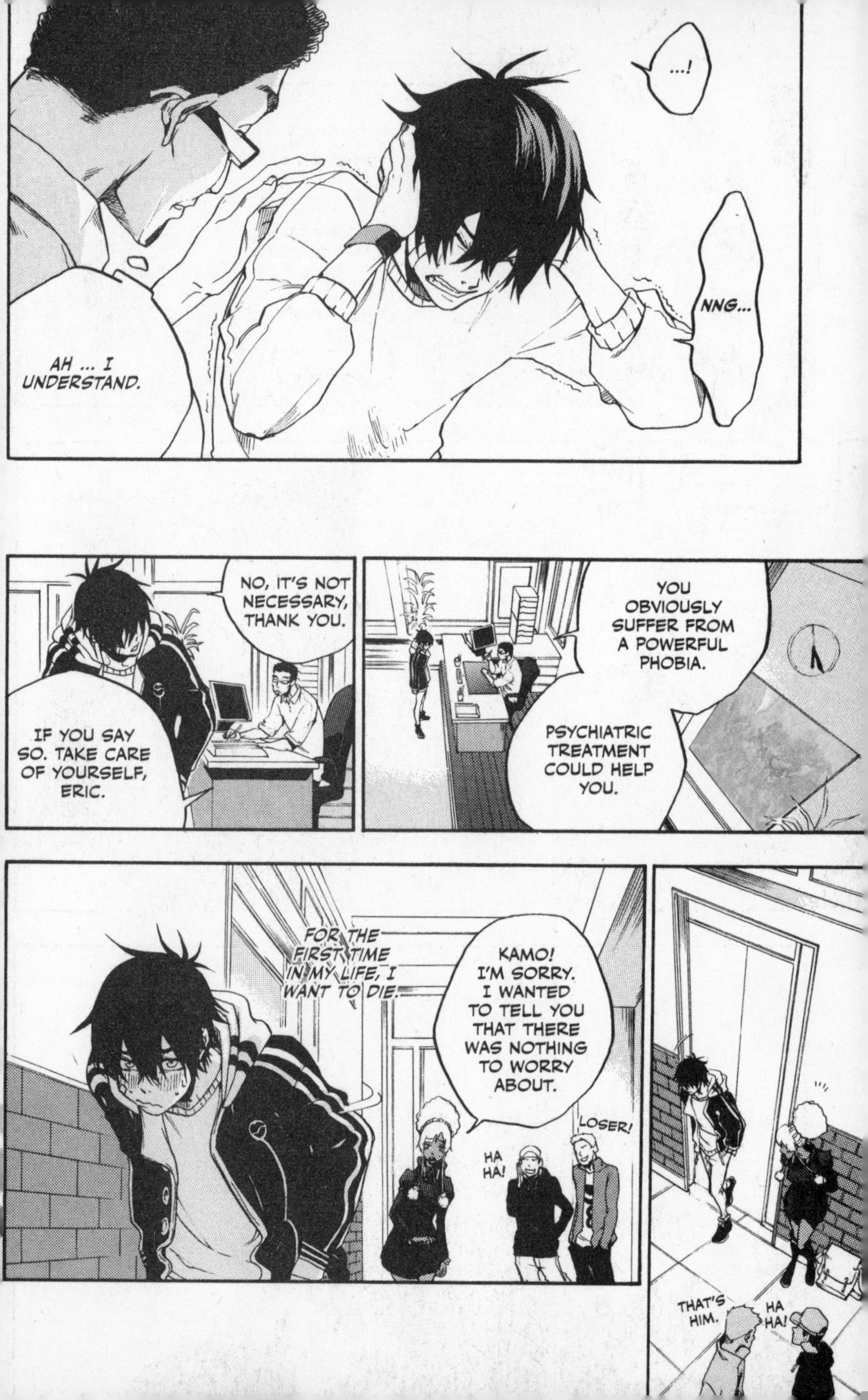
...!
NNG...
AH ... I UNDERSTAND.
YOU OBVIOUSLY SUFFER FROM A POWERFUL PHOBIA.
PSYCHIATRIC TREATMENT COULD HELP YOU.
NO, IT'S NOT NECESSARY, THANK YOU.
IF YOU SAY SO. TAKE CARE OF YOURSELF, ERIC.
HA HA!
THAT'S HIM.
LOSER!
KAMO! I'M SORRY. I WANTED TO TELL YOU THAT THERE WAS NOTHING TO WORRY ABOUT.
HA HA!
FOR THE FIRST TIME IN MY LIFE, I WANT TO DIE.

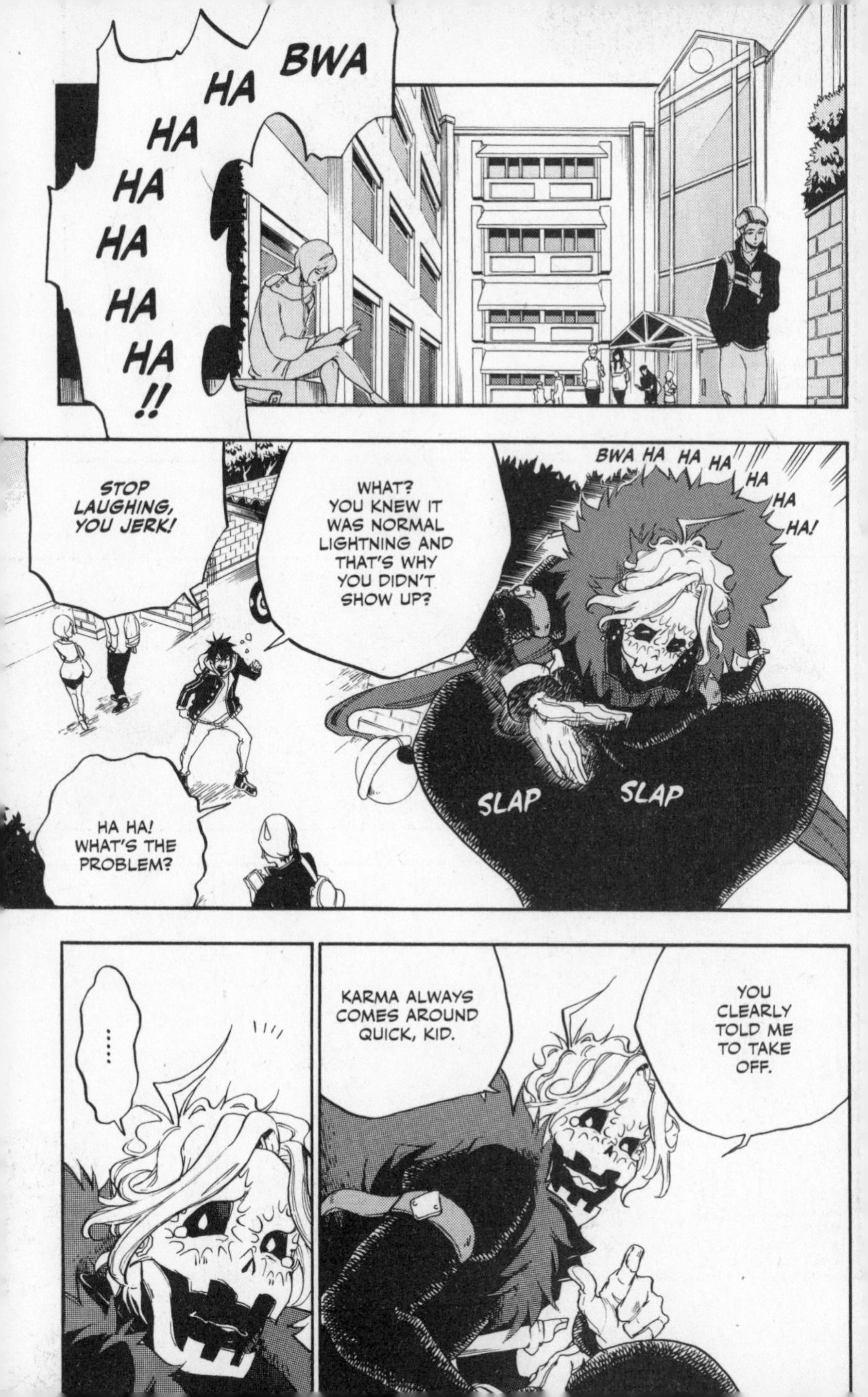
BWA HA HA HA HA HA HA!!
BWA HA HA HA HA HA HA!
SLAP SLAP
WHAT? YOU KNEW IT WAS NORMAL LIGHTNING AND THAT'S WHY YOU DIDN'T SHOW UP?
STOP LAUGHING, YOU JERK!
HA HA! WHAT'S THE PROBLEM?
YOU CLEARLY TOLD ME TO TAKE OFF.
KARMA ALWAYS COMES AROUND QUICK, KID.
……

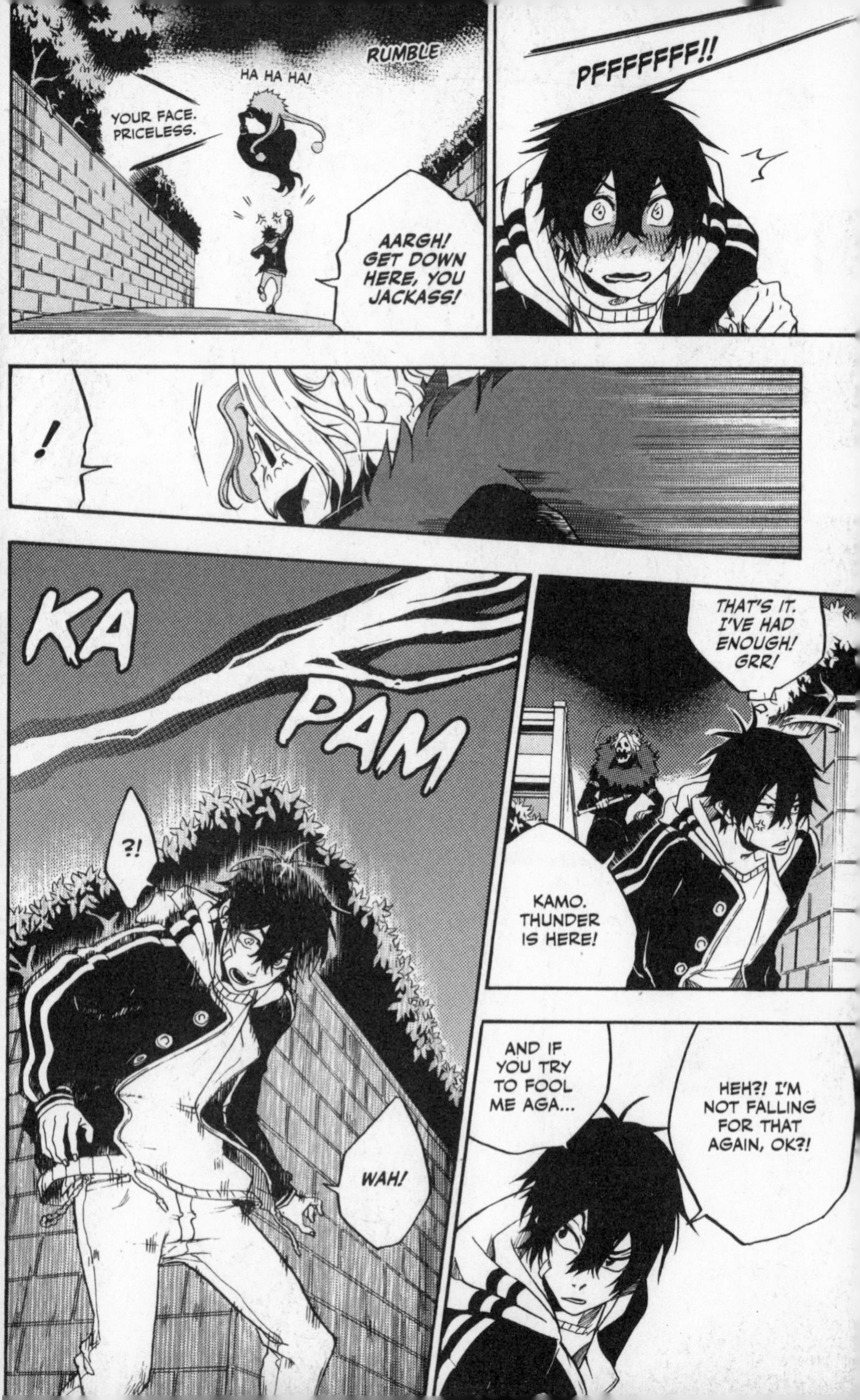
PFFFFFFF!!
RUMBLE
HA HA HA!
YOUR FACE. PRICELESS.
AARGH! GET DOWN HERE, YOU JACKASS!
!
THAT'S IT. I'VE HAD ENOUGH! GRR!
KAMO. THUNDER IS HERE!
HEH?! I'M NOT FALLING FOR THAT AGAIN, OK?!
AND IF YOU TRY TO FOOL ME AGA...
KA
PAM
?!
WAH!

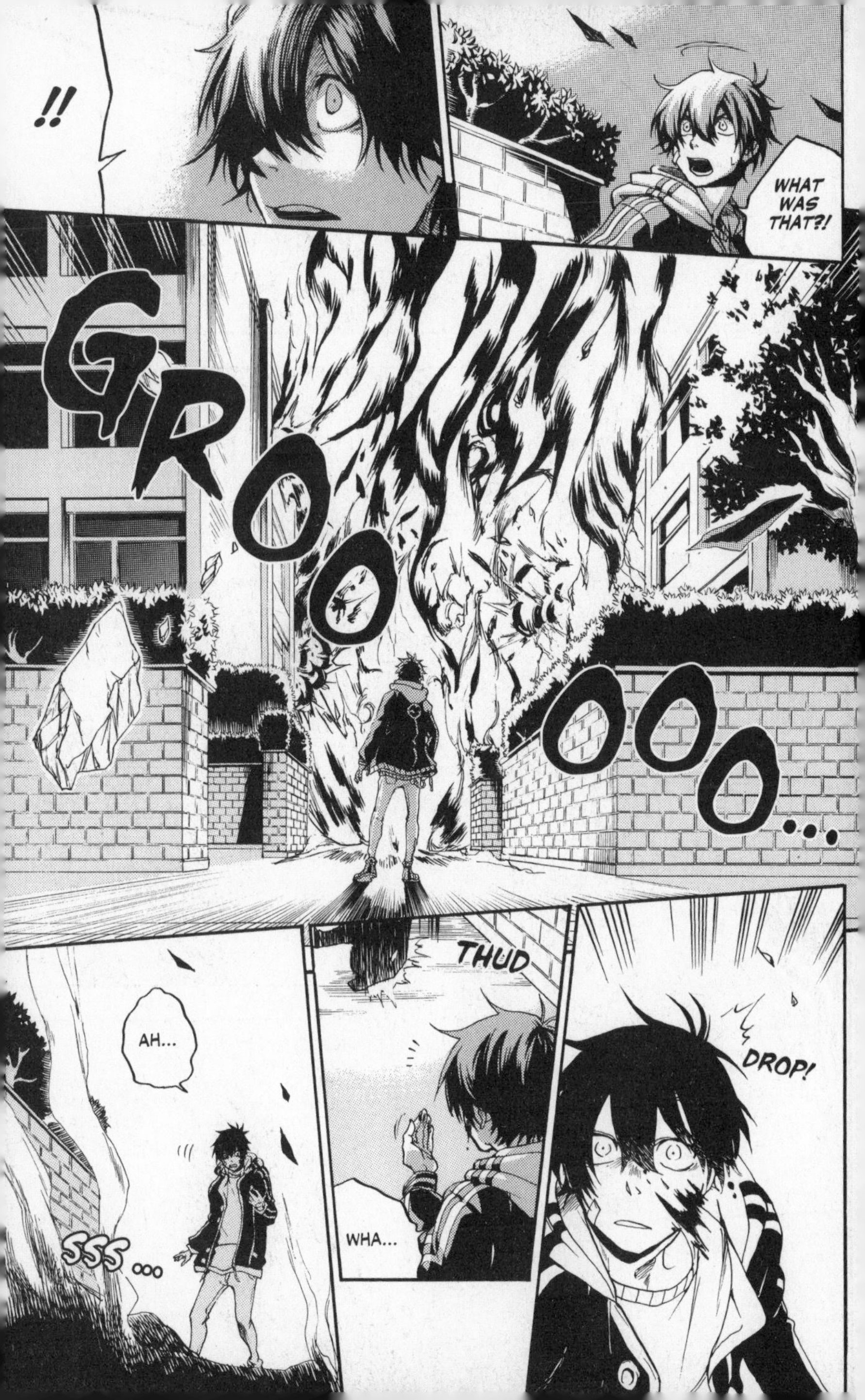
WHAT WAS THAT?!
!!
GROOOOOO...
DROP!
THUD
WHA...
AH...
SSS ooo

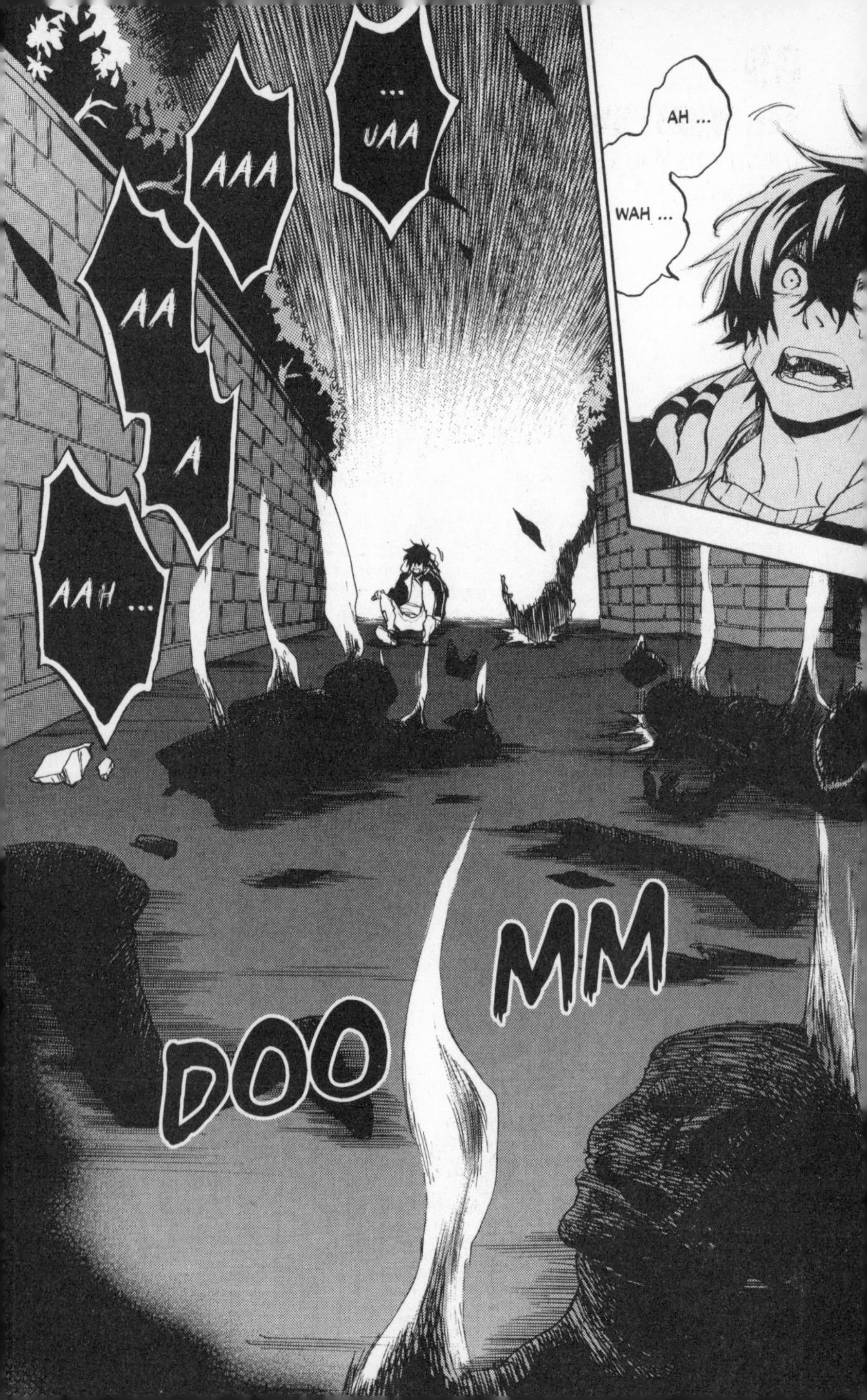
AH ...
WAH ...
... UAA
AAA
AA
A
AAH ...
DOO MM

05

DER WORTE SIND GENUG GEWECHSELT!

THE WORDS YOU'VE BANDIED
ARE SUFFICIENT!

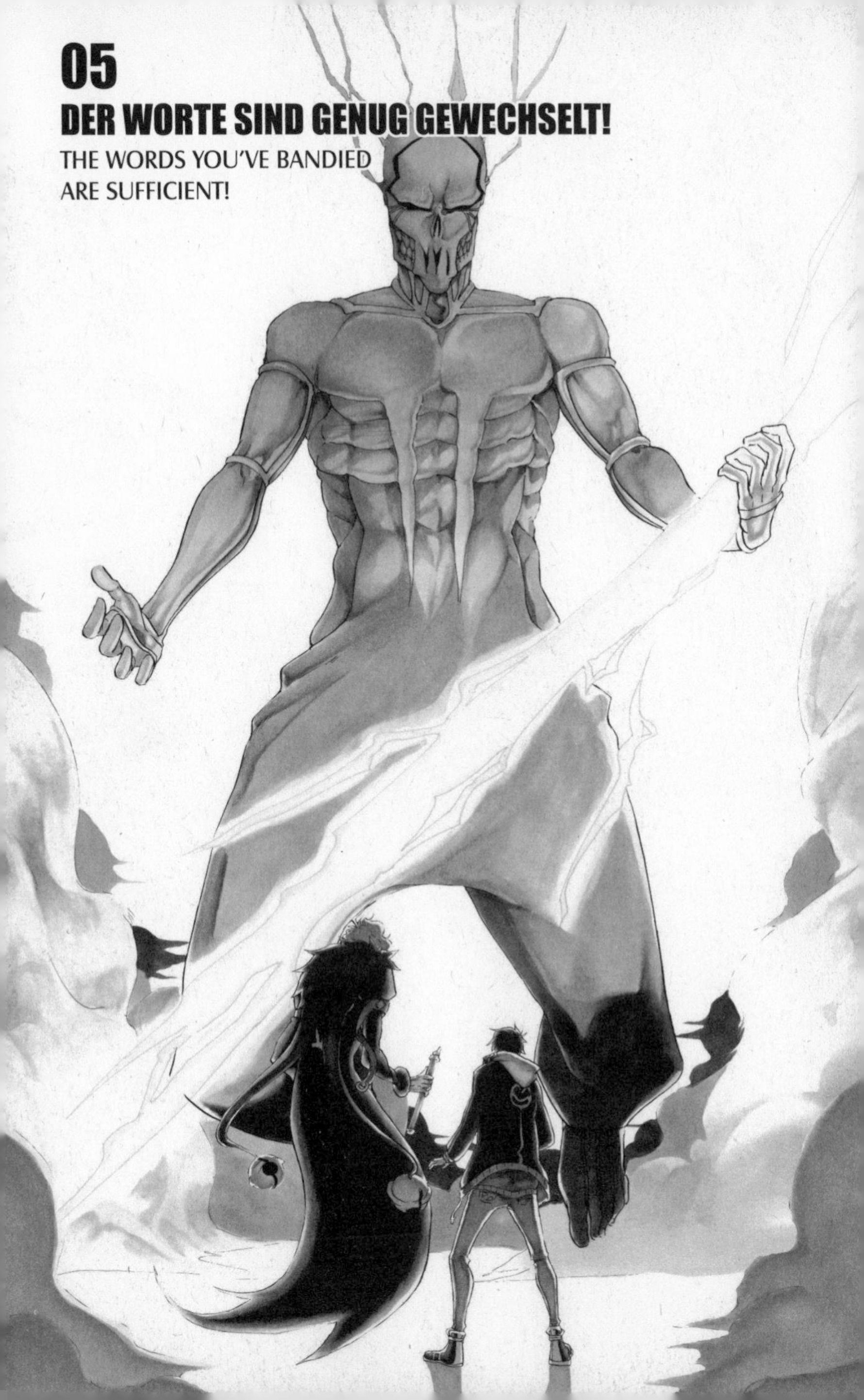

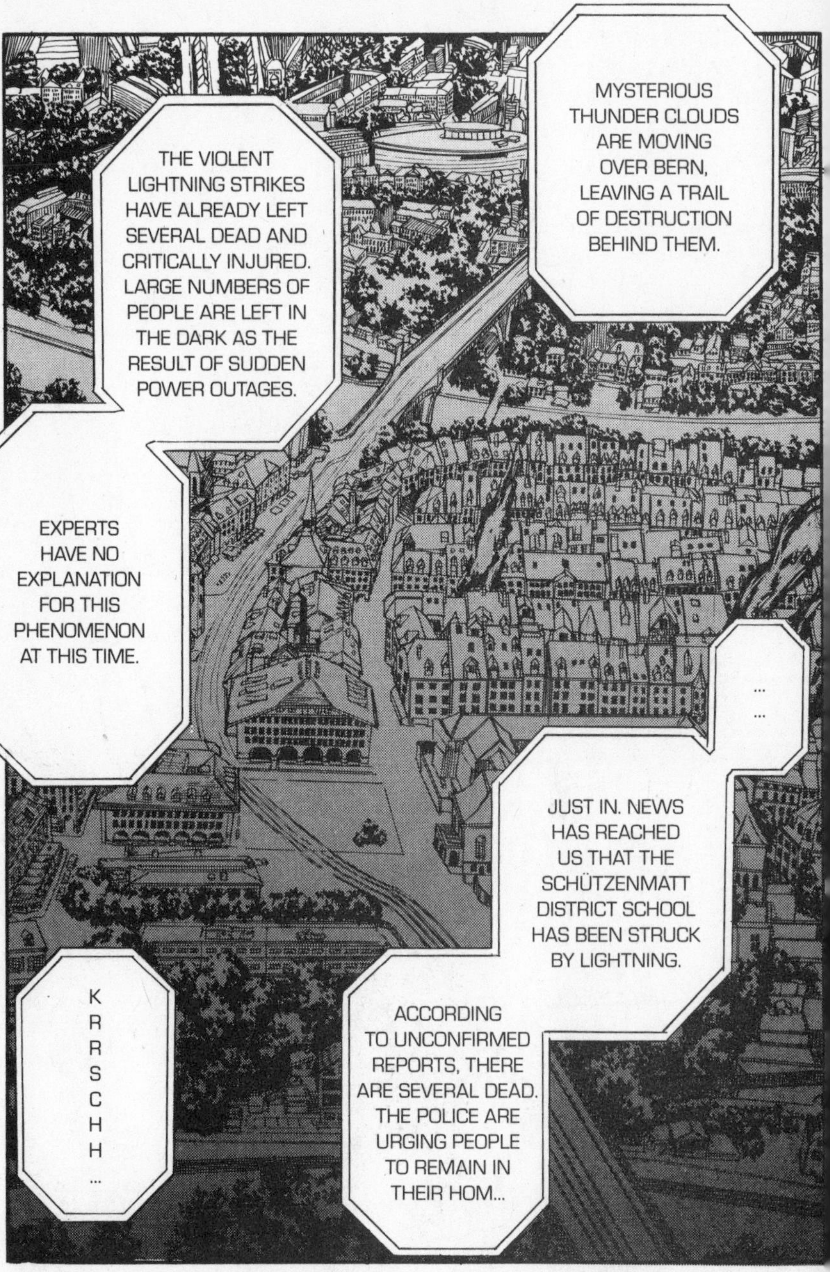

MYSTERIOUS THUNDER CLOUDS ARE MOVING OVER BERN, LEAVING A TRAIL OF DESTRUCTION BEHIND THEM.
THE VIOLENT LIGHTNING STRIKES HAVE ALREADY LEFT SEVERAL DEAD AND CRITICALLY INJURED. LARGE NUMBERS OF PEOPLE ARE LEFT IN THE DARK AS THE RESULT OF SUDDEN POWER OUTAGES.
EXPERTS HAVE NO EXPLANATION FOR THIS PHENOMENON AT THIS TIME.
... ...
JUST IN. NEWS HAS REACHED US THAT THE SCHÜTZENMATT DISTRICT SCHOOL HAS BEEN STRUCK BY LIGHTNING.
ACCORDING TO UNCONFIRMED REPORTS, THERE ARE SEVERAL DEAD. THE POLICE ARE URGING PEOPLE TO REMAIN IN THEIR HOM...
KRRSCHH...

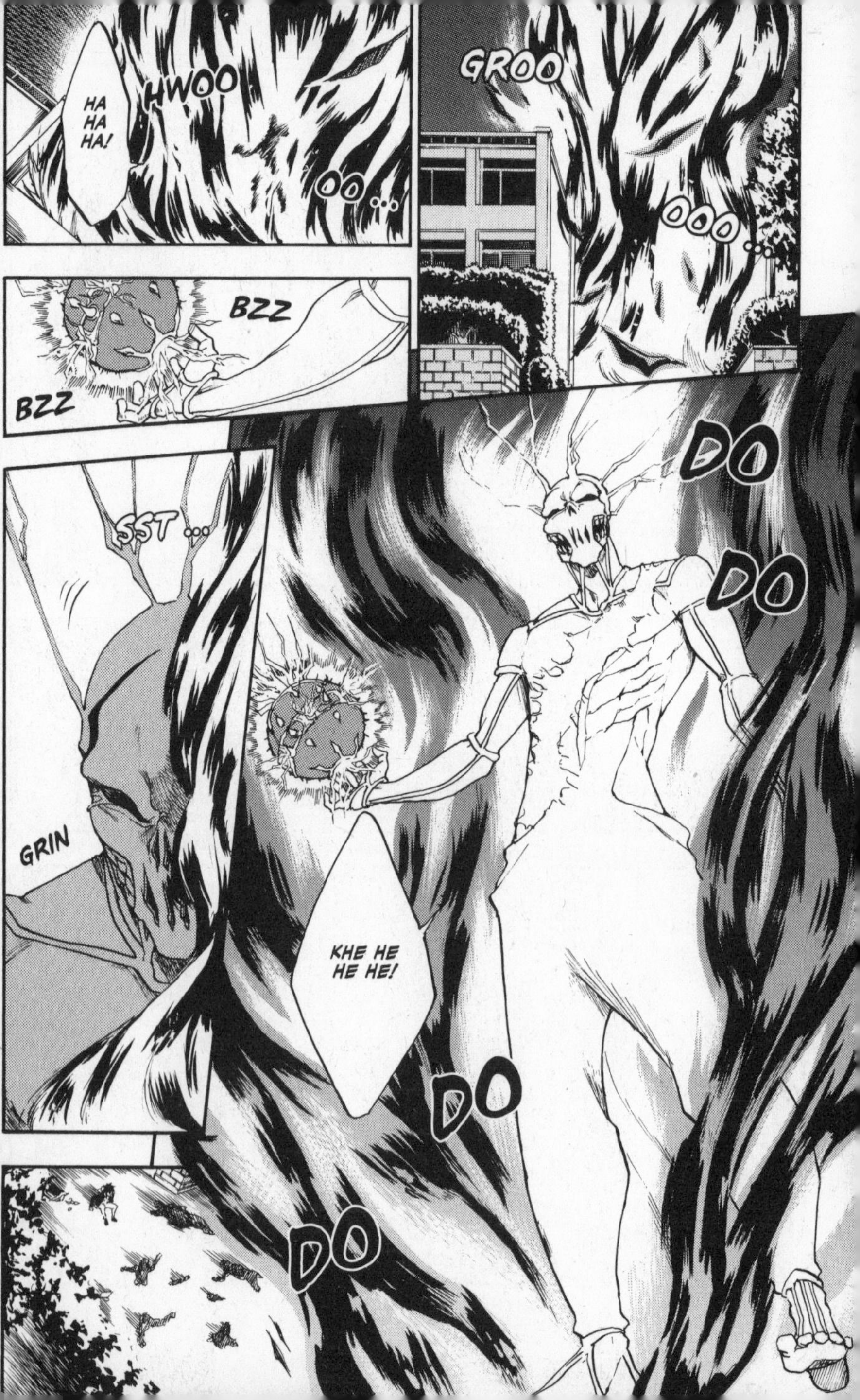
GROO
OOO...
HA HA HA!
HWOO
OO...
BZZ
BZZ
DO
DO
KHE HE HE HE!
DO
DO
SST...
GRIN

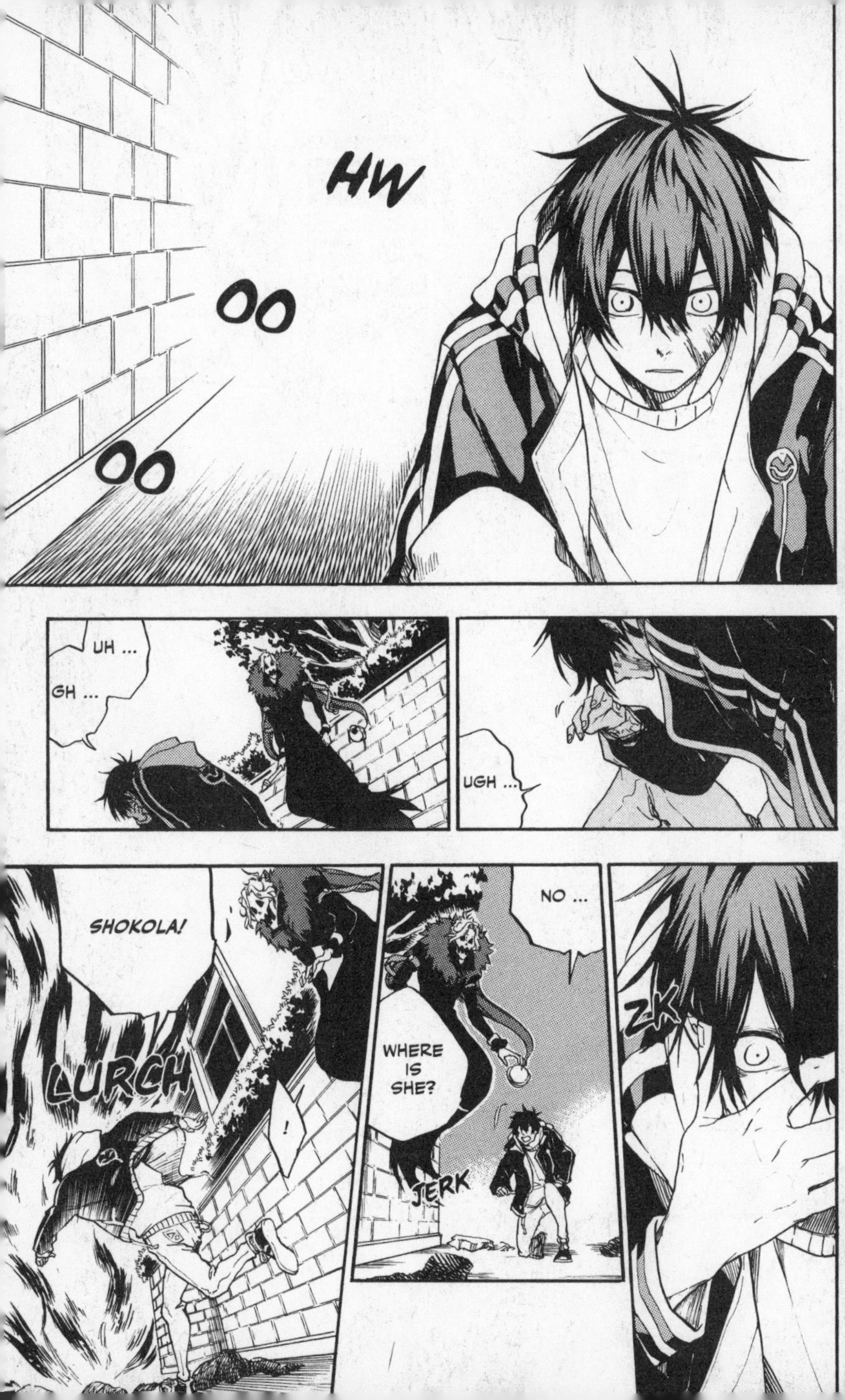
HW
OO
OO
UGH ...
UH ...
GH ...
ZK
NO ...
WHERE IS SHE?
JERK
SHOKOLA!
!
LURCH

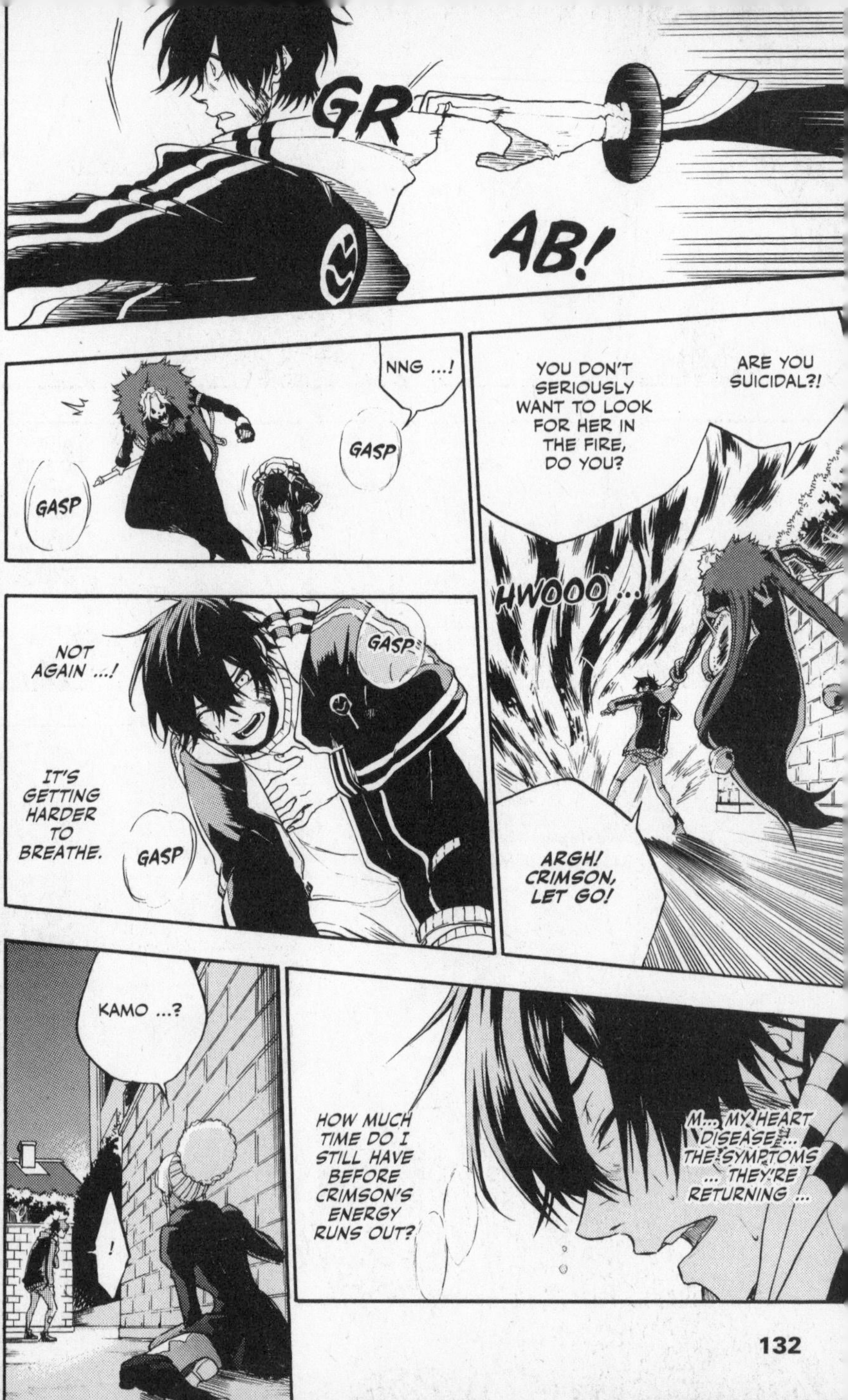
GR
AB!
ARE YOU SUICIDAL?!
YOU DON'T SERIOUSLY WANT TO LOOK FOR HER IN THE FIRE, DO YOU?
HWOOO ...
ARGH! CRIMSON, LET GO!
NNG ...!
GASP
GASP
GASP
NOT AGAIN ...!
IT'S GETTING HARDER TO BREATHE.
GASP
M... MY HEART DISEASE ... THE SYMPTOMS ... THEY'RE RETURNING ...
HOW MUCH TIME DO I STILL HAVE BEFORE CRIMSON'S ENERGY RUNS OUT?
KAMO ...?
!

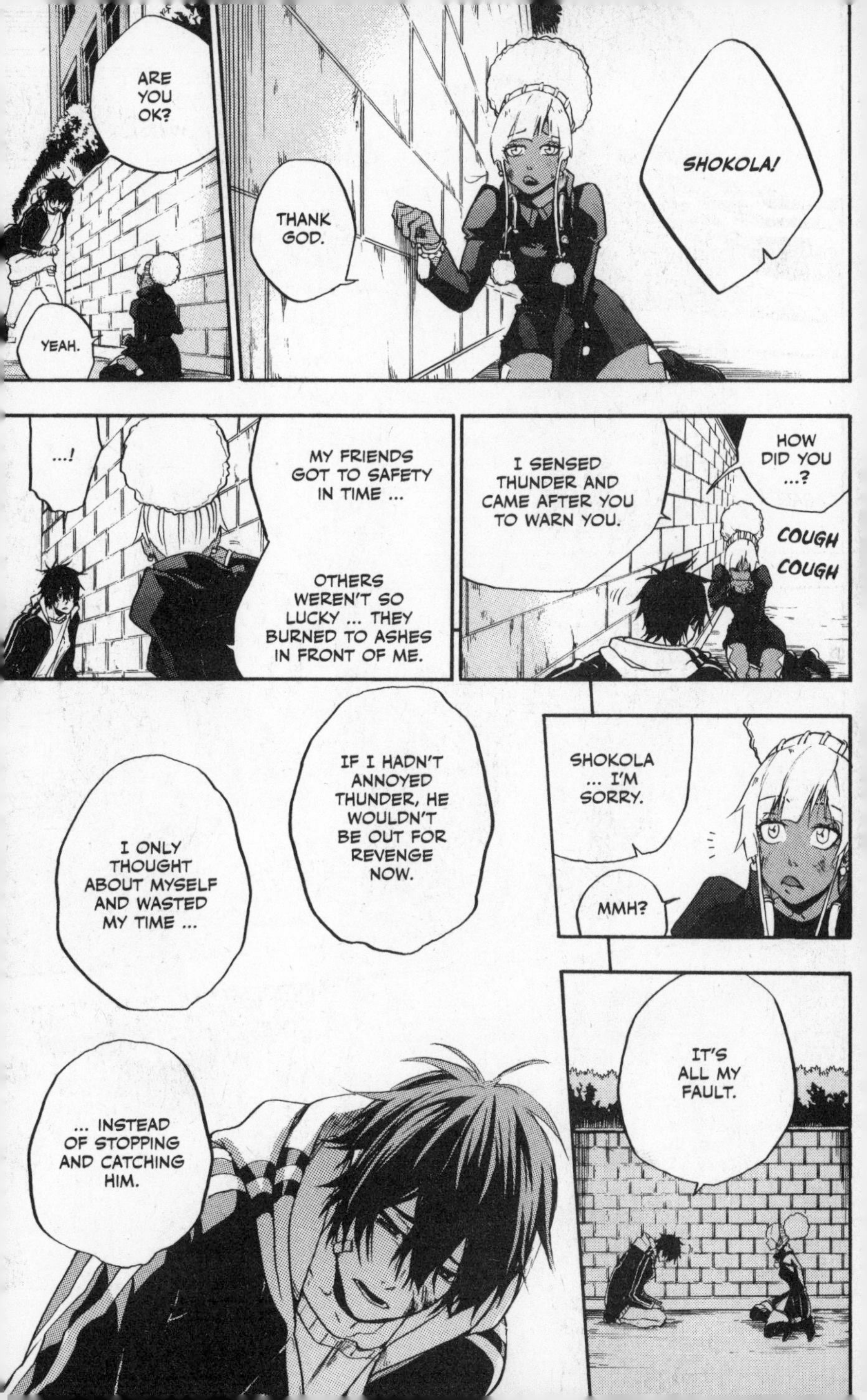
SHOKOLA!
THANK GOD.
ARE YOU OK?
YEAH.
HOW DID YOU ...?
COUGH COUGH
I SENSED THUNDER AND CAME AFTER YOU TO WARN YOU.
MY FRIENDS GOT TO SAFETY IN TIME ...
...!
OTHERS WEREN'T SO LUCKY ... THEY BURNED TO ASHES IN FRONT OF ME.
SHOKOLA ... I'M SORRY.
MMH?
IT'S ALL MY FAULT.
IF I HADN'T ANNOYED THUNDER, HE WOULDN'T BE OUT FOR REVENGE NOW.
I ONLY THOUGHT ABOUT MYSELF AND WASTED MY TIME ...
... INSTEAD OF STOPPING AND CATCHING HIM.

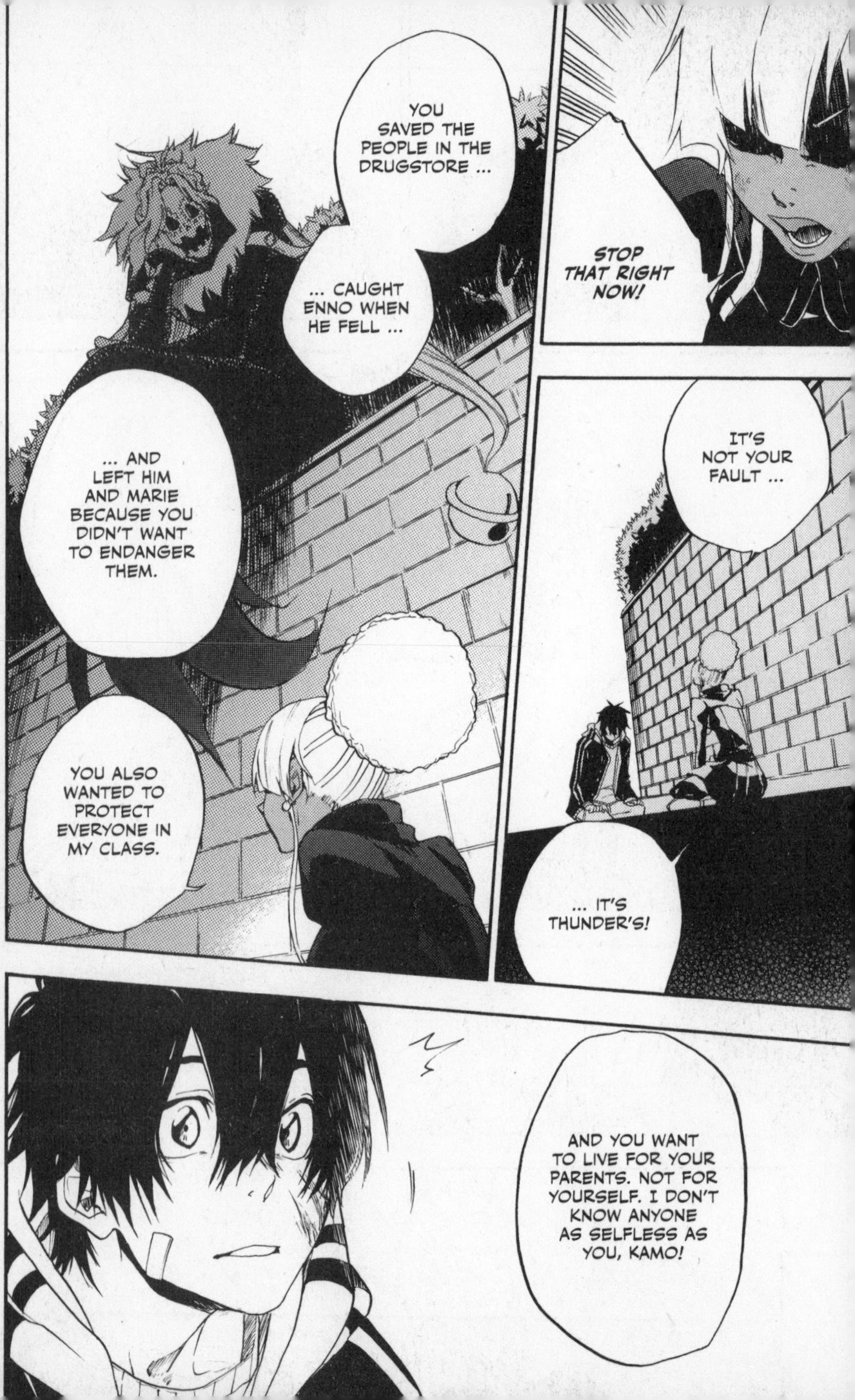
STOP THAT RIGHT NOW!
IT'S NOT YOUR FAULT ...
... IT'S THUNDER'S!
YOU SAVED THE PEOPLE IN THE DRUGSTORE ...
... CAUGHT ENNO WHEN HE FELL ...
... AND LEFT HIM AND MARIE BECAUSE YOU DIDN'T WANT TO ENDANGER THEM.
YOU ALSO WANTED TO PROTECT EVERYONE IN MY CLASS.
AND YOU WANT TO LIVE FOR YOUR PARENTS. NOT FOR YOURSELF. I DON'T KNOW ANYONE AS SELFLESS AS YOU, KAMO!

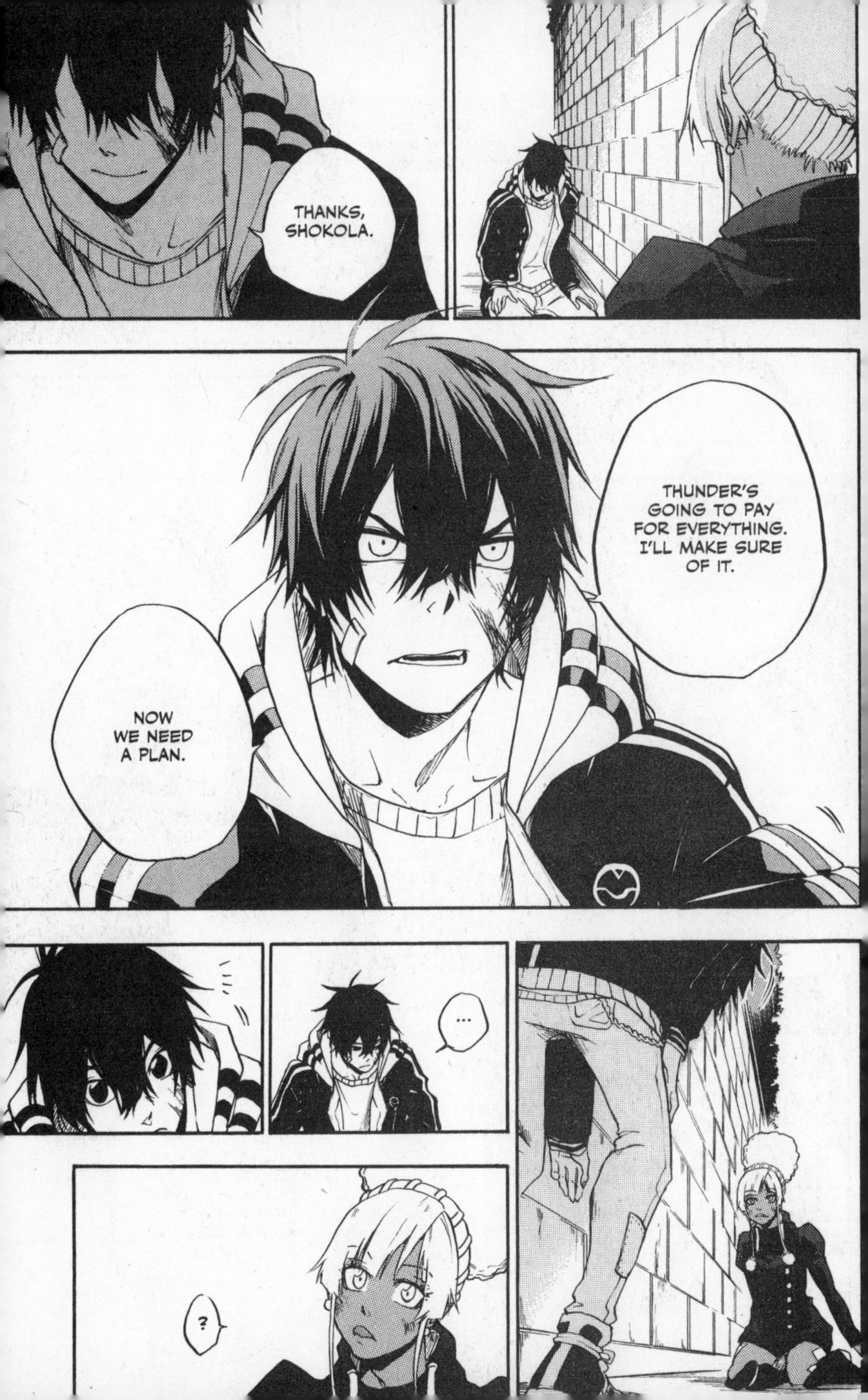
THANKS, SHOKOLA.
THUNDER'S GOING TO PAY FOR EVERYTHING. I'LL MAKE SURE OF IT.
NOW WE NEED A PLAN.
...
?

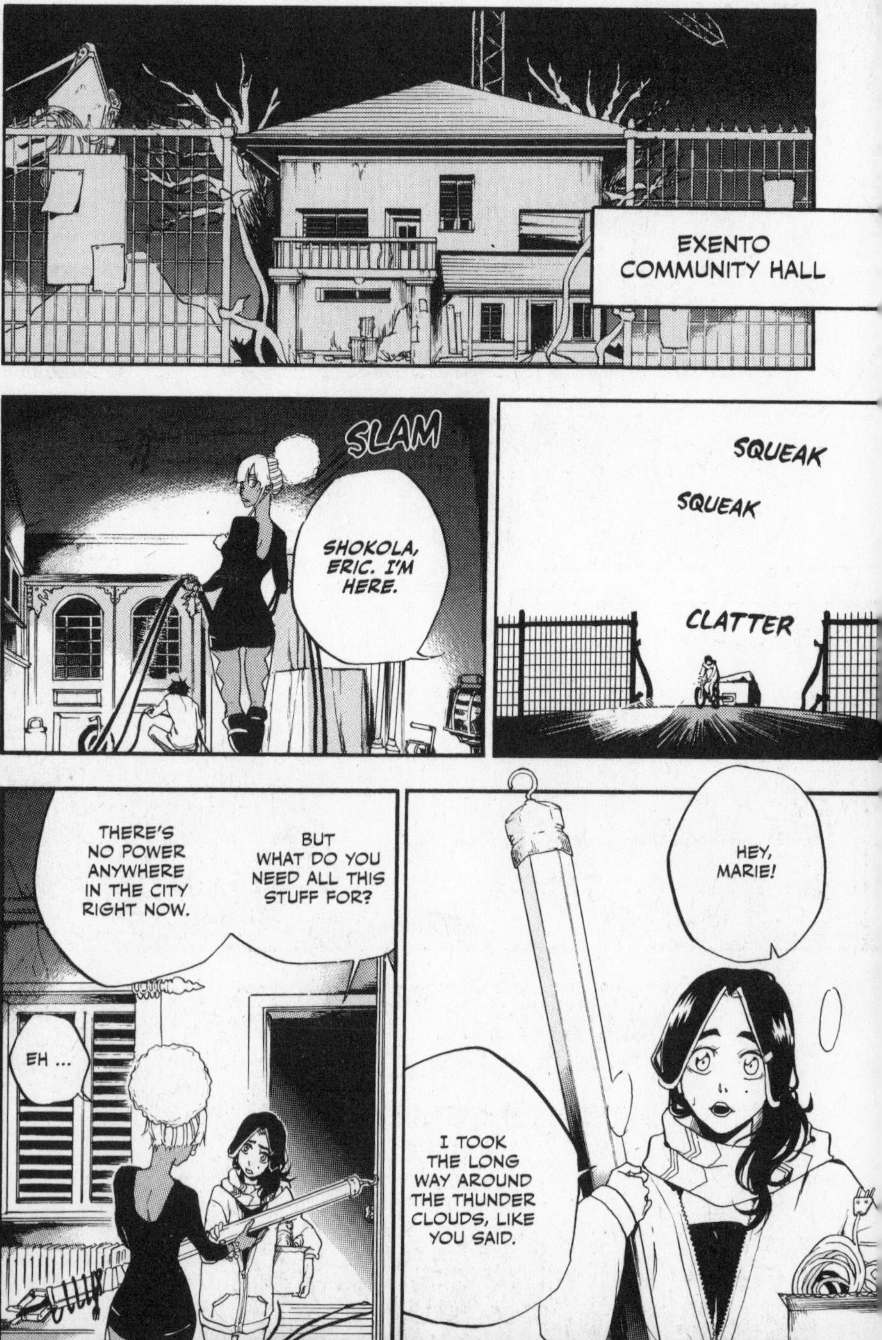
EXENTO COMMUNITY HALL
SQUEAK
SQUEAK
CLATTER
SLAM
SHOKOLA, ERIC. I'M HERE.
HEY, MARIE!
I TOOK THE LONG WAY AROUND THE THUNDER CLOUDS, LIKE YOU SAID.
BUT WHAT DO YOU NEED ALL THIS STUFF FOR?
THERE'S NO POWER ANYWHERE IN THE CITY RIGHT NOW.
EH ...

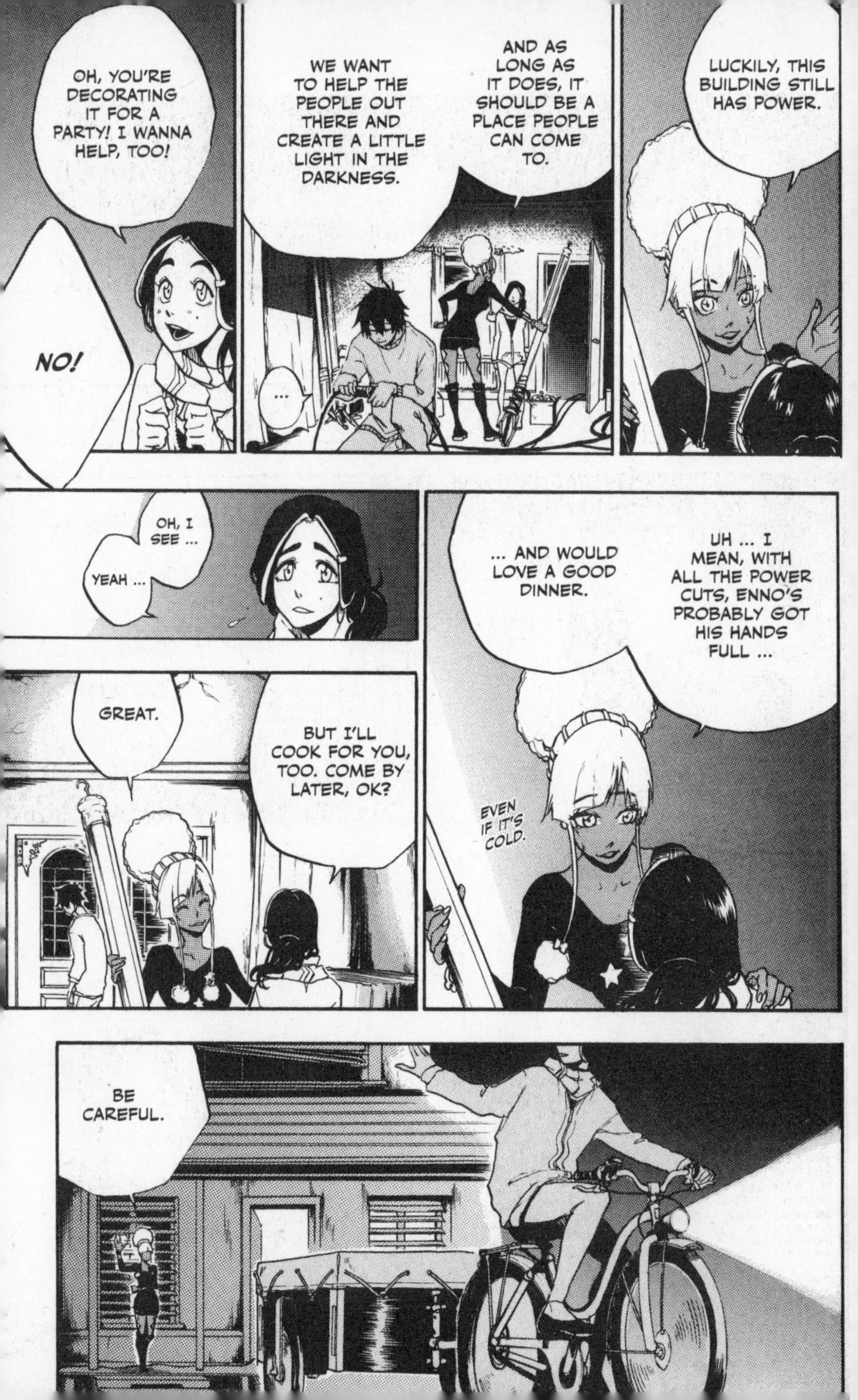
LUCKILY, THIS BUILDING STILL HAS POWER.
AND AS LONG AS IT DOES, IT SHOULD BE A PLACE PEOPLE CAN COME TO.
WE WANT TO HELP THE PEOPLE OUT THERE AND CREATE A LITTLE LIGHT IN THE DARKNESS.
...
OH, YOU'RE DECORATING IT FOR A PARTY! I WANNA HELP, TOO!
NO!
UH ... I MEAN, WITH ALL THE POWER CUTS, ENNO'S PROBABLY GOT HIS HANDS FULL ...
... AND WOULD LOVE A GOOD DINNER.
EVEN IF IT'S COLD.
OH, I SEE ...
YEAH ...
BUT I'LL COOK FOR YOU, TOO. COME BY LATER, OK?
GREAT.
BE CAREFUL.

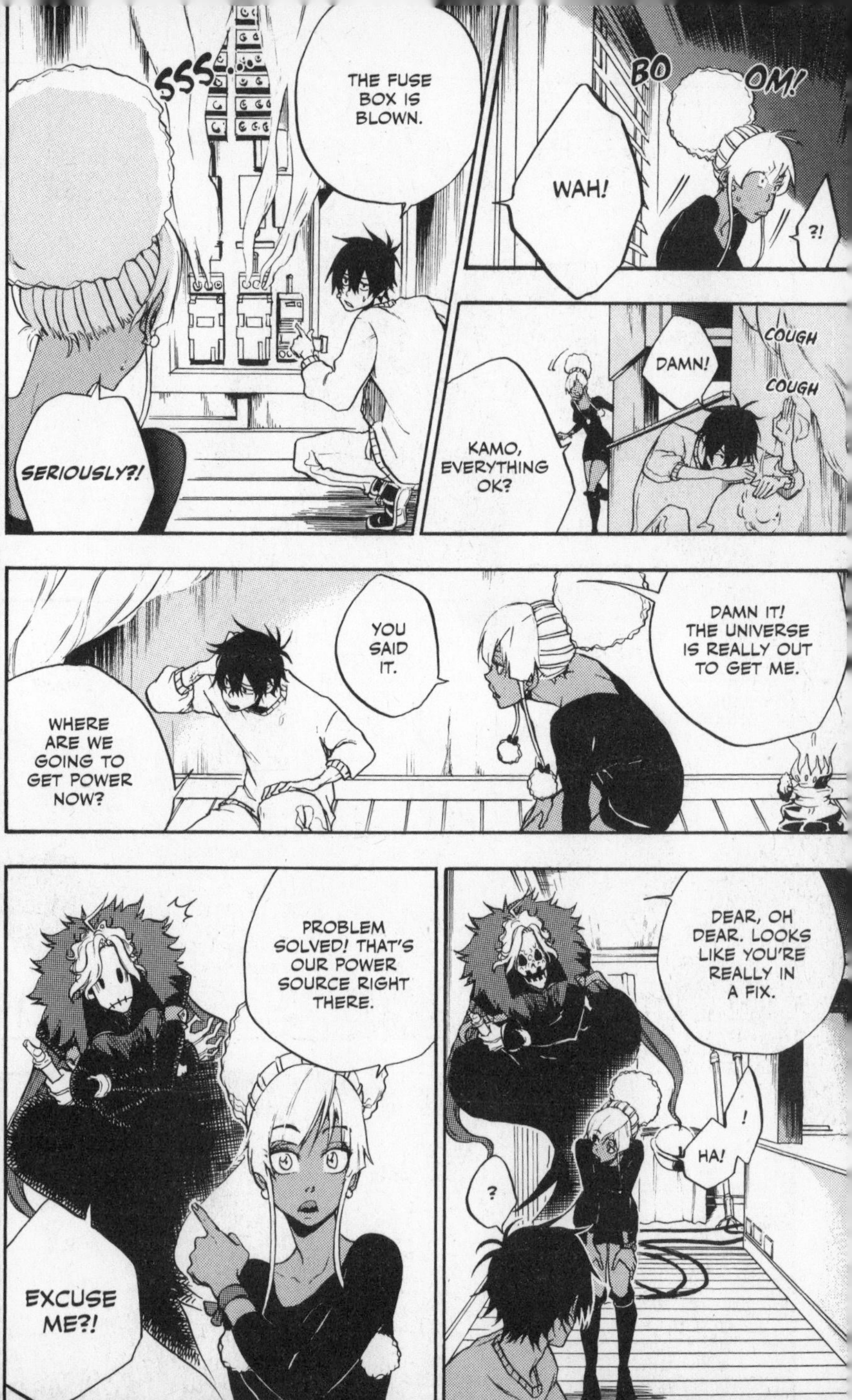
BOOM!
WAH!
?!
COUGH
COUGH
DAMN!
KAMO, EVERYTHING OK?
SSS...
THE FUSE BOX IS BLOWN.
SERIOUSLY?!
DAMN IT! THE UNIVERSE IS REALLY OUT TO GET ME.
YOU SAID IT.
WHERE ARE WE GOING TO GET POWER NOW?
DEAR, OH DEAR. LOOKS LIKE YOU'RE REALLY IN A FIX.
!
HA!
?
PROBLEM SOLVED! THAT'S OUR POWER SOURCE RIGHT THERE.
EXCUSE ME?!

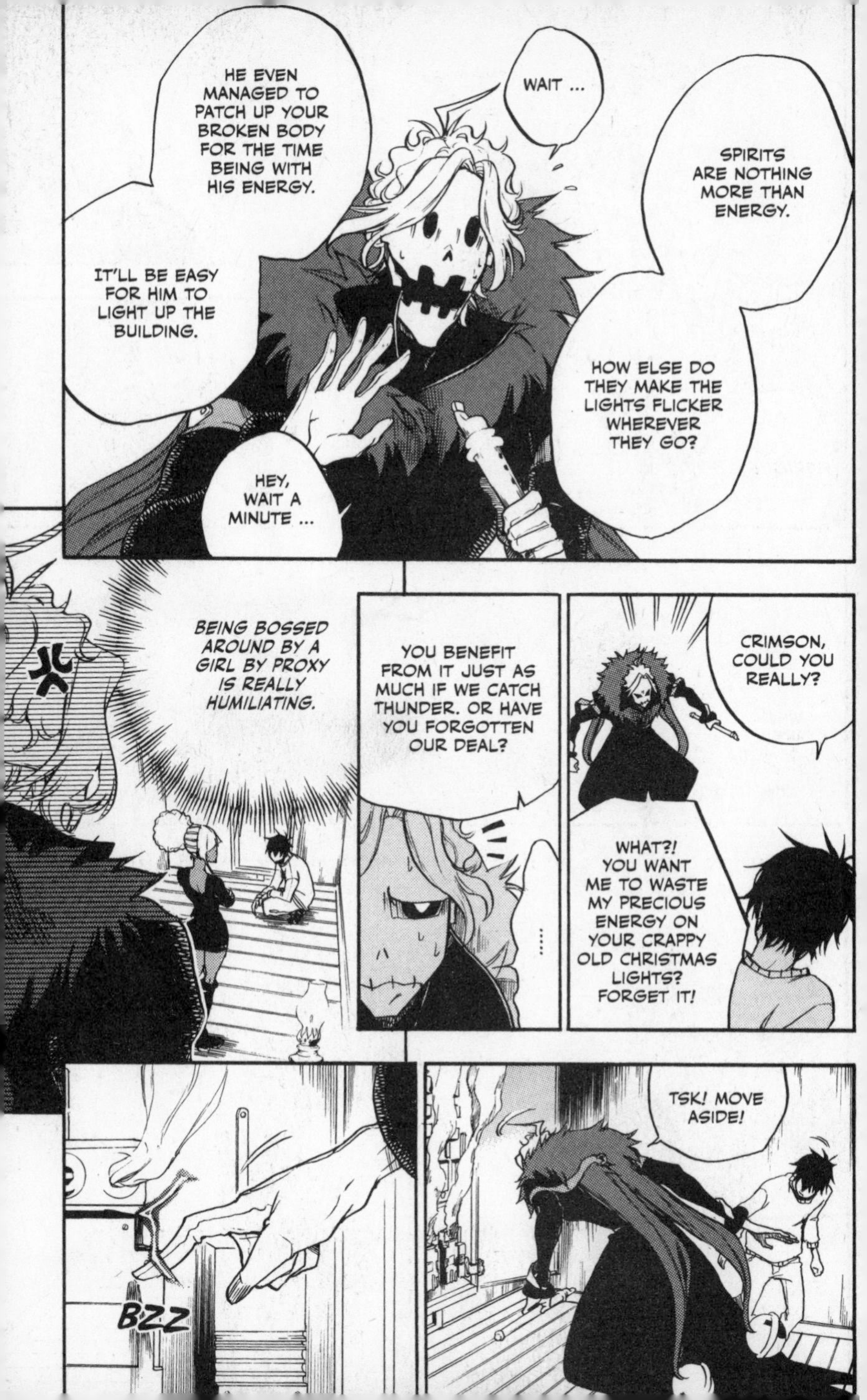
SPIRITS ARE NOTHING MORE THAN ENERGY.
HOW ELSE DO THEY MAKE THE LIGHTS FLICKER WHEREVER THEY GO?
WAIT ...
HE EVEN MANAGED TO PATCH UP YOUR BROKEN BODY FOR THE TIME BEING WITH HIS ENERGY.
IT'LL BE EASY FOR HIM TO LIGHT UP THE BUILDING.
HEY, WAIT A MINUTE ...
CRIMSON, COULD YOU REALLY?
WHAT?! YOU WANT ME TO WASTE MY PRECIOUS ENERGY ON YOUR CRAPPY OLD CHRISTMAS LIGHTS? FORGET IT!
YOU BENEFIT FROM IT JUST AS MUCH IF WE CATCH THUNDER. OR HAVE YOU FORGOTTEN OUR DEAL?
.....
BEING BOSSED AROUND BY A GIRL BY PROXY IS REALLY HUMILIATING.
TSK! MOVE ASIDE!
BZZ

...!

LOOK AT THAT.

ANOTHER SOURCE OF FOOD.

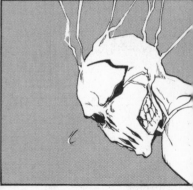

140

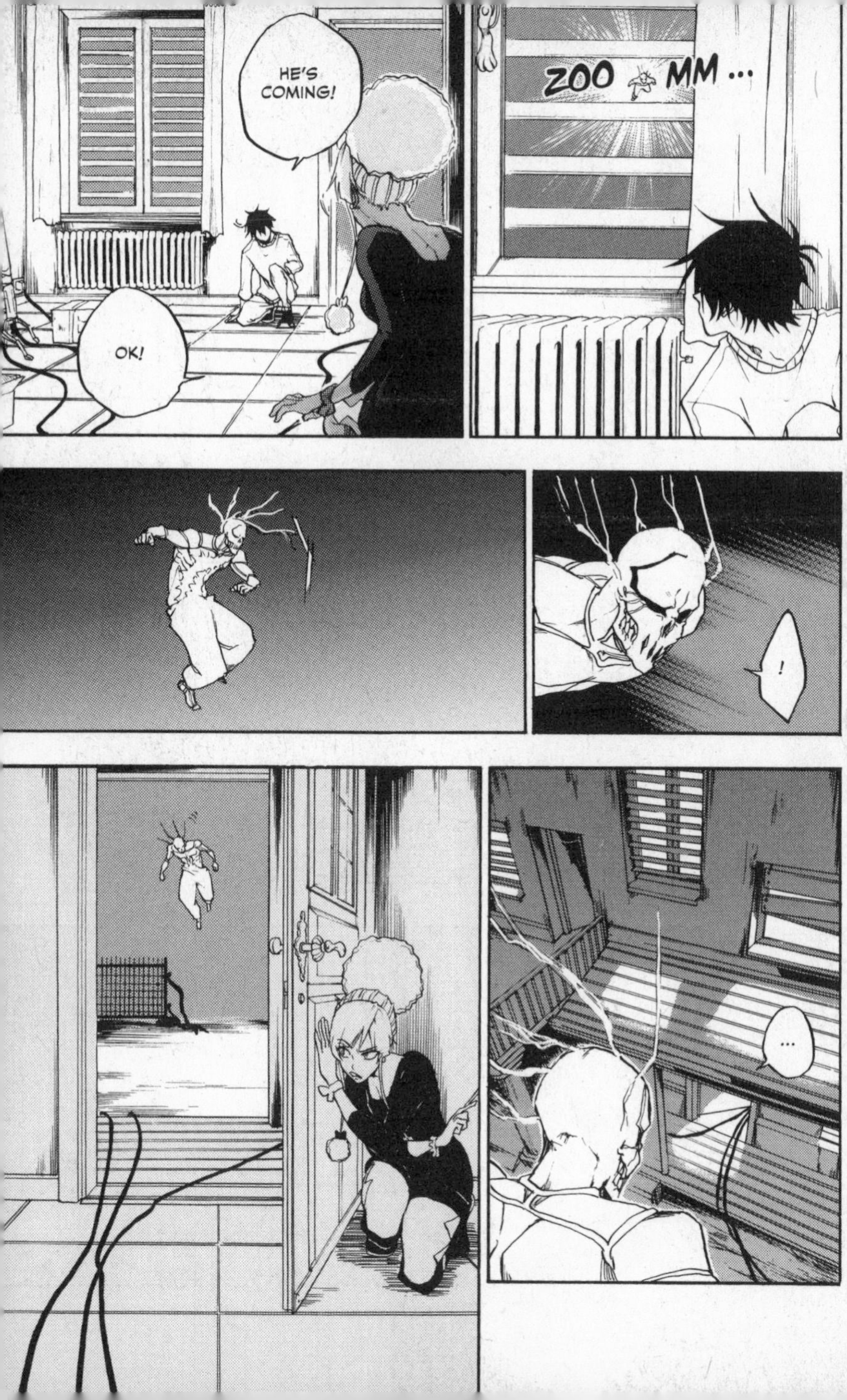
ZOO MM ...
HE'S COMING!
OK!
!
...

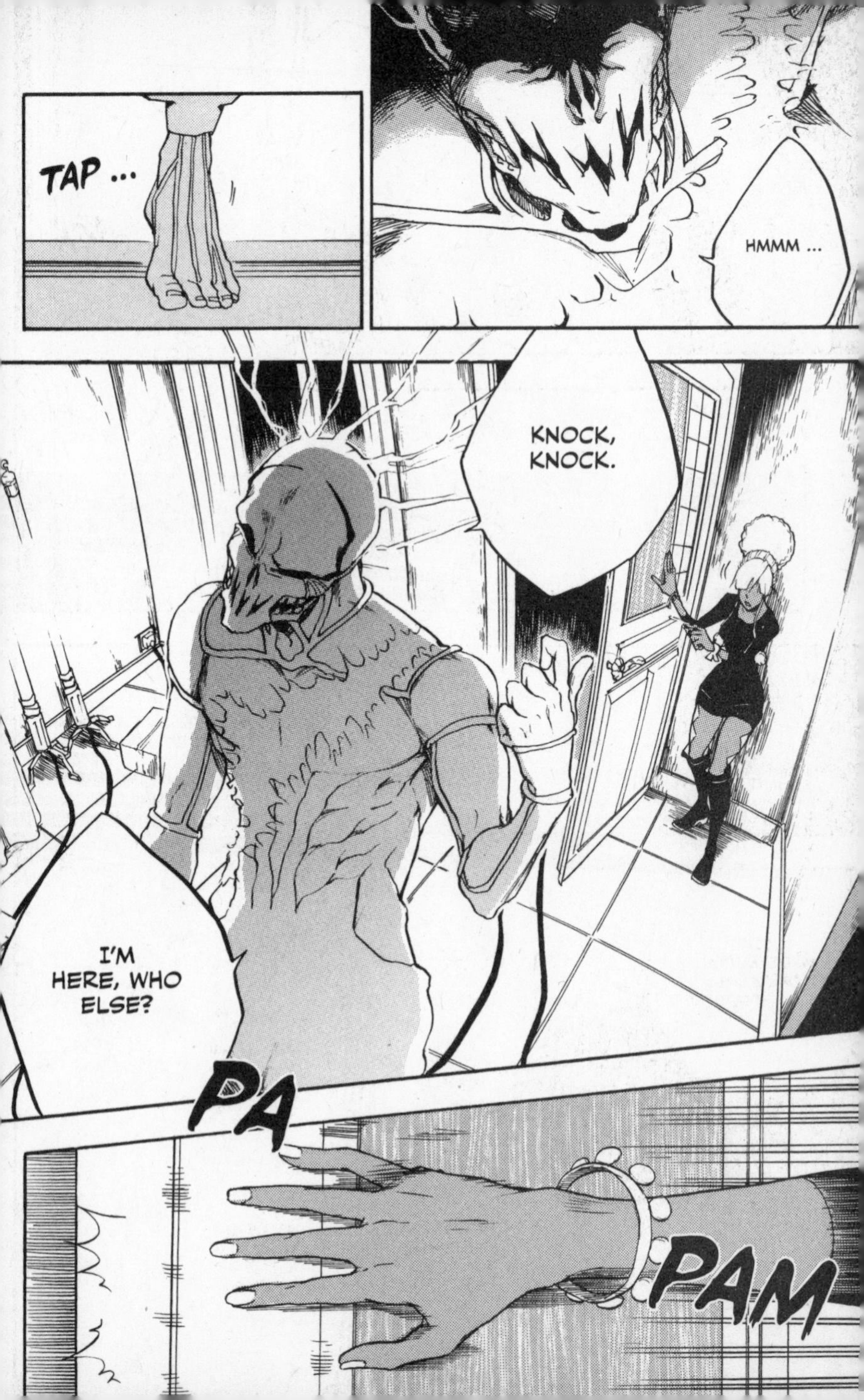
HMMM ...
TAP ...
KNOCK, KNOCK.
I'M HERE, WHO ELSE?
PA
PAM

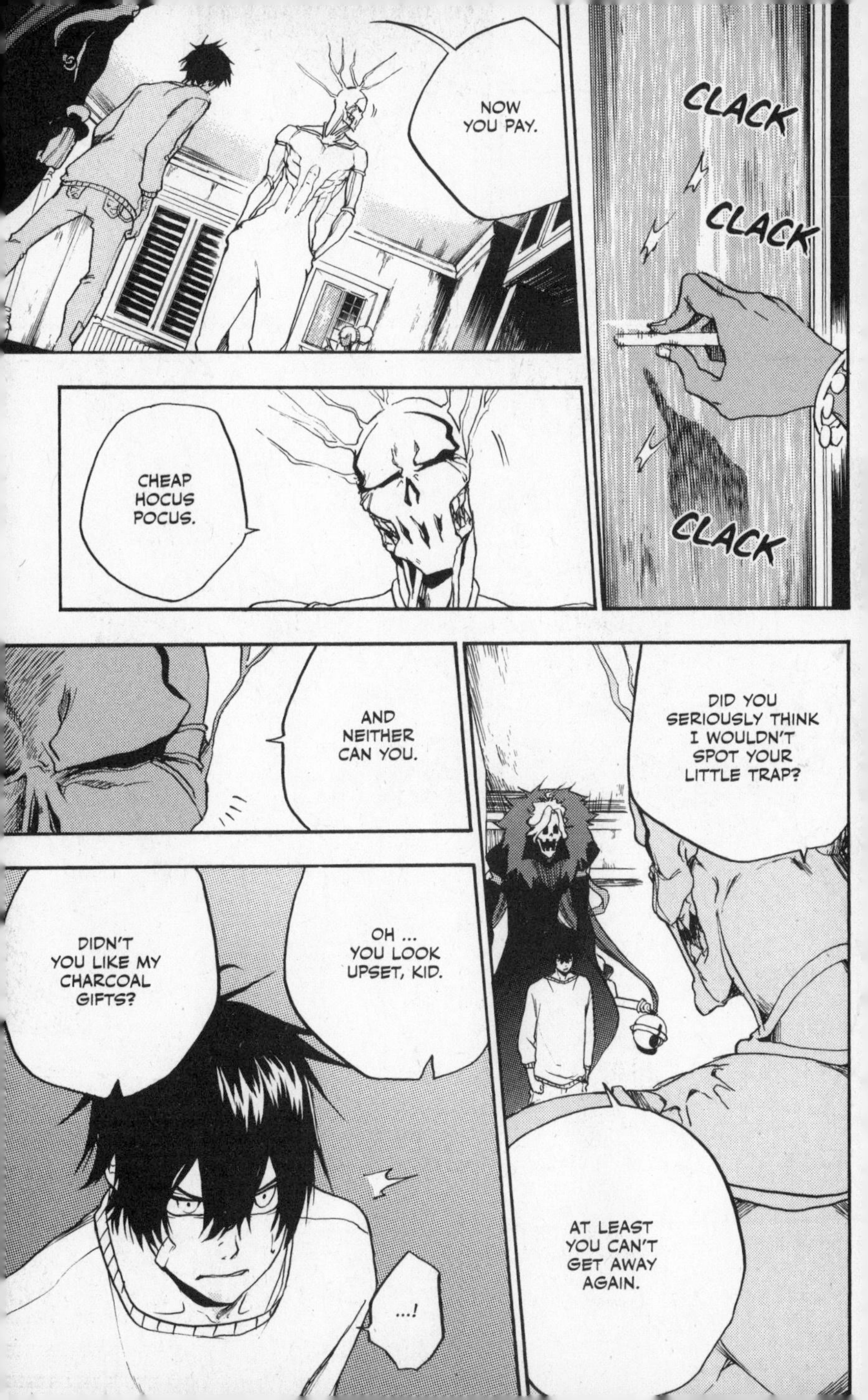
CLACK
CLACK
CLACK
NOW YOU PAY.
CHEAP HOCUS POCUS.
DID YOU SERIOUSLY THINK I WOULDN'T SPOT YOUR LITTLE TRAP?
AT LEAST YOU CAN'T GET AWAY AGAIN.
AND NEITHER CAN YOU.
OH ... YOU LOOK UPSET, KID.
DIDN'T YOU LIKE MY CHARCOAL GIFTS?
...!

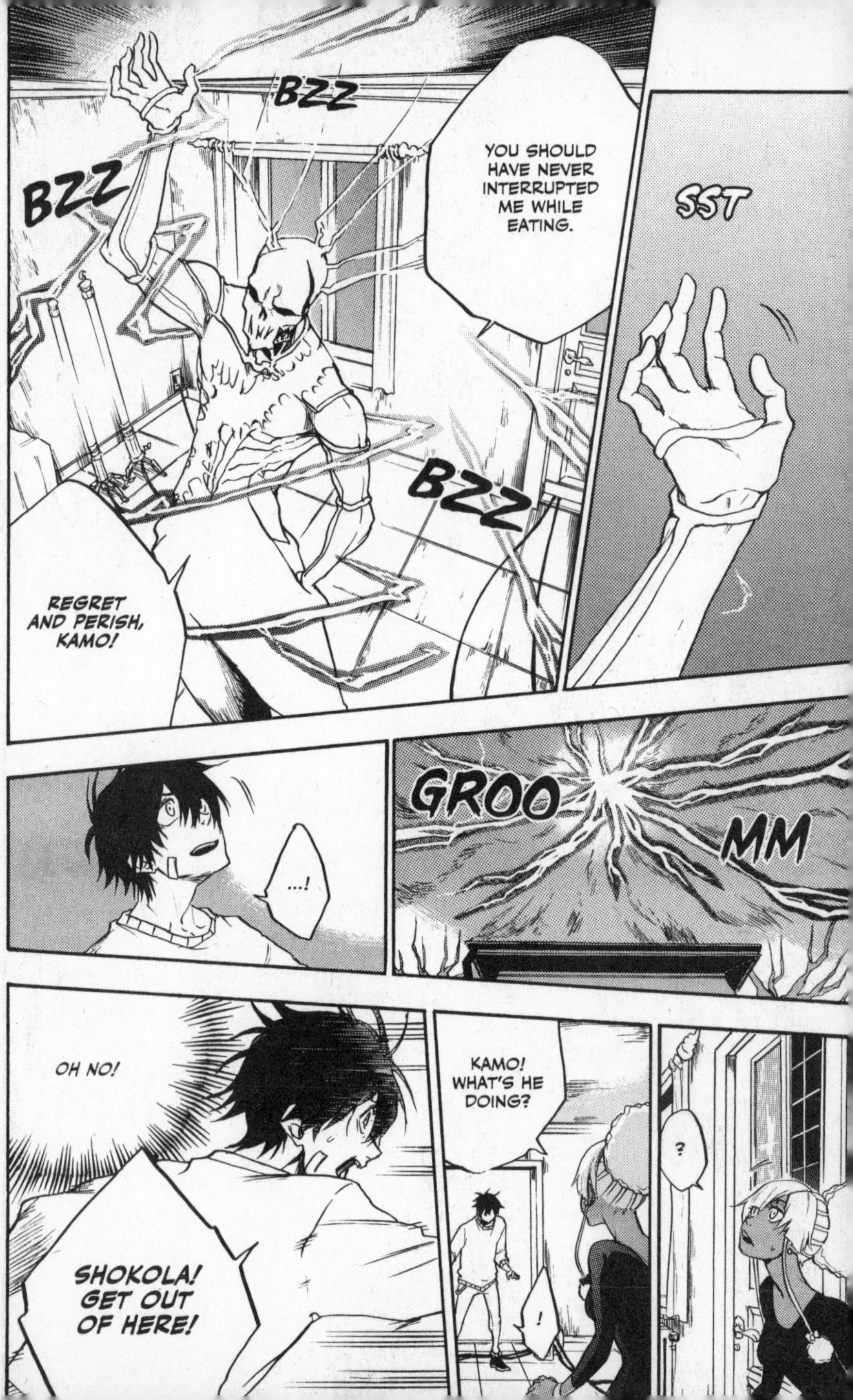
SST
YOU SHOULD HAVE NEVER INTERRUPTED ME WHILE EATING.
BZZ
BZZ
BZZ
REGRET AND PERISH, KAMO!
GROO
MM
...!
?
KAMO! WHAT'S HE DOING?
!
OH NO!
SHOKOLA! GET OUT OF HERE!

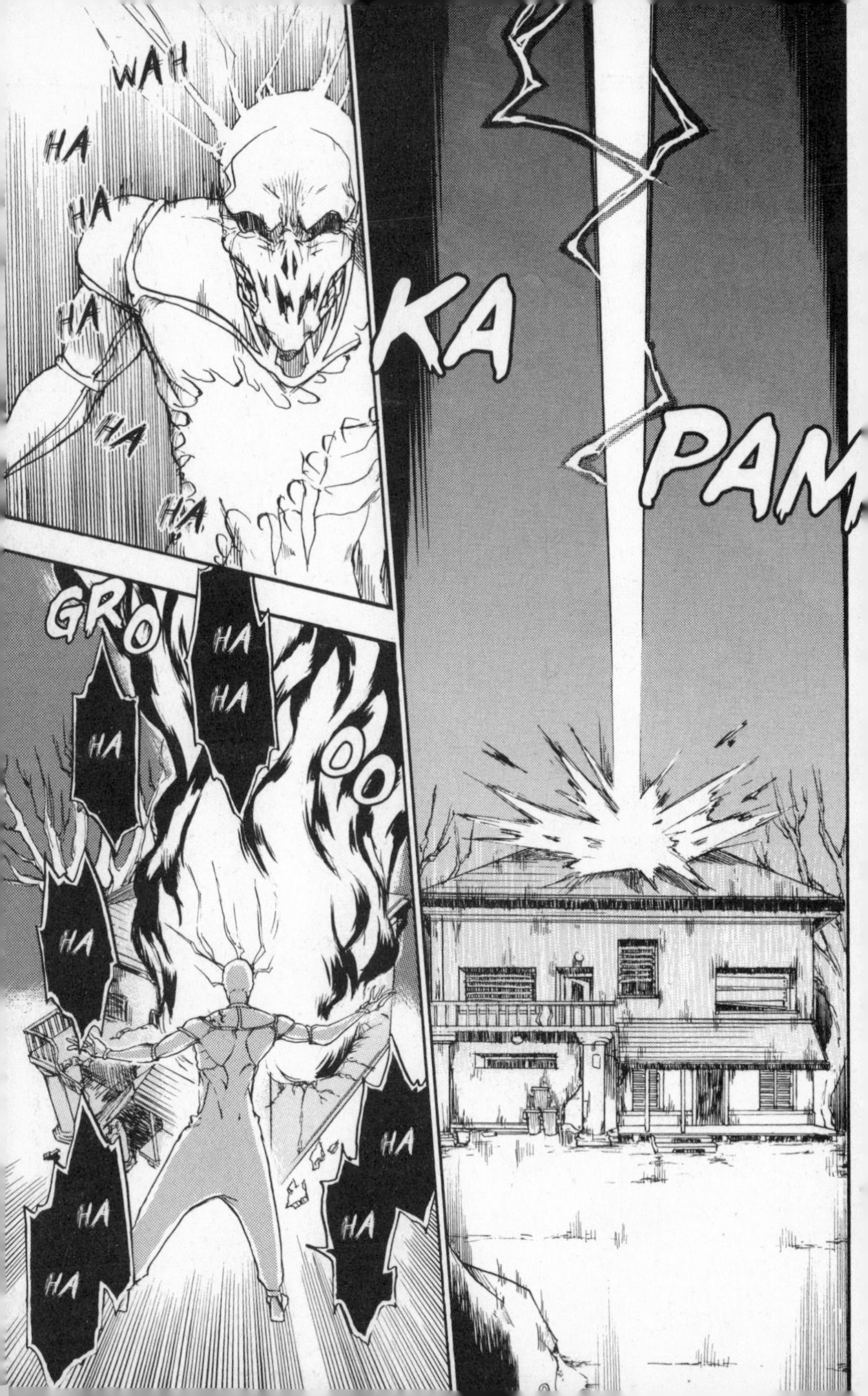
KA
PAM
WAH
HA
HA
HA
HA
HA
GRO
OO
HA
HA
HA
HA
HA
HA
HA
HA

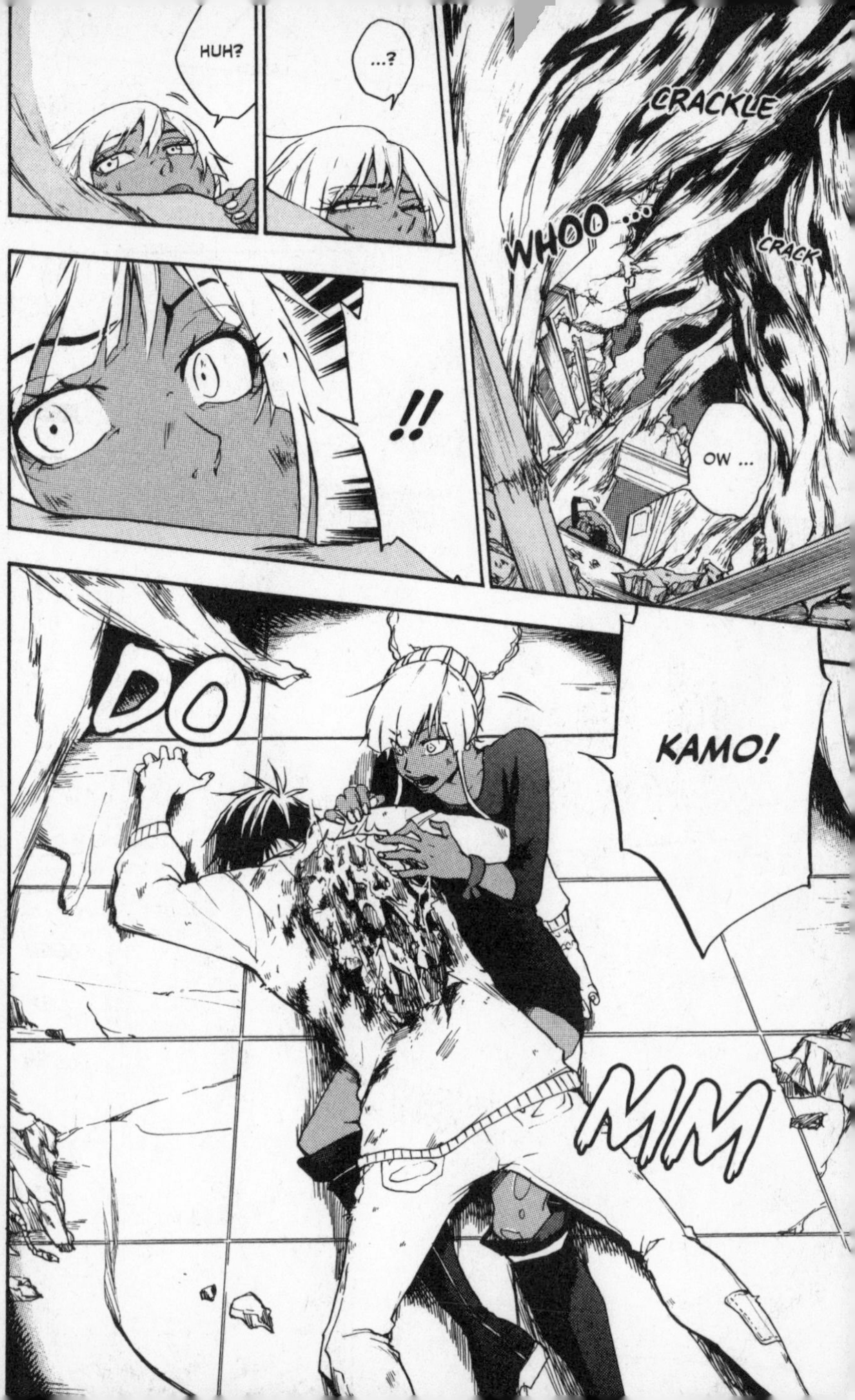
CRACKLE
WHOO ...
CRACK
OW ...
...?
HUH?
!!
KAMO!
DO
MM

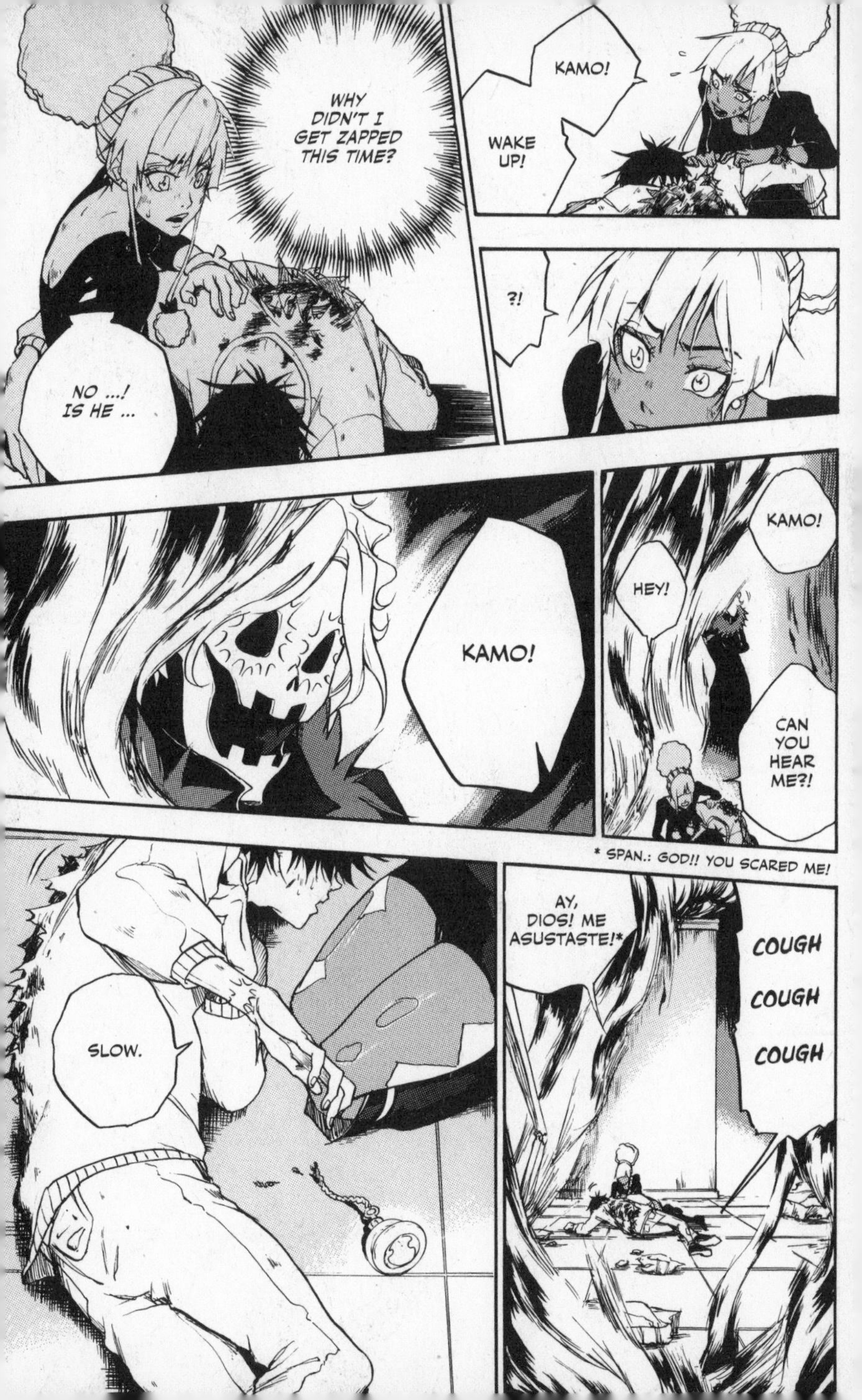
KAMO!
WAKE UP!
?!
WHY DIDN'T I GET ZAPPED THIS TIME?
NO ...! IS HE ...
KAMO!
HEY!
CAN YOU HEAR ME?!
KAMO!
* SPAN.: GOD!! YOU SCARED ME!
COUGH
COUGH
COUGH
AY, DIOS! ME ASUSTASTE!*
SLOW.

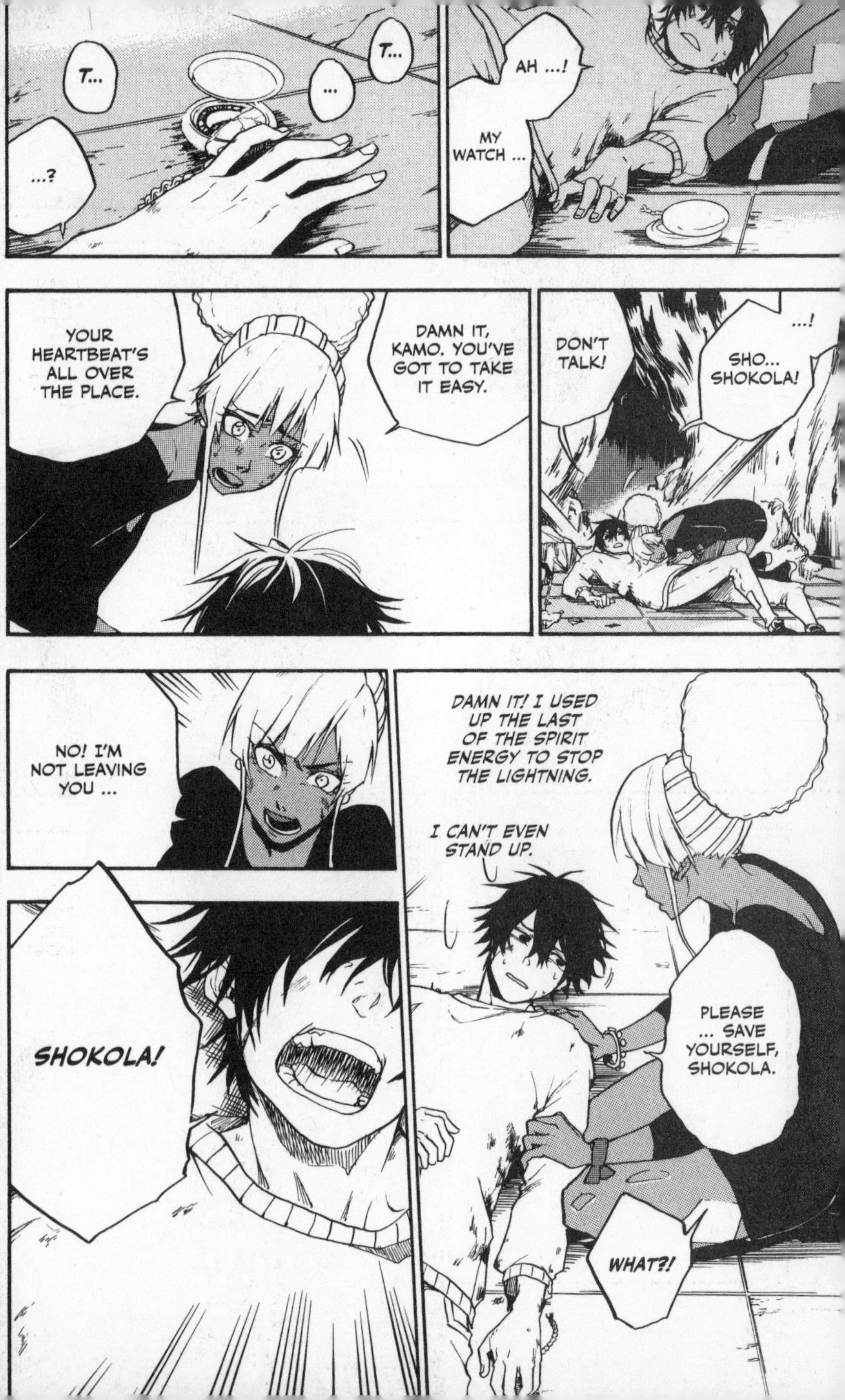
AH ...!
MY WATCH ...
T...
...
T...
...?
...!
SHO... SHOKOLA!
DON'T TALK!
DAMN IT, KAMO. YOU'VE GOT TO TAKE IT EASY.
YOUR HEARTBEAT'S ALL OVER THE PLACE.
DAMN IT! I USED UP THE LAST OF THE SPIRIT ENERGY TO STOP THE LIGHTNING.
I CAN'T EVEN STAND UP.
PLEASE ... SAVE YOURSELF, SHOKOLA.
WHAT?!
NO! I'M NOT LEAVING YOU ...
SHOKOLA!

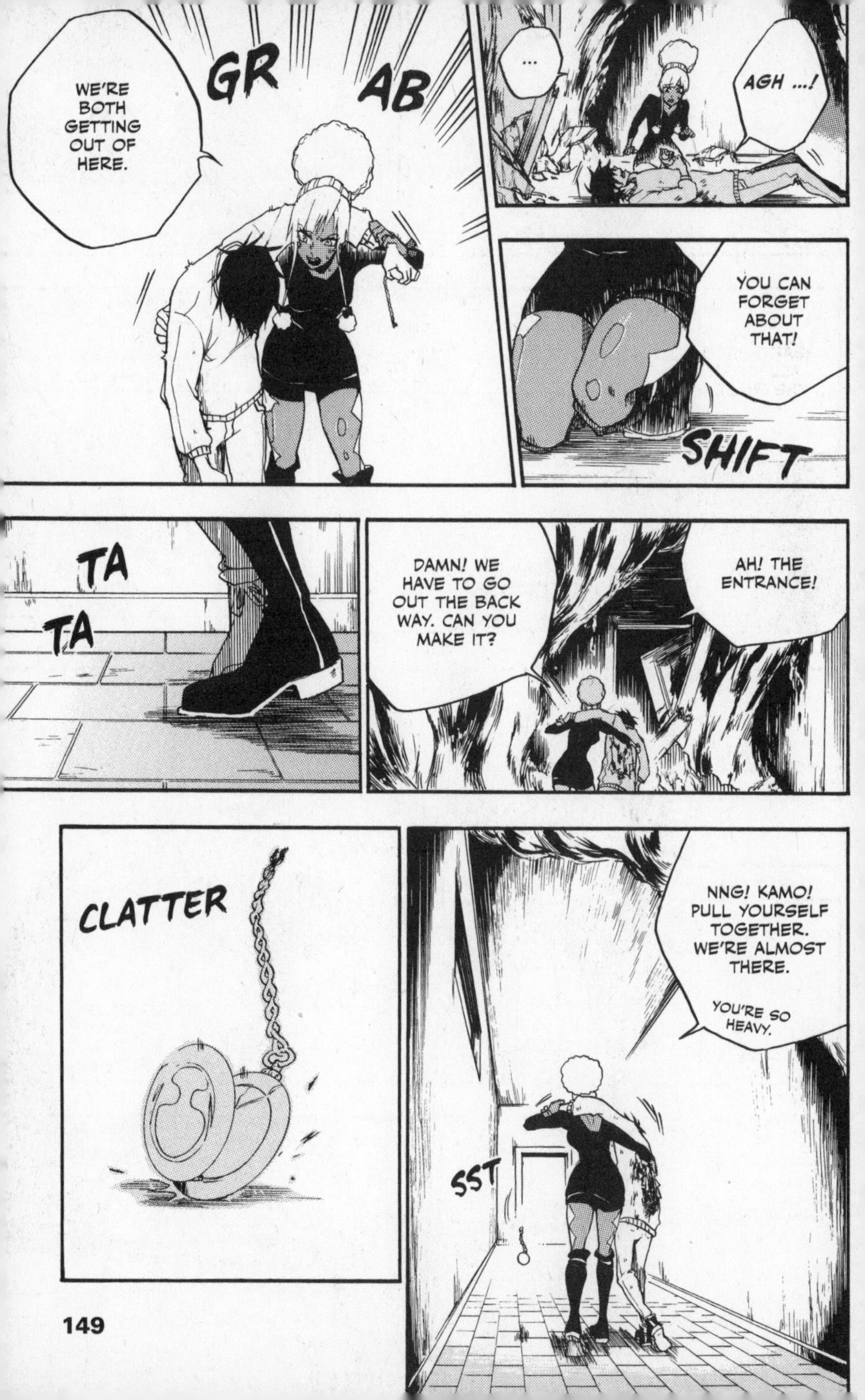
AGH ...!
...
YOU CAN FORGET ABOUT THAT!
SHIFT
WE'RE BOTH GETTING OUT OF HERE.
GR AB
AH! THE ENTRANCE!
DAMN! WE HAVE TO GO OUT THE BACK WAY. CAN YOU MAKE IT?
TA TA
NNG! KAMO! PULL YOURSELF TOGETHER. WE'RE ALMOST THERE.
YOU'RE SO HEAVY.
SST
CLATTER

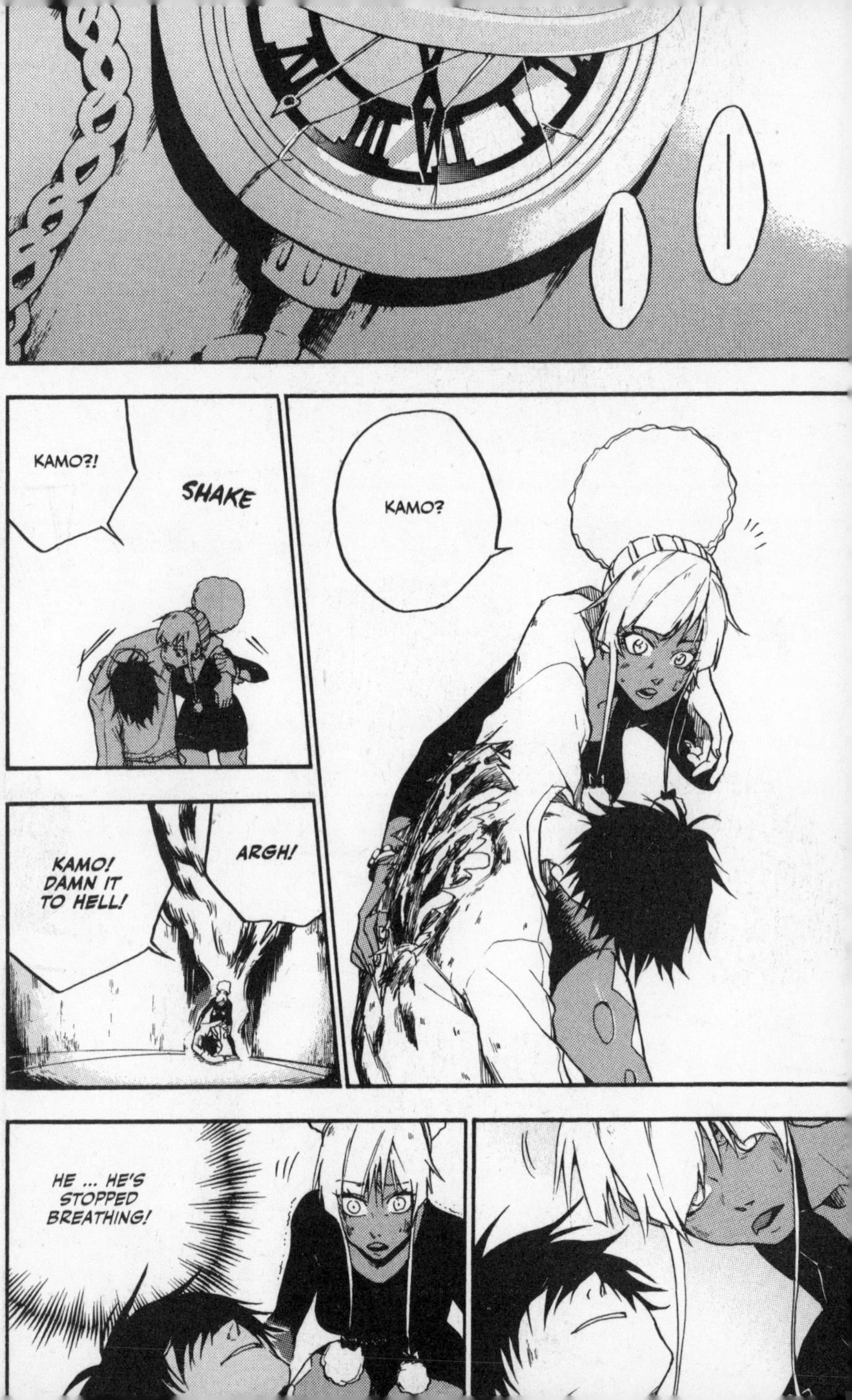
KAMO?
KAMO?!
SHAKE
ARGH!
KAMO! DAMN IT TO HELL!
HE ... HE'S STOPPED BREATHING!

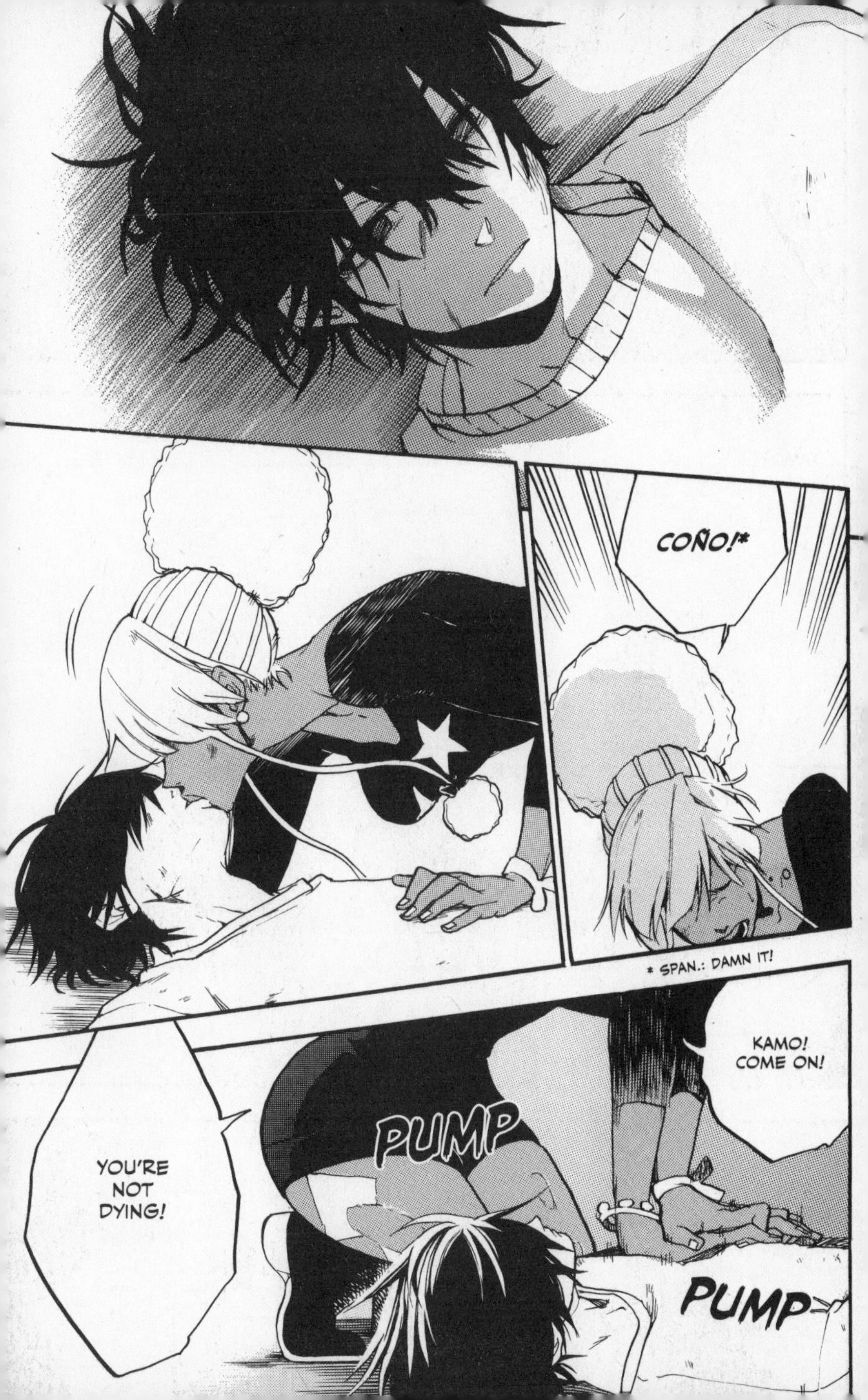
COÑO!*
* SPAN.: DAMN IT!
KAMO! COME ON!
PUMP
PUMP
YOU'RE NOT DYING!

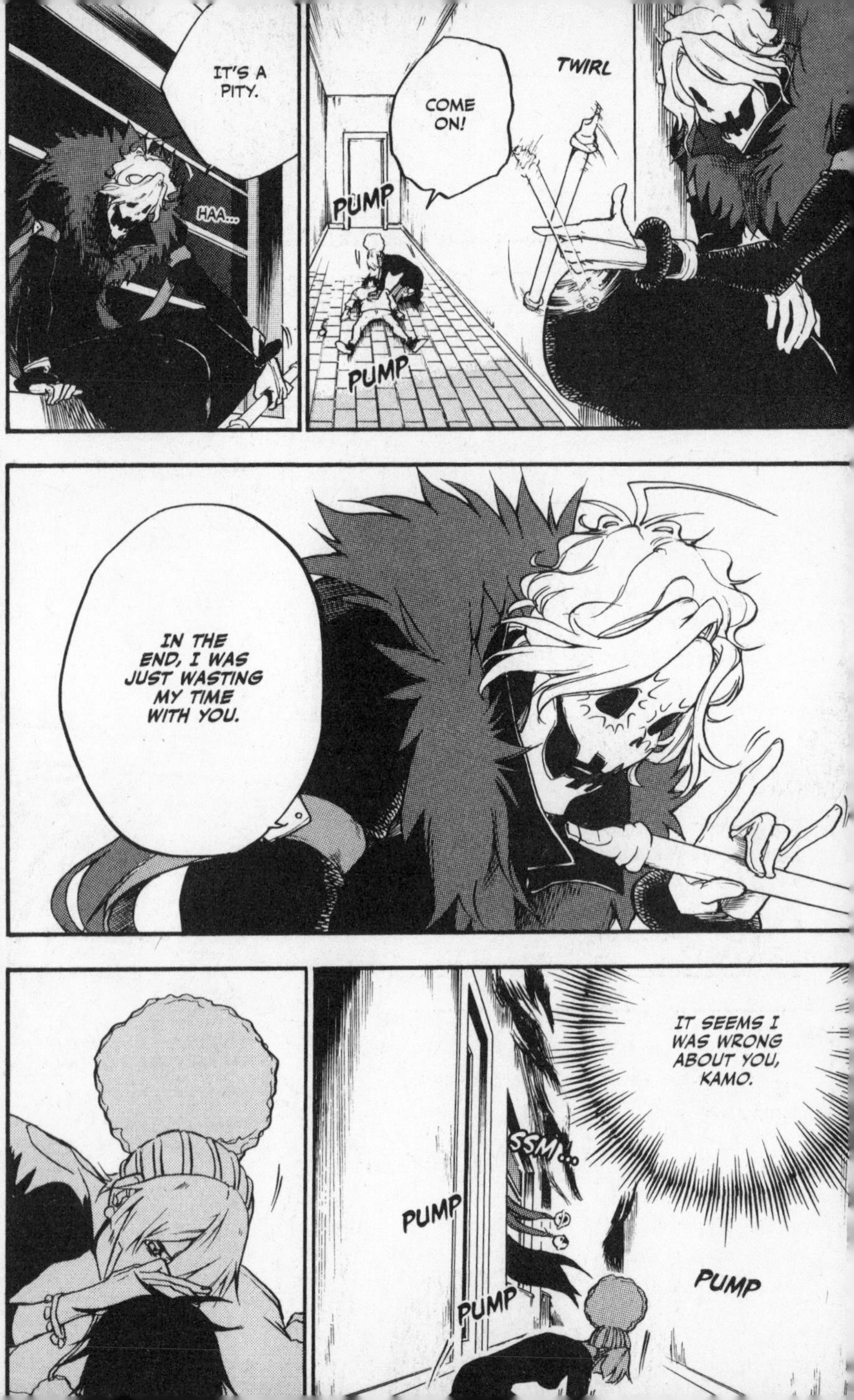
TWIRL
COME ON!
PUMP
PUMP
IT'S A PITY.
HAA...
IN THE END, I WAS JUST WASTING MY TIME WITH YOU.
IT SEEMS I WAS WRONG ABOUT YOU, KAMO.
SSM...
PUMP
PUMP
PUMP

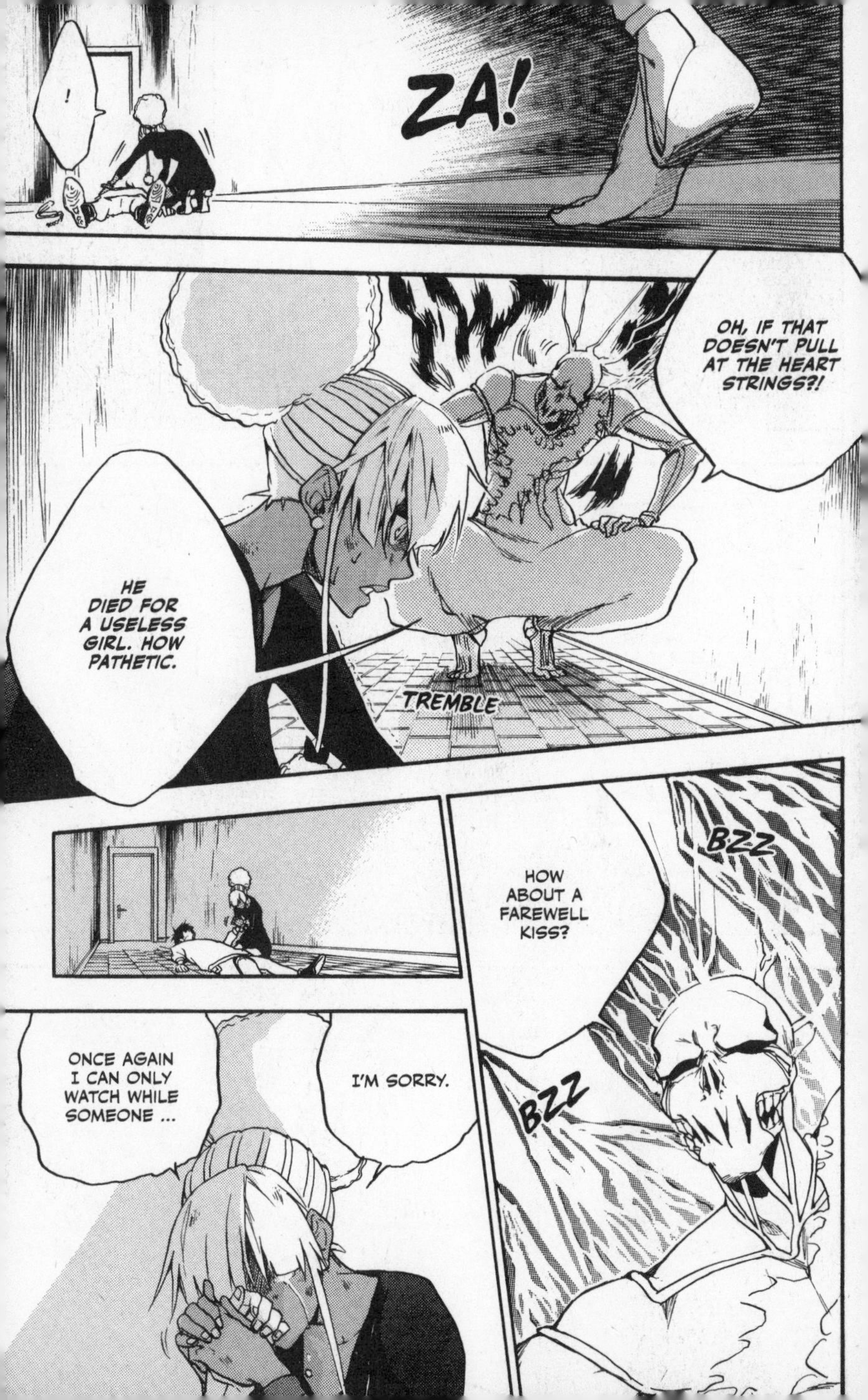
ZA!
!
OH, IF THAT DOESN'T PULL AT THE HEART STRINGS?!
HE DIED FOR A USELESS GIRL. HOW PATHETIC.
TREMBLE
BZZZ
HOW ABOUT A FAREWELL KISS?
BZZ
I'M SORRY.
ONCE AGAIN I CAN ONLY WATCH WHILE SOMEONE ...

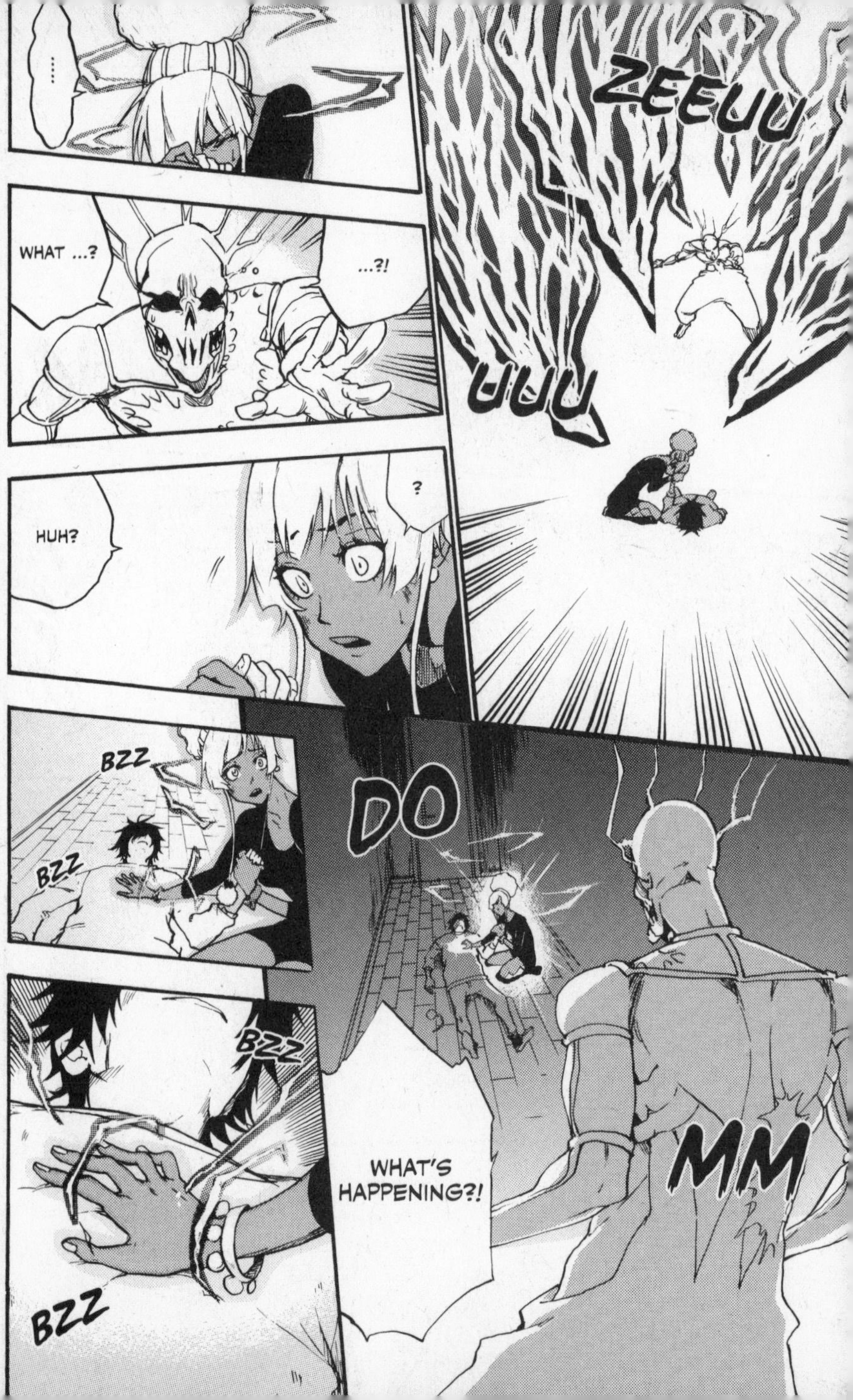
ZEEUU
UUU
......
...?!
WHAT ...?
?
HUH?
DO
MM
WHAT'S HAPPENING?!
BZZ
BZZ
BZZ
BZZ

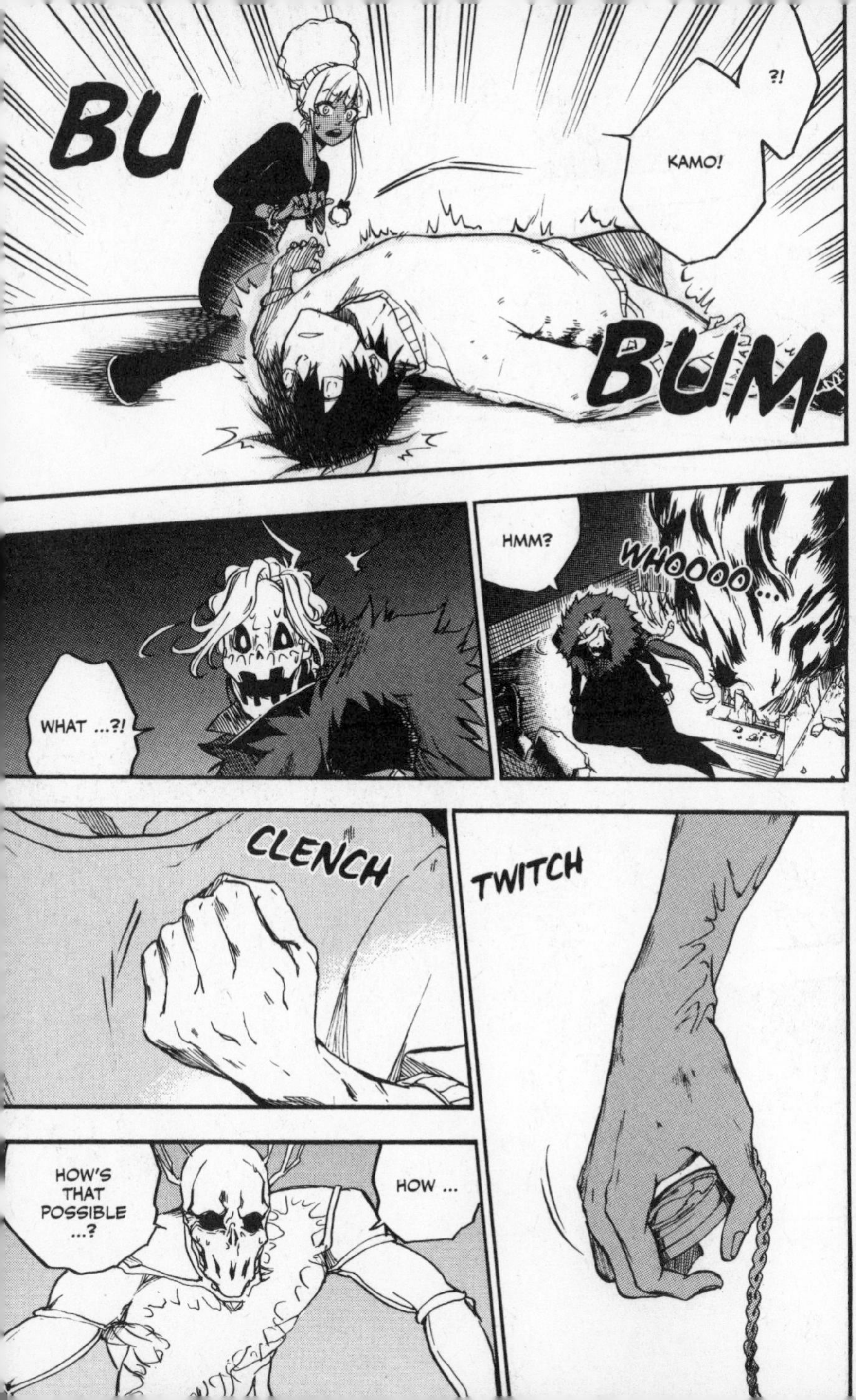
?!
KAMO!
BU
BUM
HMM?
WHOOOO ...
WHAT ...?!
TWITCH
CLENCH
HOW ...
HOW'S THAT POSSIBLE ...?

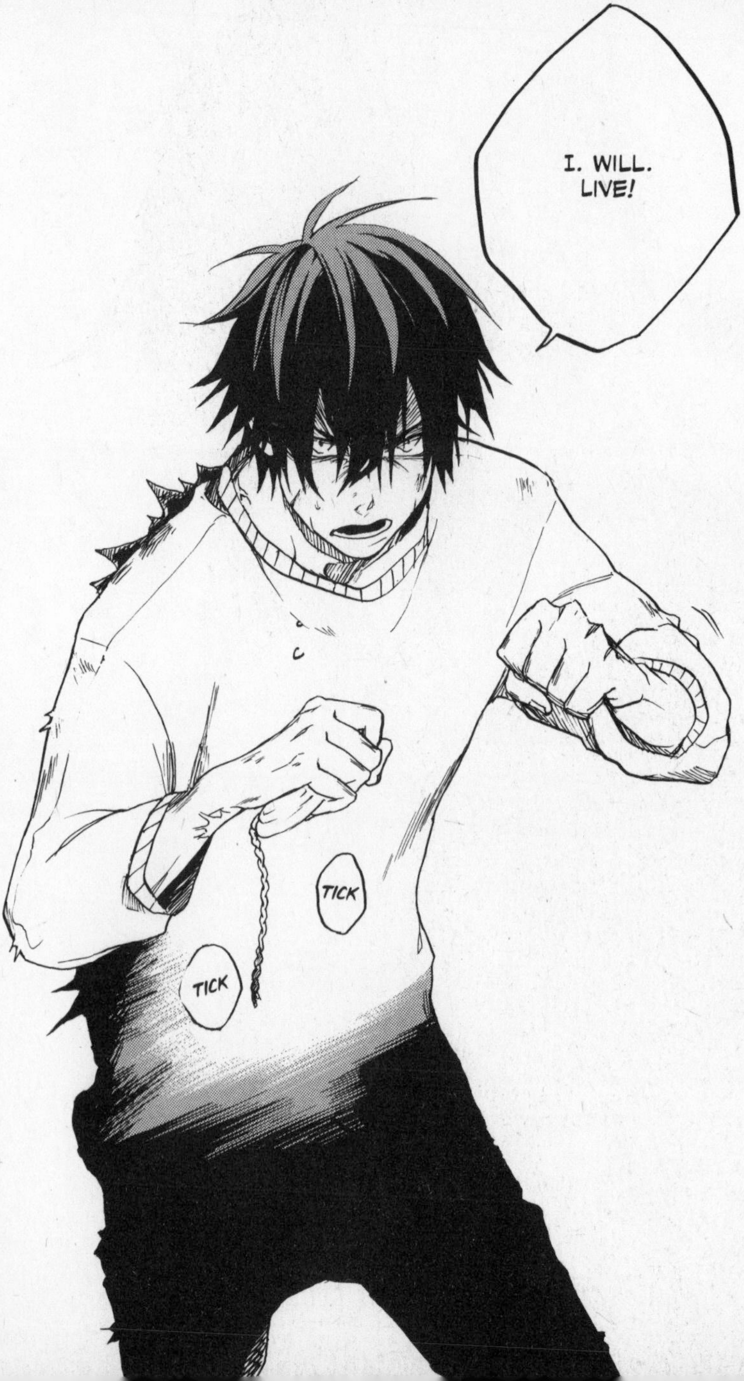
I. WILL.
LIVE!
TICK
TICK

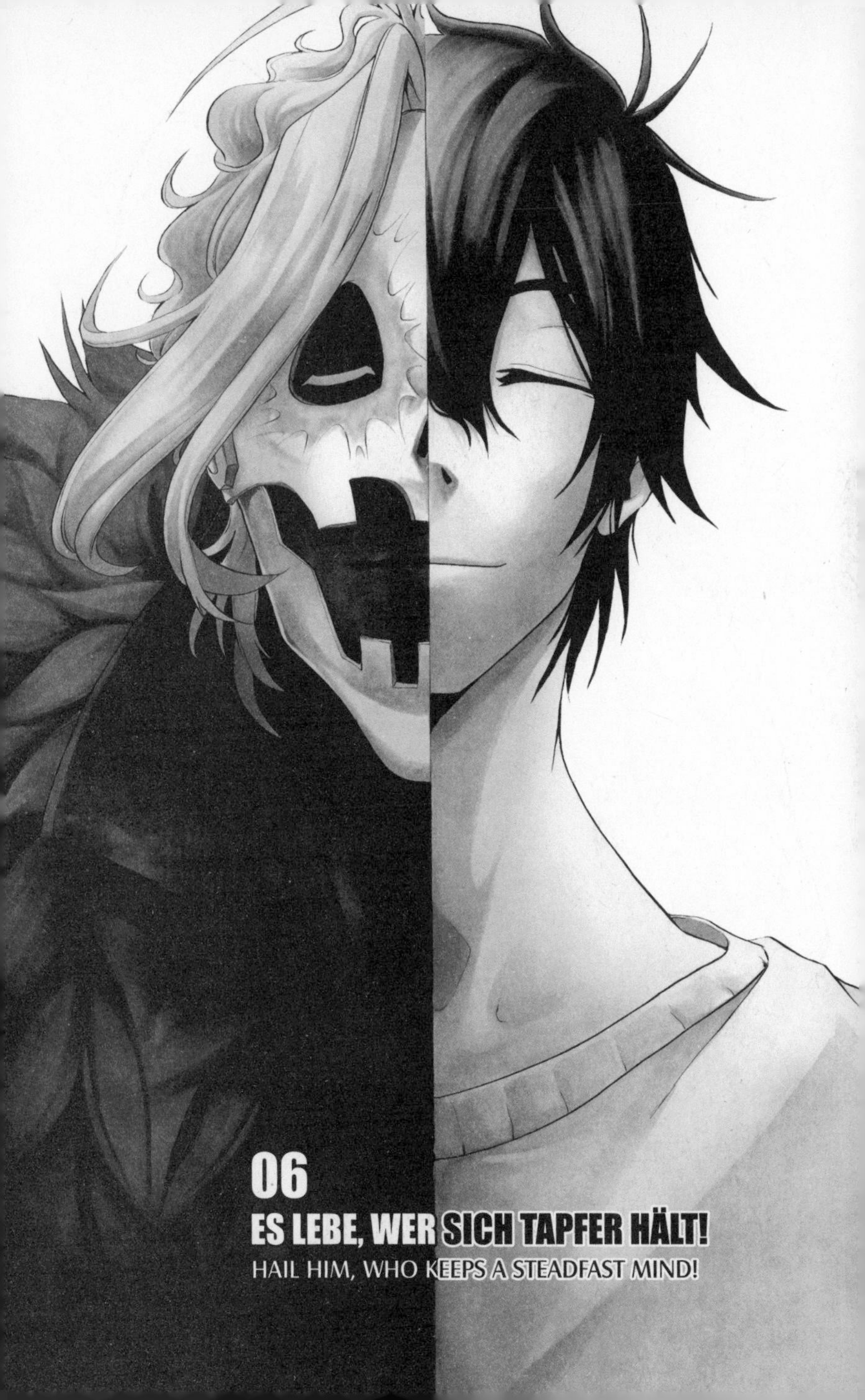
06
ES LEBE, WER SICH TAPFER HÄLT!
HAIL HIM, WHO KEEPS A STEADFAST MIND!

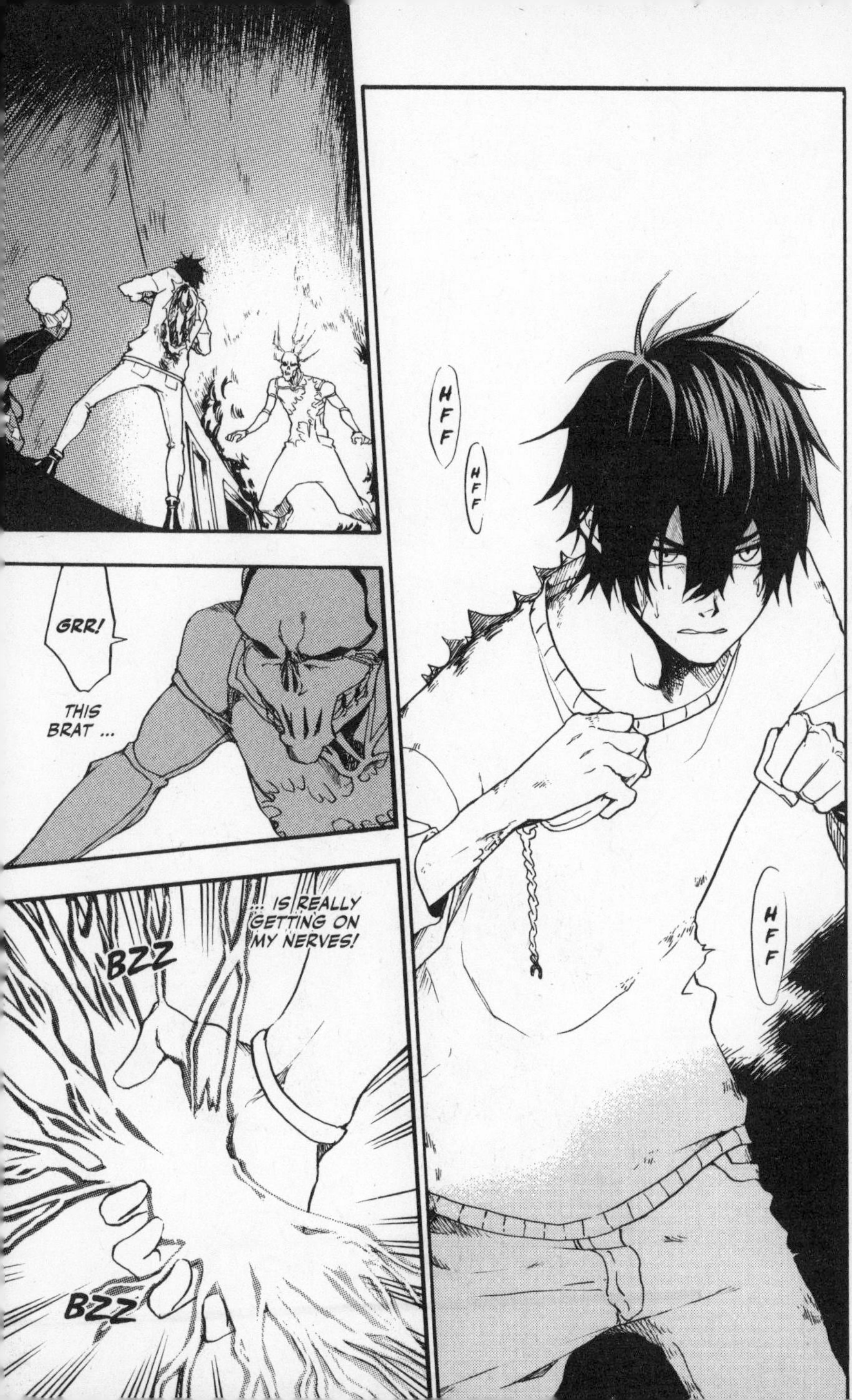
HFF
HFF
HFF
GRR!
THIS BRAT ...
... IS REALLY GETTING ON MY NERVES!
BZZ
BZZ

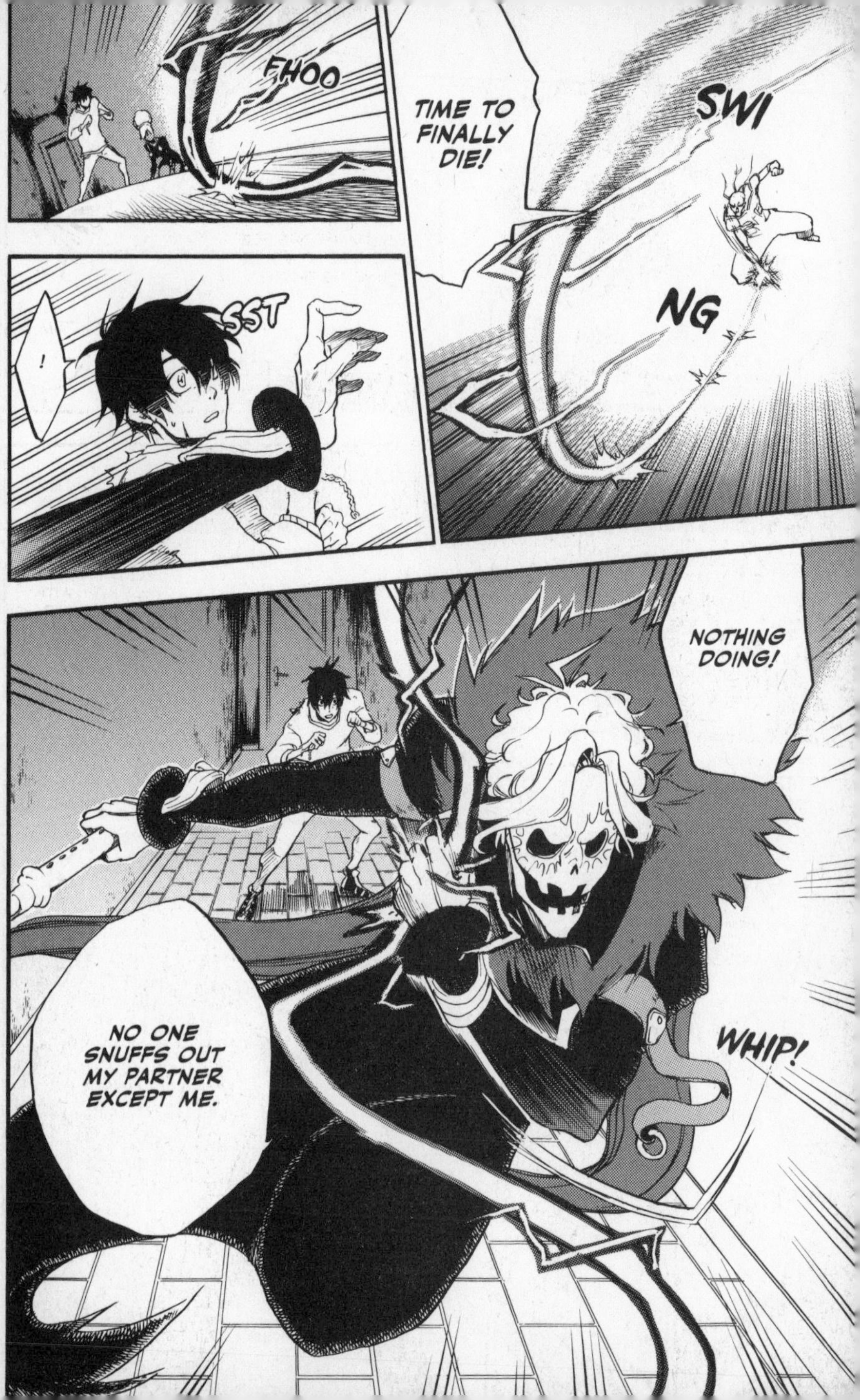
TIME TO FINALLY DIE!
SWI
NG
FHOO
SST
!
NOTHING DOING!
WHIP!
NO ONE SNUFFS OUT MY PARTNER EXCEPT ME.

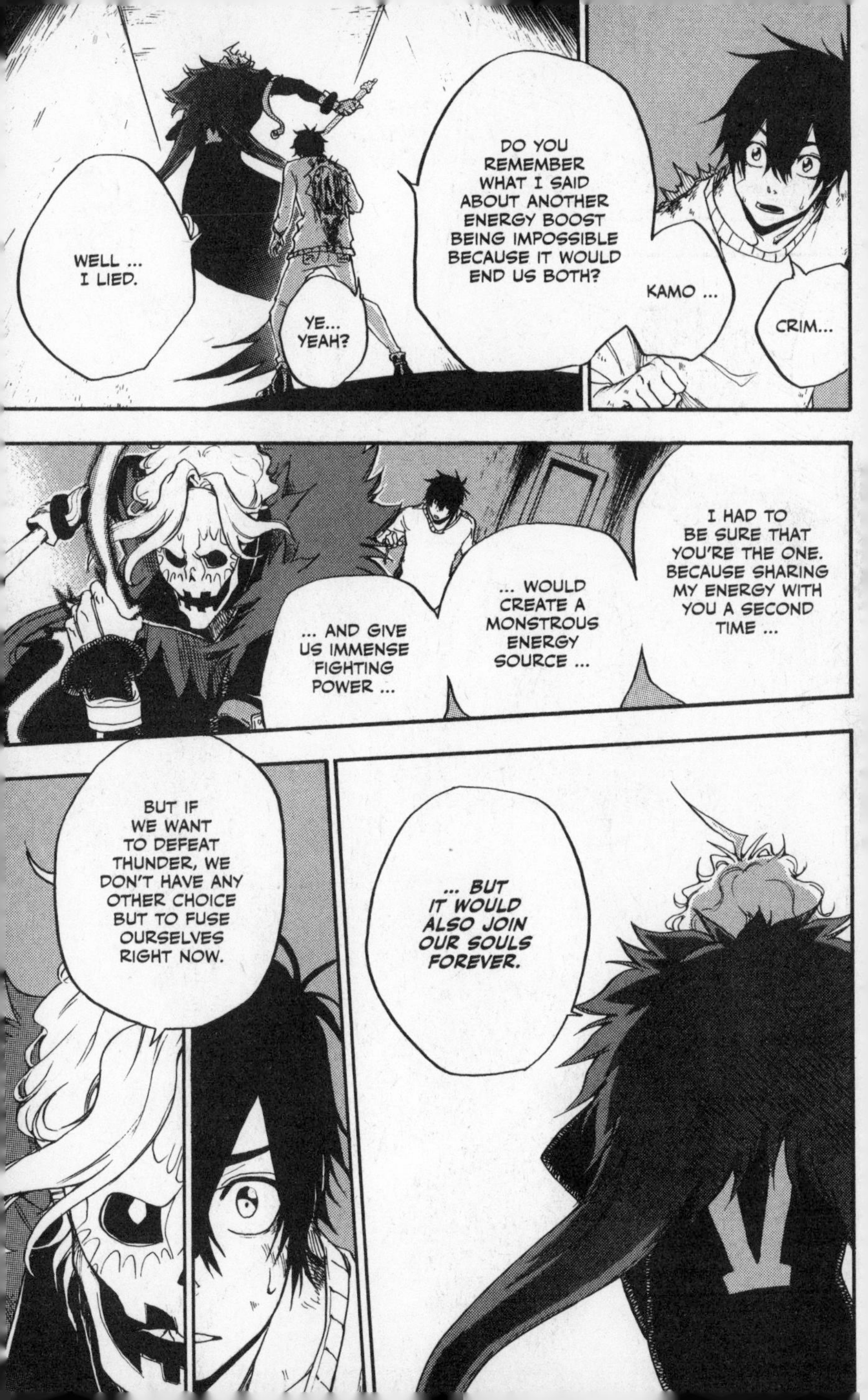
CRIM...
KAMO ...
DO YOU REMEMBER WHAT I SAID ABOUT ANOTHER ENERGY BOOST BEING IMPOSSIBLE BECAUSE IT WOULD END US BOTH?
YE... YEAH?
WELL ... I LIED.
I HAD TO BE SURE THAT YOU'RE THE ONE. BECAUSE SHARING MY ENERGY WITH YOU A SECOND TIME ...
... WOULD CREATE A MONSTROUS ENERGY SOURCE ...
... AND GIVE US IMMENSE FIGHTING POWER ...
... BUT IT WOULD ALSO JOIN OUR SOULS FOREVER.
BUT IF WE WANT TO DEFEAT THUNDER, WE DON'T HAVE ANY OTHER CHOICE BUT TO FUSE OURSELVES RIGHT NOW.

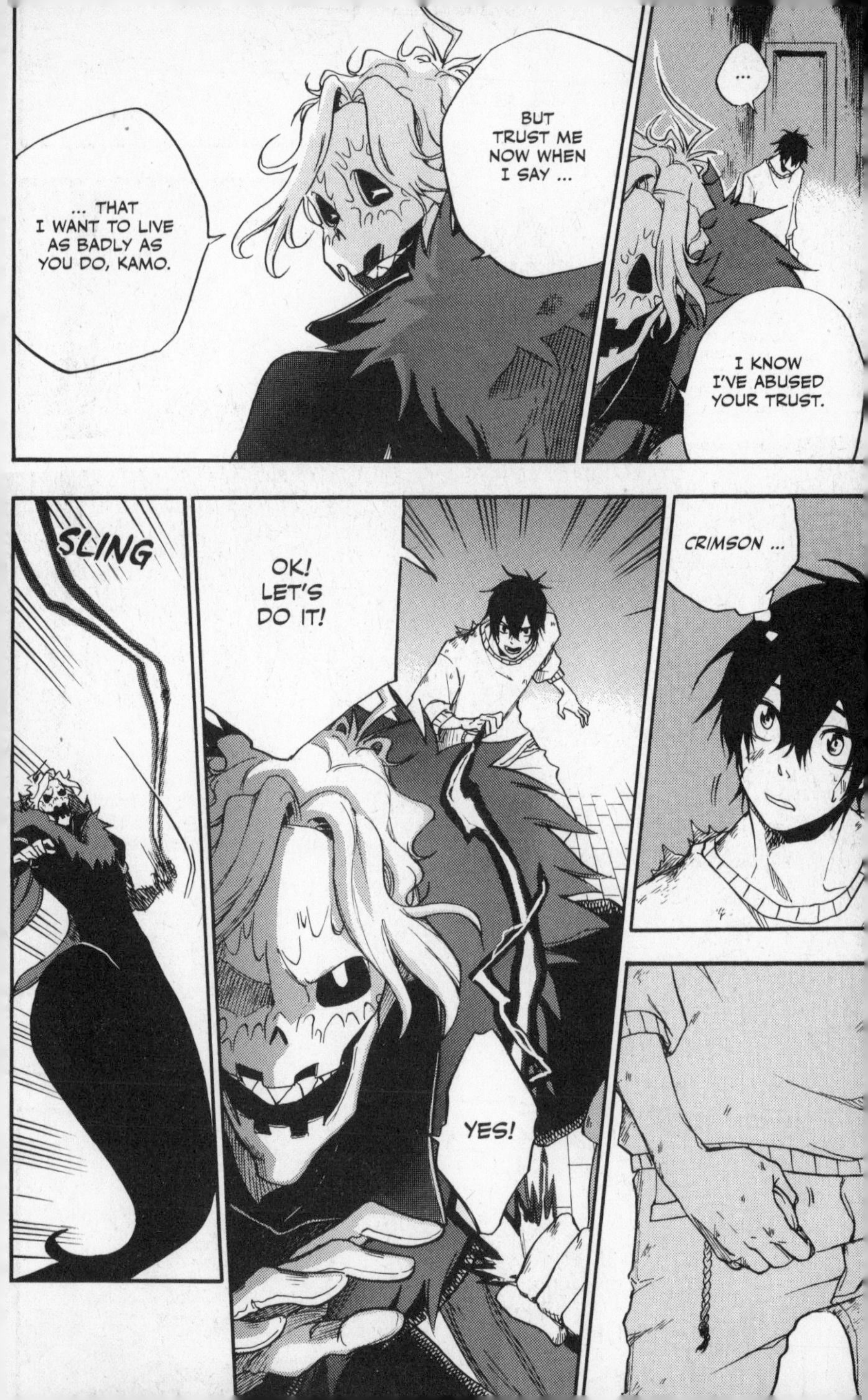
...
I KNOW I'VE ABUSED YOUR TRUST.
BUT TRUST ME NOW WHEN I SAY ...
... THAT I WANT TO LIVE AS BADLY AS YOU DO, KAMO.
CRIMSON ...
OK! LET'S DO IT!
YES!
SLING

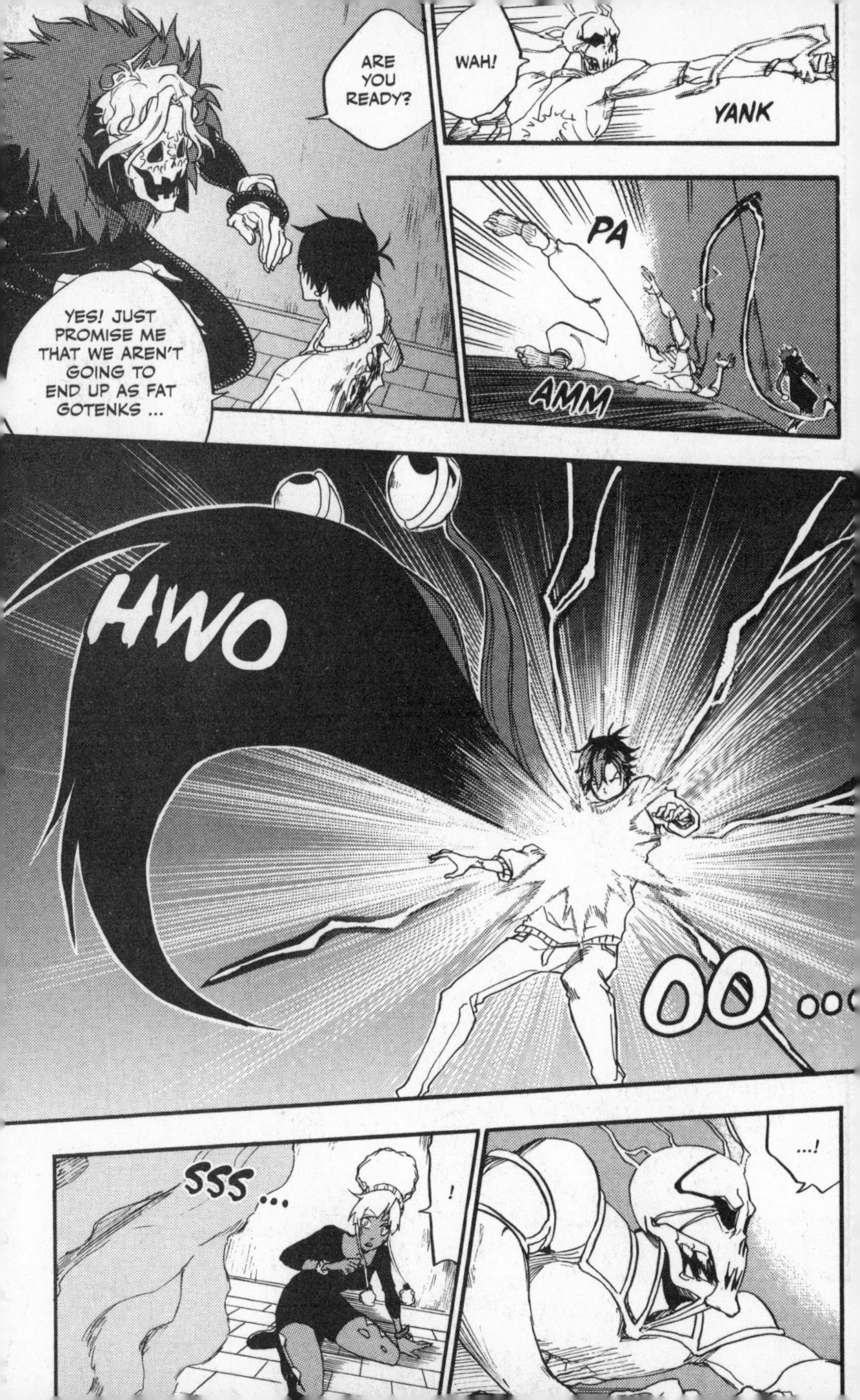
WAH!
YANK
PA
AMM
ARE YOU READY?
YES! JUST PROMISE ME THAT WE AREN'T GOING TO END UP AS FAT GOTENKS ...
HWO
OO...
...!
SSS...
!

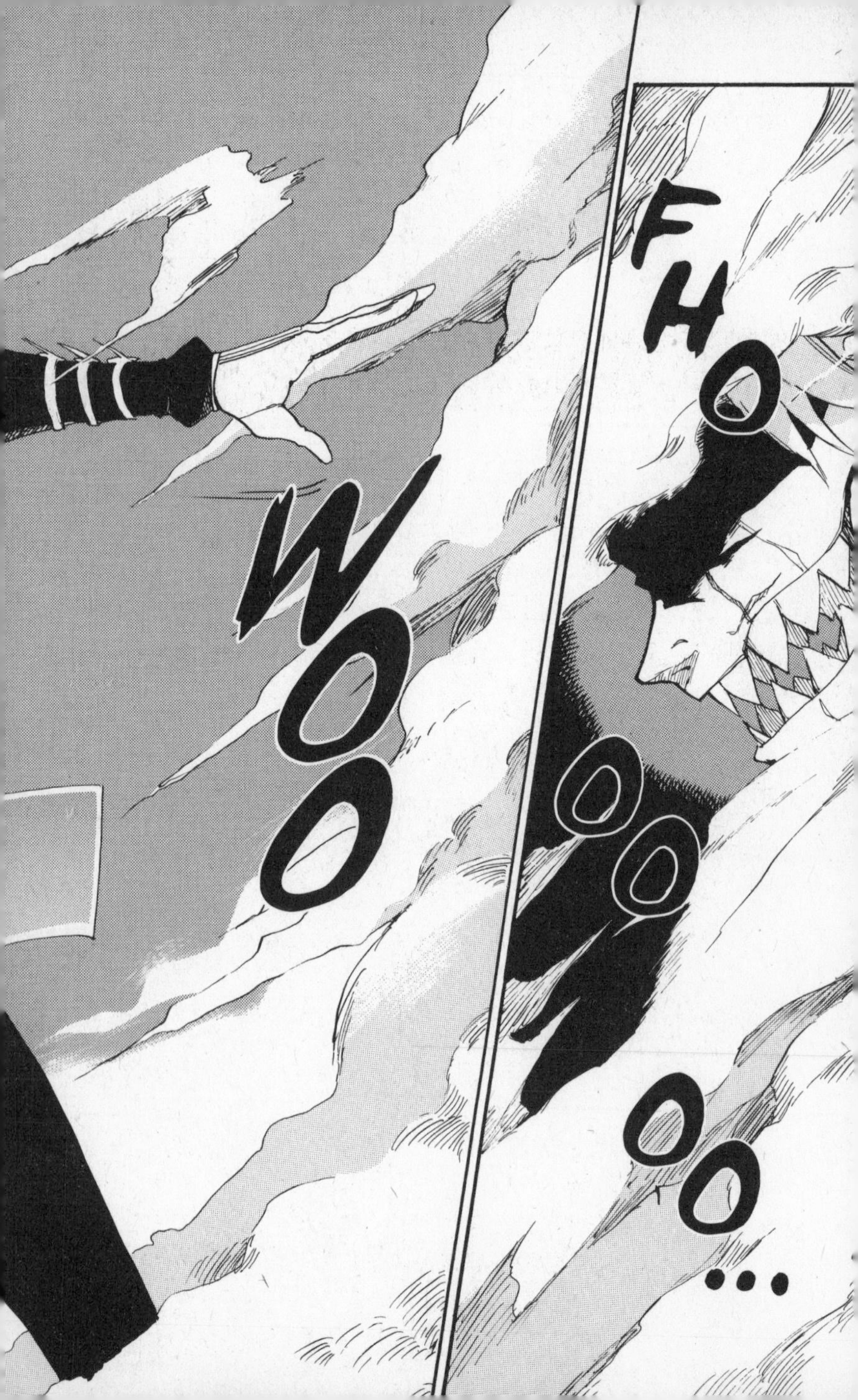
FHOOOOO...
WOO

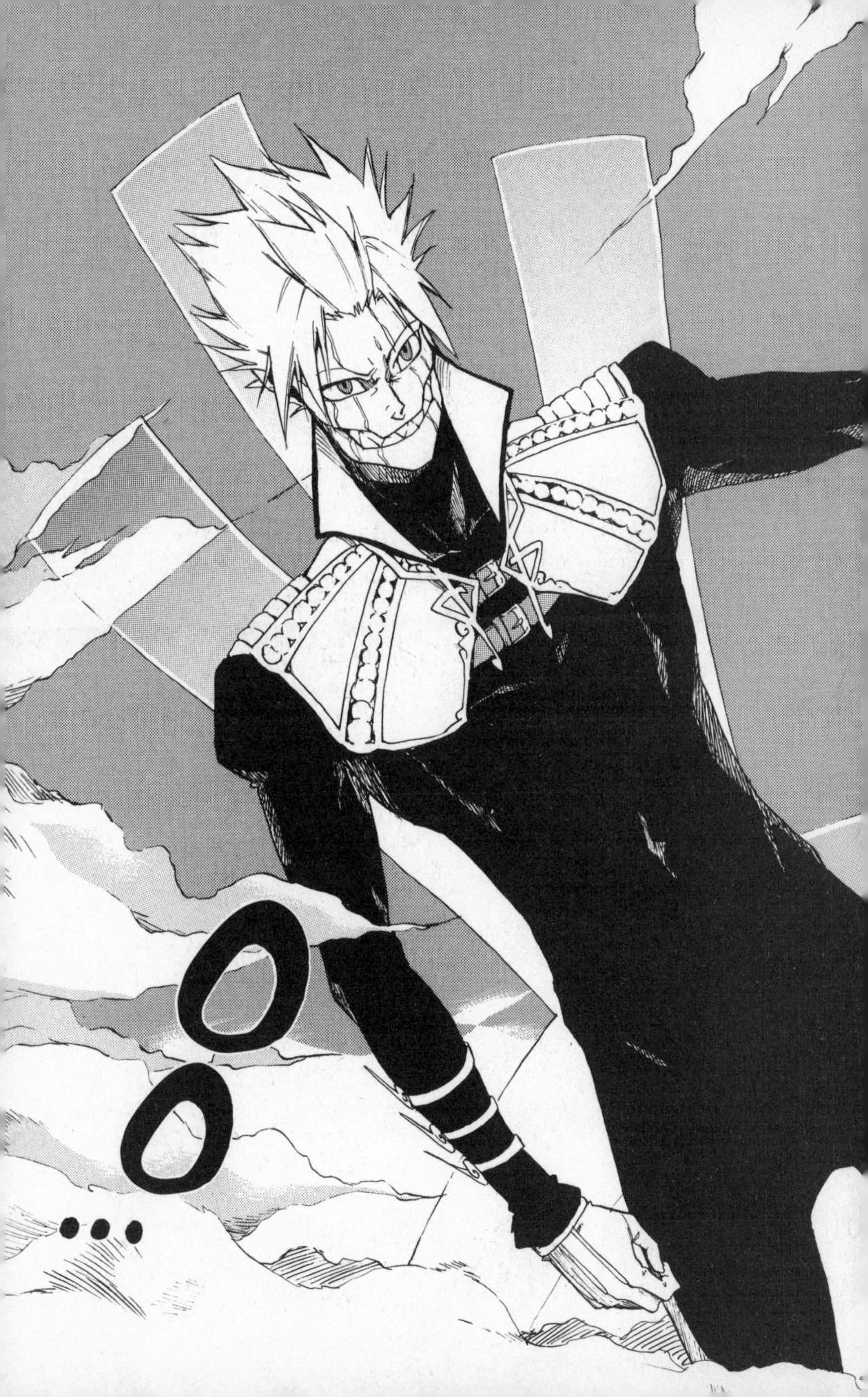
OO...

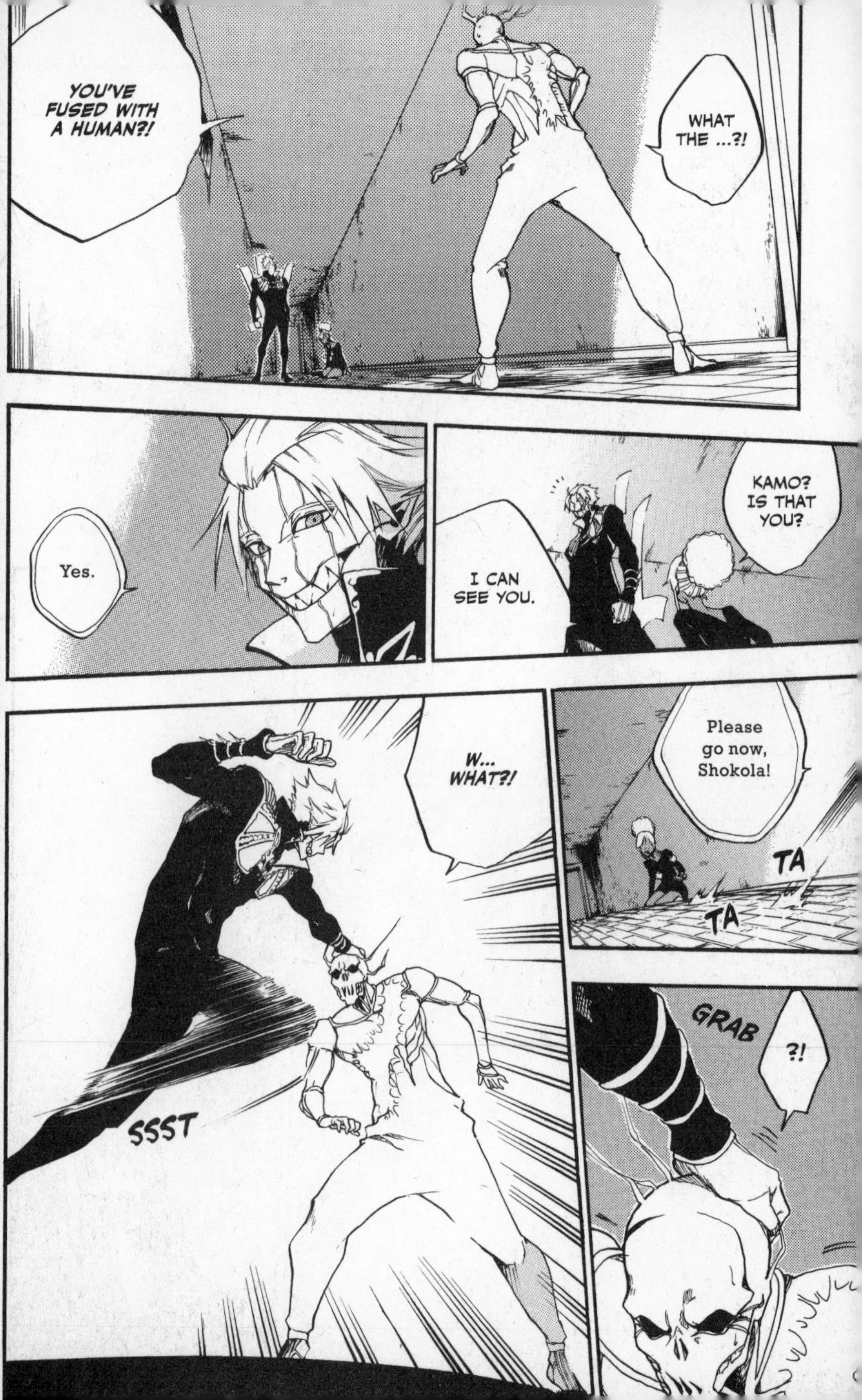
WHAT THE ...?!
YOU'VE FUSED WITH A HUMAN?!
KAMO? IS THAT YOU?
I CAN SEE YOU.
Yes.
Please go now, Shokola!
TA
TA
GRAB
?!
W... WHAT?!
SSST

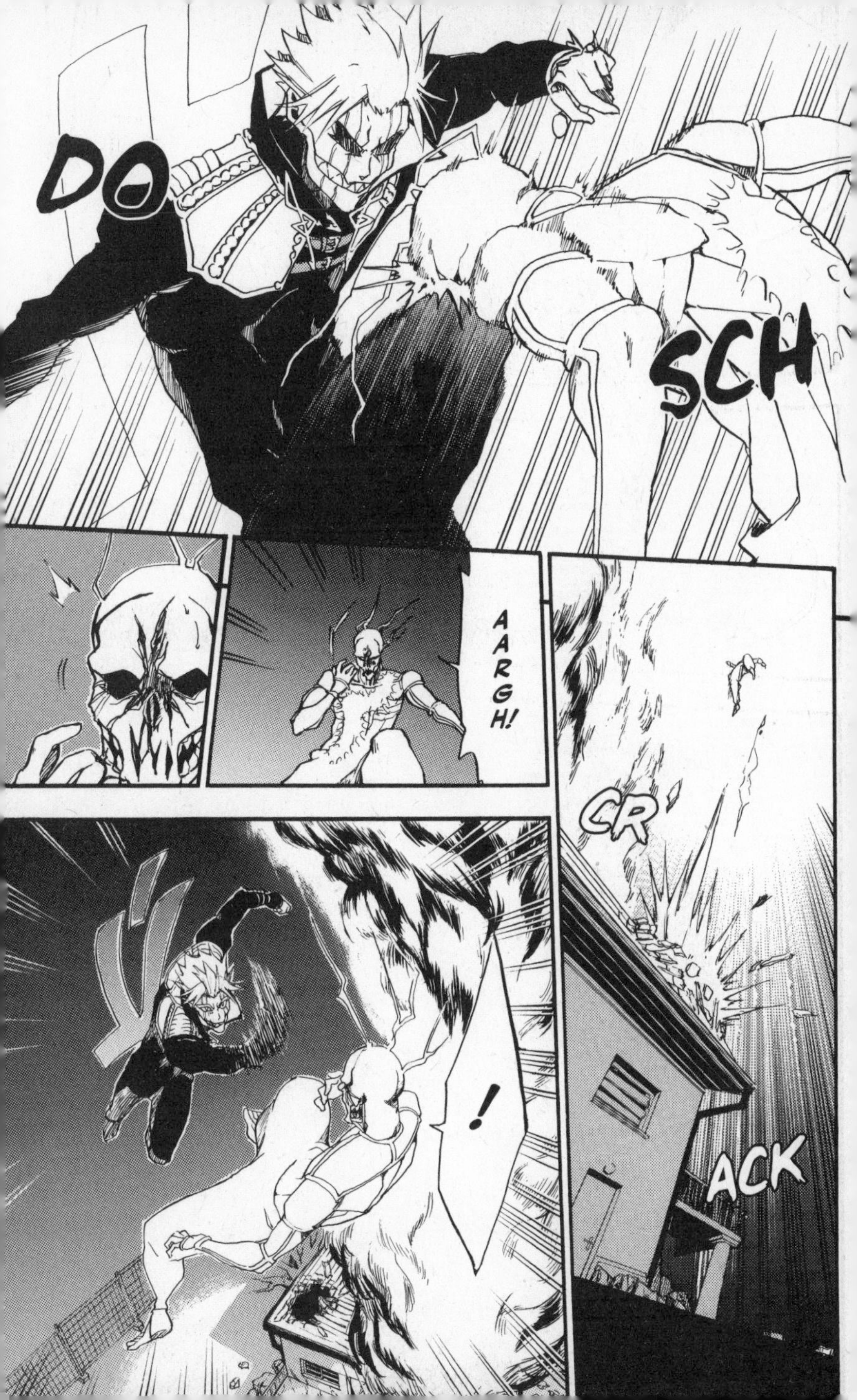
DO
SCH
CR
ACK
AARGH!
!

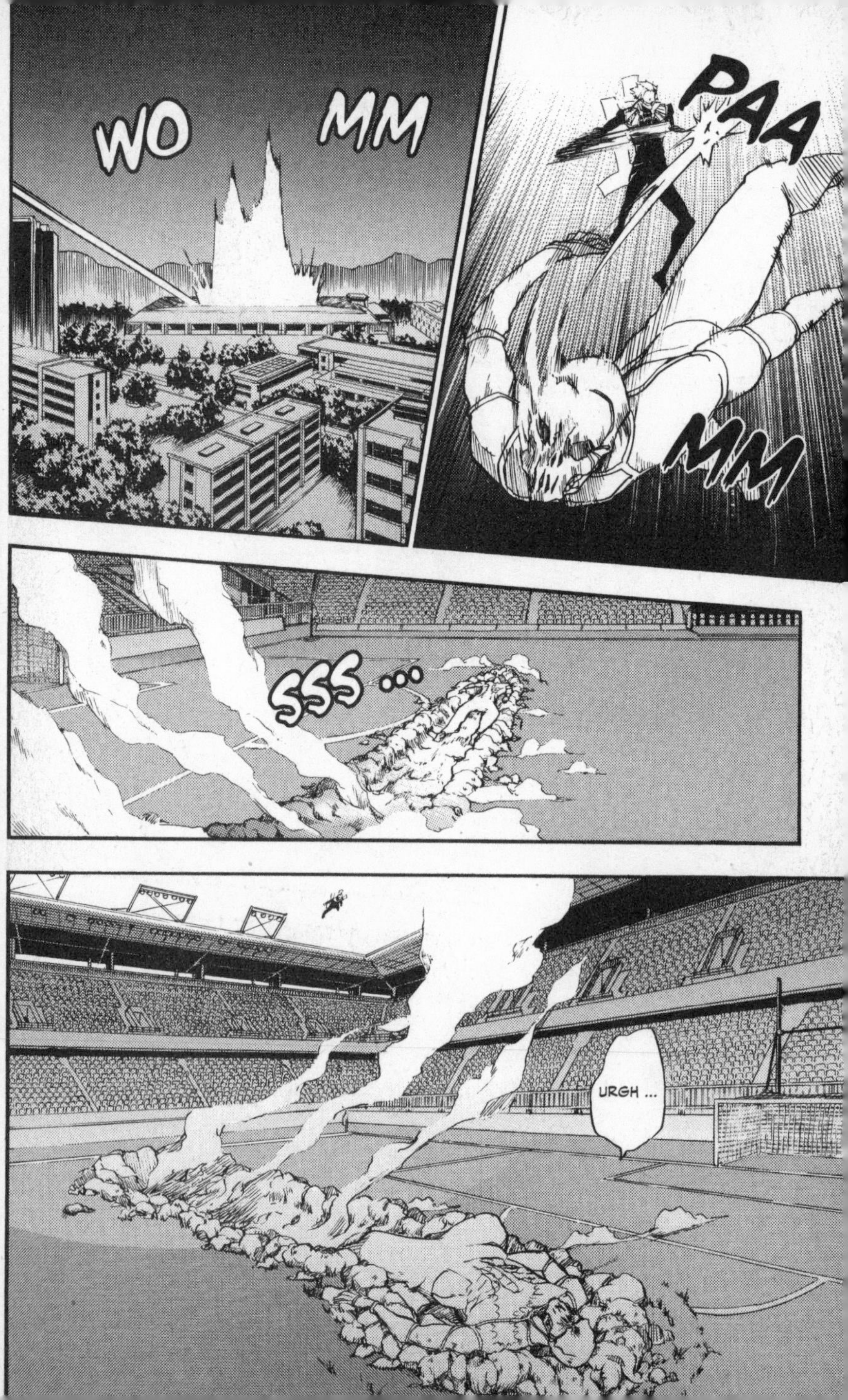
PAA
MM
WO
MM
SSS ...
URGH ...

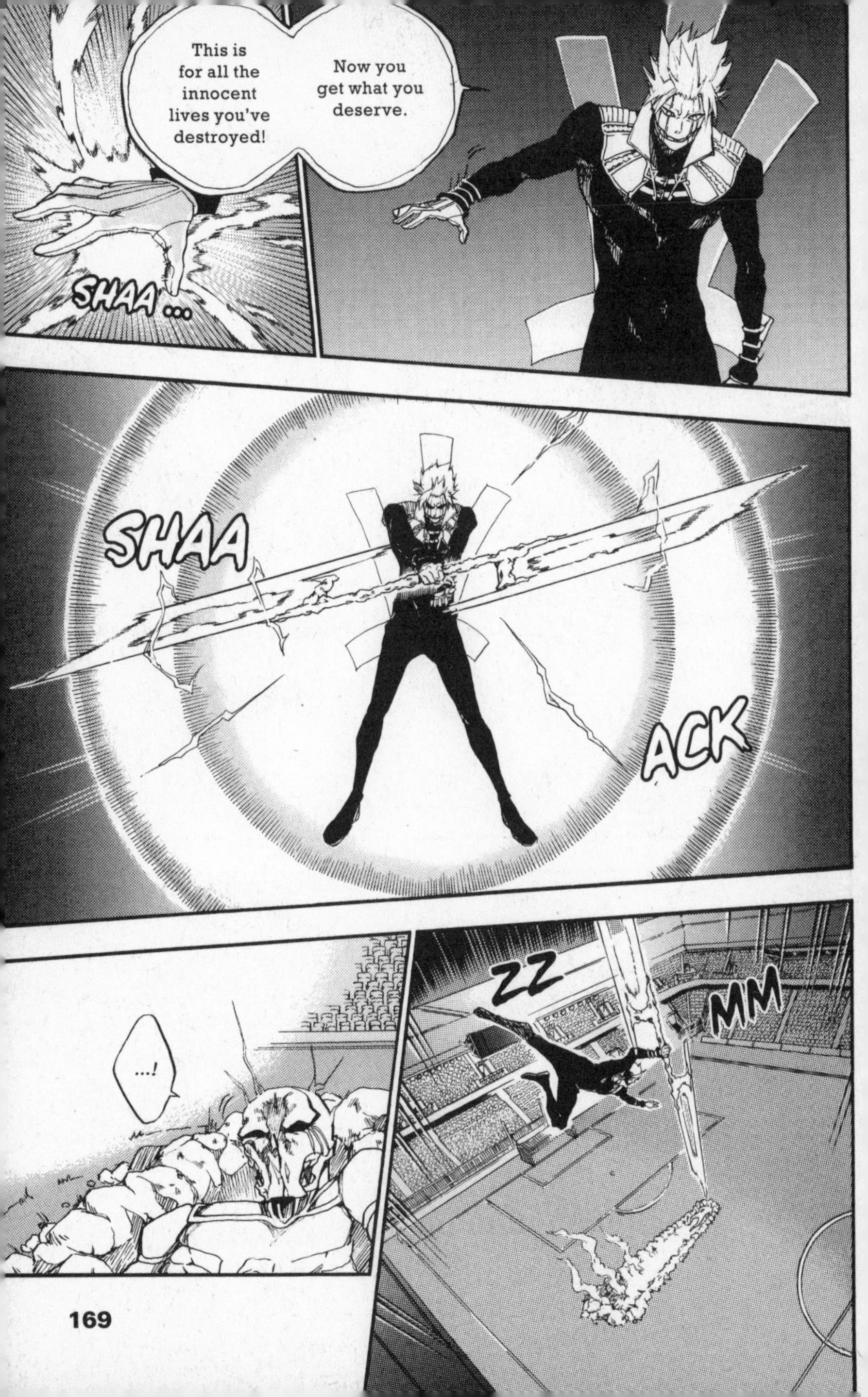
Now you get what you deserve.
This is for all the innocent lives you've destroyed!
SHAA...
SHAA
ACK
ZZ
MM
...!

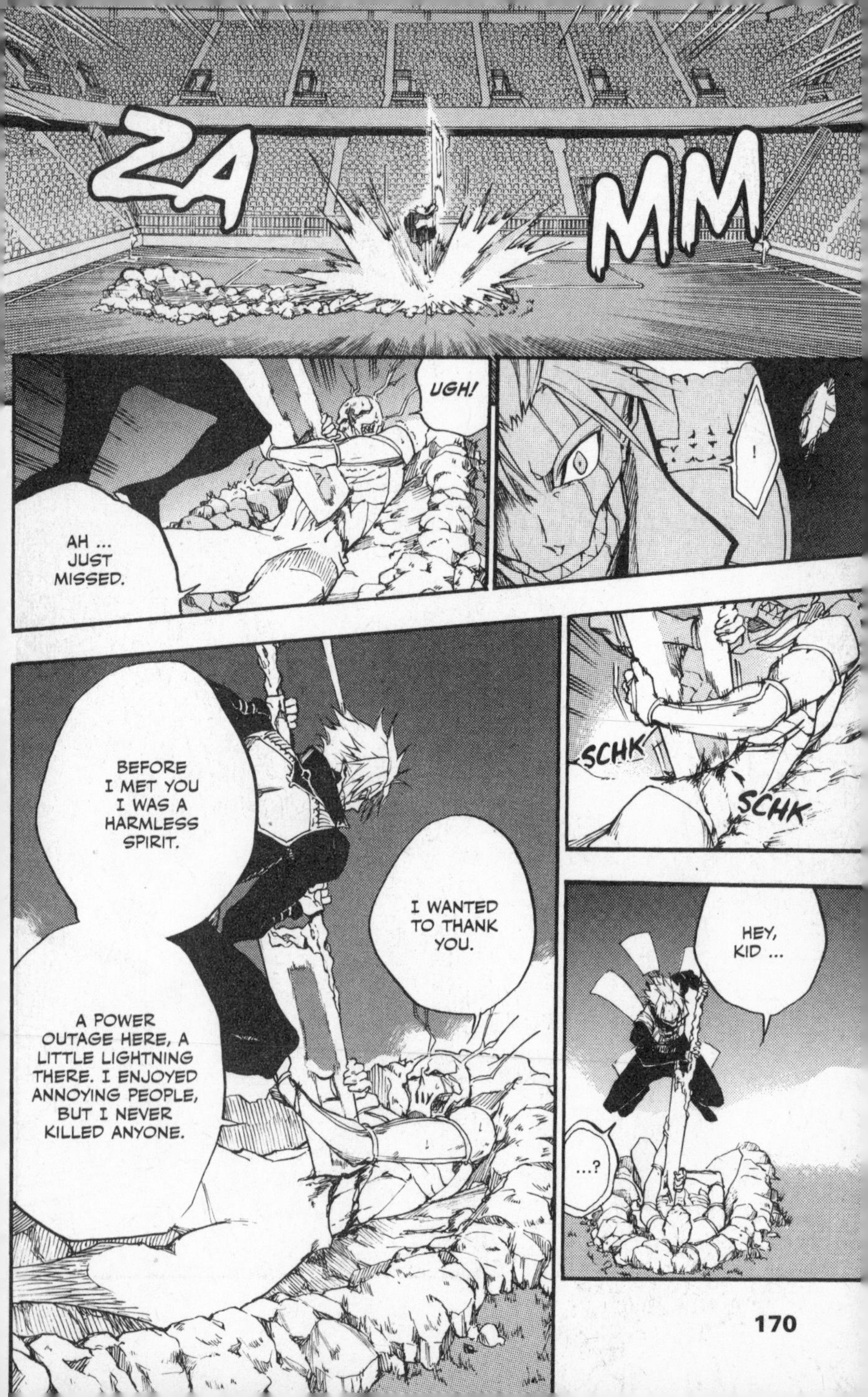
ZA
MM
!
UGH!
AH ... JUST MISSED.
SCHK
SCHK
HEY, KID ...
...?
I WANTED TO THANK YOU.
BEFORE I MET YOU I WAS A HARMLESS SPIRIT.
A POWER OUTAGE HERE, A LITTLE LIGHTNING THERE. I ENJOYED ANNOYING PEOPLE, BUT I NEVER KILLED ANYONE.

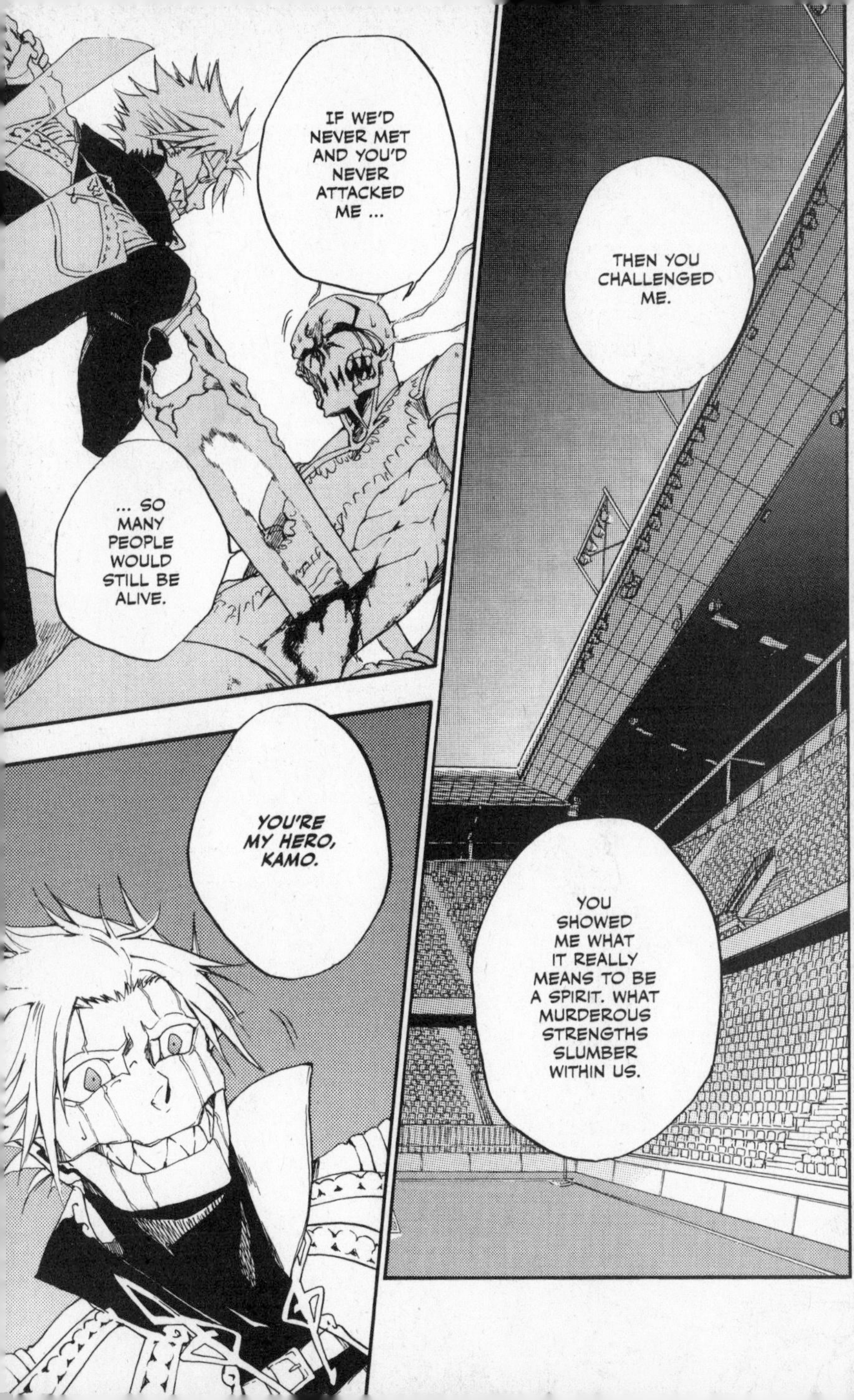
THEN YOU CHALLENGED ME.
YOU SHOWED ME WHAT IT REALLY MEANS TO BE A SPIRIT. WHAT MURDEROUS STRENGTHS SLUMBER WITHIN US.
IF WE'D NEVER MET AND YOU'D NEVER ATTACKED ME ...
... SO MANY PEOPLE WOULD STILL BE ALIVE.
YOU'RE MY HERO, KAMO.

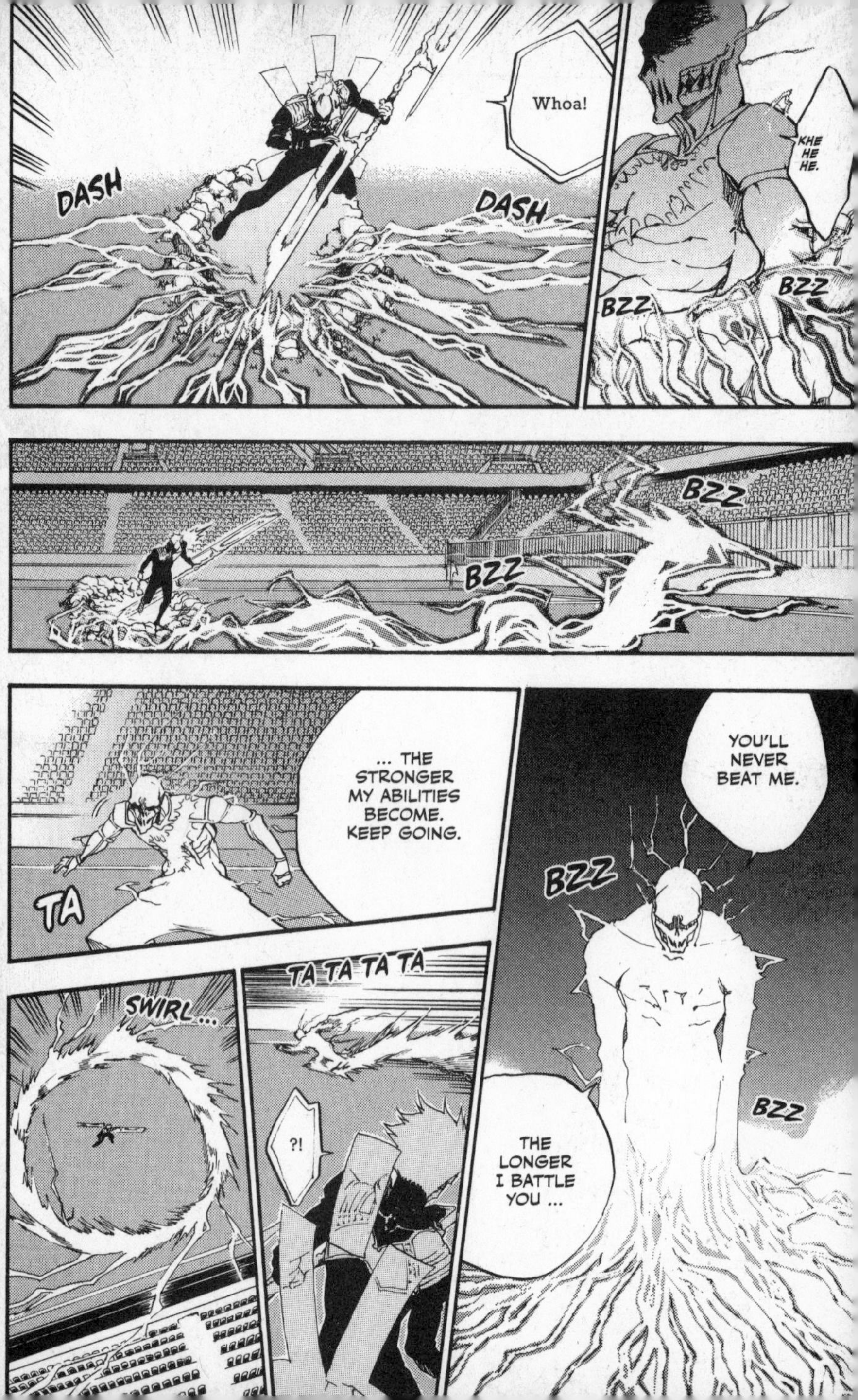
KHE HE HE.
BZZ
BZ-Z
Whoa!
DASH
DASH
BZZ
BZZ
YOU'LL NEVER BEAT ME.
BZZ
BZ-Z
THE LONGER I BATTLE YOU ...
... THE STRONGER MY ABILITIES BECOME. KEEP GOING.
TA
TA TA TA TA
?!
SWIRL ...

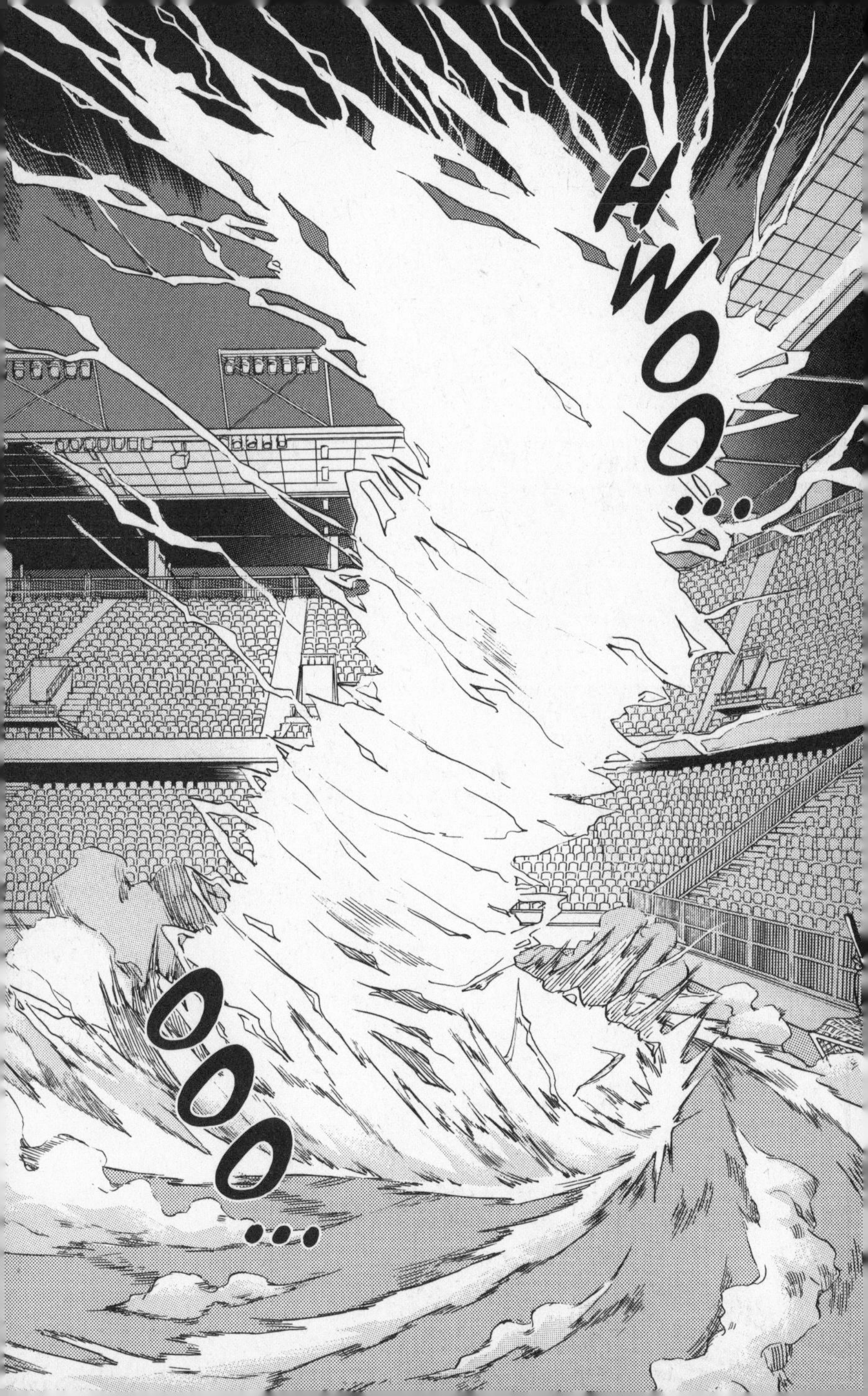
HWOO...
OOO...

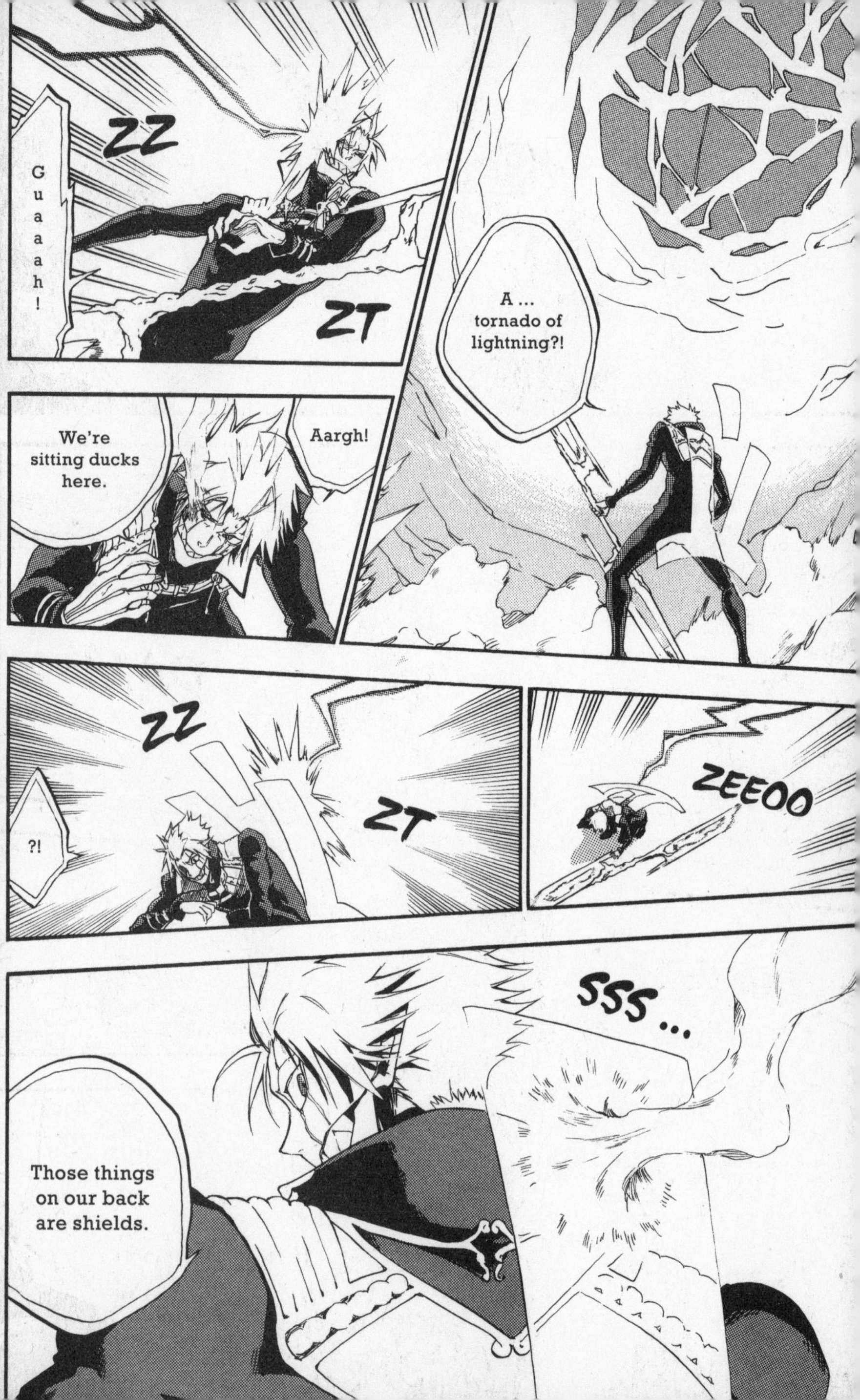
A ... tornado of lightning?!
ZZ
Guaaah!
ZT
Aargh!
We're sitting ducks here.
ZEEOO
ZZ
ZT
?!
SSS ...
Those things on our back are shields.

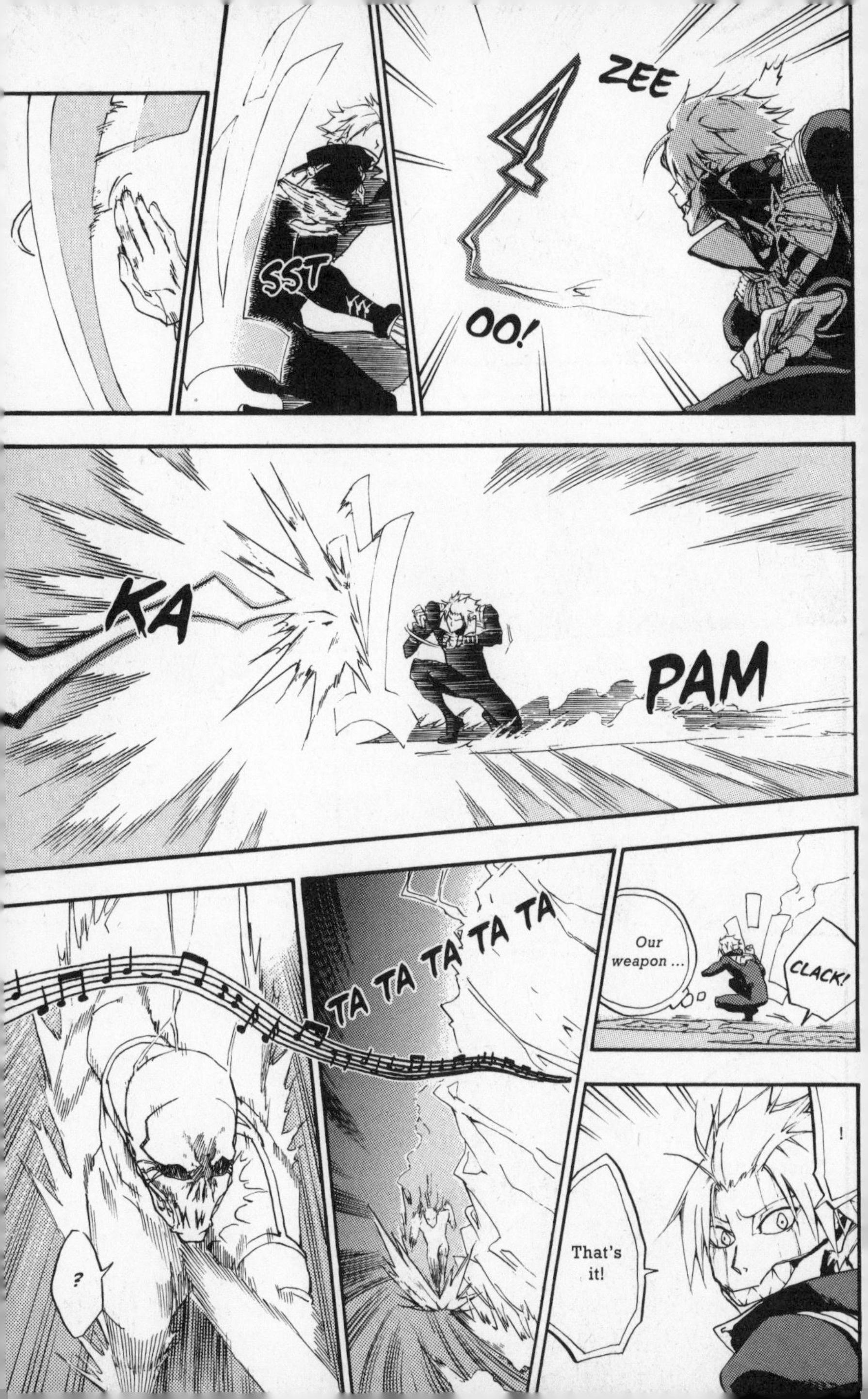
ZEE
OO!
SST
KA
PAM
!
CLACK!
Our weapon ...
!
That's it!
TA TA TA TA TA
?

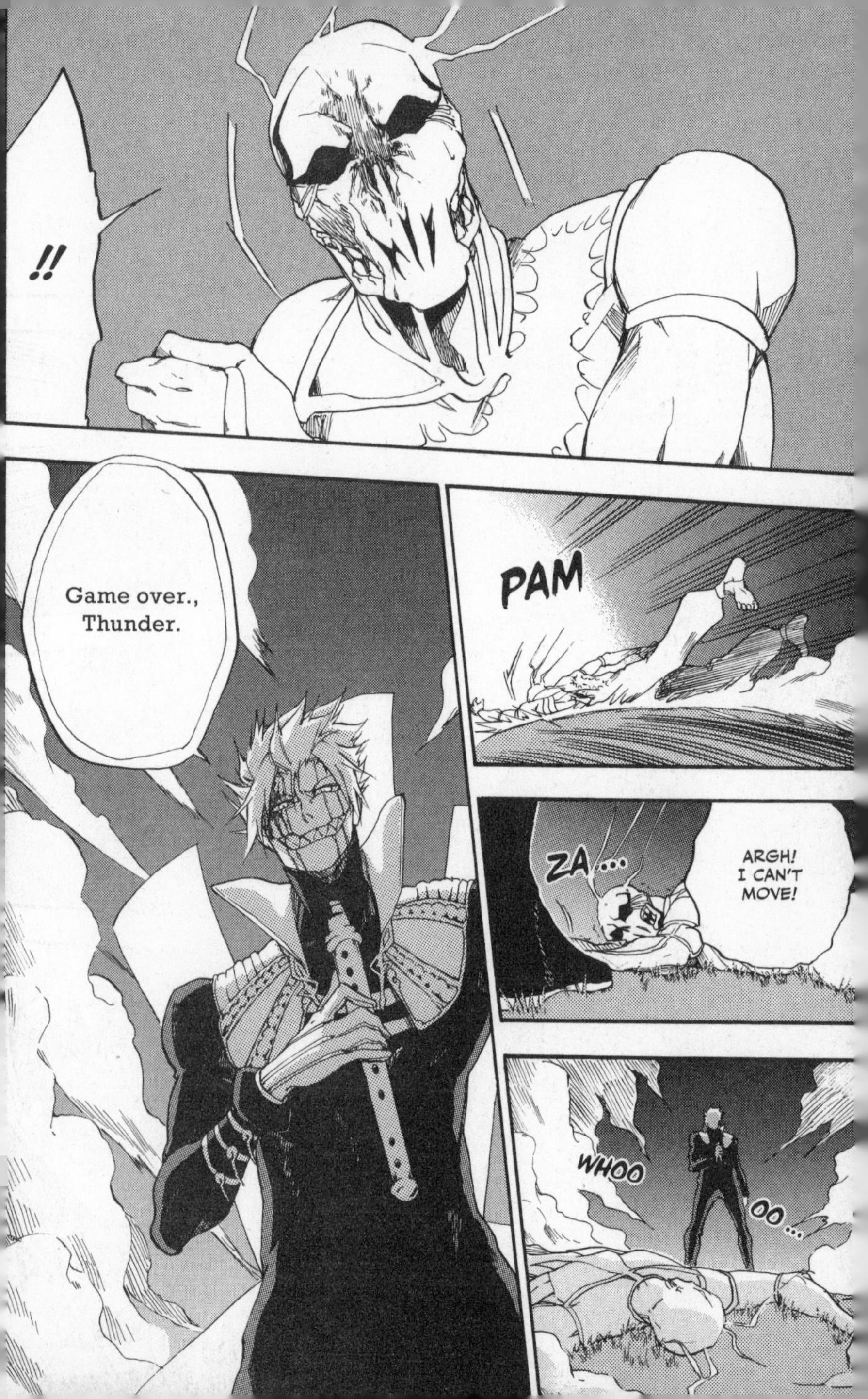
!!
PAM
ZA...
ARGH! I CAN'T MOVE!
WHOO
OO...
Game over., Thunder.

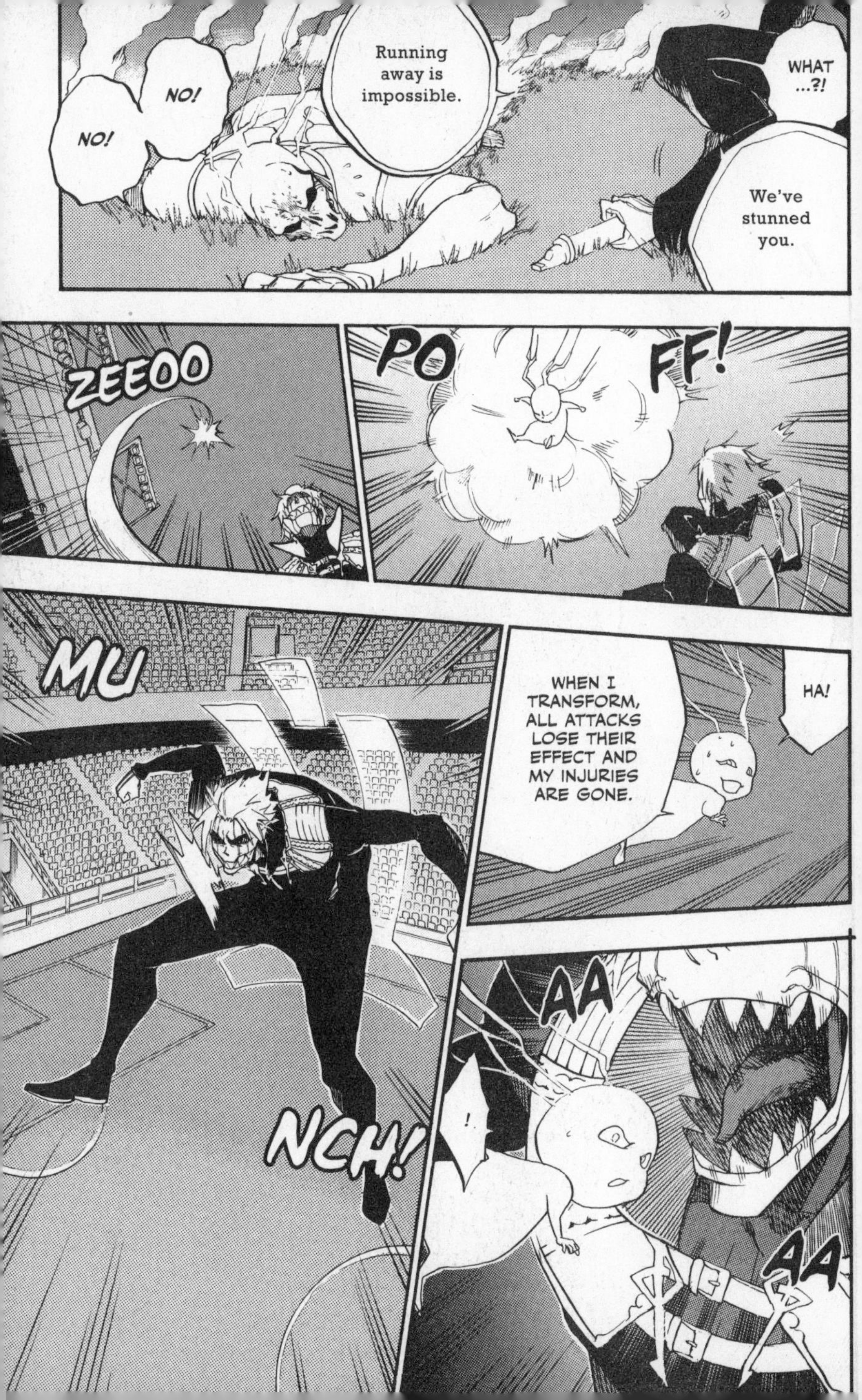
WHAT ...?!
We've stunned you.
Running away is impossible.
NO!
NO!
PO FF!
ZEEOO
HA!
WHEN I TRANSFORM, ALL ATTACKS LOSE THEIR EFFECT AND MY INJURIES ARE GONE.
AA
!
AA
MU
NCH!

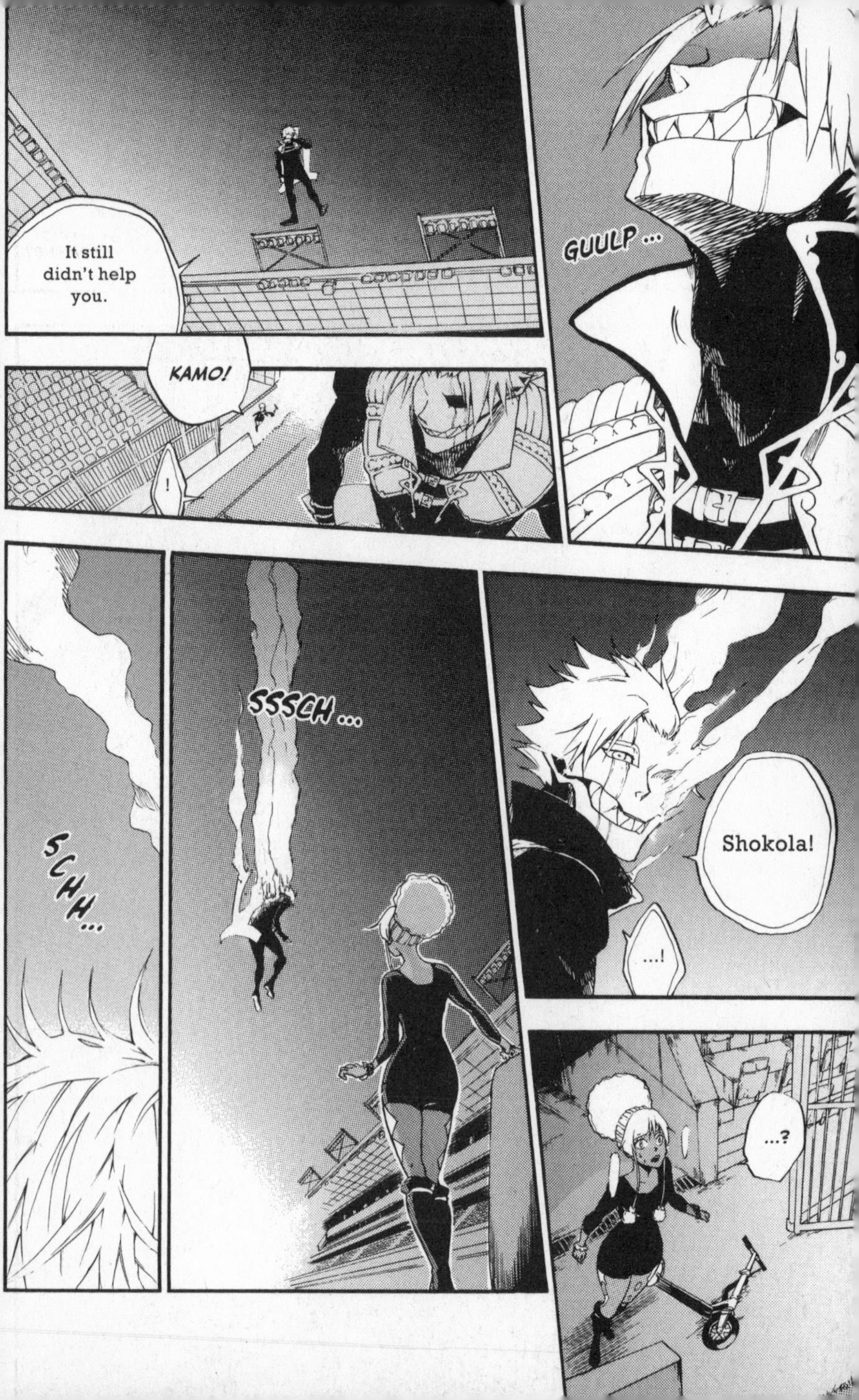
GUULP ...
It still didn't help you.
KAMO!
!
Shokola!
...!
...?
SSSCH ...
SCHH...

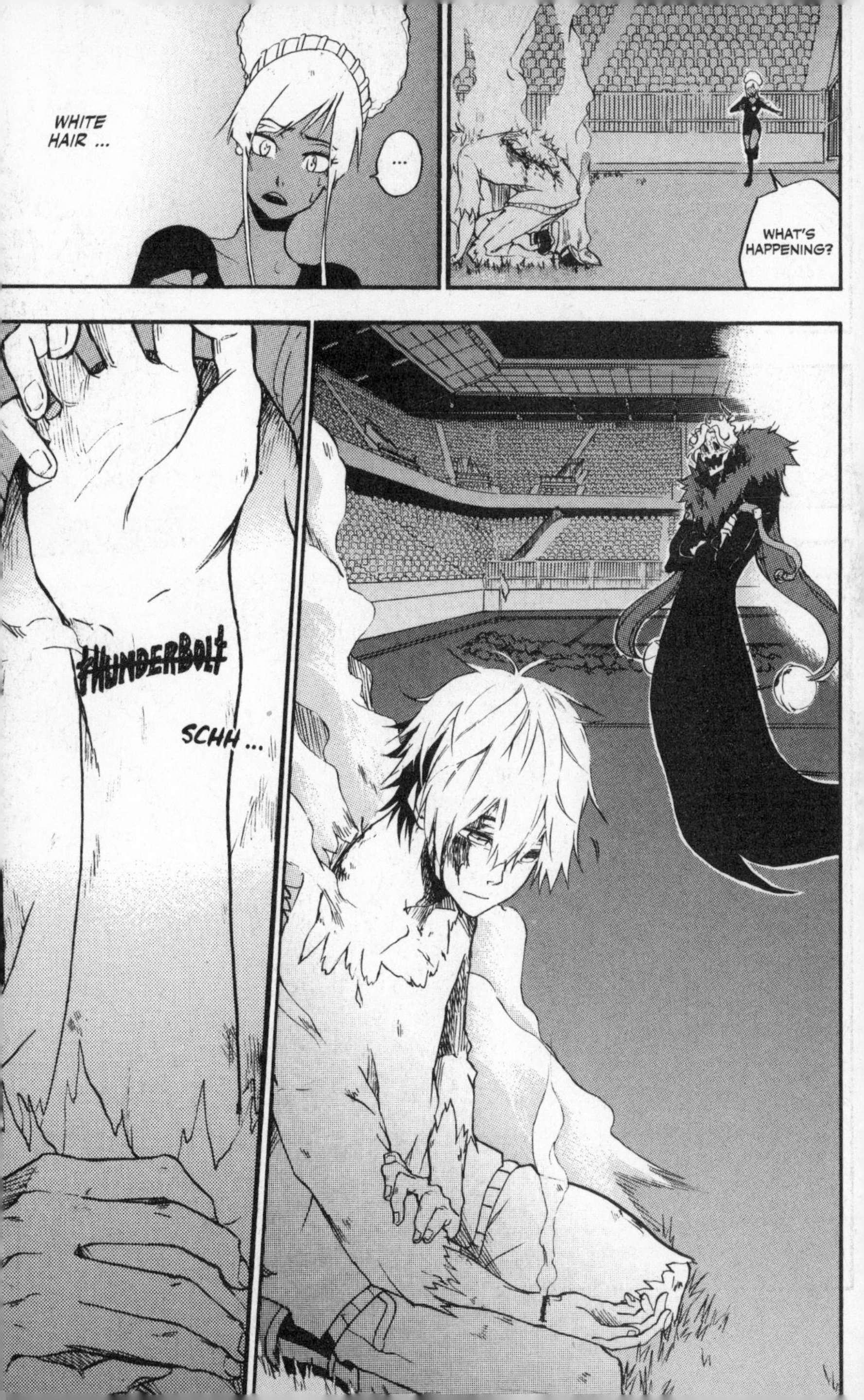
WHAT'S HAPPENING?
...
WHITE HAIR ...
THUNDERBOLT
SCHH ...

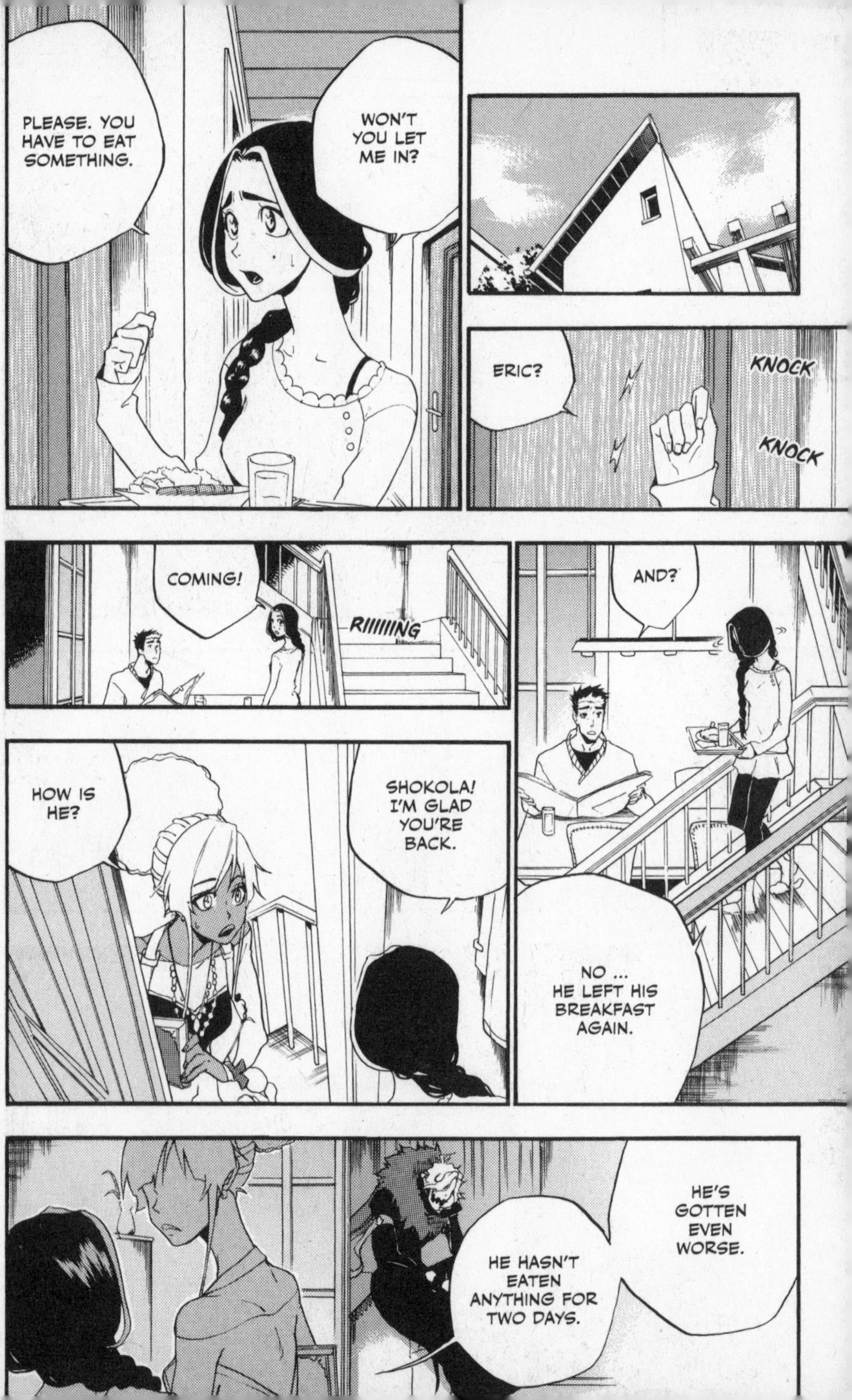
ERIC?
KNOCK
KNOCK
WON'T YOU LET ME IN?
PLEASE. YOU HAVE TO EAT SOMETHING.
AND?
NO ... HE LEFT HIS BREAKFAST AGAIN.
RIIIIIING
COMING!
SHOKOLA! I'M GLAD YOU'RE BACK.
HOW IS HE?
HE'S GOTTEN EVEN WORSE.
HE HASN'T EATEN ANYTHING FOR TWO DAYS.

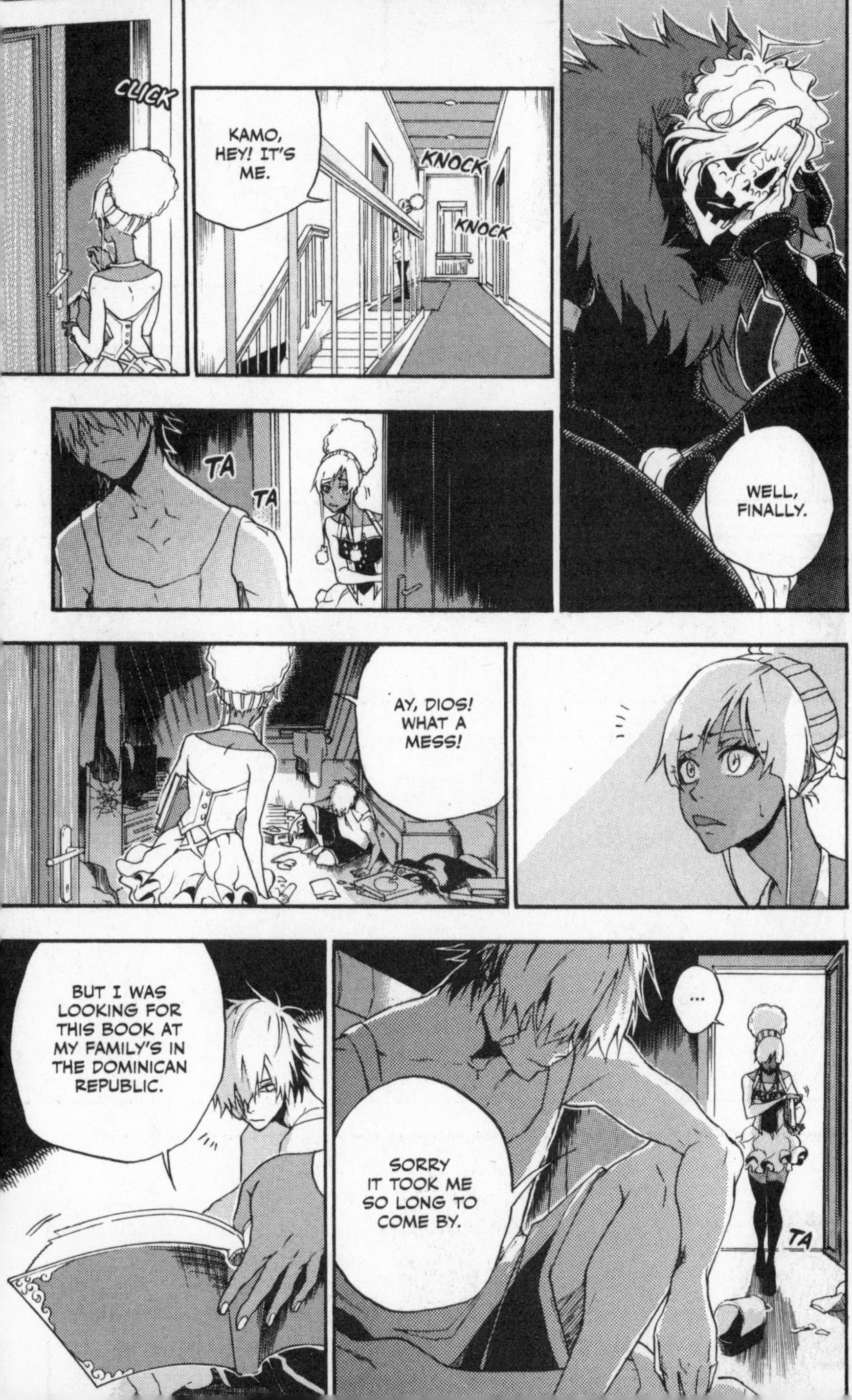
WELL, FINALLY.
KAMO, HEY! IT'S ME.
KNOCK
KNOCK
CLICK
TA
TA
AY, DIOS! WHAT A MESS!
...
SORRY IT TOOK ME SO LONG TO COME BY.
TA
BUT I WAS LOOKING FOR THIS BOOK AT MY FAMILY'S IN THE DOMINICAN REPUBLIC.

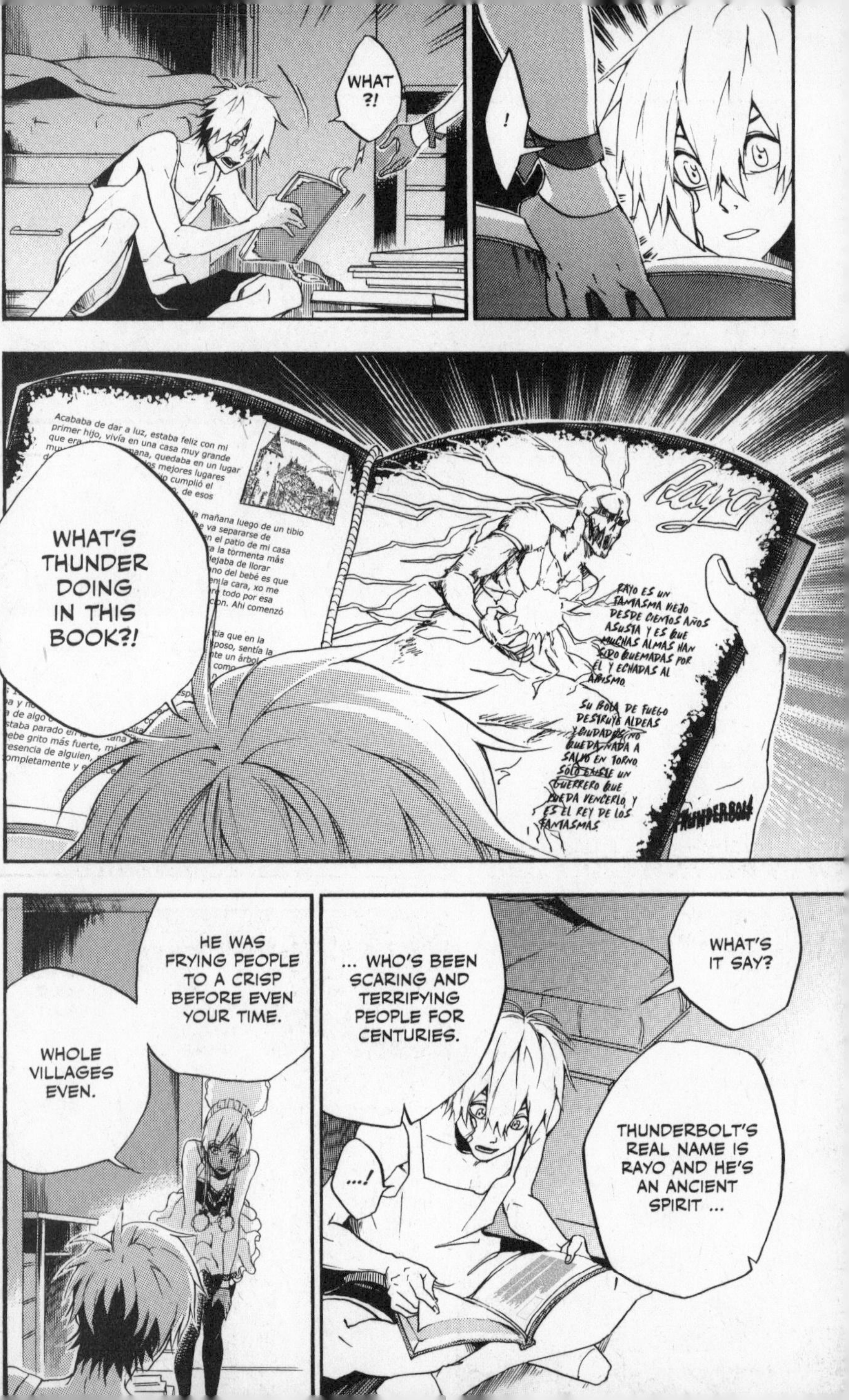
!
WHAT ?!
WHAT'S THUNDER DOING IN THIS BOOK?!
Rayo
RAYO ES UN FANTASMA VIEJO DESDE CIENTOS AÑOS ASUSTA Y ES QUE MUCHAS ALMAS HAN SIDO QUEMADAS POR ÉL Y ECHADAS AL ABISMO.
SU BOLA DE FUEGO DESTRUYE ALDEAS Y CIUDADES, NO QUEDA NADA A SALVO EN TORNO. SÓLO EXISTE UN GUERRERO QUE PUEDA VENCERLO, Y ES EL REY DE LOS FANTASMAS.
THUNDERBOLT
WHAT'S IT SAY?
THUNDERBOLT'S REAL NAME IS RAYO AND HE'S AN ANCIENT SPIRIT ...
... WHO'S BEEN SCARING AND TERRIFYING PEOPLE FOR CENTURIES.
...!
HE WAS FRYING PEOPLE TO A CRISP BEFORE EVEN YOUR TIME.
WHOLE VILLAGES EVEN.

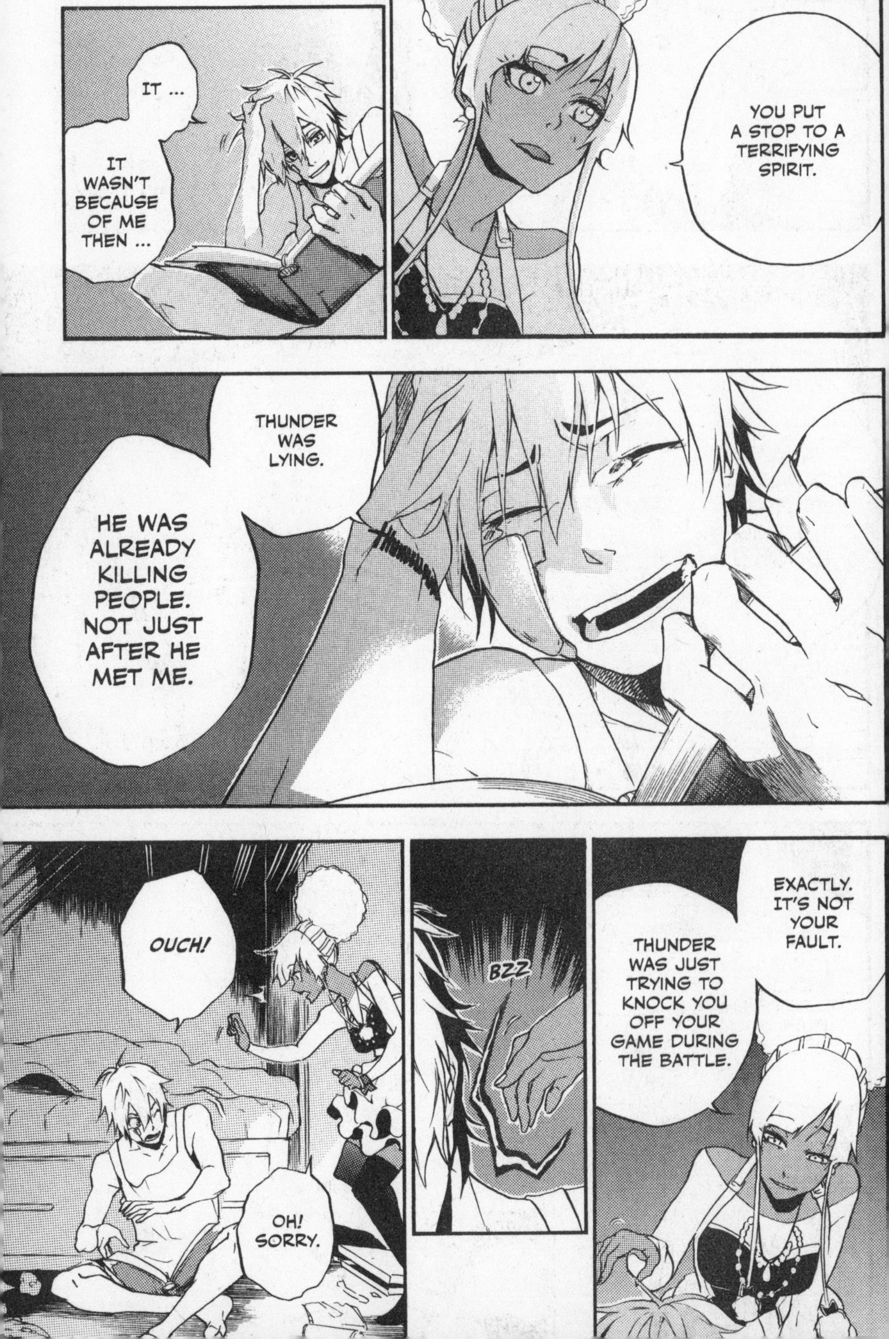
YOU PUT A STOP TO A TERRIFYING SPIRIT.
IT ...
IT WASN'T BECAUSE OF ME THEN ...
THUNDER WAS LYING.
HE WAS ALREADY KILLING PEOPLE. NOT JUST AFTER HE MET ME.
EXACTLY. IT'S NOT YOUR FAULT.
THUNDER WAS JUST TRYING TO KNOCK YOU OFF YOUR GAME DURING THE BATTLE.
BZZ
OUCH!
OH! SORRY.

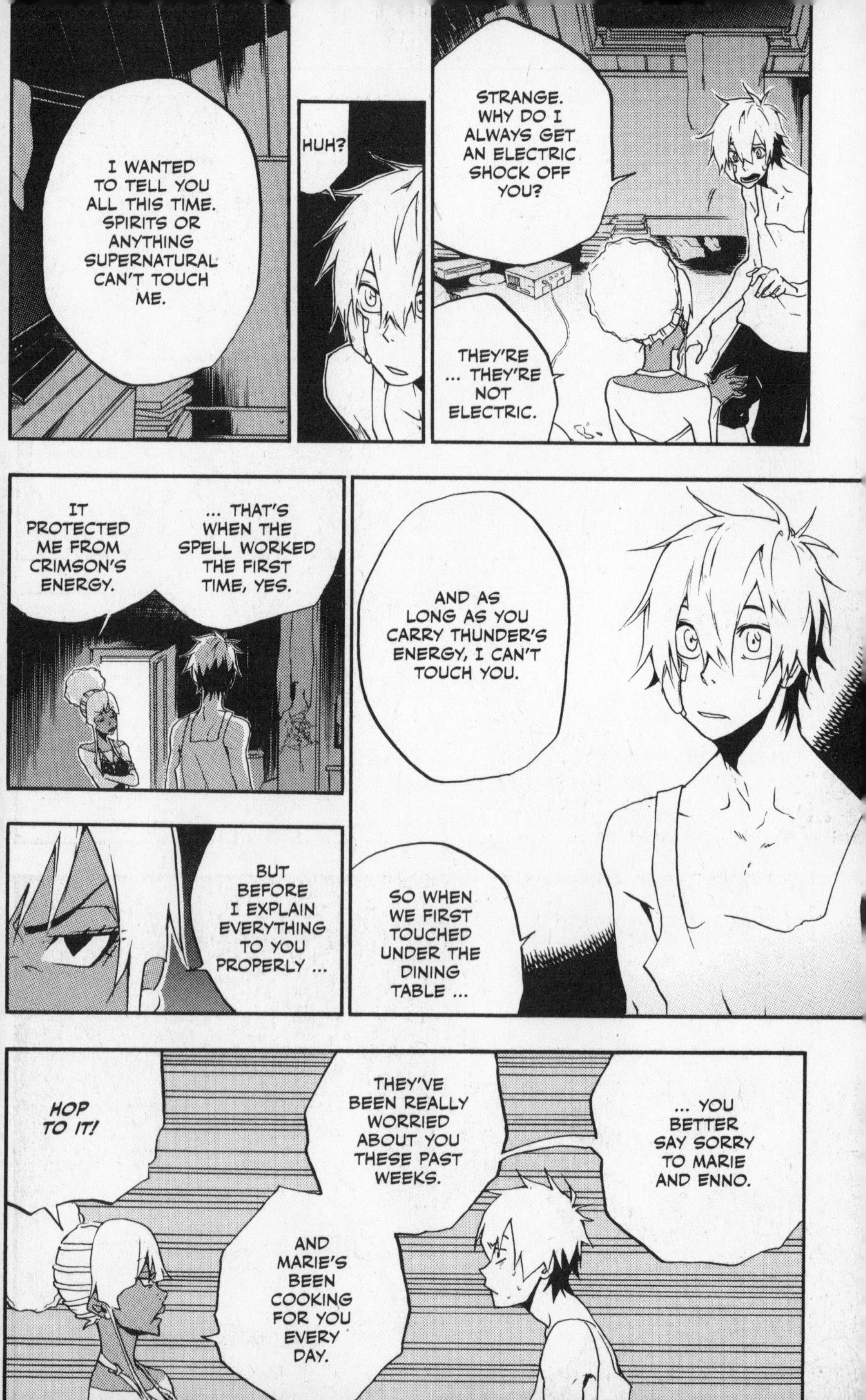
STRANGE. WHY DO I ALWAYS GET AN ELECTRIC SHOCK OFF YOU?
THEY'RE ... THEY'RE NOT ELECTRIC.
HUH?
I WANTED TO TELL YOU ALL THIS TIME. SPIRITS OR ANYTHING SUPERNATURAL CAN'T TOUCH ME.
AND AS LONG AS YOU CARRY THUNDER'S ENERGY, I CAN'T TOUCH YOU.
SO WHEN WE FIRST TOUCHED UNDER THE DINING TABLE ...
... THAT'S WHEN THE SPELL WORKED THE FIRST TIME, YES.
IT PROTECTED ME FROM CRIMSON'S ENERGY.
BUT BEFORE I EXPLAIN EVERYTHING TO YOU PROPERLY ...
... YOU BETTER SAY SORRY TO MARIE AND ENNO.
THEY'VE BEEN REALLY WORRIED ABOUT YOU THESE PAST WEEKS.
AND MARIE'S BEEN COOKING FOR YOU EVERY DAY.
HOP TO IT!

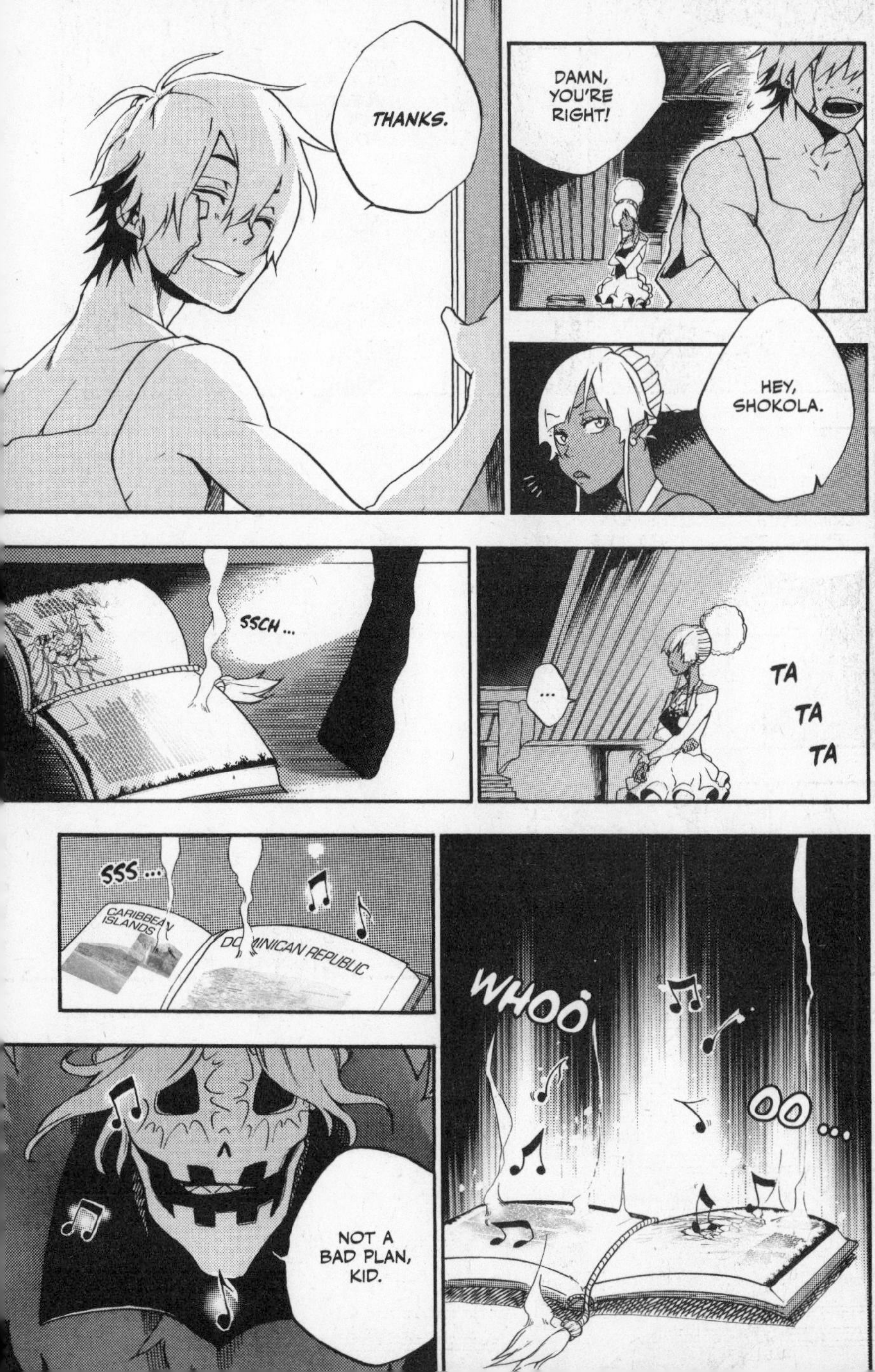
DAMN, YOU'RE RIGHT!
HEY, SHOKOLA.
THANKS.
...
TA TA TA
SSCH...
WHOOO...
SSS...
CARIBBEAN ISLANDS
DOMINICAN REPUBLIC
NOT A BAD PLAN, KID.

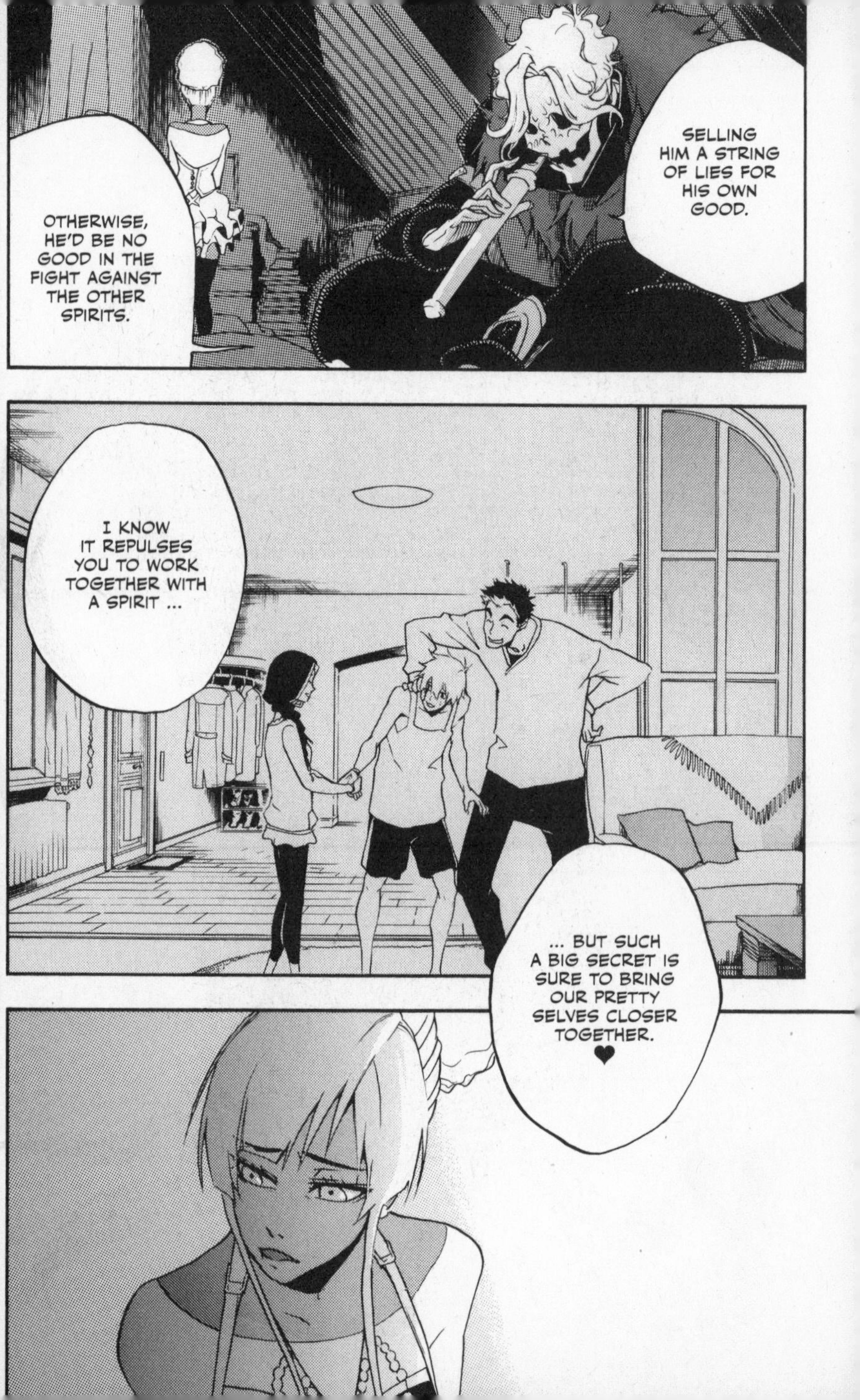
SELLING HIM A STRING OF LIES FOR HIS OWN GOOD.
OTHERWISE, HE'D BE NO GOOD IN THE FIGHT AGAINST THE OTHER SPIRITS.
I KNOW IT REPULSES YOU TO WORK TOGETHER WITH A SPIRIT ...
... BUT SUCH A BIG SECRET IS SURE TO BRING OUR PRETTY SELVES CLOSER TOGETHER. ♥

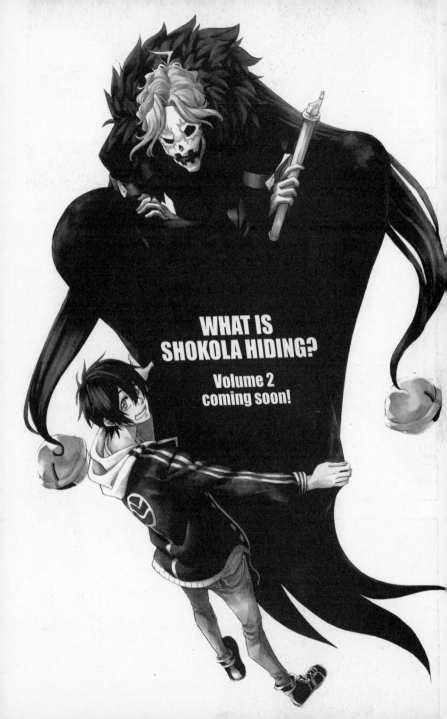

WHAT IS
SHOKOLA HIDING?

Volume 2
coming soon!

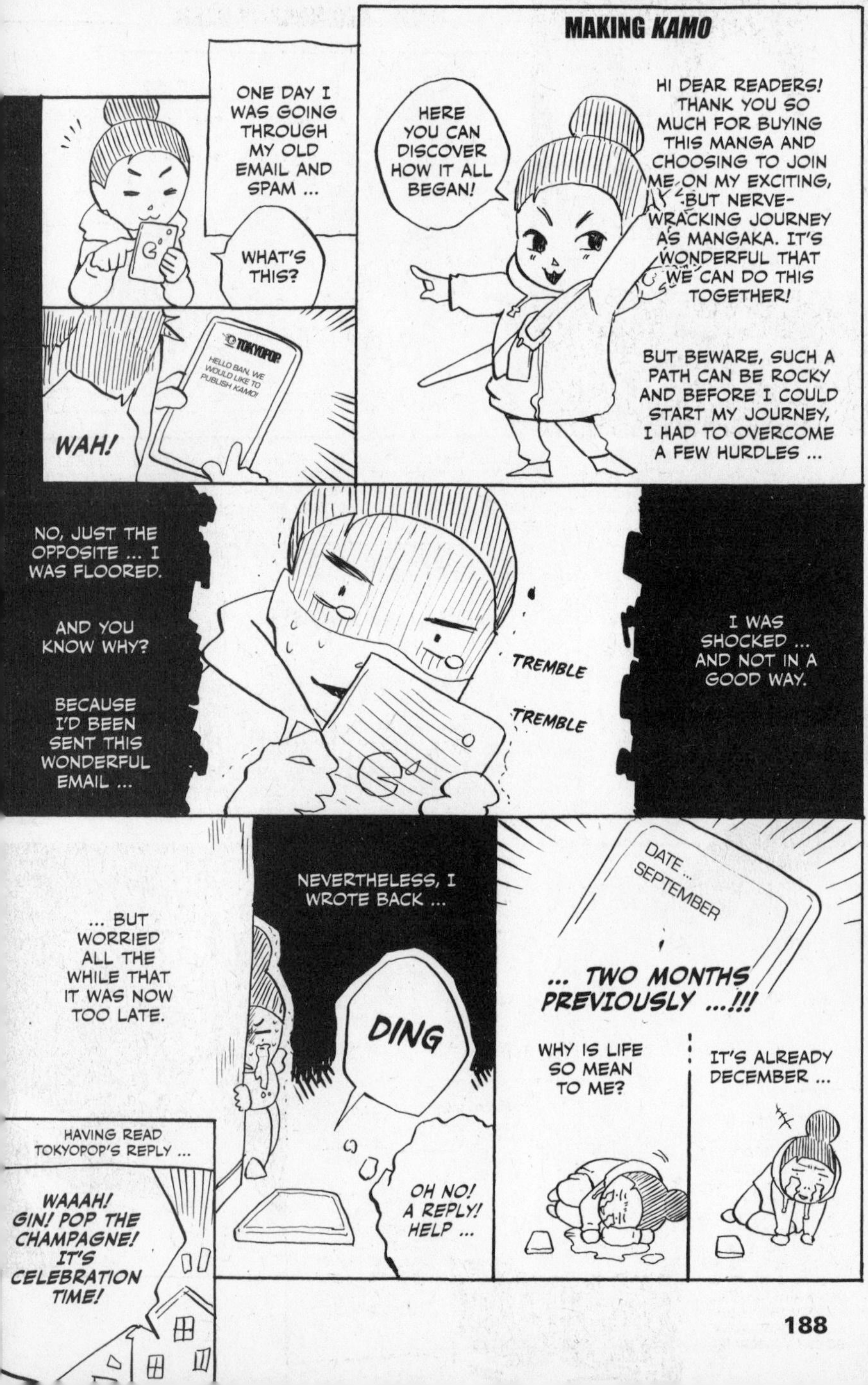
MAKING KAMO
HI DEAR READERS! THANK YOU SO MUCH FOR BUYING THIS MANGA AND CHOOSING TO JOIN ME ON MY EXCITING, BUT NERVE-WRACKING JOURNEY AS MANGAKA. IT'S WONDERFUL THAT WE CAN DO THIS TOGETHER!
HERE YOU CAN DISCOVER HOW IT ALL BEGAN!
BUT BEWARE, SUCH A PATH CAN BE ROCKY AND BEFORE I COULD START MY JOURNEY, I HAD TO OVERCOME A FEW HURDLES ...
ONE DAY I WAS GOING THROUGH MY OLD EMAIL AND SPAM ...
WHAT'S THIS?
TOKYOPOP
HELLO BAN, WE WOULD LIKE TO PUBLISH KAMO!
WAH!
I WAS SHOCKED ... AND NOT IN A GOOD WAY.
TREMBLE
TREMBLE
NO, JUST THE OPPOSITE ... I WAS FLOORED.
AND YOU KNOW WHY?
BECAUSE I'D BEEN SENT THIS WONDERFUL EMAIL ...
DATE... SEPTEMBER
... TWO MONTHS PREVIOUSLY ...!!!
IT'S ALREADY DECEMBER ...
WHY IS LIFE SO MEAN TO ME?
NEVERTHELESS, I WROTE BACK ...
DING
OH NO! A REPLY! HELP ...
... BUT WORRIED ALL THE WHILE THAT IT WAS NOW TOO LATE.
HAVING READ TOKYOPOP'S REPLY ...
WAAAH! GIN! POP THE CHAMPAGNE! IT'S CELEBRATION TIME!

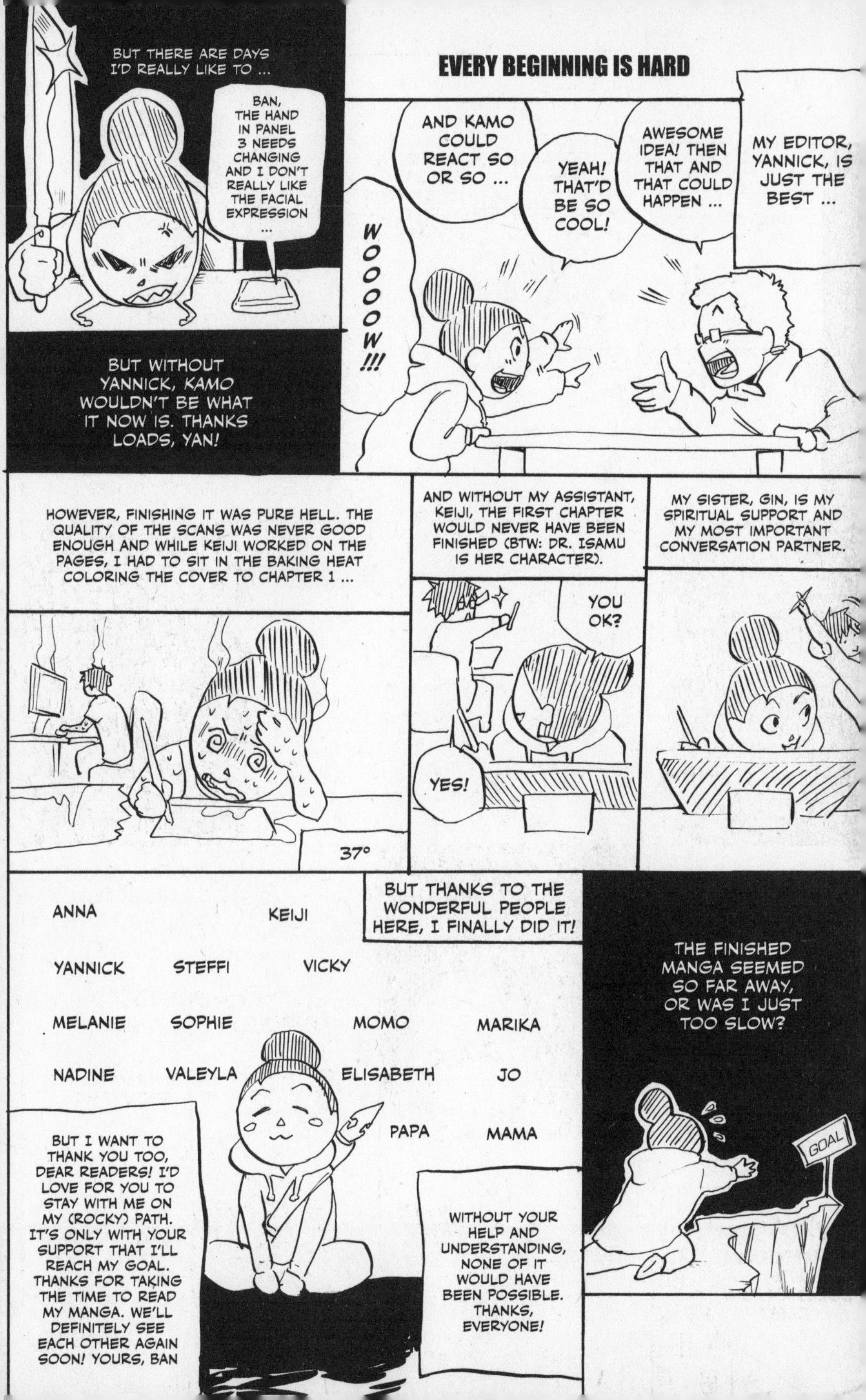
EVERY BEGINNING IS HARD
MY EDITOR, YANNICK, IS JUST THE BEST ...
AWESOME IDEA! THEN THAT AND THAT COULD HAPPEN ...
YEAH! THAT'D BE SO COOL!
AND KAMO COULD REACT SO OR SO ...
WOOOOOW!!!
BUT THERE ARE DAYS I'D REALLY LIKE TO ...
BAN, THE HAND IN PANEL 3 NEEDS CHANGING AND I DON'T REALLY LIKE THE FACIAL EXPRESSION ...
BUT WITHOUT YANNICK, KAMO WOULDN'T BE WHAT IT NOW IS. THANKS LOADS, YAN!
MY SISTER, GIN, IS MY SPIRITUAL SUPPORT AND MY MOST IMPORTANT CONVERSATION PARTNER.
AND WITHOUT MY ASSISTANT, KEIJI, THE FIRST CHAPTER WOULD NEVER HAVE BEEN FINISHED (BTW: DR. ISAMU IS HER CHARACTER).
YOU OK?
YES!
HOWEVER, FINISHING IT WAS PURE HELL. THE QUALITY OF THE SCANS WAS NEVER GOOD ENOUGH AND WHILE KEIJI WORKED ON THE PAGES, I HAD TO SIT IN THE BAKING HEAT COLORING THE COVER TO CHAPTER 1 ...
37°
THE FINISHED MANGA SEEMED SO FAR AWAY, OR WAS I JUST TOO SLOW?
GOAL
BUT THANKS TO THE WONDERFUL PEOPLE HERE, I FINALLY DID IT!
ANNA
KEIJI
YANNICK
STEFFI
VICKY
MELANIE
SOPHIE
MOMO
MARIKA
NADINE
VALEYLA
ELISABETH
JO
PAPA
MAMA
WITHOUT YOUR HELP AND UNDERSTANDING, NONE OF IT WOULD HAVE BEEN POSSIBLE. THANKS, EVERYONE!
BUT I WANT TO THANK YOU TOO, DEAR READERS! I'D LOVE FOR YOU TO STAY WITH ME ON MY (ROCKY) PATH. IT'S ONLY WITH YOUR SUPPORT THAT I'LL REACH MY GOAL. THANKS FOR TAKING THE TIME TO READ MY MANGA. WE'LL DEFINITELY SEE EACH OTHER AGAIN SOON! YOURS, BAN

HELLO DEAR READER!

I'M ONE OF BAN'S ASSISTANTS AND RESPONSIBLE FOR DIGITALLY PROCESSING THE PAGES. IT WAS ALWAYS A LOT OF FUN SEEING THE FINISHED CHAPTERS FOR THE FIRST TIME AND I REMAIN INCREDIBLY IMPRESSED BY BAN'S TALENT! EVEN JUST BY THE FACT THAT SHE WORKS SO CLEANLY AND THERE'S NOT MUCH I HAVE TO TOUCH UP ...

I'M THRILLED TO HAVE MET BAN AND HELP MAKE HER DREAM A REALITY. I WISH HER TONS OF SUCCESS FOR HER MANGA!

YOURS, VALEYLA

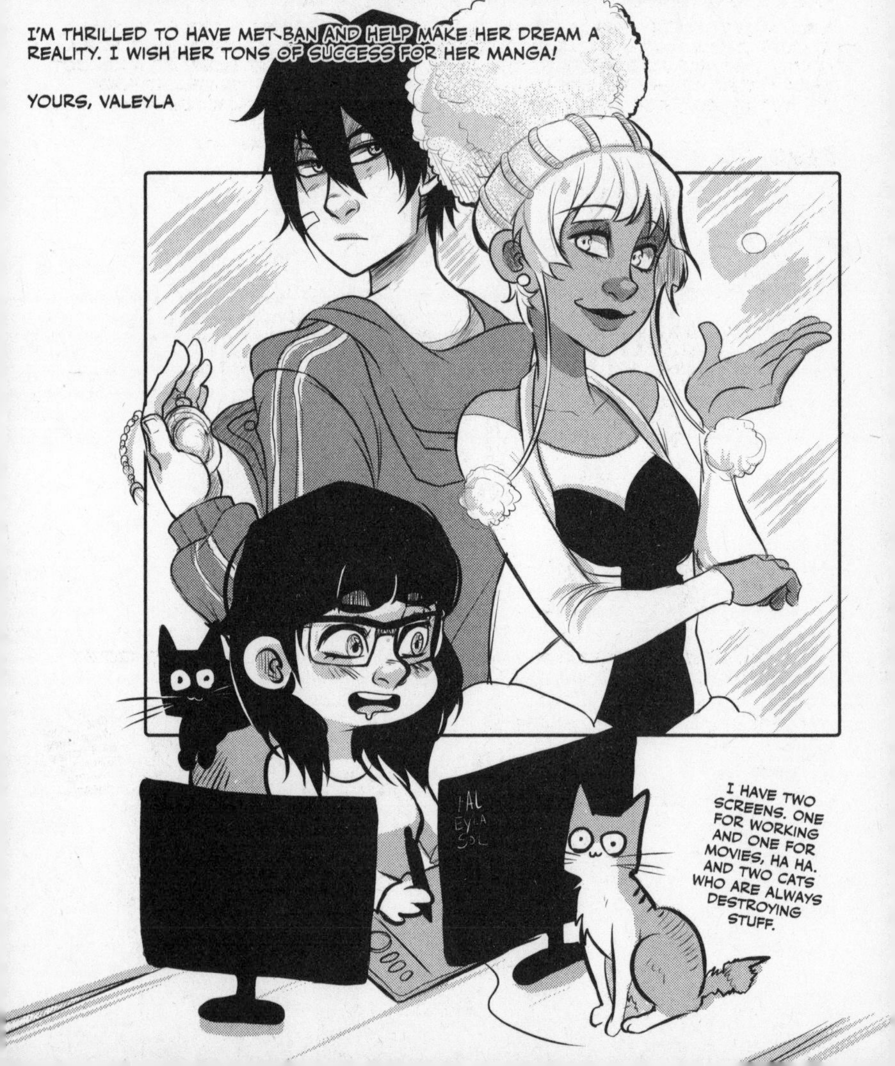
I HAVE TWO SCREENS. ONE FOR WORKING AND ONE FOR MOVIES, HA HA. AND TWO CATS WHO ARE ALWAYS DESTROYING STUFF.

IDEA AND MAIN CHARACTER

THE IDEA BEHIND *KAMO – PACT WITH THE SPIRIT WORLD* GOES BACK YEARS. I ONCE ASKED MY FACEBOOK FRIENDS WHAT SUBJECT AND GENRE THEY'D LIKE ME TO DO A STORY ON AND THE MAJORITY CHOSE A GHOST STORY. THIS RESULTED IN THE DOUJINSHI *KA-MO*, WHICH I HAD TO STOP AFTER THREE CHAPTERS WHEN TOKYOPOP PUT ME UNDER CONTRACT.

WHILE KAMO AND CRIMSON HUNT THE TWELFTH AND LAST SPIRIT IN THE DOUJINSHI, *KAMO – PACT WITH THE SPIRIT WORLD* TELLS HOW KAMO AND CRIMSON HUNT FOR A SPIRIT TOGETHER FOR THE FIRST TIME. HOWEVER, THE STORY IS MORE OF A REBOOT THAN A PREQUEL AND I'M INCREDIBLY HAPPY THAT I'M ALLOWED TO TELL IT FOR TOKYPOP AFRESH. THIS IS EXACTLY HOW I ALWAYS WANTED TO SHOW YOU KAMO.

KAMO

KAMO FROM THE DOUJINSHI *KA-MO* (2014)

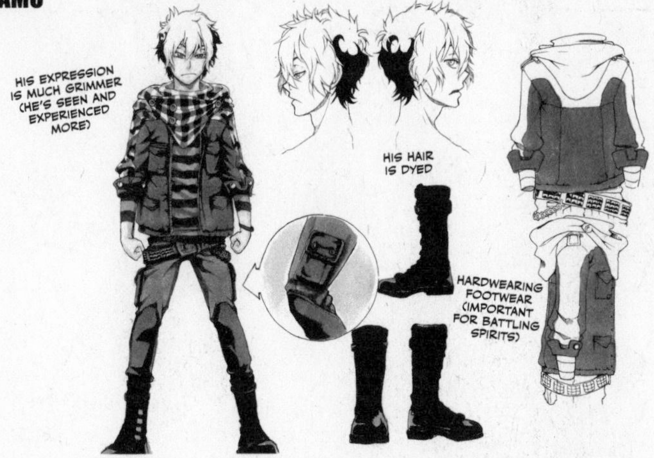
HIS EXPRESSION IS MUCH GRIMMER (HE'S SEEN AND EXPERIENCED MORE)
HIS HAIR IS DYED
HARDWEARING FOOTWEAR (IMPORTANT FOR BATTLING SPIRITS)

THE CURRENT VERSION OF KAMO WITH HIS OUTFITS IN EACH CHAPTER (2016)

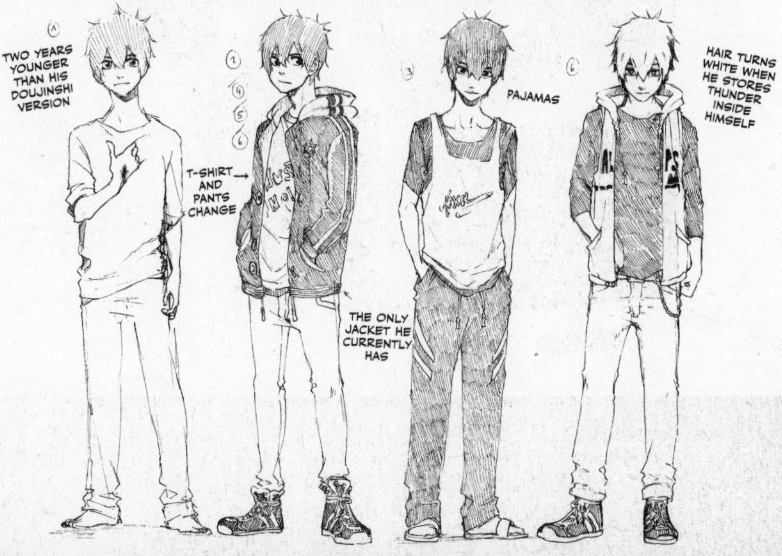
TWO YEARS YOUNGER THAN HIS DOUJINSHI VERSION
T-SHIRT AND PANTS CHANGE
THE ONLY JACKET HE CURRENTLY HAS
PAJAMAS
HAIR TURNS WHITE WHEN HE STORES THUNDER INSIDE HIMSELF

ADDITIONAL MAIN AND MINOR CHARACTERS

CRIMSON

WHEN I FIRST STARTED WORKING ON THE DOUJINSHI, DRAWING CRIMSON WAS PARTICULARLY DIFFICULT. I COULD NEVER DECIDE ON ONE SHAPE FOR HIS MASK. NOW CRIMSON IS THE EASIEST CHARACTER FOR ME TO DRAW. THIS DRAWING OF HIM IS ACTUALLY MUCH OLDER. ORIGINALLY, HE WAS GOING TO APPEAR IN A DIFFERENT STORY THAT NEVER GOT MADE.

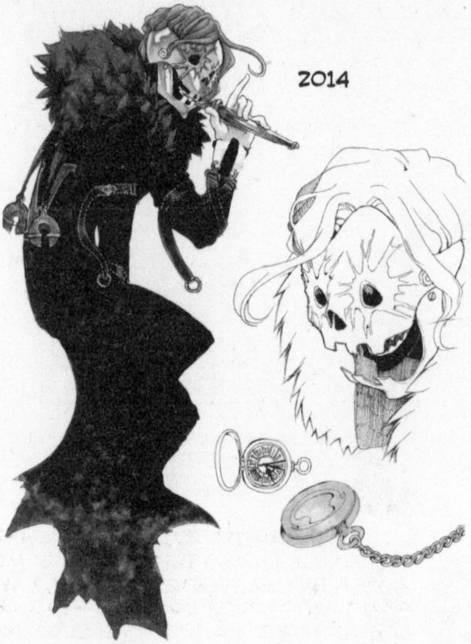

2014

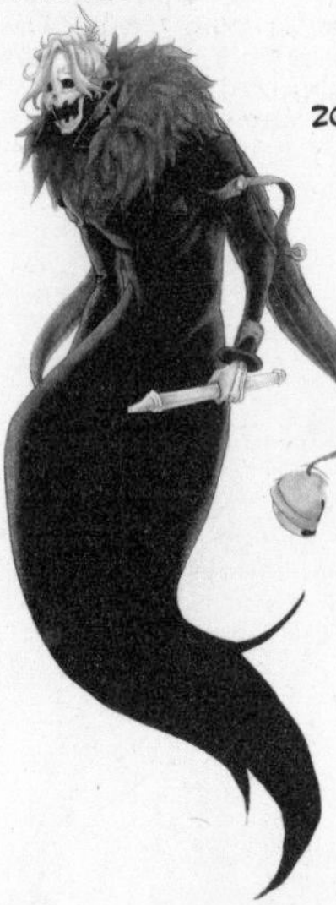

2016

SHOKOLA

THE BEST THING I LIKE ABOUT SHOKOLA IS HER TEMPERAMENTAL NATURE. THIS IS PROBABLY BECAUSE SHE HAS MANY OF MY DOMINICAN RELATIVES IN HER. OF THE THREE MAIN CHARACTERS, SHOKOLA'S DESIGN HAS CHANGED THE LEAST. ONLY HER BELOVED BULLDOG BUTCH HASN'T MADE AN APPEARANCE IN THE CURRENT VERSION YET. BUT PERHAPS THAT WILL CHANGE IN BOOK 2?

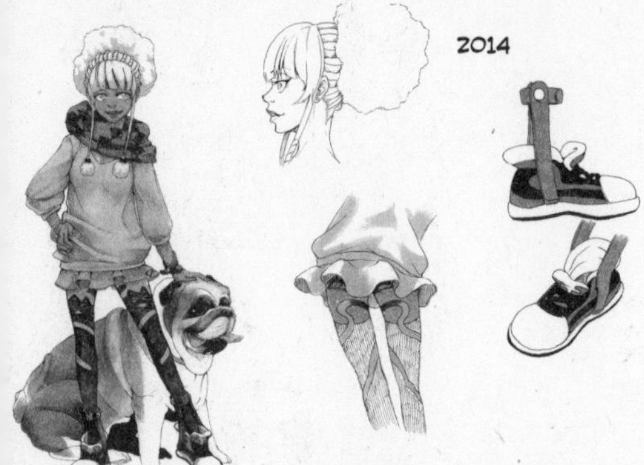

2014

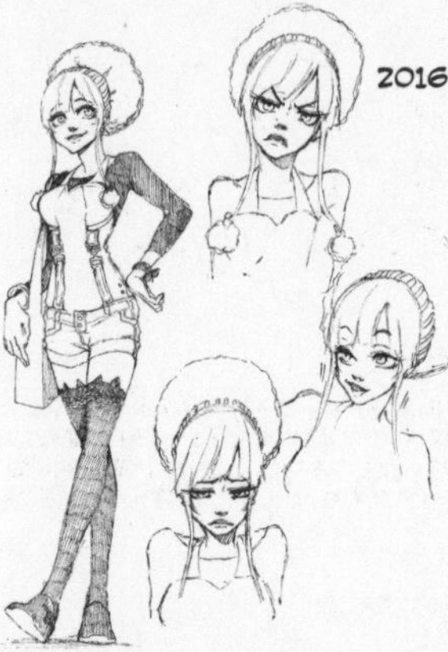

2016

THUNDERBOLT

HERE'S THE FIRST DRAFT OF THUNDERBOLT, WHICH I LIKE TO SHORTEN TO THUNDER (IN THE MANGA, TOO). THE MANY UNUSUAL AND ELABORATE MUSCLE LINES ON HIS LIMBS HAVE DRIVEN ME ABSOLUTELY CRAZY AS AN ARTIST (WHAT WAS I THINKING WHEN I DESIGNED HIM?), BUT HE'S REALLY GROWN ON ME OVER TIME.
I WISH WE HADN'T HAD TO SAY GOODBYE SO SOON.

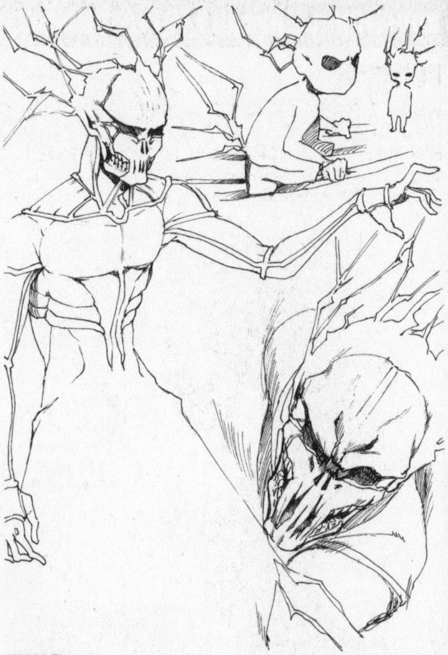

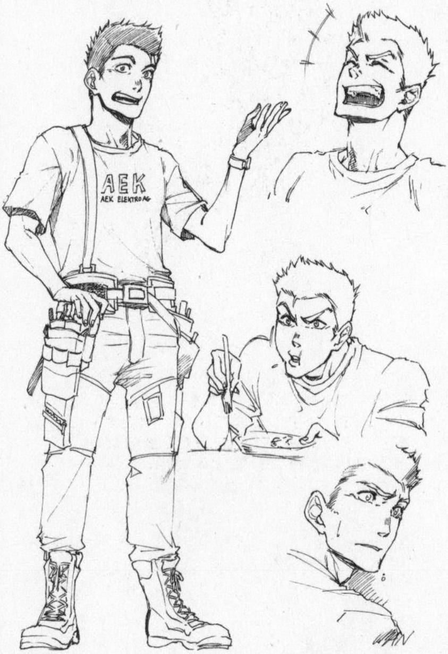
AEK

MARIE

MARIE WAS ALSO PLANNED, LIKE CRIMSON, FOR ANOTHER STORY. THEY WOULD HAVE EVEN MET EACH OTHER BECAUSE MARIE WAS TO BE HAUNTED BY CRIMSON.

ENNO

I ALWAYS WANTED TO CREATE A CHARACTER LIKE ENNO. IT WAS IMPORTANT TO ME TO HAVE A FATHER FIGURE FOR KAMO, WHO GIVES HIM A ROOF OVER HIS HEAD AND WHO LOOKS AFTER HIM. WHEN HE LOST HIS WIFE A FEW YEARS AGO, ENNO PROMISED HER THAT HE AND THEIR DAUGHTER WOULD LEAD A HAPPY LIFE. DESPITE THE MANY SLING AND ARROWS OF FATE, ENNO IS A PURE OPTIMIST.

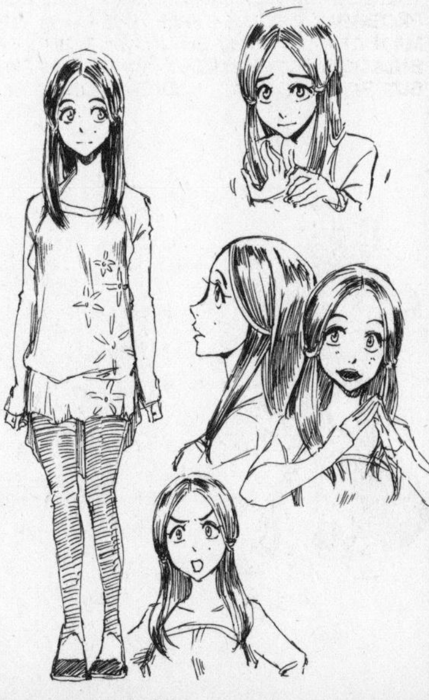

THE KAMO/CRIMSON FUSION

THERE ARE ALSO NATURALLY COUNTLESS DRAFTS OF THE FUSION OF KAMO AND CRIMSON. IN THE SECOND BOOK, IT WILL EVEN GET ITS OWN NAME, BUT I DON'T WANT TO GIVE THAT AWAY JUST YET. ;)

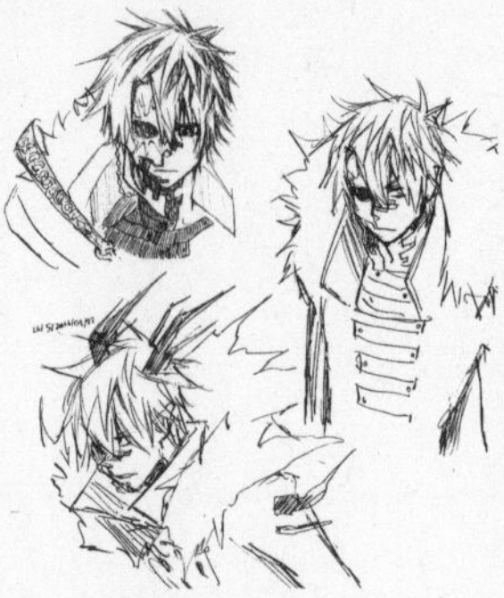

1.
I BEGAN WITH ABSOLUTELY NO IDEA OF HOW TO DESIGN THE FUSION. I JUST KNEW THAT IT HAD TO REPRESENT A COMBINATION OF KAMO AND CRIMSON (VERY IMAGINATIVE, I KNOW).

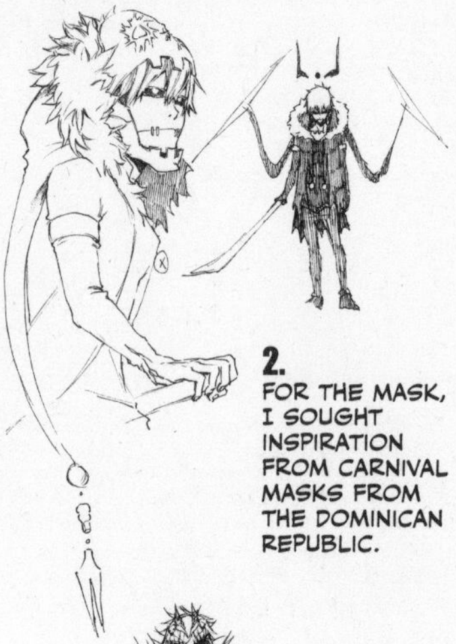

2.
FOR THE MASK, I SOUGHT INSPIRATION FROM CARNIVAL MASKS FROM THE DOMINICAN REPUBLIC.

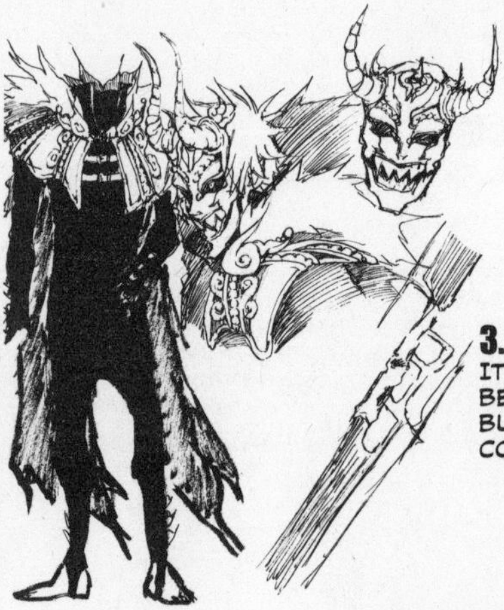

3.
IT SHOULD BE DEMONIC BUT STILL COOL.

4

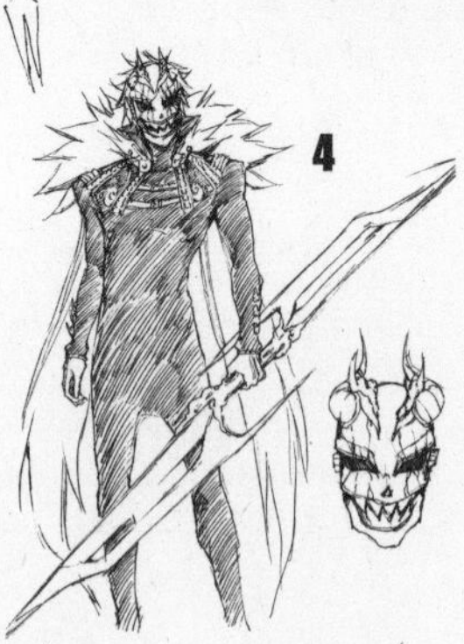

I THANK MY SISTER, GIN, FOR SUPPORTING ME DURING THE FINAL VERSION.

5

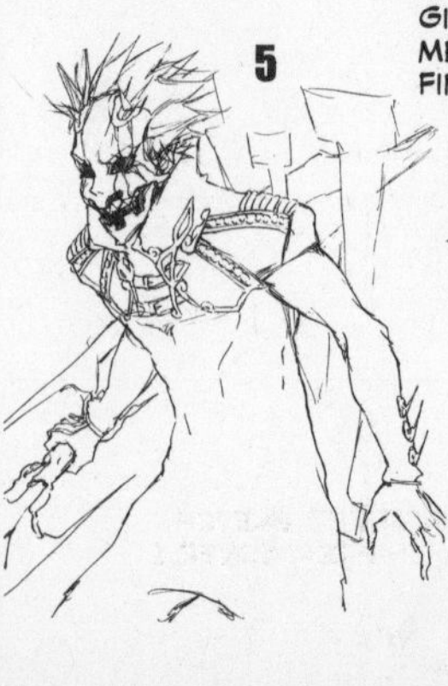

6

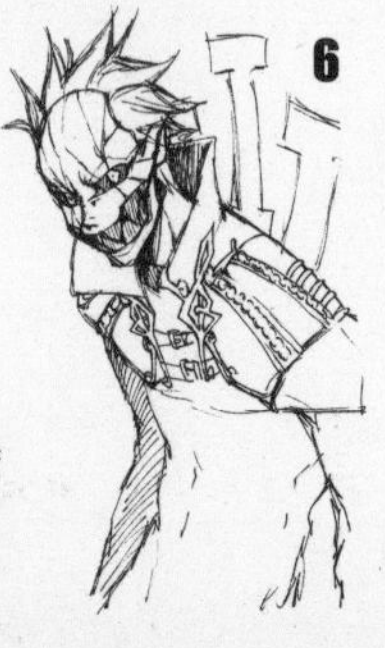

7

8

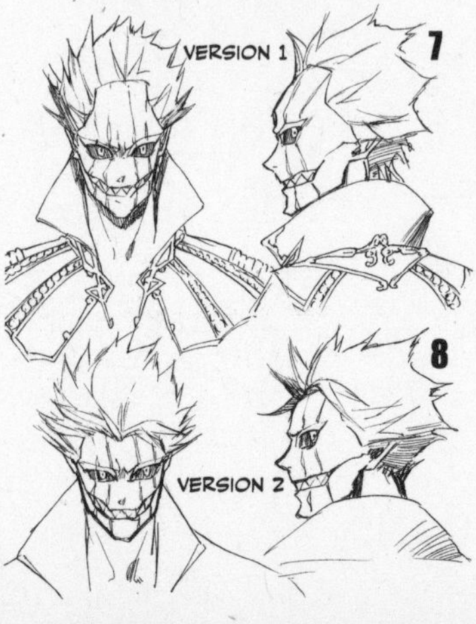
VERSION 1
VERSION 2

ALTERNATIVE COVER DESIGNS

I ALSO MADE A LOT OF DESIGNS FOR THE CHAPTER COVERS (AND A LOT ARE UNDERSTATED). TO BEGIN WITH, I SIMPLY DREW WHAT CAME TO ME; LATER, I TRIED TO FIND THEMES THAT COMPLEMENTED THE CHAPTER.

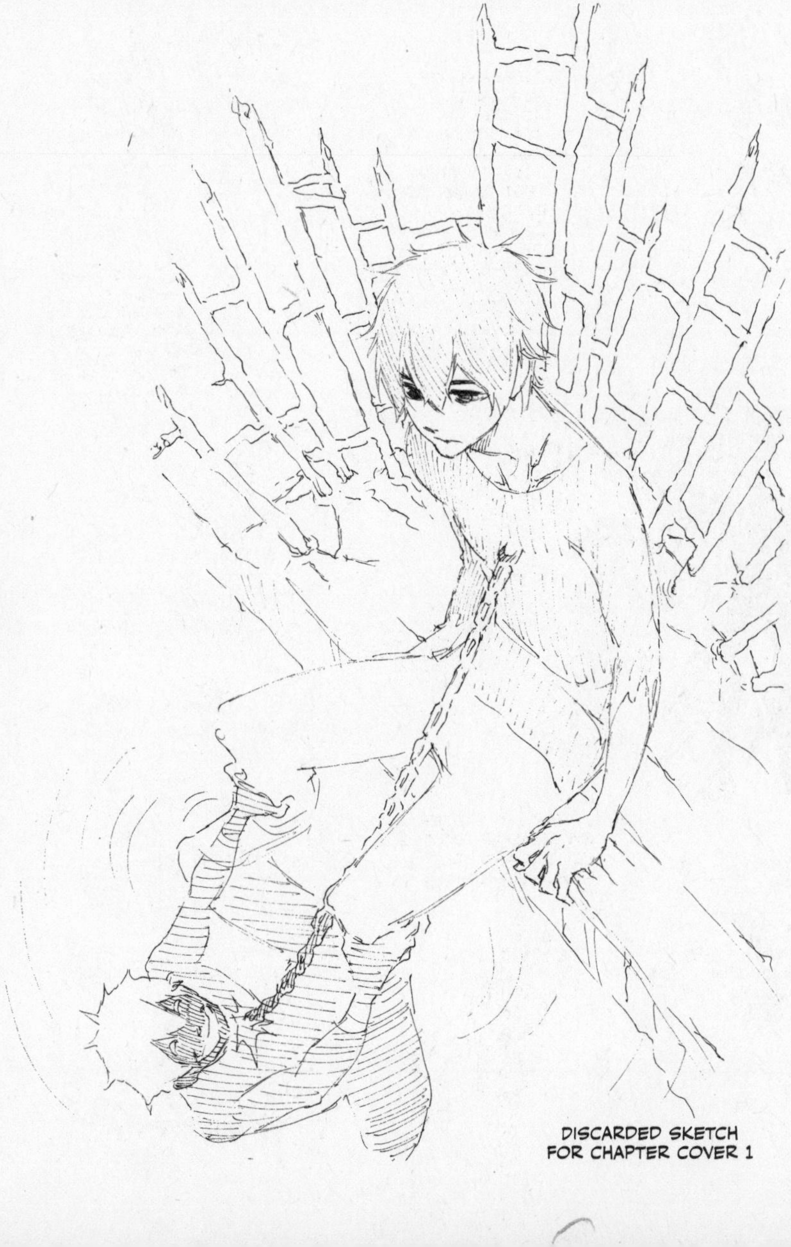

DISCARDED SKETCH
FOR CHAPTER COVER 1

SOME IDEAS AND THEMES WERE INSTANTLY GOOD AND THEN LIGHTLY CHANGED. THIS COVER WAS ABOUT PUTTING MORE FOCUS ON SHOKOLA AND KAMO (SORRY CRIMSON, THERE WASN'T ANY SPACE LEFT FOR YOU).

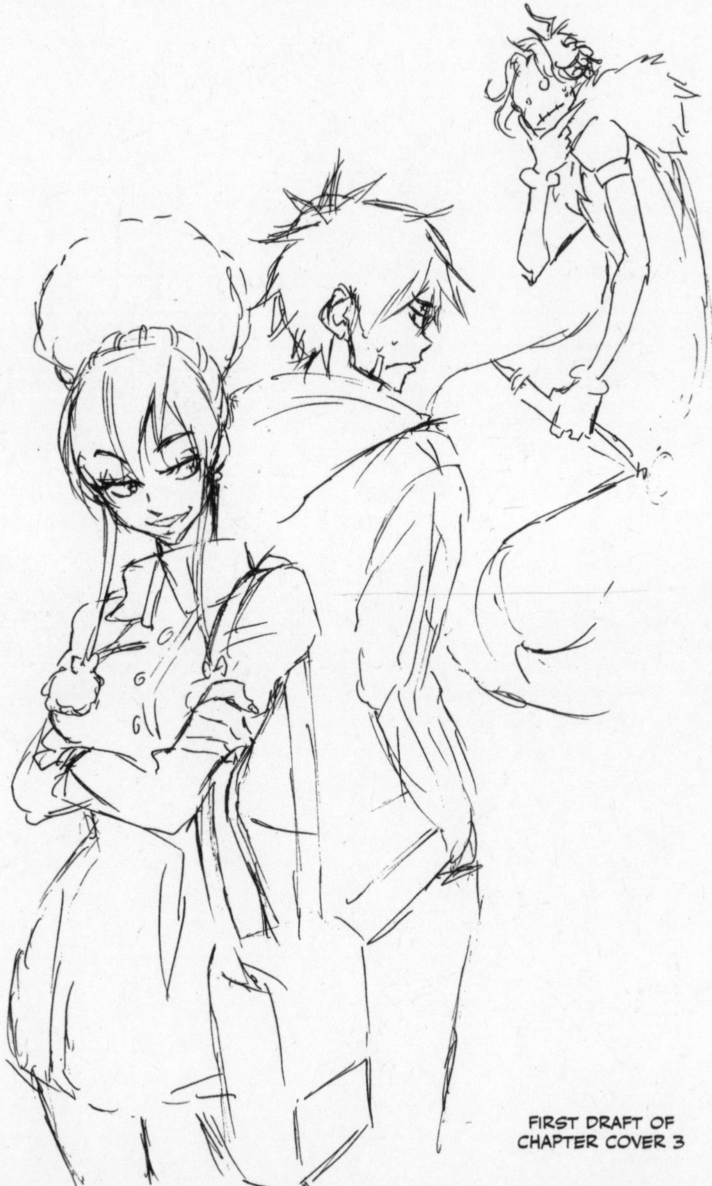

FIRST DRAFT OF
CHAPTER COVER 3

HOWEVER, SOMETIMES YOU HAVE TO WATCH OUT THAT THE COVER DOESN'T GIVE TOO MUCH OF THE CHAPTER AWAY. FOR THIS REASON, IN THE FINAL VERSION, YOU SEE HALF OF CRIMSON'S FACE AND NOT OF THE FUSION.

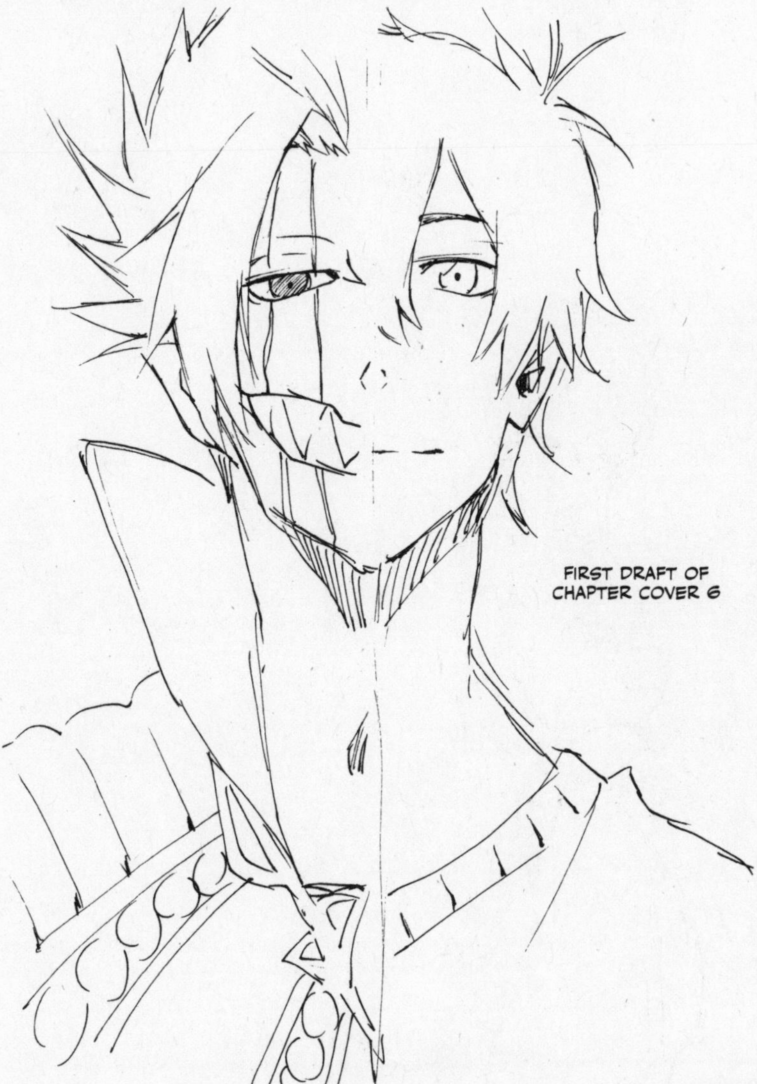

FIRST DRAFT OF CHAPTER COVER 6

TOKYOPOP
• PRESENTS •

INTERNATIONAL WOMEN of MANGA

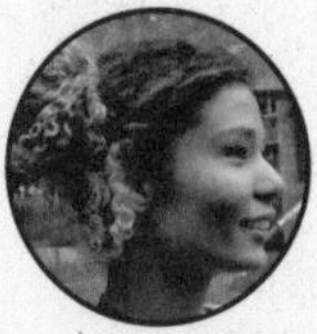

NANA YAA

GOLDFISCH

An award-winning German manga artist with a large following for her free webcomic, ***CRUSHED!!***

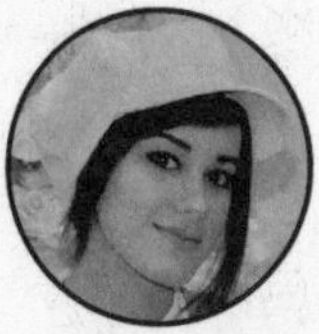

Sophie-Chan

Ocean of Secrets

A self-taught manga artist from the Middle East, with a huge YouTube following!

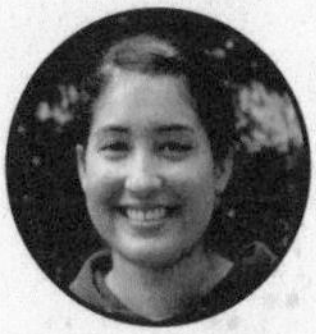

Ban Zarbo

KAMO
PACT WITH THE SPIRIT WORLD

A lifelong manga fan from Switzerland, she and her twin sister take inspiration from their Dominican roots!

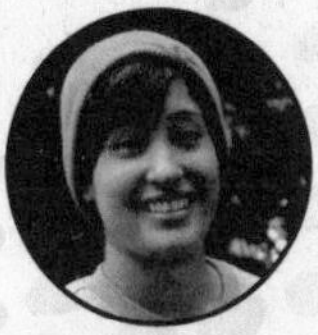

Gin Zarbo

UNDEAD MESSIAH

An aspiring manga artist since she was a child, along with her twin sister she's releasing her debut title!

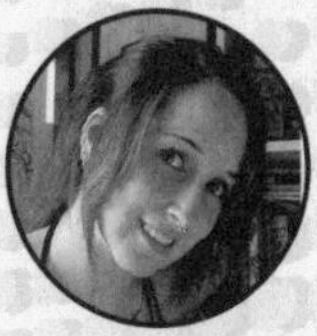

Natalia Batista

Sword Princess Amaltea
Natalia Batista

A Swedish creator whose popular manga has already been published in Sweden, Italy and the Czech Republic!

TO LEARN MORE PLEASE VISIT OUR WEBSITE

www.TOKYOPOP.com

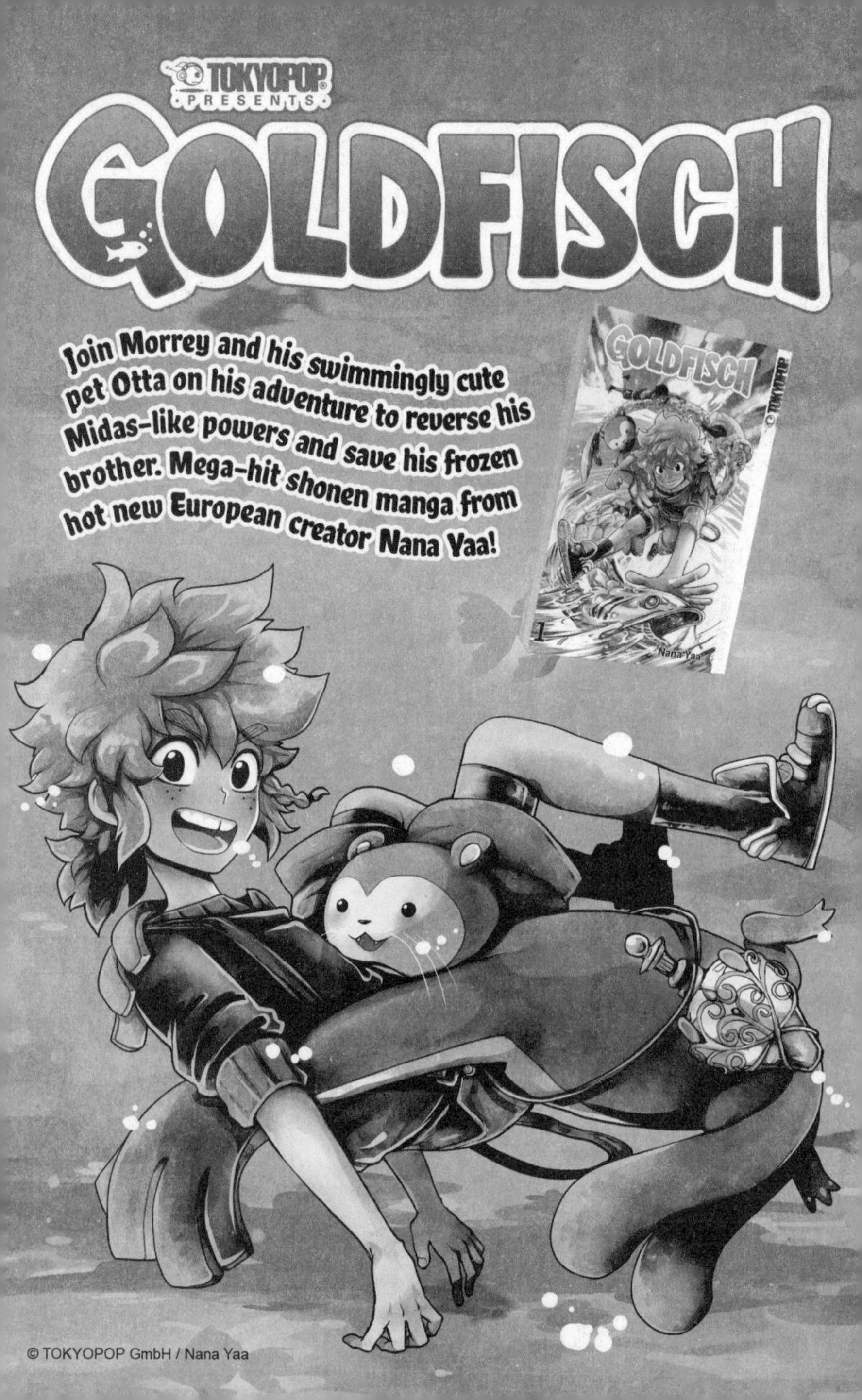
TOKYOPOP PRESENTS
GOLDFISCH
Join Morrey and his swimmingly cute pet Otta on his adventure to reverse his Midas-like powers and save his frozen brother. Mega-hit shonen manga from hot new European creator Nana Yaa!
GOLDFISCH
TOKYOPOP
1
Nana Yaa
© TOKYOPOP GmbH / Nana Yaa

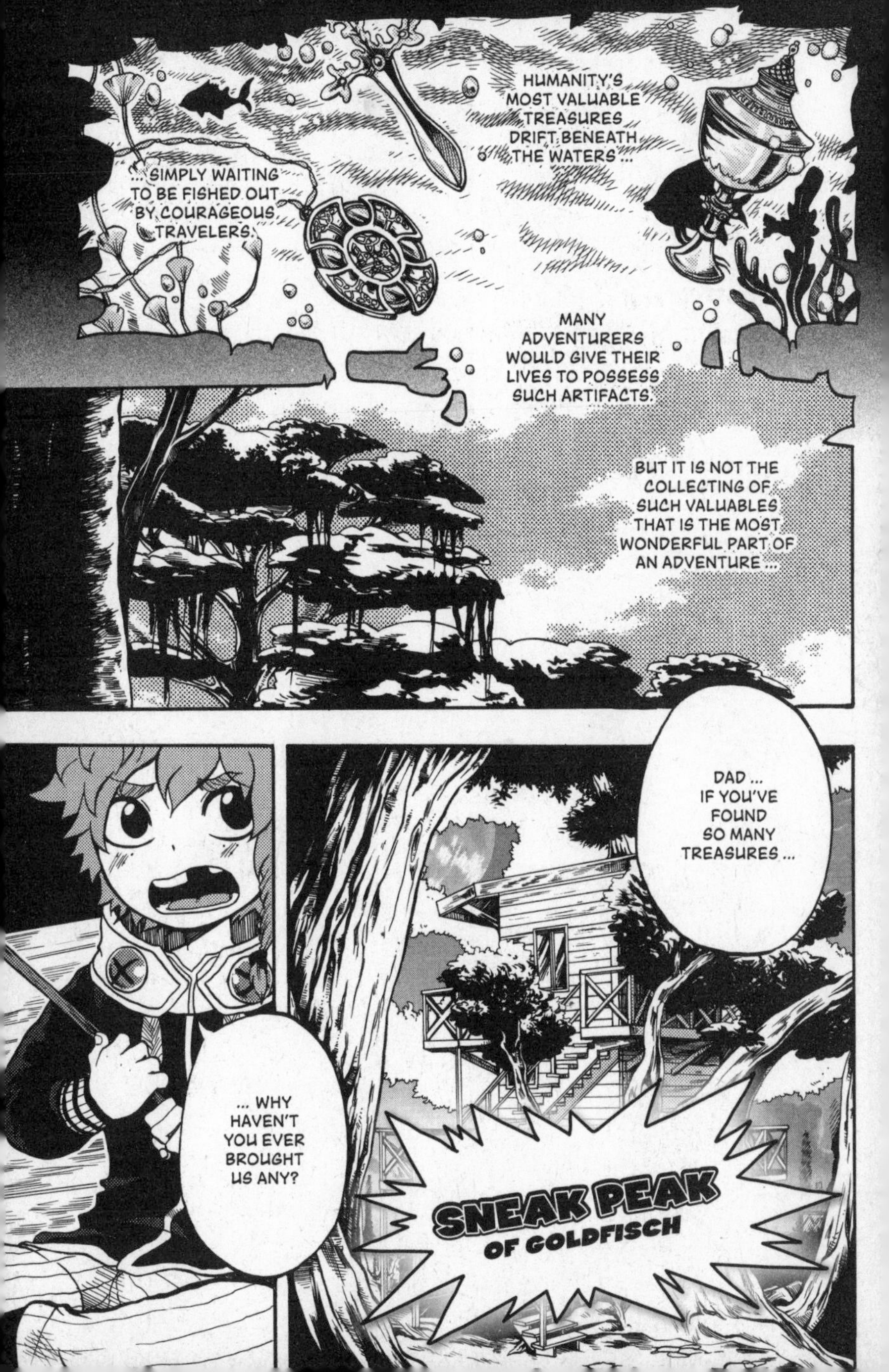
HUMANITY'S MOST VALUABLE TREASURES DRIFT BENEATH THE WATERS ...
... SIMPLY WAITING TO BE FISHED OUT BY COURAGEOUS TRAVELERS.
MANY ADVENTURERS WOULD GIVE THEIR LIVES TO POSSESS SUCH ARTIFACTS.
BUT IT IS NOT THE COLLECTING OF SUCH VALUABLES THAT IS THE MOST WONDERFUL PART OF AN ADVENTURE ...
DAD ... IF YOU'VE FOUND SO MANY TREASURES ...
SNEAK PEAK OF GOLDFISCH
... WHY HAVEN'T YOU EVER BROUGHT US ANY?

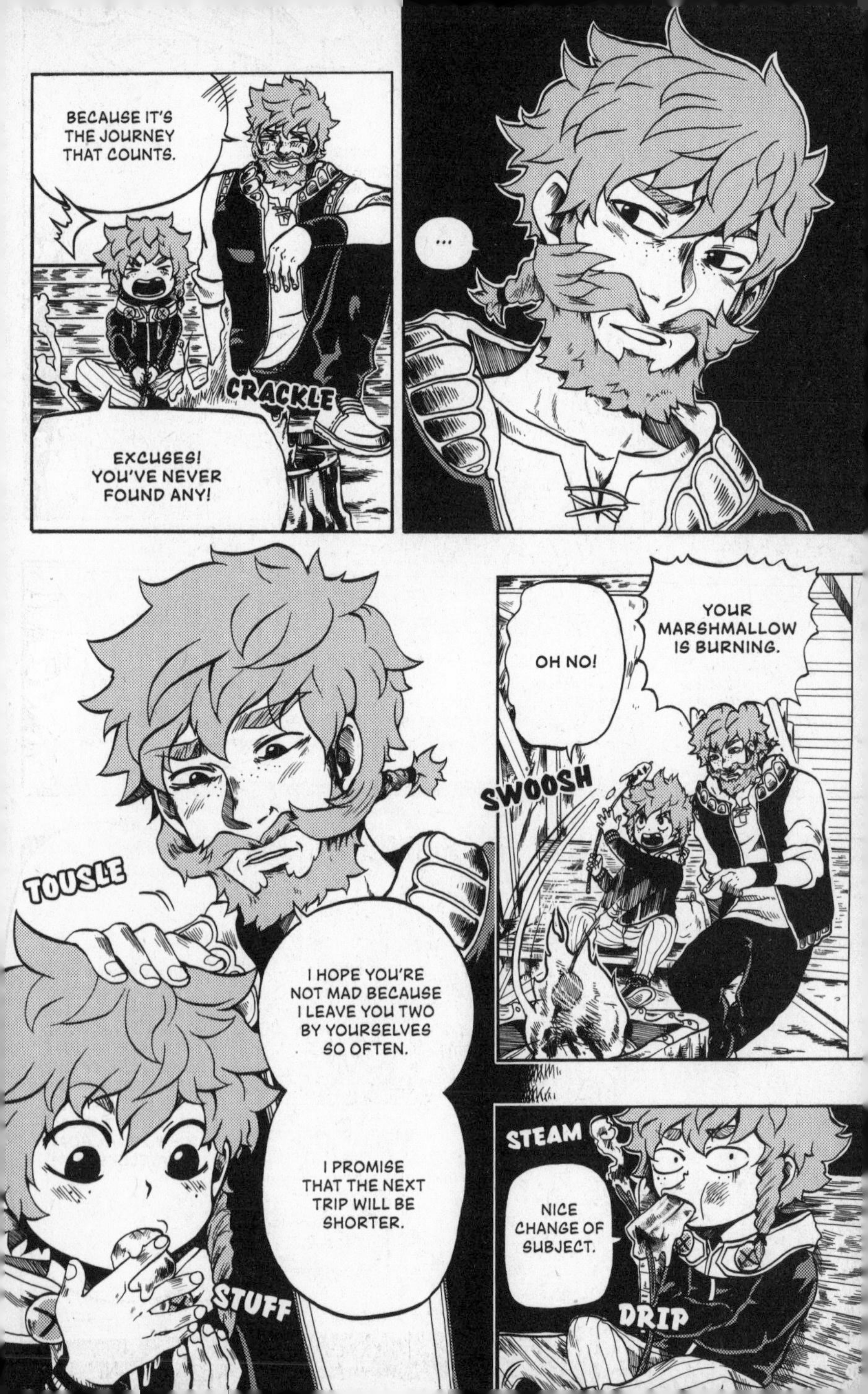
...
BECAUSE IT'S THE JOURNEY THAT COUNTS.
CRACKLE
EXCUSES! YOU'VE NEVER FOUND ANY!
YOUR MARSHMALLOW IS BURNING.
OH NO!
SWOOSH
STEAM
NICE CHANGE OF SUBJECT.
DRIP
TOUSLE
I HOPE YOU'RE NOT MAD BECAUSE I LEAVE YOU TWO BY YOURSELVES SO OFTEN.
I PROMISE THAT THE NEXT TRIP WILL BE SHORTER.
STUFF

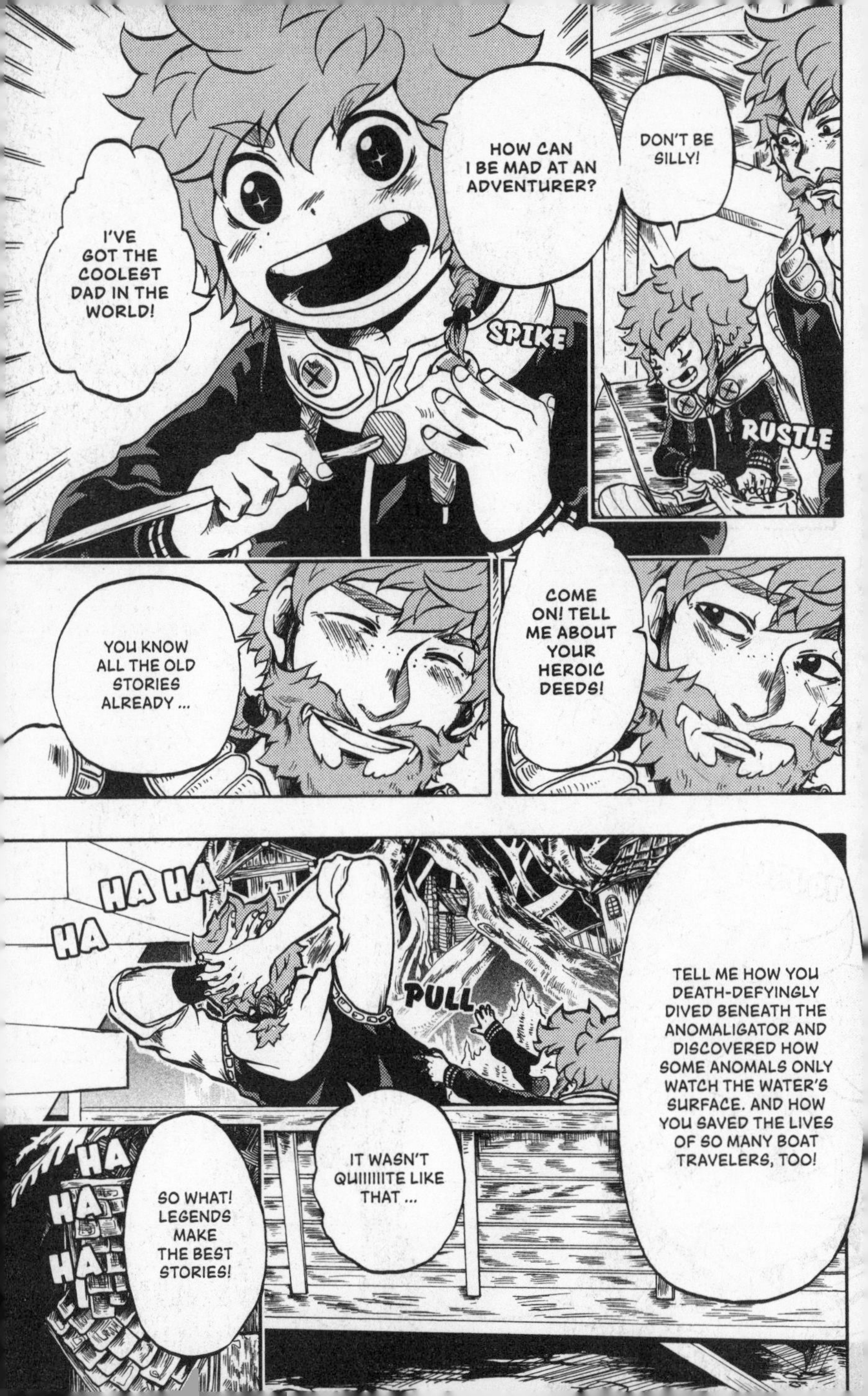
DON'T BE SILLY!
RUSTLE
HOW CAN I BE MAD AT AN ADVENTURER?
I'VE GOT THE COOLEST DAD IN THE WORLD!
SPIKE
COME ON! TELL ME ABOUT YOUR HEROIC DEEDS!
YOU KNOW ALL THE OLD STORIES ALREADY ...
TELL ME HOW YOU DEATH-DEFYINGLY DIVED BENEATH THE ANOMALIGATOR AND DISCOVERED HOW SOME ANOMALS ONLY WATCH THE WATER'S SURFACE. AND HOW YOU SAVED THE LIVES OF SO MANY BOAT TRAVELERS, TOO!
PULL
IT WASN'T QUIIIIIITE LIKE THAT ...
HA HA HA
SO WHAT! LEGENDS MAKE THE BEST STORIES!
HA HA HA

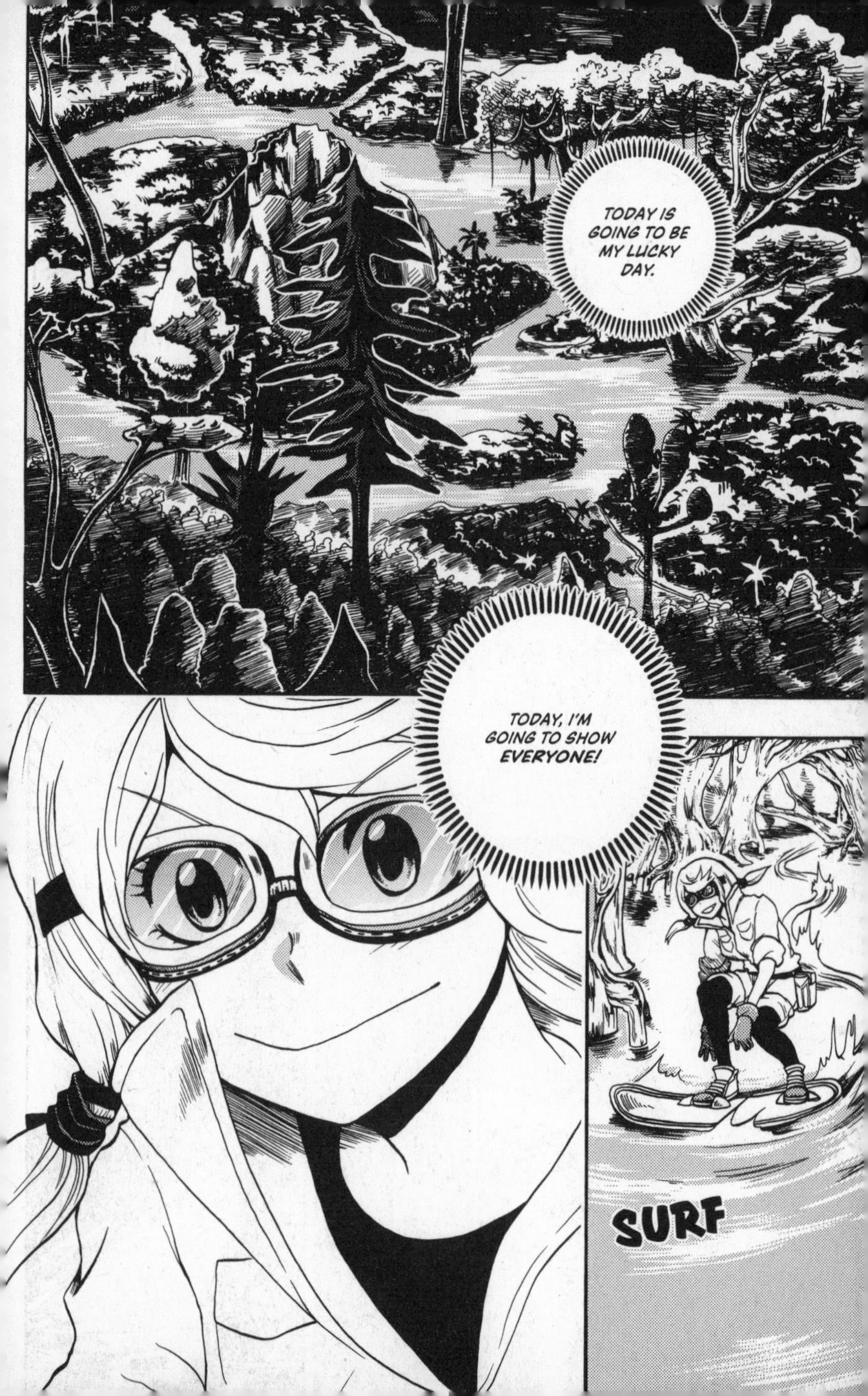
TODAY IS GOING TO BE MY LUCKY DAY.
TODAY, I'M GOING TO SHOW EVERYONE!
SURF

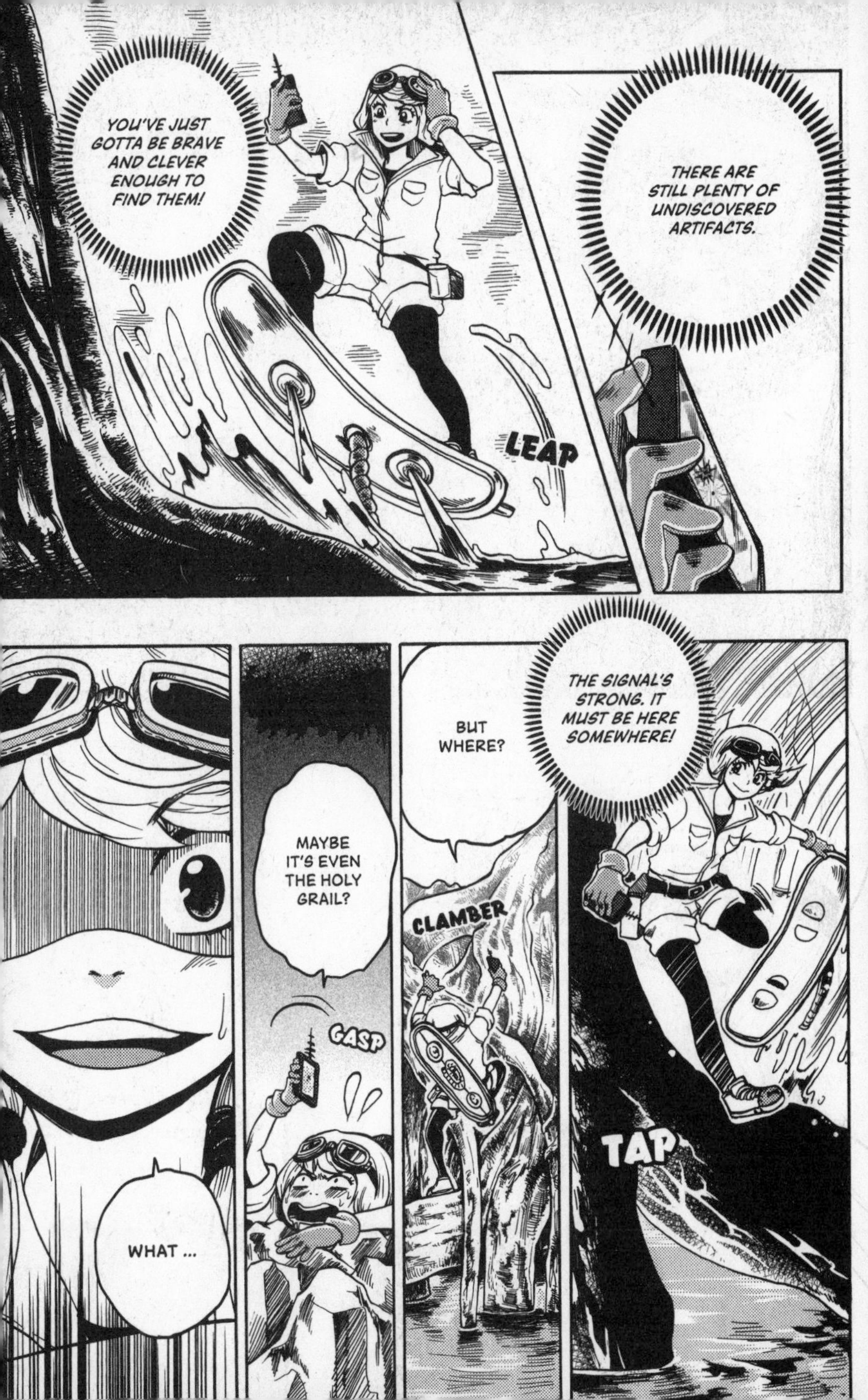
THERE ARE STILL PLENTY OF UNDISCOVERED ARTIFACTS.
YOU'VE JUST GOTTA BE BRAVE AND CLEVER ENOUGH TO FIND THEM!
LEAP
THE SIGNAL'S STRONG. IT MUST BE HERE SOMEWHERE!
TAP
BUT WHERE?
CLAMBER
MAYBE IT'S EVEN THE HOLY GRAIL?
GASP
WHAT ...

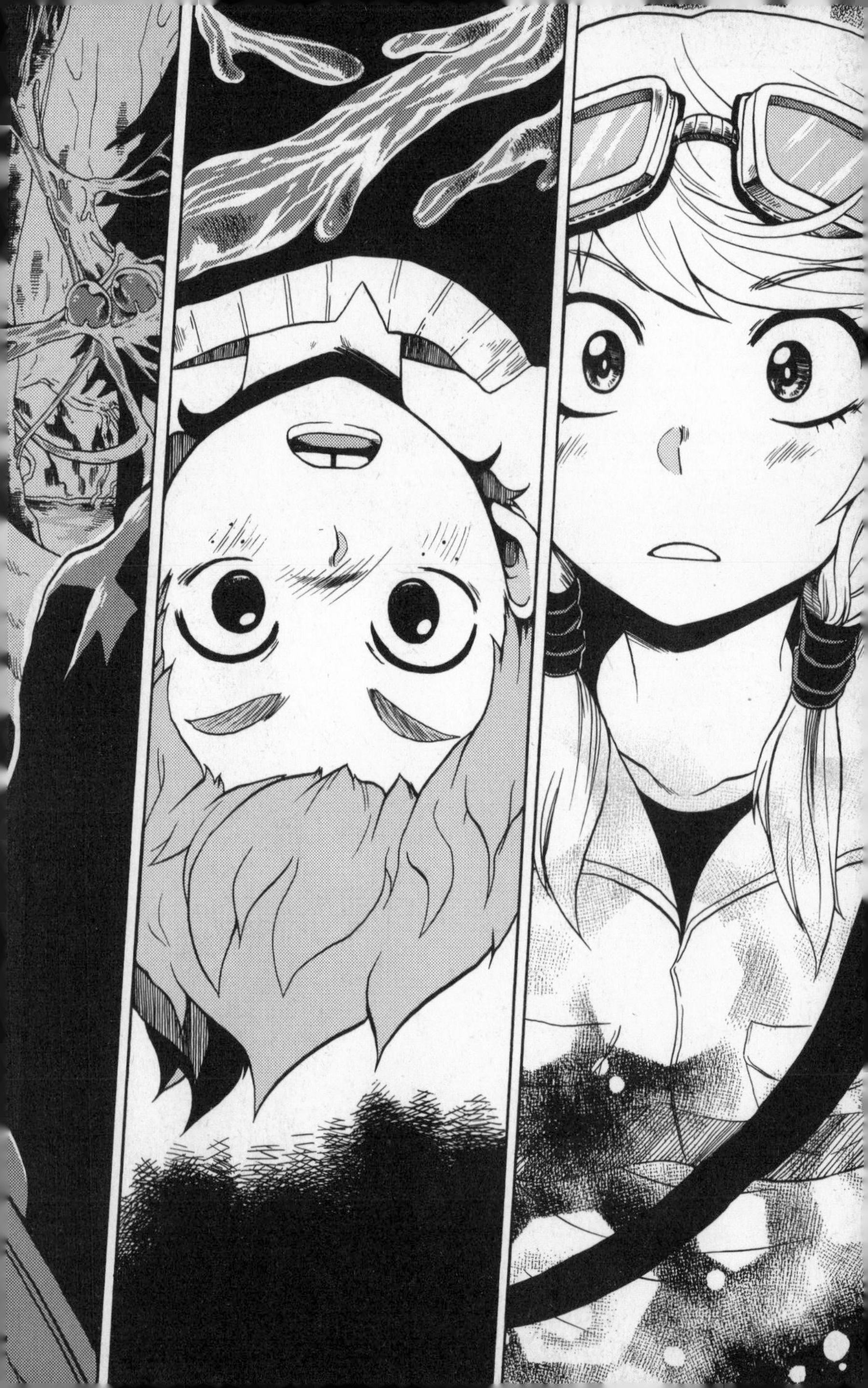

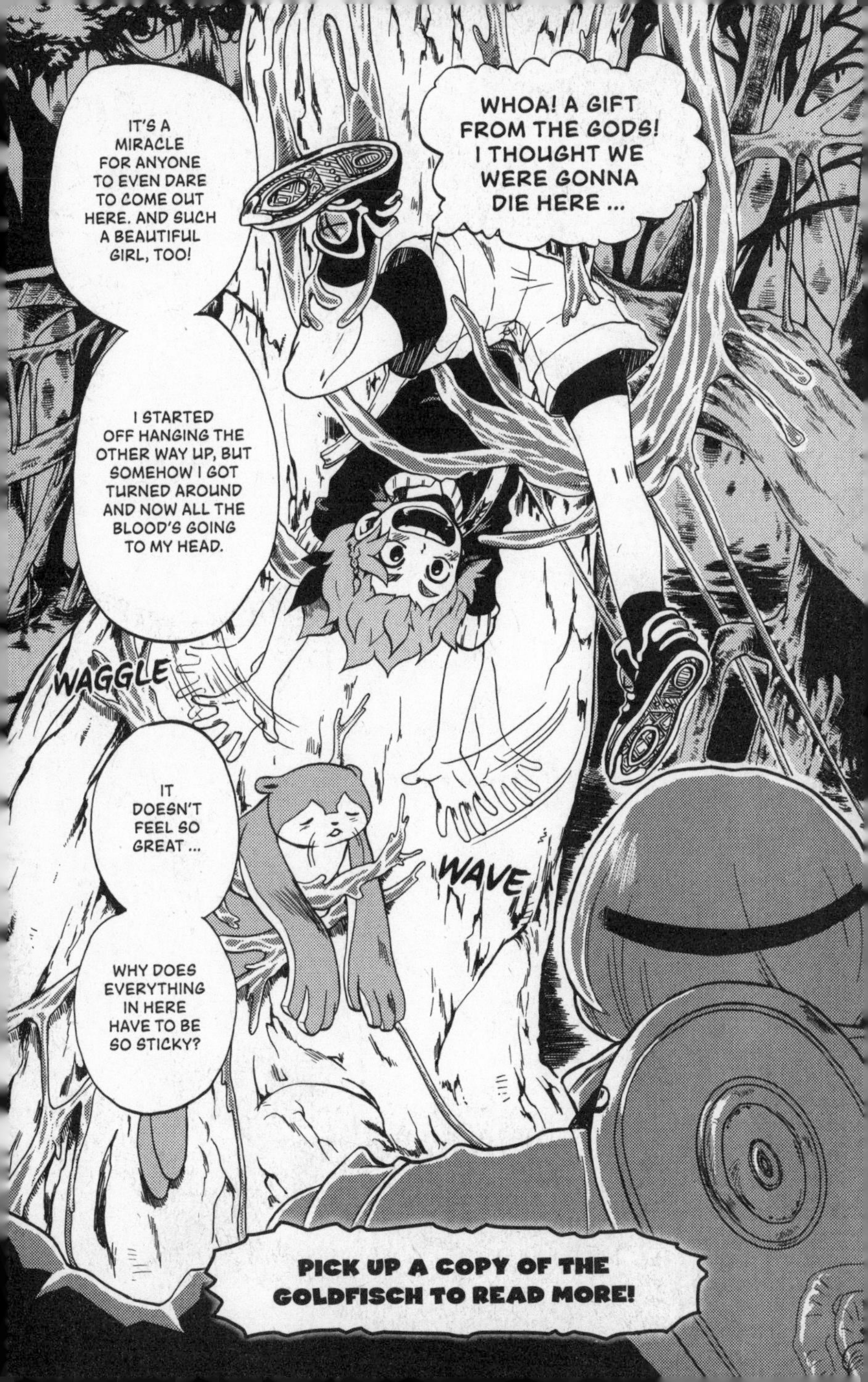
WHOA! A GIFT FROM THE GODS! I THOUGHT WE WERE GONNA DIE HERE ...
IT'S A MIRACLE FOR ANYONE TO EVEN DARE TO COME OUT HERE. AND SUCH A BEAUTIFUL GIRL, TOO!
I STARTED OFF HANGING THE OTHER WAY UP, BUT SOMEHOW I GOT TURNED AROUND AND NOW ALL THE BLOOD'S GOING TO MY HEAD.
WAGGLE
WAVE
IT DOESN'T FEEL SO GREAT ...
WHY DOES EVERYTHING IN HERE HAVE TO BE SO STICKY?
PICK UP A COPY OF THE GOLDFISCH TO READ MORE!

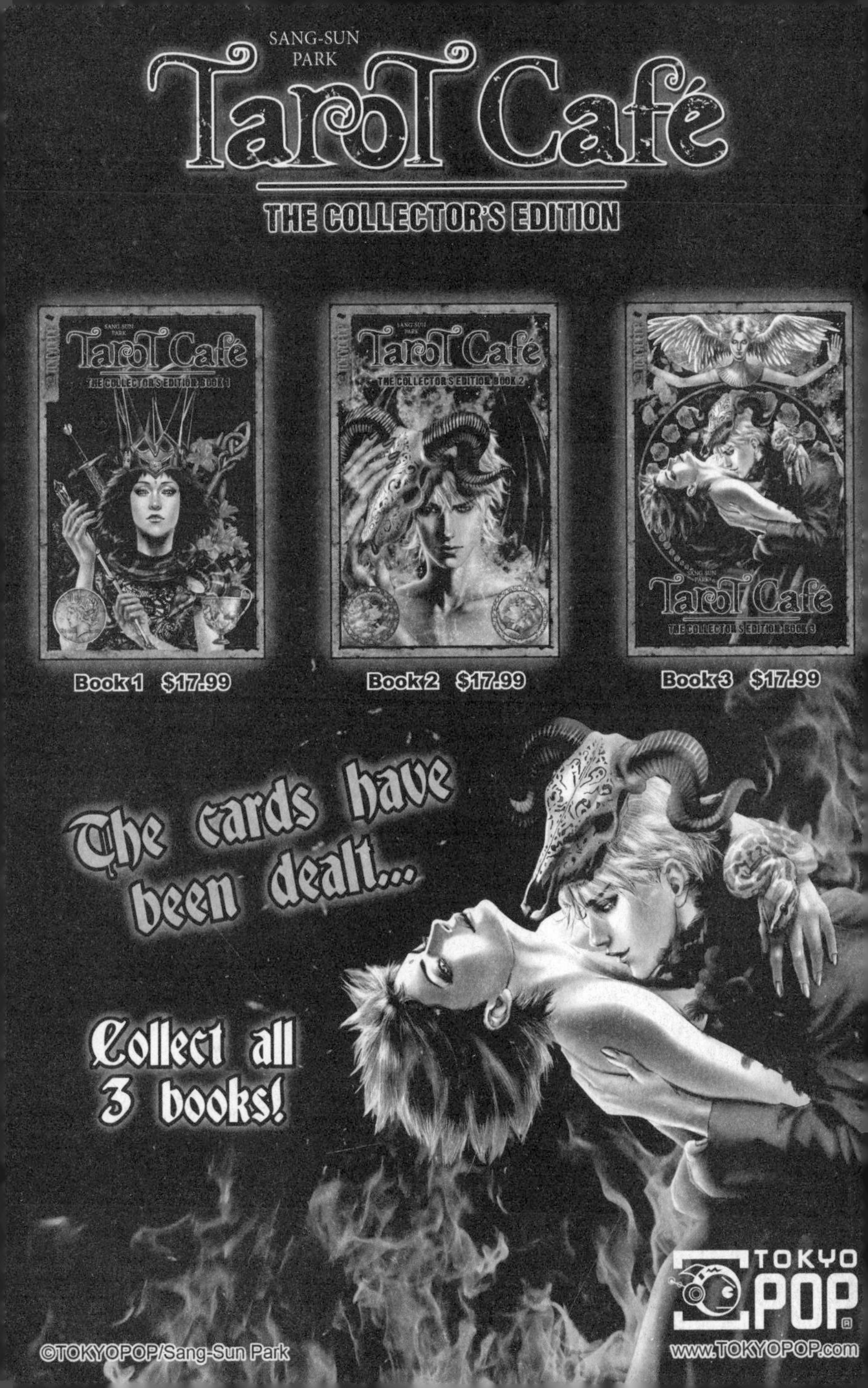
SANG-SUN PARK
Tarot Café
THE COLLECTOR'S EDITION
Book 1 $17.99
Book 2 $17.99
Book 3 $17.99
The cards have been dealt...
Collect all 3 books!
TOKYOPOP
©TOKYOPOP/Sang-Sun Park
www.TOKYOPOP.com

THE AUTHOR

IT WAS HER MOTHER WHO INTRODUCED BAN TO ANIME AND MANGA AS A YOUNG GIRL. EVEN BACK THEN, BAN KNEW THAT SHE WANTED TO ONE DAY BECOME A MANGAKA. BORN IN 1993, THE SWISS NATIVE WITH DOMINICAN AND ITALIAN ROOTS, HAS NOW, MANY YEARS LATER, REACHED HER GOAL: *KAMO* IS HER FIRST PUBLICATION WITH A PUBLISHER AND IS BASED ON THE DOUJINSHI *KA-MO*, WHICH SHE SELF-PUBLISHED IN 2014. INSPIRATION FOR HER MOSTLY SUPERNATURAL STORIES COMES FROM SAGAS AND MYTHS FROM THE CARIBBEAN.

BAN'S TWIN SISTER, GIN, IS ALSO A MANGAKA. TOGETHER, THEY NOT ONLY SHARE A STUDY IN THE SWISS HAMLET OF LANGENDORF, BUT A MASSIVE MANGA COLLECTION, TOO

FACEBOOK: BANZARBO
TWITTER: BANZARBO
INSTAGRAM: BAN_ZARBO